SO SHALL YOU REAP

Also by Marilyn Wallace

A SINGLE STONE
PRIMARY TARGET
A CASE OF LOYALTIES

MARILYN WALLACE

So Shall You Reap

You Reap

A PERFECT CRIME BOOK

DOUBLEDAY

New York   London   Toronto   Sydney   Auckland

A Perfect Crime Book
PUBLISHED BY DOUBLEDAY
a division of Bantam Doubleday Dell Publishing Group, Inc.
666 Fifth Avenue, New York, New York 10103

DOUBLEDAY is a trademark of Doubleday,
a division of Bantam Doubleday Dell
Publishing Group, Inc.

Library of Congress Cataloging-in-Publication Data

Wallace, Marilyn.
  So shall you reap / by Marilyn Wallace.
    p.   cm.
  "A Perfect crime book."
  I. Title.
PS3573.A4266S6   1992
813'.54—dc20   92-934
                                                               CIP

ISBN 0-385-42214-8
Copyright © 1992 by Marilyn Wallace
All Rights Reserved
Printed in the United States of America
August 1992
First Edition in the United States of America

10 9 8 7 6 5 4 3 2 1

For Judith Greber, whose friendship is
As Good As It Gets.

Acknowledgments

The town of Taconic Hills can't be found on any map. Since it exists only in my imagination, I've taken ongoing diabolical delight in populating it with scoundrels and curmudgeons that might not be found in the other towns in my well-loved Columbia County.

Creating Taconic Hills has been a pleasure, and not only of the solitary kind that comes with writing.

Thanks, first, to my editor, Kate Miciak, for encouraging me to find my place, and helping me find my voice.

For country hospitality and wisdom (research is such a lovely burden!), my true gratitude goes to Anita and David Orlow, Jean and Bruce Kimball, Harold and Alice Seletsky, Larry, Helen, Janet, and Alan Lampman, Polly Masters, and Margaret Adams.

For support, literary and otherwise, I'm grateful to Judith Greber, Susan Dunlap, and to the Saturday Group: Joan Cupples, Lucy Diggs, Caroline Fairless, Mary Rose Hayes, Cary James, Kermit Sheets, Katie Supinski, and Liz Thompson.

As always, thanks to my husband Bruce—first reader, first listener . . . *first*, and to my sons, Mark and Jeremy, who enrich so many things in my life, including being a writer.

And thanks, especially, for strength and sanity, to my agent, Molly Friedrich.

SO   SHALL   YOU   REAP

Girls don't usually have their own trees.

I did. Whenever Dad went into one of his silent, seething burns if someone mentioned taxes or the church, or when Mrs. Crezinski was out running errands, I scrambled up into the arms of my tree.

Even now, I can see that smaller Sarah waging a battle to create herself, seeking the hard company of the oak tree and claiming it as a place to keep her secrets. My throat closes up as I watch that fierce child puzzle out what to bring to a classmate's birthday party or how to make a straight part in her hair, questions any other girl could ask her mother.

My tree, a towering oak with bark the color of deer antlers and a thick canopy of branches sturdy enough to let a full-grown adult climb twenty feet above the ground, chose me the week before my tenth birthday, tipping the occasion toward significance.

Since that day nineteen years ago, I've seen something of the world beyond Taconic Hills, my tiny hamlet halfway between the Hudson River and New England. I sought the sanctuary of my oak tree often last year, during the events surrounding the bicentennial of our small town, a celebration that brought me—and, indeed, all of Taconic Hills—to the edge of a precipice.

But when I was not quite ten the world was an altogether more circumscribed place, populated by Dad and Mrs. Crezinski, the apple-faced widow who cooked and cleaned and generally looked after us. Nearly everyone else, it seemed to me then, was a marker, like a hedgerow or a stone wall: essential to defining boundaries but not invested with much personal meaning. I had, by then, concluded that my mother was never coming back. I had even succeeded in convincing myself that her absence meant nothing to me.

I loved the quarter-mile walk alone up the dirt road to the top of Vixen Hill after the school bus left me off. As a child, I spent as much time as I could out-of-doors, forever assigning meaning to the patterns of fireflies against the night sky or to the keening cry of the doves at twilight, certain these were secret messages, if only I could manage to understand them.

That warm October afternoon, I stopped to watch a mallard fly in a confused circle above a field of corn stubble, enchanted by the sparkle of emerald at his throat. He seemed to be looking for something, his mate perhaps, or the pond. Hurrying ahead so I could point him out to Mrs. C., I got a sharp, empty feeling in my stomach when I remembered she had an appointment with the dentist in Millerton and that no one would be home.

As I knelt to tug up my socks—I'd outgrown everything over the summer, even my socks—I heard a dry rustling at the far edge of the field where the corn hadn't yet been cut. I felt the hot gaze of someone, some thing watching me. Reluctantly, I straightened and looked around. The shadow of a passing cloud made its way to the mound of the hill, disappearing when it reached the pines. Papery cornhusks rippled in the breeze.

Nothing there, I told myself, and I started to sing "Yellow Submarine" at the top of my lungs to frighten it away. By the time I reached the first rise of the hill and caught sight of our boxy white house, I had almost forgotten my unease. With the shades drawn and the door shut, the old house seemed to be ignoring me, dozing while a chorus of crickets chirped in the tall grass near the pond across the road. Beside the pond sat Vixen Hill Lodge, shuttered and empty, hunkered down in a thicket of goldenrod and other weeds that circled the rambling old structure.

A sudden thunk echoed from the general direction of the pond. I spun around. I thought I saw a shape, bent over as if an invisible weight pressed on its back, then two eyes, shadowed by a shock of hair. Or was it all only a trick of the light pouring through the shrubs?

Then Queenie, our brown-and-tan all-purpose pet, cow herder, and watchdog, yapped and bounded down the hill toward the pond.

When I dared to look again, whatever had been there was gone.

My chest, tight with unaccustomed fear, opened at the sight of Queenie galloping toward me, fur rippling and gleaming in the autumn sun. Her big, barking presence made me brave, and I dumped my books and jacket on the picnic table in our front yard and sprinted across the road. Queenie veered off to the right and I, too, ran toward the grassy space between the willow and the old oak. And then the crickets stopped; a sudden silence poured over me until I felt small and cold.

I skidded to a stop. A pitchfork had been stuck by its tines deep into the rough, mossy bark of the massive oak. Sweaty, cottonmouthed from the terror that crept up from my stomach, I tried to turn away but my legs were frozen in place.

All at once the crickets started a racket. Queenie leaped at me, dog breath steaming in my face, and I fell backward, smashing my elbow painfully against the knobby root that pushed out of the ground at the base of the tree. I squeezed my eyes shut. *When I look again,* I prayed, *make the pitchfork be gone.*

It wasn't. The top was broken off so that only a hand's height of ragged wood remained, what was left of the shaft weathered to a lovely gray, like the feathers on the underside of a dove's wings. The three tines gleamed with the brightness of glass. Its sudden appearance in this beloved place—*my* place—was so terrible I could barely look at it.

Someone *had* been on my hill; I hadn't imagined those eyes peering at me through the bushes. And it wasn't someone who belonged here. Neither Dad nor Mrs. C. would stick a broken pitchfork in the tree and just leave it there. A chill, like the shadow of the cloud in the cornfield, passed over me.

Grasping the stunted handle, braced against the tree, I pulled the pitchfork free.

I examined the glinting metal, somehow surprised that I didn't see even a single drop of blood. Drawing my finger along the round shank of one tine, I pressed until the point nearly pierced my soft flesh.

I had to get rid of the thing. That it terrified me so completely was reason enough to act immediately; the explanation for its power didn't matter.

I heaved it as hard as I could and it sailed out over the pond just far enough to miss the weeds and the boulder and come down with a noisy splash. I stood for a long time, watching until the algae-slick surface was calm.

Then I ran across the grass and sat on the ground, my back pressed against the trunk of the old oak. A breeze stirred the dry leaves overhead and murmured to me that I would be safe here, that the tree would heal and be whole again. With Queenie sprawled across my feet, I sat unmoving until Mrs. C. came home. I never told her or Dad about the pitchfork; I couldn't bear having them think I was afraid.

I wonder if it would have changed things if I'd told them. But you can never know for sure and I still prefer not to ask certain questions.

I understand now that examining the past too closely can be dangerous.

February 1991

When packing bees for wintering-over, it is best to push two colonies together on a hive stand. This creates a dead air space, which protects the colonies from bottom moisture, but care must be taken to keep out mice, snakes, and other predators.

—*Everywoman's Guide to Beekeeping,* Revised Edition

One

The great serrated teeth of the backhoe bit into the earth and lifted a scraping of dirt, then disgorged its load beside the deepening hole. Hard and dark in contrast to the snow around it, the soil at first came up in slices, in ribbons, in small frozen strips, carved out by the power of the machine. No rich, loamy scents would well up from that hole; the cold had sealed all the smells of life deep in the ground. Even the miserly light that drifted around the branches of a lone chestnut tree and slid down from the plain white steeple of the Taconic Hills Methodist Church was without warmth. It was a proper day for a funeral.

I watched the work from the cab of my pickup truck, fascinated by the patience of the operator, woolen earflaps pulled down close to his head as he repeated the procedure, each time coming up with only scant pickings in the bucket. The snowplow on the road in front of me was maneuvering a full turn and I couldn't go anywhere until it finished. I'd made my honey deliveries and this season's sap run had only just started, so I wasn't in a hurry. I had more than enough time to get ready for the funeral of the Reverend Edward Fitzhugh.

Death, in Taconic Hills, is a social occasion, an opportunity to break routine and put on Sunday clothes and take a drink in the middle of a weekday. The weather, which had been unforgivingly cold for weeks, was sure to contribute to an excellent turnout. Besides, the Reverend Fitzhugh's funeral would be a grander occasion than most, since he was a neighborhood curiosity as well as a man of

God, and the manner of his death had been the subject of some speculation.

"Say what you will about him, Edward Fitzhugh was an important figure in this town before his illness," Ruth Hoving, my mother-in-law, had announced two days earlier as the town buzzed with the news of Fitzhugh's death. She ran her hand along the rough surface of the mantel on my fieldstone fireplace. "I do agree, though, that he'd developed some unusual habits in the past few years."

"Unusual? He never went anywhere, never talked to anyone. Maybe walking in endless circles around his own flower garden was unusual. But, always singing Broadway show tunes under his breath? Always dressed head to toe in black? At least that's what the kids who've seen him in his yard say." Peter's blue eyes flashed with questions. "Come on, Mother, the man had been unable to do a thing for himself for five, six years, maybe more. He couldn't drive a car or fix a sandwich or read a newspaper. I doubt the poor fellow knew where he was going. Anyone know how long he'd been out there?"

"Don't talk nonsense. With all that cold and snow, it wouldn't have to be too long." Ruth's face was screwed into the stern look she'd always used to bring Peter into line.

I wondered whether she'd noticed that it hadn't worked for years.

"Doesn't take long to die of exposure," she went on, "when all you're wearing are flannel pajamas and a bathrobe and cracked leather slippers. Tears freeze in your eyes on days like that."

"If the milk-truck driver hadn't spotted his bathrobe belt on that pricker bush, the sheriff might have not have found Ed until the snow melted. Two miles from his house . . . I still don't understand how he got that far," Peter insisted.

"Before his illness"—and here Ruth's voice dropped because everyone knew that whatever kept Fitzhugh from the pulpit for a decade had little to do with physical problems—"he was the most dynamic church speaker in Columbia County. That man brought many a strayed Christian back into the fold."

I didn't point out that, however charismatic Fitzhugh had been, he hadn't enticed my father one inch closer to the inside of a church. And while this wasn't the time to repeat the stories of the minister's occasional indulgence in a few too many tranquilizers, I was curious about her response to some of the other rumors about him that had sprung up like weeds in a summer garden. "Did he really have a drinking problem? I understand his wife was in Albany that day, trying to get some state agency to continue his disability payments."

"Alicia Fitzhugh had Marge Hoysradt come in to give him his lunch. He was all right when Marge left at twelve-thirty." Ruth turned from the fireplace and laced her fingers together, holding her hands loosely at her waist, a figure of perfect control and propriety. "He was a fine minister, a man who cared for his flock and inspired us all. When he was at his best, no one could deliver a sermon like Edward Fitzhugh."

Her eulogy had a purpose, I knew. She was not a casual woman and I often suspected that the small world of Taconic Hills ran itself according to a silent set of orders that Ruth Hoving, regal, silver-haired, and quintessentially Yankee, issued each morning while her coffee brewed.

She moved to the old camelback sofa, examined the fringe on the Navaho blanket I'd tossed over it to cover an ancient food stain, and then sat down, poised on the edge of a cushion. Her brown eyes fixed me with a forthright gaze. "Walter has business in Hudson and Peter will be in Chatham on Wednesday. I'd like you to drive me to the funeral, Sarah."

What she meant was that I was expected to attend. Left to my own choice, I wouldn't go to the funeral of a man who was nothing to me —but rebellion for its own sake was a perversity I seldom gave in to anymore. With Ruth, I was often tempted, often sorely aware that her efforts to mold me into a proper wife for her only son consisted mostly of filling the gaps of my social education. I found myself gritting my teeth in frustration.

That Ruth Hoving evokes such feelings in me has as much to do with me as it does with her; I don't take well to being mothered.

My mother left Taconic Hills when I was four years old. Vanished, as far as I was concerned, although the year I was twelve, two letters arrived from New York City, my name and the address printed in strong blocky letters and in vivid green ink. By that time, I had hardened myself against her. It was a habit, even at twelve, to think of my own feelings as dangerous; denying my mother access to my heart was a protection, to keep her from hurting me again. I threw the letters in the trash, unopened. Helen Lambert once forgot my father's ban against talking about my mother and told me that she had a voice so sweet the berries jumped off bushes into her apron. All I knew—all I *wanted* to know then—was that she walked out and

Dad burned every one of her pictures and forbade everyone to mention her name. Kindness from Ruth Hoving always carried a high price tag; it was further tainted for me when it was maternal.

"When do you want me to pick you up?" I asked.

"Ten before noon will be time enough. I think I'll wear my navy suit," Ruth had said, rising and smoothing her hair, "and if it's really cold, my boots." As though she were talking to herself. As though she were not trying to make sure I understood the requirements for this particular event.

The snowplow continued on its way and I started along the newly cleared road to home, caught by a sudden contrary longing to show up at the funeral in my jeans. It would look like a spiteful dishonoring of the dead; even I knew that. Still, I enjoyed the moment's pleasure the thought brought me.

"Sarah, my dear, you *do* look elegant."

That was all, but it was said with a smile that signified my burgundy wool dress and I had passed muster. Satisfied, Ruth pressed forward into the crowd and I followed her to a pew in the middle of the church. From our seats, I had a fine view of the proceedings. A pine lectern served as the pulpit. A large wooden cross looked down from the wall behind it, and baskets of white and coral gladioli formed a border along two sides of the altar. Carved candlesticks had been placed beside the lectern; the flames dipped and guttered as the choir filed in. The small, plain church was soon filled to overflowing with familiar faces.

The service seemed endless, hymn after hymn, speech following speech. I spent most of my time looking for architectural oddities, like the mismatched boards in the chancel floor, and the place on the window trim where years before the painter had missed a spot. When that bored me, I assessed the crowd as discreetly as I could. Peter, his eyes on his polished shoes, sat between Ben Yarnell and Walter near the rear door. The three men, splashed by jeweled light from the stained-glass window, looked too big for the pew section they'd squeezed into. Except for my father, everyone was here: Jeanie and Clayton Boice, Deeny Lambert and his parents, Ike Kronenburg, Grady and Patsy McClosky. All the farmers; all the storekeepers; all the members of families who had lived in Taconic Hills forever: Edward Fitzhugh had drawn quite a crowd of mourners.

But I was no mourner. Having cried when Mrs. C. died when I

was fifteen, I knew sorrow. I felt none of it for Fitzhugh, a man who, in my memory, I had never even seen. I sat on the cold pew, the heat from the press of bodies heavy around me, and thought not about Edward Fitzhugh but about my father, Roy Stanton.

Dad would be furious if we held a church service to mark his death and on that point I had promised that when the time came I would let no one, not Peter or Walter or Ruth Hoving, push me toward respectability. The idea of my father's death took me by surprise: he hadn't been sick and he wasn't prone to accidents. But he was near Edward Fitzhugh's age and this unadorned room, candles flickering in wooden sconces along the bare walls, made his death seem an inevitability I'd never admitted. I was glad not to think about it anymore when the service was over and the congregation rose to leave.

Glad, that is, until I realized I was in a receiving line. I prepared to offer condolences to the new widow. Alicia Fitzhugh was a tight, dour woman with hair the same golden blond as the hay that lay in drifts each summer waiting to be baled on the Kronenburg farm, the kind of person who pushed her cart through the Millerton Super determined not to make eye contact with anyone. She and her husband and my father and all the other social eccentrics were so much a part of Taconic Hills that people rarely thought of them as odd. They simply absorbed them into the fabric of the town, blotted them up so they didn't stand out too much, secretly glad of their existence since by their very strangeness they proved the normalcy of everyone else.

At least here, at her husband's funeral, no one expected Alicia to smile and sing out gay greetings. As the line inched forward, I followed Ruth, who nodded to everyone and chatted with Jeanie Boice about the weather and the high price of heating oil. I spotted Peter in the narthex, his mouth curving into a smile when he saw me.

A pair of somber clergymen supported Alicia, her reddened eyes barely visible behind a black mesh veil. The dazed look of the newly bereaved fit like a second veil over her face. Ruth leaned forward and kissed the widow's cheek, and the small, blond woman nodded and said thank you through pale lips.

And then I was standing in front of her. Before I could offer the few words I'd prepared, Alicia Fitzhugh lifted her veil and jerked back, her eyes showing great white circles around the dark pupils. "Julia," she whispered.

My heart pounded and my lips were suddenly so dry I couldn't open them. My feet wouldn't move me out of her way; I was stone.

Ruth took my hand and tried to lead me away. "Alicia's disoriented from her grief," she whispered. "And the resemblance *is* striking. Come, take me home now."

But I forced myself to complete the ritual. Despite the knife of pain that ripped at my throat, Alicia Fitzhugh would receive my condolences. I wouldn't allow myself to run away or to appear unstable. "I'm sorry for your loss," I said, not touching her, not kissing her cheek, wanting only to be gone.

"Julia," she repeated, and I fled into the crush of people in the vestibule, shaken that anyone, even a woman lost in the confusion of mourning, had called me by my mother's name.

As though he'd heard a silent summons, Peter appeared at my side. He put his arm around my shoulder and led me through the crowd, and I leaned into him. His frown asked questions he didn't say aloud: *What's wrong? What has upset you?*

"She called me Julia," I whispered.

"She probably hasn't slept and she certainly isn't thinking clearly." Peter's hand gripped mine as we were swept by the crowd toward the door. "She didn't know what she was saying."

But *I* knew what she had said, and it disturbed the fine fiction of my mother's nonexistence that I'd worked so hard to maintain.

Two

The sun felt good on my back as I made my way along the stand of sugar maples. I was glad to be busy, grateful for the chance to quiet the sound of her name in my head. *Julia. Julia.* It woke me in the middle of the night, pursued me if I dared to doze off before dinner from the sheer exhaustion of not sleeping more than four hours at a time. Emptying sap into the five-gallon gathering bucket, hauling the filled-up bucket to the holding tank in the back of my pickup truck—the activity warmed me quickly enough, and the promise in that watery sunshine was welcome. It helped put me in a dream of spring.

Something in me always rises at sugaring time, a habit of believing in the future even though I know deep down that the midday warmth is a trick. The sap only flows for a couple of weeks, when the temperature rises high enough during the day to coax you out of your second pair of socks. I get to seeing in my mind's eye the shadblow and forsythia brightening the roadsides. What I forget every February is that the nights are still dead-winter cold and very, very long.

It amazes me that I can know and forget in the same day.

I was halfway down the row of old maples that border the long drive leading to my mother-in-law's house when I heard footsteps breaking the crust of the snow behind me. I replaced the cover on an emptied bucket, set it back over its tap, and turned in time to see Peter hurl a snowball at me.

"No mercy for saboteurs," I warned, scooping up a handful of snow. My well-tamped snowball sliced a sharp arc into the air and then cut to the right and up. Peter bobbed, feinting to his left; the snowball caught him on the edge of his jaw. As if in applause, a woodpecker's rat-a-tat echoed from the woods.

The only way to keep myself from suffering a snowy revenge was to attack. I ran toward him shouting apologies, the deep drifts forcing my legs high with each step, but Peter knew me well enough to disbelieve my display of contrition and was already patting a fresh gloveful of snow into shape. I laughed and leaped at him, knocking him onto his back.

"Truce," I demanded, flattening my body against his. Even through the layers of clothing, I was aware of my breasts against his chest, of my thighs pressing his. I thought about how it would be to make love right there and have the heat from our bodies melt chaotic depressions into the snow, but I wouldn't chance Ruth or Walter Hoving seeing us, and I let the desire pass away.

Peter wriggled beneath me and narrowed his eyes. He'd been acting his February self lately, as though some inner intensity was struggling to warm him and protect him from the cold. The first time I noticed it was the first year, really, that I became aware of him.

I was eleven; Peter was fourteen, a high school sophomore. The morning had been bitter, the sky filled with a steely light, and my school bus was late, but I ignored the pain that frosted the tips of my ears and my fingers as I watched the high school bus drive up, its windows steamed and cloudy.

Except for one.

The clear circle rubbed into the next-to-last window was filled with a shadowed face, slender but not at all childish. His blue eyes were fixed on me as though he could see my bones clear through my coat and my sweater and my skin. A curl of dark hair sat in the center of his forehead like a horse's forelock, only silkier. The bus pulled away but the boy's head kept turning so that his eyes were locked onto mine until the last possible second.

Since that day I've learned that like the wheel of the seasons, Peter has cycles, too. Perhaps if I'd grown up differently, I might have absorbed the knowledge of how to soothe away his moods and that would have been the end of it. Loving a placid, temperate Peter would be like living in a world where it was always May and I couldn't bear that.

The high whine of a chain saw in the woods behind us cut through the quiet. I bent my head to kiss him but he rolled me over and pinned me beneath him. Snow trickled down my collar, a vivid, disorderly contrast to my hot skin; Peter caught my wrists with his hands.

"No fair! You're taking advantage." I gasped as he undid the top snap of my workshirt and kissed his way past my throat to the swell of my breast. I squirmed under him, feeling the edge of my excitement give way to anger at my immobility.

He lifted his head long enough to take a breath and cast a devilish grin at me. "Love or war, all's fair."

"Just remember you said that," I muttered. Then I hiked up his jacket and stuffed a fistful of loose snow in the waistband of his pants.

Peter yelped; he leaped to his feet, opened his belt, and danced around shaking snow down his pants leg, all the while looking at the trees, at his pants, everywhere but at me.

I got up, too, and busied myself with emptying the next sap bucket, filling the air with splashes and metal clangings that covered the sound of my breathing.

"Mother wants to see you before you go to the sugarhouse. She said to tell you it's important and that you should come up to the house before you start boiling off." Peter lifted the gathering bucket and set it down beside the snow spattered maple tree. I walked behind him, kicking up grainy clumps of snow with the toe of my boot, aware for the first time that a chill was working its way to my core, starting at my feet and my fingers.

If Ruth Hoving requested your presence, Lord knows, whether you were her daughter-in-law or the sheriff's deputy, you paid attention. A momentary vision of Ruth—sitting at her kitchen table, wearing a strap undershirt and holding a tumbler of cheap red wine as she received visitors, dispensed favors, and called in debts graciously—made me smile.

"What's so urgent?" I rescued a floating spider from the sap and emptied the last bucket, then turned to Peter, who leaned against a bent birch, arms folded across his chest.

"You know the bicentennial to-do that's planned for Labor Day weekend? Mother and Dad and the rest of their gang came up with a new idea. Jeanie and Clayton suggested they do a play. Dan Lambert wants it to be a reenactment of the establishment of the grand and glorious town of Taconic Hills.''

The bicentennial had been mentioned at Sunday dinner at Ruth's house but I'd paid little attention at the time. I'd been more interested in Peter's description of an intact old butter churn he'd found in a barn, and had listened with feigned indifference to talk about Doc Verity's visits to Alicia Fitzhugh, who was still, Ruth had reported disapprovingly, in a state of emotional shock.

"What does the bicentennial have to do with me? I've already agreed to donate ten pints of Sweets honey and maple syrup for them to sell at the booth with the Ladies' Auxiliary brownies and pumpkin bread. From each according to her ability—I'm contributing my own way." My jaw tightened and my fingers curled around the bucket handle.

Peter rubbed his hands along his thighs and blew cottony puffs of breath into the air. "Mother asked me if I'd take the role of Stefan Schiller," he said mildly.

"You mean, the lawyer?" I tried to remember a ninth-grade project on local history. The only Schiller I could dredge up was a child born on a long, hard winter passage across the Atlantic, whose parents died shortly after their arrival in the colony. I dug deeper in my memory. I could see the cover I'd fashioned out of brown construction paper, and the silver musket I'd glued in the center. That helped; I remembered more. The boy's father was a German Palatine, one of the mercenaries brought over by Queen Anne in 1710 to work the land for the Livingstons. His mother was a farmer's daughter.

Peter cupped his ears in his gloved hands. "Stefan was a *bookkeeper*, for the Livingstons. Sort of inherited his connections and his position from his father."

More of the history came back to me. Stefan's father had married a Van Rensselaer, not a bad position to be in when the old leasehold system was dismantled and the land-rich Livingstons and Van Rensselaers were forced to distribute their vast acreage. "It probably wasn't uncommon, even then, for someone to marry money and power and pass the benefits on to his son."

Peter colored under my gaze.

"I didn't mean *that*." I watched him decide whether or not to take my remark as a personal insult. "The shoe doesn't fit, Peter.

Ruth didn't have enough of an inheritance to influence Walter. Tell me more about this play."

"The drama's pretty much built in—Stefan and his wife Emily and the other locals had what Mother has taken to calling 'adventures.' She did a lot of research and now Ben Yarnell's going to write a play."

The tension dissolved from between my shoulders. I half expected him to say that Ruth wanted me to write the script. She was capable of dragging in the fact that I'd graduated from college with a major in English literature. Never mind that I'd specialized in Chaucer. I'd gone to college to prove to myself that I wasn't choosing Taconic Hills out of fear or ignorance and I returned home with a B.A. and the ability to tell off-color jokes in Middle English.

"Ben's perfect, but I'm surprised he agreed. He's always going on about how he gets paid paperboy wages for doing three full-time jobs. How can he do the research and write the play and still be editor, reporter, and photographer for the *Columbia Journal?*"

"Says he'd rather be busy than have time to worry about where new advertising revenue's coming from." Peter's shoulders lifted in a shrug. "Anyway, he said yes."

If Ben was eager to be involved in the pageant, that was *his* business. "You still haven't told me. Why does your mother want to see me?"

Peter shifted his weight, lifting each foot out of the snow and then staring at his boots. "She wants you to play Emily."

Anger pulled the knot tight again, this time in my chest. This, just when I thought Ruth finally accepted that my good works would be different than hers. She was a woman of committees and events; those activities made me restless, anxious to be outside again among the things I understood best. I slammed the brimming bucket down on a snowless patch of ground and jumped back to keep from getting splashed.

"I can't do it. I won't have time for all that. Memorizing lines. Rehearsals in August. That's the start of the fall honey season—"

"Just go talk to her, okay? I have to finish installing the heating system in the Chatham house. Another cold snap, the pipes might freeze. I'll be home late. Poker game tonight." Peter brushed my cheek with a kiss and turned toward the road.

I watched him retrace his steps through the snow, suddenly aware that my toes were so cold they felt like fat little grapes inside my boots. I'd warm them in Ruth's house when I stopped to apologize for not being in her play. I hauled the bucket to the truck, my gait stiff as I tried to keep the sap from sloshing over the sides. Thick with leaves, the fine-mesh filter over the holding tank caught another brown spider when I poured in the sap. I'd had no real surprises this year—no drowned mice, no soggy squirrels. Through the trees at the top of the drive, I spotted Peter's van in time to return his smile and a wave as he drove off.

At the crest of the knoll, the imposing white Colonial stood sentinel watch over the sweep of lawn and the pond below. An icicle hung from the shuttered living-room window, looking as big around as the ash saplings that Peter cuts every fall when he thins the woodlot. The lower windows caught the sun; the four dormers receded into shadow. I wasn't sure whether I really did see a silhouette slip into the darkness of the house and then peer out from behind the starched Priscilla curtains in one of the upstairs bedrooms. Ruth Hoving couldn't *really* be everywhere and see into everyone's heart, even if it sometimes seemed as though she knew everything.

I was getting the full treatment. Ruth suggested we have our tea in the living room by the fire, and the prospect of warm toes momentarily overcame my wariness. Legs outstretched, I nestled among the faded chintz flowers of one of the wingback chairs that flanked the shallow fireplace, waiting in the hushed cheeriness of her red, blue, and brass Americana while she puttered in the kitchen. The gleam of rich mahogany warmed even the dark corners of the room, sending light spinning from the surfaces of the butler's table with its polished brass hinges to the stork-legged reading stand on which a massive black leather Bible rested, its grosgrain placemarker faded with one hundred fifty years of touching and smoothing. A comforting wintery smell, apples and a burning fire and the cedary echo of Christmas wreaths, settled like fragrant powder on every surface.

I watched the flames, content to let them dance or fizzle as they would. Usually I poke fires, shift logs, do what I can to entice the flame to burn brighter. Ruth never pays the slightest attention to her fires and yet they blaze merrily at the same steady glow. It was how she did everything—effortlessly yet effectively, and with a gracious control that was absolute.

Porcelain cups and saucers tinkled against the enameled tray, announcing her entry into the living room. She set the tray on the butler's table, lifted a lump of sugar with silver tongs and dropped it into one of the flower-sprigged cups, then repeated the procedure.

My jaw clenched and I sat straighter in my chair, nearly knocking over her knitting basket and spilling all the neatly wound yarn, the knitting needles and hooks and whatnot.

Putting sugar in my tea was a simple, hospitable act, really, but it felt like another brick in the maternal wall she was building around me.

"I'm proud of you, Sarah," Ruth said between sips.

I must have made a face because she smiled with that condescending crinkle that made me want to upend all the precious little trinkets in her curio cabinet.

"I mean, doing so well with your business. I see Sweets labels all over. Your honey is the only brand they carry in that cute little store in Great Barrington. Did you know that?" She shook her head and smiled. "Of course you knew. And you've done it all by yourself and I'm very proud."

I pounced on the opening. "Thanks, Ruth. In fact, I'm afraid I can stay only a few minutes. I have two hundred gallons of sap in the truck and—"

She held up her hands as if to protest my need to explain. "I know. I'll come right to the point. Jeanie and Clayton Boice and Dan Lambert agree with Walter and me that the bicentennial celebration is the perfect time to put on a play. It will get everyone— weekenders and old timers—involved and working together. The ideal opportunity for cooperation, don't you think?"

She didn't wait for my response. "I ran into your father not an hour ago at Oblong Books in Millerton. Roy Stanton—now there was a challenge. But even *he* said that if he didn't have to speak in public, he'd take a part, and he'd let us use his garage if we needed the space to build things."

If Dad had agreed to find time for Ruth's pageant, either she'd coerced him with one of her implied threats or else he'd already been convinced that the project was in some way necessary. He seldom did anything but work at his garage, carve small figures from wood scraps, or play solitaire—and *he* bristled at Ruth's bossiness even more than I did.

"You know what Ben's going to write about, don't you?" Again, she didn't bother to wait for an answer and I didn't bother to offer one. "Stefan Schiller and his wife Emily established one of Columbia

County's first independent farms, right here at the crossroads. Nothing but rocky land and they turned it into a prosperous farm. Of course, it wasn't easy. Tests—my goodness, they were tested constantly."

Aren't we all, I thought as I waited for her to get to her point.

"Life was difficult for everyone around here in those days. Gunther Meier, a worker on Stefan's farm, sent an entire shipment of spoiled milk to Albany. Livingston was so angry he nearly took away the land. Stefan's mother was bitten by a rabid dog on the Fourth of July—what a terrible death that must have been." She paused as if to consider the full horror of it and then went on. "Arnold Peck, the forge foreman, was killed when a keg of gunpowder exploded at the forge.

"And everything took so much *time*. Stefan and Emily had to stop work on their new home for weeks because they were stricken with some illness. Influenza, I think, from the way the symptoms are described. Poor things, when the house was nearly done, they had a fire and were forced to start again. He was a stalwart pioneer, and even though she was a Livingston and aristocracy, she was his perfect helpmeet. They kept on. Well, Stefan did, for years, until he was shot in a hunting accident. He became a widower when he was hardly more than thirty-five, poor thing."

That Emily died young seemed to count for nothing to my mother-in-law.

I sipped my tea, wondering what was remarkable in that tale and why the time was so perfectly right to reenact the story now.

Ruth set her cup on the saucer and reached with her other hand into a pocket for a tissue. She blew her nose, then bent to retrieve something that had fallen onto the braided oval rug. The object in her hand seemed to draw the light to it.

It was a gold cross, not more than two inches high, with pewter stars, eight-pointed, at the end of each bar. *Sharp. Those points at the end of the stars were so sharp.* A chill swept over me; I tried to look away, but the sight of the cross held me.

Images, sounds, swam before me. A dark place, someone screaming.

Spiderwebs clinging to my cheek.

The cross glinting in a shaft of light.

The smell of turpentine, and then darkness.

"My dear, are you all right?" Her hand lying gently on my shoulder, Ruth's apparent concern frightened me.

Where had all that come from? I saw that my fingers were clamped down over the scar on my right arm. I took a slow, deliberate breath, but the room threatened to go on spinning.

"I'm sorry. I've been working outside all morning. Must have made me light-headed. That cross," I said, forcing myself to look away from it so I could breathe again, "have you always had it?"

Ruth frowned and held it up. "This thing? It's odd, isn't it? A *crux stellata*, someone called it, a starred cross. Ages and ages ago I was a Sunday-school teacher. Each year we got a little gift. This was one of them. I was going to have it made into a pin, but I put it in my pocket and forgot it was here."

I offered a smile to prove that I was fine and Ruth nodded and sat again in her chair. The cross still lay in her hand—I stared at the reindeer on my socks and then at the pattern in the rag rug and at the leaping fire.

She pocketed the cross and fixed the folds of her skirt, and went on as though there had been no interruption. "It's a wonderful story, really, this tale of the Schillers, proof positive of the power of courage, persistence, and love." She fairly glowed with pride, as though Stefan and Emily were her own children. Then the light in her eyes dimmed and her mouth drooped. "Columbia County has changed so since you and Peter were younger, New York City people making it hard for children who grew up here to buy homes, over-paying for anything sitting on a half decent piece of land—falling-down shacks, old barns."

The contempt in her voice made my cheeks burn. Last year, when Peter found out that Vixen Hill Lodge, a barn that had been converted into a hunting lodge in the 1950s, was for sale, I could barely contain my excitement. Just across the road from the house where I grew up and where Dad still lived, the property included the pond and my oak tree. We scraped together a down payment and Vixen Hill Lodge became ours. Our *old barn* was the place where we would create our joined life.

She went on talking as though she meant nothing disparaging. I doubted that.

"City people paying ten times what these properties are worth. Still, once it's jam, it can't be strawberries anymore." Ruth's cup and saucer were rock-still in her hands. "And now Jim Dembowski's son,

Nick, is preparing to go before the zoning board in the fall and ask for a variance, when plans and perc tests and such are done."

She was almost whispering. When Ruth talks about things that make her angry, her voice gets softer and softer, as though what she's saying is unspeakable. "They say he's planning to sell three hundred acres of pine woods to a developer who wants to put in townhouse condominiums. Imagine—a *farmer* thinking he can solve his money problems by desecrating the land. Nothing less than the survival of Taconic Hills is at stake. The bicentennial will generate the kind of community feeling we'll need to defeat Dembowski."

Nicky Dembowski couldn't do without Izod shirts and a Mustang in high school. Still, it was hard to believe he'd sell out so egregiously. All I could think of were huge yellow machines flattening the land, sculpting uniform driveways to lead to ill-made identical houses that would fall to ruin within ten years. All this he would inflict on the wildness of my hills, my woods and swamplands.

"The pageant," Ruth said, "must be the cornerstone of our efforts to keep the developers from taking over. There's been some talk that a development will be good for the county—help expand the tax base and bring in new money. We have to fight that notion, Sarah. It's imperative to remind everyone what a precious thing we have here. This play is how I mean to do it. Bring the past back to life and heal the community."

Bring the past back to life . . . I shivered with prickly unease at the idea of reviving those long-ago lives to serve our own purposes. Hadn't Stefan and Emily Schiller and all the other early settlers already done their share for Taconic Hills two hundred years ago?

Clearly, Ruth had no such misgiving. She leaned forward, her pale eyes glittering with excitement. In a second, I knew, she would pat her hair. I felt well and truly trapped. Saying no to Ruth would be like declaring that I was ready to infect Taconic Hills with an unknown but deadly disease.

"You're absolutely the perfect person to play Emily Schiller." Now she *did* touch the fine silver hair at the nape of her neck. "You even look like her. Tall. Slender, strong. And your hair. It's perfect. They say she had masses of dark hair. She wore *hers* in two plaits, like an Indian."

As though fitting the description would allow me to step into Emily Schiller's life the way one would step into a suit of clothes.

Maybe my mother-in-law's world really was as neat and simple, as *tidy* as it seemed.

"Don't you think Margaret Kimball, that lawyer from Manhattan, would be a better choice?" Another victim ought to suit, as long as she had dark hair. I felt myself scrambling for purchase on a rapidly eroding slope.

Ruth smiled. "Ah, Margaret's playing Mary Schiller, Stefan's mother. Clayton Boice will be the forge foreman, but I still haven't filled one or two roles. I need someone to play Klaudia Weigelt. Stefan became the young woman's friend after he saved her from marauding fur traders. Alicia Fitzhugh, when she was younger, would have been perfect. According to the Historical Society booklet, Klaudia was dainty and blond, with eyes like—I think the pamphlet says emeralds but I'm not sure about that. Maybe it was lapis. Klaudia dropped from sight—no one's sure what became of her—and Stefan married Emily shortly afterward."

Ruth, it seemed, wanted me to play the woman who was our hero's second choice.

She leaned toward me and laid her warm, dry hand atop mine. "You're the one for this role. You must do this, Sarah. For Taconic Hills."

And God and country? Even if I didn't agree with her tactics, Ruth had chosen her weapons and had engaged her troops in the fight against Dembowski. If I were leading the charge, my choice would be different, but I could scarcely decline to join her effort. Still, I wanted to delay her moment of victory.

I set the fragile china cup on its saucer and stood. "I'd like to give it some thought. You know how busy I'll be when rehearsals start and—"

"Of course, dear. You think about it. Call me tomorrow when you've decided." Ruth rose, too, and smoothed the white lace runner on her oak apothecary chest with long, graceful strokes. "You'll make a wonderful Emily. You're so clever."

She didn't have a thought that I might refuse. She'd called me clever, after all, and had decreed that I was just what the town needed to be rescued from the scourge of developers. I fought my anger: I wouldn't give her the satisfaction of seeing that she'd unnerved me. And clever or not, I still had all that sap to boil. I threw on my jacket, scarf, hat, and gloves, mumbled something about calling her, and then hurried out into the brittle sunshine.

Winter quiet in Taconic Hills is different from summer stillness. Nothing moves in the cold—no low buzz of farm equipment, no bird sounds or breezes sifting the grasses. I heard no dogs yapping in the fields and no children shouting, even though I stood listening for movement or voices. The quiet became so dense that I had a sudden urge to shatter the silence.

I pressed the gas pedal to the floor, let the roar of the engine mix with my own roaring anger, and sped off in low gear.

Patches of ice still lurked in the spots on the road where the pine trees blocked the sun. I tried to give all my attention to driving but I kept thinking about Ruth, about Nicky Dembowski's development, about the Schillers, and the way everything circled around that cross. Despite all the whirl in my brain, I had regained a measure of calm by the time I reached Vixen Hill. Driving does that for me; sitting high up in the cab of my truck works best of all.

The sight of Vixen Hill Lodge flooded me with pleasure. This was *my* place, our haven, and if Ruth had something against old barns, that only made it sweeter for me.

Years earlier, the barn had been converted into a rustic inn; the biggest stone fireplace I've ever seen dominated the huge central room. Sixteen-foot-high ceilings soared above the big room and a bay window looked out over rolling hills and marching stands of ash, oak, chestnut, and hickory. A porch ran along the west side of the house; a greenhouse nestled up to the south wall. The kitchen boasted a pantry the size of a small bedroom, an eight-burner stove complete with griddle, and a window overlooking the pond and my oak tree.

When we bought the place, shutters tilted at odd angles, their hinges dangling uselessly. The mottled-gold kitchen linoleum was pitted and scarred, the upstairs bedrooms all leaked in the heavy rains, and stubborn mildew in the downstairs bathroom dotted the ceiling with bearded green growth and laid a film of black mold on the window ledge.

But we were fixing it up, little by little. The most ambitious project was the kitchen renovation, scheduled for March. No matter what improvements we subjected the rest of the house to, Peter and I had agreed that the weathervane, a smiling mother fox with her tail curved gracefully around two kits, would stay. We planned to be here a very long time.

I pulled around to the backyard and parked at the sugarhouse, a label that lent false dignity to the setup I'd rigged behind the house last winter. It was really nothing more than two tubs on legs, a propane stove for sterilizing bottles, and tarps to keep the woodpiles dry. Peter had suggested I convert the outbuilding at the far end of my father's land into a proper sugarhouse, but my father's little shed seemed steeped in darkness. On the days I had to drive past it to get to the Vixen Hill hives, I averted my eyes, scarcely able to look at it without feeling the skin tighten on my scalp. Besides, it was too small, and it wasn't mine.

Thick clouds bunched around the sun. Short, lacy shadows fell onto the snow through the bare branches of my oak tree as I raised the siphon tube to my mouth and drew up the sap, holding some in my mouth. No wonder the Iroquois drank sap as a tonic; I savored its cold, barely sweet freshness while it gurgled steadily into the tubs. I tilted the tank to empty the last dribbles, then started the fire, laying on some extra kindling to speed the boiling.

Stately bubbles rolled in to the middle of the pans; wisps of steam drifted toward the trees. It would take hours of boiling; for every gallon of syrup I bottled, I'd have to boil away thirty gallons of sap. In those hours, my mind would wander into a quiet I'd interrupt every now and then to stir the syrup or to shake a couple of drops of top milk into the pan when it threatened to boil over.

Above the far end of the field, a pewter sky streaked with afternoon gold reached down to cast an eerie brightness on the patches of snow. A shadow flickered at the edge of the woods as the fire breathed and stretched, creaking in the stillness.

A doe, graceful and nervous, emerged from the woods, walking point for a fawn who bent her head to nibble among the woody undergrowth. Oblivious, safe under the watchful eye of her mother, the fawn poked and snuffled among the hummocks. Then, alerted to some unseen danger, the doe twitched and cocked her head. Silently, I urged them to watch over each other. The doe turned toward me and I stood to meet her gaze, pleased that she had heard me. At my movement, she led the yearling out of the clearing. Like a dream fading, they vanished into the woods and I was alone again.

Lengthening shadows signaled that most of the waiting was over. I leaned into the steam, inhaling to check for that caramel-candy smell that meant the syrup was approaching the critical stage.

Droplets clung to my face, an icy glaze of moisture that I wiped away with my sleeve. Much of the clear liquid had boiled away and the sap had turned a thick, glossy amber. The hydrometer float came to rest exactly at the hot-syrup mark. The sample was perfect—Fancy grade and ready to bottle.

With heavy tongs, I lifted the burning logs and set them in the brick-edged ring where they would provide heat and light for the rest of the operation. I skimmed tiny floaters of ash from the syrup with a cheesecloth-covered paddle, then pulled on my asbestos-lined gloves. When I turned the spigot, syrup flowed into the first bottle in a thin ribbon.

The work went well, rhythmically, quietly. I had fifty pints filled and capped before I noticed the inky darkness that lay tight against the hills. The cold slowed me a bit but I took a few quick breaths to get the blood moving into my fingers and toes, and grabbed the last rack of bottles.

The purr of a car engine broke the quiet, and I gritted my teeth in response.

I was here to make maple syrup, to succumb to the trance of my own measured, precise movements and to complete a task I loved, not to entertain visitors. The glare of headlights made it difficult to see much; the car was small, foreign, but that was all I could tell in the darkness. Around Taconic Hills, you get to know vehicles and their owners, and this was one I had never seen. I lifted the last rack of sterile bottles from the stove and set an empty one under the spigot. The way the day had gone, I thought angrily, there was little chance that the driver would have the good sense not to interrupt my work.

The car door slammed and a woman in a hooded leather jacket, dark slacks, and city pumps picked her way around the hard ruts in the driveway, making careful progress in my direction. A dainty leather purse hung from her shoulder; thin, lilac-colored stockings showed beneath the hem of her slacks.

"Excuse me, Peter Hoving was supposed to stop by to talk about some work on my house. I thought he said four o'clock. But maybe he meant here. I didn't write it down. Is he around?" Her voice was rich and low, and somehow familiar.

"He's not here." I capped the full bottle and set another under the flow.

She came closer and knelt beside me; her head barely reached the top of my shoulder. She had a strong, straight nose and a full mouth.

In the light of the flickering fire, her face was deeply shadowed but I had the feeling that I'd seen her somewhere before. Spicy perfume cut through the cold air.

"What's this?" she asked as she reached out for one of the bottles. "You shouldn't—"

Her cry of pain interrupted my warning. She snatched her hand away, the beam of the car's headlights brightening the tears that sprang to her eyes.

The bottle under the spigot started to overflow; syrup congealed in a sticky stream as it cooled, spilling precious ounces onto the ground. My hands shaking with anger, I twisted the spigot to keep from losing any more of my Fancy syrup—now I'd have to stop my work to see to this woman. I couldn't ignore the sharp intake of breath between her teeth; she was clearly in pain.

I scooped up a mound of ash-darkened snow from the drift beside the woodpile. "Stick out your hand," I ordered. "I was about to tell you that it was hot maple syrup but you—"

"I'm always doing things like that," she said, her voice thinner now and cracking. She didn't wince when I covered her palm with the snow. "Thanks. I'm sorry if I mucked things up. I didn't mean—"

"Keep ice on this and it will be all right. Peter won't be home until late." I stuck a pan under the spigot and opened it again. The only way to save the remaining two or three pints would be to finish them off in the kitchen, and even then I wouldn't be able to put a Sweets label on them.

Her pretty face wrinkled in a frown. "Late? He won't be home until late? I thought he was going to—" All at once, the frown disappeared and she was smiling. "I'll be at home tomorrow morning, if you don't mind telling him that Catherine Delaney stopped by."

"If I remember," I said curtly as I loaded the first rack of filled bottles onto the truck.

She shook the melted snow from her hand and walked with straight-backed dignity to her car. She bent to examine her palm in the glare of the headlights. The hood slipped off her head and blond curls tumbled out, falling onto her narrow shoulders in a silky cascade, the way I imagined Alicia Fitzhugh's hair would look if she undid her tight coil. What color were her eyes? I wondered. Emerald? Lapis?

She slammed the car door and backed all the way down the drive-way, her right arm flung across the back of the seat the way country boys do when they're traveling in reverse.

The fire sputtered and crackled, sending a shower of sparks raining down onto everything. I dumped a bucket of water over the glowing coals, stirred them with a stick, doused them again, and ran my fingers through the ashes. Cold, utterly cold.

That done, I went into the house, poured some Scotch into a wineglass, and sat down in the living room to wait for Peter.

Three

In the cold and dark of early morning, I regretted the attack of territoriality that had caused me to snap at Catherine Delaney. Frustrated because I couldn't understand the images provoked by the sight of Ruth's starred cross, I had used Catherine as a target. That strange piece of metal—it wouldn't leave me alone, lurking in my mind when I should have been paying attention to other things, prodding me awake before I'd slept enough to feel rested.

Peter had tiptoed in during the deep, quiet hours when the moon cast a dusting of silver on the fields and trees. Surprised to find me curled on the sofa under the Navaho blanket, surprised to see an untouched glass of Scotch on the table, he led me to our bedroom, his breath a little beery as he kissed me good-night. Gently, he helped me out of my jeans and shirt and then fell asleep almost instantly. I huddled under the quilted coverlet, restless, finally drifting off. When I awoke, we were turned away from each other, each toward our own wall, only our feet touching.

There was no use pretending I'd fall asleep again. I made my way down the shadowy hall to the dining room to start the morning fire in the Ashley. Prince, the grandson of my beloved Queenie, shifted and stretched from his sleeping place under the harvest table in the center of the room. The blue floral rug now wore a permanent haze of honey-colored dog hairs, but the stove provided Prince's winter warmth so I didn't mind. He tilted his head to follow my progress past the highboy. With carved pineapples and gargoyles climbing from its legs to the borders of its upper shelves, it was a frequent topic of discussion between Peter and me. *He* loved it; I wished I would wake up one day and find the grotesque thing gone. So far, it hadn't obliged me.

Shivering from the cold that seeped up from chinks between the wide boards of the pine floor, I crumpled a sheet of newspaper and tented up a handful of kindling sticks in the stove, then held a match to the paper until it flared into bluish flames. Dark smoke curled into the room, stinging my eyes.

I'd forgotten to open the flue. Prince's whuffle as he pattered into the kitchen was ample comment on my performance so far this morning. Coughing, I jumped up and turned the handle, then knelt in front of the stove, muttering about my own incompetence until the smoke streamed up the broad stovepipe and the flame burned orange.

Even awake, it seemed, Catherine Delaney and that bizarre cross wouldn't leave me alone. To make a strange matter worse, both were connected to Ruth. But I was being foolish. Life was more than a power struggle between Ruth and me. Yet when I tried to get beyond that, I heard only an inner voice warning me about the dangers of disturbing the past.

I lay four larger pieces of wood on the fire, closed the door, and damped the flue before I went to the kitchen to make coffee. The large room was chilly; a draft streamed around the weather stripping where the ill-fitting window sash gaped. Outside, a cardinal pecking at a suet ball in my old oak tree was the only spark of color in the gray landscape. The leafless branches of the tree seemed haphazard, out of control, and the snow looked unclean. It cheered me to see the clouds moving closer, promising fresh snow and perhaps even a storm. Winter's fierceness would be a welcome relief, despite bringing the sap run to an early halt.

I settled into a chair beside the window and watched the sun struggle to break over the hill, first lighting the snow with pink and amber, then giving way again to a flinty gray.

I had taken only a sip of my coffee when Peter ambled into the kitchen, raking his hands through his tumbled hair. Warm from sleep, he held me close and reached beneath my sweater to rub my back. He lifted my chin with his hand, his mouth cool and minty, the kiss a pleasant greeting. "You talk to Mother? You going to help her keep Taconic Hills safe for her grandchildren?"

I pulled away from him, fighting my desire to yell, and counted to five as I tried to catch my breath. "I am going to speak to your mother later, and yes, I am going to do the play. I thought we weren't going to talk about having children until the spring."

"And *I* thought you'd agreed to actually consider the possibility instead of hiding from it." He turned his back to me, pouring coffee.

"It frightens me. Not childbearing, you know that. But the constancy. The commitment. What if I can't handle it?" *Like Julia couldn't,* I wanted to scream. Instead, my words were barely audible.

In reply, Peter took my cold hands and kissed each finger with his warm lips, his breath on my skin soothing and somehow substantial. When he leaned back into his chair, he let go of me but held my gaze with his. "Okay, new subject. What did you mumble last night about Catherine Delancy?"

At the sound of her name, my stomach twisted again. I hated my own mean-spirited wish that she would just go away. I didn't like feeling small and petty. Well, *tall* and petty: Catherine was the dainty one. "She wants you to call her this morning. Says you missed an appointment yesterday. At her house at four."

Peter's forehead furrowed. "Must be her blue-blood Connecticut background that makes her think she's always right. You'd think someone who could memorize an hour's dialogue would be able to remember that I said *Friday.*"

"An hour's dialogue?" Ben hadn't even written the play yet. A flash of scarlet shot across my field of vision as the cardinal flew to an uncertain perch on the bare lilac bush near the back door.

He shrugged. "She rebelled against Mommy and Daddy by going off to New York to act in some daytime soap. 'As Time Goes By.' Now she's decided she's really a painter, so she quit her TV career and bought the Hetherton house on Wilkie Bridge Road. Wants to convert one of the bedrooms into a studio. It needs new windows, shelves, a skylight, lots of work."

Maybe I'd seen her, heard her voice on some trailer during a break in the evening news. Maybe she played a pampered, devious woman, and I'd been reacting to *that* person. The tight fist in my stomach relaxed its grip.

"She's the solution to Mother's last casting problem." Peter poured more coffee into our cups, then leaned against the stove. "That unfilled role in the play—Mother needed another city person to balance the cast. If you give her half a chance, you might find out you like her. She's smart and nice. Pretty down-to-earth, really, despite Mommy and Daddy and finishing school in Greenwich.''

"She's already agreed to do it?" Saying it aloud only confirmed something I knew as soon as I saw Catherine Delaney's blond hair tumble to her shoulders.

"Mother met her in the general store yesterday afternoon. You know Ruth—she just came out and asked her to take the part of Klaudia Weigelt and what could the poor woman do? You sound like you've got something against her." He set his cup in the sink and then stood looming above my chair. "Are you jealous?"

"Of course not." But I said it too quickly. I tried thinking generous thoughts to sweep away the mental picture of Catherine Delaney and Peter poring over blueprints together, but it was no good. An edge of sarcasm leaked into my voice. "At least Ruth gets to have one professional in her play."

"Cut that out, Sarah. The whole world will not disintegrate if you admit someone stirs up feelings in you. Come on, say it. Tell me you feel something. Jealousy. Insecurity. Anxiety. *Something.*" He'd hardly unclenched his jaw; his speech ended with an exasperated hiss, like a balloon collapsing in on itself and forcing out all the air.

"Don't you know I wish I could?" I stared at the tabletop, paying too-careful attention to the uneven grain and to the tiny nicks and scratches in the surface. *The points of the stars were so sharp.*

He stood back, fixing me with a knowing look. "You haven't gotten over it, have you? Being called Julia, I mean."

In that instant, every tiny doubt I'd ever had about the advantages of marriage as a condition of my life evaporated. Peter knew me so well. He could name what was bothering me and thus take away some of its power. *Of course* I was still suffering the effects of being called by her name. It had taken so much energy over so many years to keep Julia Stanton in shadow that I had none left when Alicia fixed a glaring light on her.

"You know, you're letting a woman you haven't seen in twenty-five years endanger our marriage." He said it simply, as though he were telling me he was leaving for work or that I had spilled salt on the table. "Everyone you become attached to is *not* going to leave you, Sarah."

I wanted him to say: *I won't.* But he didn't, not then, although he had said it countless times, until I thought I'd heard it enough. I studied his mouth, the way his lower lip looked as though someone had left the impression of a touch in its center. I watched him watching me; when he looked away, I felt as though part of him had been left inside me.

"Even just thinking about it makes me . . . I'm afraid of what I might discover or what it will mean." I shivered when he touched my cheek and then brushed away a stray hair.

"Slow down, Sarah. It's like being scared of thunder or being afraid to drive in a snowstorm. It's fear that makes a situation dangerous."

To be stopped by fear—no, that was for other people. *I need to deal with this,* I thought. Habits two decades old would be hard to break; my father was sure to be furious when I spoke her name. Still, it was that or continue to let Julia Stanton rule my life from her place in the darkness.

I waited to be slammed back down to earth by the rough hand of reality reminding me that learning about Julia Stanton was an impossible idea. Instead I felt free and light, as though I were floating on a wave of gentle elation.

The morning collecting went quickly. Twice I had to break a thin layer of ice before I could pour the sap out of the buckets. A change was in the air, but for now I was happy to fix on immediate tasks. Solitude, work, and long hours among the elements—these had always been my tonics. The faster I worked, the better I felt, and by the time I reached the last stand of maples, I was humming "Ode to Joy" and marching briskly from tree to tree, emptying buckets with easy abandon.

The holding tank in the truck was only half-full. I'd have to wait another day or maybe even two to boil off; the only thing I had to do was check my Thursday hives, part of the rotating schedule that brought me practically full circle around the county each week. Twelve hive sites, one hundred seven hives—in winter, I could check them all in a week, in about an hour a day. The prospect of an afternoon puttering in the greenhouse and pretending it was almost spring pleased me, and I headed for the post office to see if my pumpkin seeds had come in yet.

I cut across East Taconic Road and, still singing, pulled up at the post office, a homey bungalow built by one of Deeny Lambert's ancestors who never came back from Teddy Roosevelt's charge up

San Juan Hill. It sat on the southwest corner of the crossroads that constituted the town proper.

The general store and an antique shop with a small café in back, all in weathered wood, occupied the northwest corner. The store was the brainchild of a Manhattan advertising dropout who, in 1968, tried selling scented candles, brown rice, and red lentils, then switched to pepper Brie and bottled water. Finally, in 1987 Deeny and his wife Nancy took over. After that, Campbell's soup, Coca-Cola, Genessee beer, and Charmin kept a steady stream of customers stepping up to the stamped-metal cash register.

Opposite that was Doc Verity's house, the side-entrance office a familiar if not altogether welcome sight. All my childhood inoculations, a total of seventeen stitches (eight that start at my hairline, so that it looks like I have an extra part above my right eye), and all the usual illnesses—I couldn't count the times I'd waited for her to reach into the paper bag under her desk and pull out a remedy or a treat to make me feel better. Less than a quarter mile down the road, the Taconic Hills Historical Society and the *Columbia Journal* each occupied small frame houses on either side of a parking lot big enough for ten cars. There were seldom more than four filling any of the spaces.

The ownership of the fourth corner had been under dispute for so long that everyone simply took turns mowing the weeds to make our little village look like the rural paradise we wanted it to be.

At eleven o'clock on a February morning, though, the only action in town was at the post office.

Jeanie Boice had been the postmistress since the days when I had to stand on my toes to reach the counter. Warm brown eyes magnified by wire-frame glasses enliven her plain round face. Good-humored and optimistic, she's one of those institutions that gives small-town living its good name. I sometimes wished she'd say something unpleasant or let a single testy comment slip out, but she never did. Mostly, I had come to believe that she was as accepting as she appeared.

"How's the sap?" Jeanie leaned both elbows on the wooden counter and rested her chin in her hands, squinting as I pulled the door shut. She would measure the sap run by my expression, no matter what my words said, and I loved her for that.

"About the same as last year. This weather won't hold beyond the afternoon." I nodded out the window at the spiteful snow sky. It was looking more and more like it would bring the kind of storm that would linger for days.

Jeanie reached into one of the numbered cubbyholes and pulled out a square padded envelope that sported a glorious orange pumpkin on its front. "Seeds," she said matter-of-factly. "That's all."

"Thanks, Jeanie." I was about to grab my packet and head for the door but I stopped. Jeanie Boice had worked behind this counter forever and knew everyone and everything about them—and liked them anyway, even the outsiders. A shiver of excitement ran through me as I realized that once I started, there was no calling this off. I was about to change the old rules and she was sure to notice. I searched for an opening but my mind wouldn't settle anywhere. If you know nothing at all, I reminded myself, anything is a beginning. "Now, this is just between you and me—and don't ask me why I'm asking, okay?"

Jeanie waited for my question, her blunt, chafed hands resting easily on the counter.

The brightly colored seed packet was the first object I saw. "Julia Stanton—was she a gardener?" I asked, surprised by my own words.

"Sarah." She leaned toward me, her brows knitting together and her mouth open.

"It's all right, Jeanie. Tell me about her. Please."

The silence that followed seemed endless. Jeanie's eyes went somewhere far away and her face offered no clue to her thoughts. When she started to talk, it was in a voice at once tentative and husky. "Flowers. She was taken with flowers. Your mother grew the biggest zinnias I ever saw, the whitest snowdrops, the most fragrant lilac bushes in this part of the county. She even took to saving her own seeds and pretty soon she developed early-blooming cosmos and special colors of dianthus."

I envisioned a tall, thin woman, her milky-white face shaded by a broad-brimmed straw hat, bending over rows of dainty blossoms to pluck out the offending weeds. It was a peaceful scene, and I allowed myself to enjoy it.

"She got to be kind of an expert. When people found out what she was up to out there on that hill, they started asking her for help. Whatever anyone asked of her," Jeanie said, her voice turning melodic over its usual gruff heartiness, "she went out of her way to try to do for them. Someone wanted forsythia cuttings, she'd leave her own vegetable garden half-dug and go take a cutting for them.

Someone's delphiniums got black rot, she'd spray 'em with some secret concoction. And while she was gone doing that, the aphids would get her roses. Generous—Julia Stanton was very generous."

To everyone but me. Maybe she simply had no sense of limits, no ability to say no. What Jeanie was calling generosity could have been a need to ingratiate herself to people she wanted to impress, a community whose acceptance she desperately courted.

Jeanie nudged the pumpkin seeds toward me, watching my face with an earnest look that made me glad she'd been the first person I asked about Julia. But I'd heard enough for now. Little bits at a time —it was all I could afford to let in without feeling overcome, swallowed up by a new reality. Dimly, I knew that one of my struggles would be to hear the good things. It was my old trick: trying to prove she was selfish enough, hateful enough so that I could go on blaming her for leaving, and not feel the loss as pain.

"Thanks, Jeanie. See you later." I grabbed my packet and started for the door, but it sailed open and Ben Yarnell blew inside, rubbing his hands and grinning.

Ben fancied himself something of a big brother to me, but his protectiveness often went a step or two too far. Then he'd rely on his joshing humor to get him out of trouble. And it worked, most of the time. Today, though, I wanted only to take what I'd learned from Jeanie and examine it again, privately.

"Hey, Sweets. How goes the flow?" He hit my shoulder with his open hand as though I were an old football buddy.

Jeanie tried to hide her smile, making a great show of turning away to sort the mail, although I knew she'd hear—and remember— every word Ben and I exchanged.

I was going to disappoint both of them. I would *not* let Ben Yarnell prod me into a round of time-wasting banter by calling me Sweets. I had work to do, things to consider.

"Three hundred gallons yesterday, less today." Suddenly the hot air and Jeanie's lavender scent were too much. I tried to edge around Ben to reach the door. "Well, see you sometime."

"Ruth snag you yet?" His dark eyes grew mischievous and the tiny cracks in the winter-dry skin of his lips stretched as he smiled. "I sit at my desk and conjure up these people. Every damn time I write a scene with Emily in it, I see you. You're going to do it, aren't you? After all, like the rest of us, you've got plenty of free time on your hands, right? 'Time on my mind; you on my . . .' Are those the words? Did I get the tune right? Anyway, you've got the pioneer spirit written all over your face and . . . what?"

"I'll probably have to miss some rehearsals. I get very busy in August." All his jabbering—I didn't have time for this, especially now. I peered over his shoulder at the door, took a step in that direction.

"We're *all* busy. I'm huffing and puffing to keep my creditors distracted, for instance. But you're going to come to Monday's meeting and pledge your participation because you want to save Taconic Hills from Nicky Dembowski and the marauding developers, right, Sweets?" He stood as though he were planted on the floor, his strong legs spread in a wide V and his arms folded across his chest. "So, what are you going to wear in the fire scene? Appropriately tattered homespun, I hope. Will you play Emily as the siren or the martyr? You know," he said with new gravity in his voice, "you're like her in quite a few ways."

"Don't tell me you subscribe to Ruth's theory of casting according to hair color?"

"You're linked to Emily by more than that. She didn't make syrup, but did you know she was a beekeeper? Her letters keep referring to her checking her skeps. What's that?"

"Straw hives. The wooden ones weren't invented until the mid-nineteenth century. I wonder why Ruth didn't mention Emily's bees." I knew, of course. She always held back ammunition; perhaps she was planning to fire that round if I refused her. "Well, okay, that's *one* thing old Emily and I share."

"And even better, she went after what she wanted," he said, his eyes narrowing as a smile tugged at the corners of his mouth, "with the same quiet and elegant determination to be in charge of her own world that you have."

"Is that the same as being the perfect—what did Ruth call it—the perfect *helpmeet* to her man?" I liked Ben's Emily better than Ruth's. At that moment, the discrepancy hadn't yet become a source of concern.

Ben's pleasant face twisted in a grimace. "She might not have been the Mother Teresa of her time, exactly, but she was a brave woman, our Emily. She drowned trying to save a drowning neighbor. Early in the honey harvest, the year of her thirtieth birthday, she's walking along with this pot of comb honey. The way I picture it, she's humming a church song, watching a fat robin rooting in a patch of dirt, when she hears this cry. Sets the pot down, runs to the pond, tries to save this burly lumberjack who's flailing away in the water. But he panics, pulls her down and, well, so long woodcutter and bye-bye Emily."

I gulped a breath to dispel the choking feeling in my throat and then wondered at my reaction: I'd always loved water—ponds, streams, the rain—and I was a strong swimmer. The sensation passed, and despite my desire to get to the hives and finish my outside work, and to reflect on what Jeanie had told me about Julia Stanton, I was curious to hear what Ben had learned about Emily Schiller.

"How'd you find out about her? That was two hundred years ago."

"I've read a carload of old letters, even some of Emily's in her very own fine, loopy handwriting. The good people at the Historical Society have preserved them in plastic sleeves. Numbered. Indexed. Great job. Came from attics all over the county. There are other connections between the two of you, Sweets. For one thing, she married the son of one of the most influential women around and immersed herself in a life of hard physical work that kept her close to the land and—"

My laugh, loud and whooping, surprised even me. I might have expected this from Ruth, but from Ben it was a curious departure from his usual cynical self.

He looked wounded by my laughter and by my inability to share his beliefs. "Maybe it isn't much, but that . . . and your hair and . . . Oh, hell, forget it. All that stuff about the fire and Emily's first fiancé—a thief, according to charges brought against him by Livingston. *She* was the one who exposed him, if you can imagine that. And the business of hanky-panky between Stefan and Klaudia Weigelt—nothing like that in your life or in Peter's. You, in all your rational glory, are, of course, pooh-poohing any thought that you might have a—let's call it a *spiritual* connection to some character from two hundred years ago. Am I right, or is this Paris?"

Ben's telling was so much more intriguing than my mother-in-law's sanitized version. Still, the uneasiness I'd felt when Ruth mentioned reviving the past surfaced again, and I wanted to whisper that we'd be better off leaving the Schillers alone. Instead, I made elaborate looking-out-the-window motions.

"Nope," I said when I turned around to face him again.

"Nope?" A frown creased Ben's brow.

"No Eiffel Tower."

Ben's laugh rolled out in a boom. "You're okay, Sweets. Just don't go getting all metaphysical about this."

"I'm an intelligent human being, perfectly capable of reading a script without—"

"Of course you are." The laughter disappeared from his voice. "I hope I can follow my own advice. See you Monday night at the meeting." He stepped away from the door and asked Jeanie for his mail.

I frowned at his back, trying to read from his posture what all this meant but he was hunched over the counter absorbed in a sheaf of envelopes and magazines. Jeanie disappeared into the rear room; I said good-bye loud enough for them both to hear and then I stepped outside into the bracing cold and the wind, holding the hazy image of Julia Stanton close to me.

Clayton Boice, Jeanie's husband, was coming up the walk. His white hair, a permanent squint from trying to see through the cataract in his right eye, and failing hearing marked his age. Before his retirement, he'd been a teacher at the Copake School and the de facto medical staff if it was one of the days the traveling nurse wasn't there. As a child, I never minded cuts and fevers; Clayton's bushy eyebrows and gravelly voice always meant kindness and comfort to me, and he maintained an endless supply of lollipops to pull out of a drawer or a pocket whenever the situation required. By November of anyone's first year in his school, Clayton knew your favorite flavor. The one time he'd offered me a green one was after I'd gotten the wind knocked out of me when I fell on the climbing bars. I'd frowned and told him that he'd made a mistake, but then he grinned and handed me an orange sucker, and said, "Now I know our Sarah's all right."

"Weather's going to change, Sarah. Wicked storm coming, but for now it's real pretty. Cold, though. Too cold."

"You looking forward to spring, Clayton?"

"Whispering? Who's whispering? I'm talking loud and clear." Clayton's smile was serene; I wondered if anyone had ever suggested that he have his hearing tested.

And as I looked at his plain, strong face I realized that Clayton had been in high school about the same time as Julia had.

"Clayton, was Julia Stanton a good student?"

His frown and the tilt of his head as he offered me his good ear made me wonder if he'd understood my question. I tried again, talking louder, nearly shouting. "Julia Stanton—was she a good student?"

This time he heard me.

"You sure you want to talk about this?" His expression altered subtly.

"Yes." I nodded at the same time, to make sure he knew exactly what I meant.

"Now, don't forget, she was a stranger. Family came here halfway through high school and all the boys were smitten, me and Roy and Jim Dembowski, and . . . the girls, well . . . fifteen is a hard age for young people as it is and Julia wasn't like everyone else, with her painting and her scarves. Always wore some scarf or another around her neck except in the very hottest part of summer." Clayton's face softened, as Jeanie's had just minutes earlier. "She made B's mostly, and A's in French and art. She used to say that someday she was going to Paris. Most daring thought anyone expressed around here, those days. What Julia was really good at was painting. Pretty scenes. Flowers mostly. I believe she could have been a famous painter. She talked about going to that school in Paris to study painting. . . ."

His voice trailed off and I followed his gaze to the porch. Ben looked down at us distractedly, his pile of magazines and envelopes precariously balanced in the crook of his arm. Clayton's hand touched the bill of his cap, and he went on up the steps past Ben and into the post office.

"Hey, Sweets," Ben called as I started for my truck, "you drive carefully. Looks like it could get dangerous out there."

Ben and Clayton were right: change was coming. The temperature would take a precipitous drop some time in the next twenty-four hours and wouldn't budge out of the teens for days. Another sap season was drawing to a close, but my bees were always here, always part of my life.

Winter work was simple: all I had to do was check the hives for signs of predators or other physical problems. Activity at one of my Vixen Hill hives had been ominously slow, but I couldn't open it for several weeks because of the cold, and I felt frustrated at the lack of real work. These winter chores were almost too easy, too lonely without the company of the busy, flying creatures.

I parked in the packed-dirt turnout and followed the path I'd made the week before through the snow, crossing two hundred feet of flat meadow that Tim Talley kept in alfalfa. Talley's pond was shaped like a teardrop, round and fat at the top, tapering almost to a point toward the spillway of an old dam site. In the weeks that the sap had been running, the pond ice had thinned and blackened, and the rush of water over the spillway was, that afternoon, a great, pounding roar.

Julia Stanton, gardener, painter. Quiet occupations, a simple woman who worked the earth and loved the natural beauty that surrounded her. I saw that it was possible that I'd fall in love with her and then be even angrier that she'd taken herself away from me. I reminded myself of the rest of the picture that Jeanie and Clayton had sketched, of a woman so eager for approval she let other people make endless demands on her, and my disdain comforted me.

The cold seeped through my gloves; my nose tingled. I marched to the rickety footbridge spanning the head of the spillway, a twelve-foot-wide narrowing of the pond that dropped off steeply to the rocks below. The swirling water hissed and frothed; I watched it leap up to grab a pine cone that had been perched on one of the rocks and bounce it down the slick, sharp facets of stone until it was carried away by the rush of the current.

Shivering, I continued across the old bridge, two logs running across the pond, joined together by slats nailed to each log.

Everything looked in order. The tarpaper around each hive was intact, the tiny dots of yellow that peppered the snow near the entrances to each box a sign that the bees were thriving and still keeping house. I was relieved; one winter when we had little snow, I couldn't check so easily for fecal matter and I'd discovered that a family of mice had gotten to the honey stores of several hives. The bees inside had starved to death.

Had Emily Schiller ever had that problem? How many hives had she kept? I could hardly imagine someone in a long skirt tramping through the snow and bitter cold to see if her bees were wintering safely.

The far hive, in shadow, emitted a whirring hum that meant trouble. The bees were working too hard to keep warm; they would use up their winter rations early. I made a mental note to get Dad or Peter to come out with me next week and move the hive to a warmer spot.

Dad: I had to talk to him about Julia. Surely he would be upset at this abrupt change of the rules, this breaking of a silence we had scrupulously kept for so many years. I would have to tread carefully, but the sooner I did it, the less time I'd have to consider, and to lose courage.

No one answered. The house was unlocked; in Taconic Hills, only week-enders felt the need to lock their doors. But it was an unspoken rule among the three of us, Dad and Peter and me, like not opening a diary that your best friend had dropped, like not reading your husband's mail: unless an emergency arose—and that hadn't happened in the six years I'd been married—we only went inside each other's homes if we were invited.

Almost relieved that no one answered, I turned to go back to Vixen Hill Lodge when my father's voice called me back.

"Hey, Sarah. Don't you know enough to come in out of the cold?" His grizzled head motioned me inside and I followed his plaid flannel shirt into the hall and then up the stairs.

I shed my outer layer in front of his stove, a fifty-five-gallon oil drum with a door and a pipe hole cut into it and legs welded on so that it stood a full twelve inches off its brick platform. The room was fragrant with wood: wood from the fire, wood that he had carved into bears and squirrels and deer, and from the piles of shavings he collected in boxes.

As his callused fingers worked an eight-inch piece of pine with a small whittling knife, soft curls floated to a newspaper on the floor. His hands moved without apparent attention from him, fashioning a buck with a noble rack of antlers.

Despite the heat I felt chilled and I moved close to the stove. This was a terrible idea. For as far back as I could remember, Dad showed his anger by a clamping down—of his jaws, so that no words or even sounds could escape, and of his clawlike hands—on whatever was within his grasp. When I was a child, this rigid paralysis was more terrifying to me than an explosion of shouts and screams. It was the potential, the fury feeding itself and swelling inside him that I feared.

"Dad?" I began.

He brushed a hair from his forehead and tugged at his ear; he looked so at peace that I almost couldn't get the words out. "Can you tell me . . . I've started to try to find out about . . ."

What should I call her? *My mother?* That sounded too personal for the relationship; she was the woman who had borne me and then left.

He raised his thick white eyebrows and rubbed a hand over the stubble along his jaw. Deep lines creased the space above his nose and bracketed his mouth in a grimace. His pants and shirt hung loosely on his gaunt body and the fierce light in his normally watery eyes made me certain he knew what I thinking. "Just say it, Sarah. What's on your mind?"

I started over, where it had all begun, with her name. "Julia. Julia Stanton. I need to find out who she was, what she was like. I can't pretend anymore. I need to know if she was ill or unstable, if something happened that drove her away, if she just couldn't stand the pressures of being alone here on this hill with a small child, if . . ." A choking sob finally burst from me and a flood of tears, grown huge from years of being held back, spilled over onto my face.

A great, shuddering sob shook my body, and my fists pounded my thighs. Dad sat unmoving, his face more hawklike than ever. I caught my breath and wiped my eyes with the back of my hand and forced myself to go on.

"For a long time," I said raggedly, "I thought she'd left because I'd done something bad. I prayed to God: 'Tell me what it was,' I said every night before I fell asleep, 'and I'll apologize. I'll fix it if I can.' I took my special things, my fishing reel, my Indian drum, my blue marble, even the turtle—you remember the little box turtle— and I left them under a bush for God to take in trade, hoping He'd bring her back. It didn't work, of course. And the worst of it was that I didn't even know what I'd done. He never told me."

Dad got to his feet. He loosened his grip on the whittling knife and laid it on the table. "Nobody to blame but Julia."

For once I wished he would say something to comfort me, but he didn't. He said, "She was evil."

"I don't think she was evil," I said when my voice returned, "but what she *did* was." Acts that hurt other people were evil, no excuses, no mitigating circumstances, but I hated the finality of labeling a whole person that way, even Julia Stanton.

A scowl hooded his brown eyes in darkness and I could fairly feel the crackle of indignation along his spine. His face was pale with anger. "Only evil people," he snapped, echoing the words I'd heard him say countless times, "do evil things."

The old anger flashed through me, a scorching bitterness that had burned away my childhood tears. "Look what you've done to yourself, thinking like that. It's turned you into a sour old man, and I don't want that to happen to me."

But seeing Dad's twisted features, I realized he wasn't mad at her. It was *me*—I was the one he glared at, I was the one he looked like he wanted to choke. As Alicia Fitzhugh had unsettled me, so I had reminded my father that the black emptiness in his heart bore a name: Julia Stanton. A livid red crept up his neck to his cheeks until finally he turned away and stuck his big hands in his pockets. "You better go home," he said, and he stalked into the hall.

I called after him and started to follow him down the stairs. "It's not over, Dad. I'm going to find out about her."

He looked up at me, reaching out to steady himself; groping, his hand found the banister and he said nothing and he made no attempt to get out of my way.

"I'll talk to you later," I muttered as I pushed past him, shoved the door open, and fled across the road to Vixen Hill Lodge, running hard, out of breath, leaving behind the shell of my father, whose deterioration into sullen self-righteousness had been swift and steady over the years.

I stumbled inside. Prince stared up at me expectantly with his bright eyes, but I dropped my things on the sofa and ran straight back to the greenhouse.

The small room, its glass wall speckled with condensation, was steamy and close. I tossed aside strips of old washed and ironed sheets hanging like hair ribbons waiting to tie up the summer's beans and tomatoes. Panting, I hauled out a bag of potting soil from beneath the hotbed and plunged my hands into the dirt, its woody, fecund richness overpowering, almost sickening.

I smoothed several inches of potting soil on the flat bed, covering the electric coil completely.

I patted the soil and mounded up twenty hills until they looked like little volcanoes. I poked a finger into the center of each mound, then dropped three flat tan pumpkin seeds into the holes. I covered the seeds with a half inch of dirt, then sprinkled the mounds with a fine spray of water.

I moved through these tasks with none of the usual calm I felt when I had my hands in earth.

And then I realized that I was seeking comfort from the very acts in which Julia Stanton had probably taken solace, and the thought that I might be like her in other ways, too, terrified me.

Four

In the days before the bicentennial meeting, I immersed myself in the rhythms of syrup making and cold. Questions about Julia formed in my mind at odd moments, when I'd pause to make even the smallest decision. Would she thin this seedling or leave it to grow? Would she intersperse kindling with bigger pieces of firewood to make a neat stack from the heap and tangle of newly split logs? Would she chose white or gray thread to repair the tear in the bee veil? I was collecting absurdities, and I struggled to put her out of my mind for a while.

I lectured myself on the dangers of imagining, but it did no good. Julia was with me now, all the time.

The smell of wet wool and rubber boots too near a heating vent almost overpowered me as I stomped the snow from my shoes. The two classrooms of the Little School, as everyone called it after the Big School was built in the fifties, were lit by the same milk-glass fixtures that had hung from the wooden ceiling when I was a student. One-piece desks with hinged tops still filled most of the floor space, even though children hadn't stored papers, crayons, and the occasional frog in them for years.

I eased into the classroom; because I was late, I had to settle for standing room. I'd gotten a call that one of my hives had been knocked over by a bear, the very same bear, the caller said excitedly, seen rummaging in the town dump the week before. I thought it was too cold, too early in the year for bears to be poking among garbage and beehives, and indeed the only footprints had been made by someone's size-ten snowmobile boots. I had righted the hive, ignoring the few testy bees who had flown at me more in confusion than anger. The entire event, phone call to finish, had cost me two hours.

Attending this meeting cold and hungry didn't make me any better disposed to the occasion, but I tried to keep my crankiness to myself as I listened to Ben Yarnell. His storytelling voice filled the room, skillfully catching everyone in the net of his tale, casually reeling in listeners and then playing out his lines as he pleased. Long-limbed and relaxed, he leaned against the teacher's desk, its red-gold wood dull under the pale light.

"The Livingstons," he said, "were lords of the manor, the British eqivalents of the Dutch patroons. The whole thing was a throwback to feudalism, so the system generated periodic rebellion by the indentured, landless workers. But there were opportunities, as there always are, for the clever person, and the Livingstons quickly recognized in Stefan's father the qualities of a fine bookkeeper: precision, care with details, discretion about family secrets, and unfailing punctuality."

I blushed under his direct gaze and teasing smile. From his seat in the first row, Peter turned to look at me, as did several others. So much for invisibility.

"Skip ahead to 1760, the year of Stefan's birth, and then fast-forward, fife and drums in the background, to 1777. Stefan's father joins the ragtag group that holds off Burgoyne at Saratoga, leaving Stefan, apparently an only child, and his mother to manage the Livingston accounts."

Ruth was pricked either by Ben's story or her own silent thoughts to search for me. Her stony expression relaxed when she noticed Jeanie and Clayton Boice watching her. I dipped my head to acknowledge her silent greeting, pleased that her eyes lingered for a moment on my old down vest, her way of letting me know that my casual attire hadn't escaped her attention.

"Stefan—an interesting fellow," Ben said as though he'd just this minute come to that conclusion. "Fended off fur traders who attacked his beautiful young neighbor, Klaudia Weigelt. I suppose the good fräulein came up with an appropriate way to thank him, although there's some speculation that Emily didn't much appreciate the young lady."

Ben conveniently neglected to specify Emily's response to Klaudia, but from what he had said in the post office the other day, a well-developed streak of genteel vengefulness wouldn't have surprised me. I was beginning to understand Emily, and to appreciate her independence. I looked around for Catherine Delaney and found her standing in the doorway, her expensive coat still buttoned to her neck and her cornsilk hair glinting with drops of melted snow, as though strewn with sequins. I should inquire about her hand, later, when the business of the evening was completed, but I wasn't sure my well of solicitude went that deep.

"Like any legend worth his salt, Stefan Schiller had more than his share of challenges. During the Revolution, while his father was away, Stefan and his faithful dog served as messengers. Tramping through the snow, fording rivers, bringing news to the revolutionary forces. Stefan's dog never made it back from one of their missions. Got snagged in some bear trap was what Stefan said in a letter, but our hero made it safely back through enemy lines."

Made it through enemy lines—I smiled to myself at the aptness of Ben's words to describe how I would feel when the evening was over. It was a bit of an exaggeration, but not much.

"Stefan's wedding," Ben continued, "was an adventure all by itself—seems the minister didn't show up. Methodist ministers traveled a fair amount those days, like circuit riders, and Stefan and his bride and their guests and all the baked hams and roasted chickens and pies waited for hours and hours. Near midnight, they finally pressed a friendly Lutheran cleric into service, cousin to one of the forge foremen, and went on with the wedding. The minister, they found out next day, made a wrong turn in the thick of the blizzard and ended up dead in a field. Frozen stiff, he was, and covered with snow."

Just like Edward Fitzhugh and his wanderings, and his similar, snowy death. If Alicia Fitzhugh were here, surely she'd see the connection.

"As Ruth has pointed out," Ben went on, "Stefan and his wife had plenty of opportunities to give up. They had to postpone working on their house when they—most of their neighbors, too—got sick. When they finally did get the house built, a fire burned the whole thing to the ground, and they had to start again. And Stefan's mother, good woman though she was, was bitten by a mad dog during a Fourth of July celebration and she died of rabies. Ever the troupers, Stefan and Emily kept going, they persevered, and Taconic Hills was born."

Ben cut the air with a theatrical flourish and leaned forward again to look directly at me. "For anyone who came in too late to hear Ruth's opening remarks, the good news is that planning for the bicentennial celebration is going very well indeed. The committees are set and the actors have been chosen. To do a really good job of bringing the past to life for the benefit of Taconic Hills, we knew we'd have to find exactly the right people for each role, and Ruth and I are very pleased, very confident, that we've cast this play perfectly, exactly as it should be."

The strength of his conviction disturbed me. His words were too close to the ones Ruth had used to talk about the past serving the needs of present-day Taconic Hills. I didn't want to believe that Ben and Ruth had some secret reason for urging me to take the part of Emily, or for waiting for Catherine Delaney to appear from thin air to fill the role of Klaudia Weigelt.

"And that, ladies and gentlemen, concludes the business portion of this meeting. Your patience will be rewarded by coffee and doughnuts, thanks to Jeanie, Marge, and Helen." He hopped from his perch and settled into one of the folding chairs at the side of the room. As though confirming that the meeting was adjourned, the big coffeepot gurgled noisily in the corner. Jeanie Boice set out a jar of powdered creamer and a box of sugar cubes on the long library table under the window; Marge Hoysradt pulled down a sleeve of Styrofoam cups from the supply cabinet: the Ladies' Auxiliary was working on automatic, slipping unconsciously into their roles as handmaidens, as though they had been born to serve.

The crowd bunched together in chattering clusters and I caught Catherine Delaney watching me. A friendly smile lit her face, her pale delicacy again reminding me of blond, petite Alicia Fitzhugh, or at least the Alicia Fitzhugh who might have come to such a meeting twenty-five years earlier.

All those years ago . . . Alicia Fitzhugh must have known Julia well enough so that even at her husband's funeral she was reminded of my mother when she saw me. Was I really so like Julia that other people, my father perhaps or Ruth, thought of her whenever they saw me? Did they ever, then, look past the resemblance to Julia Stanton and see me, Sarah, a person formed by the exercise of will?

I pushed the thoughts aside and made small talk about the

weather with Jeanie and Marge until I could free myself and inch through the crowd toward Peter. I had made my appearance; all I wanted as a reward was a cup of hot soup in front of my own fireplace.

As I approached the middle of the room, a palpable tension, like a swarm of angry bees, split the dry, hot air and I followed the pointed stares of the crowd to the source of the disturbance. My father and Ruth stood practically nose to nose in front of the wooden supply cupboards, engaged in a private war that was becoming more and more public as conversation stilled and everyone listened to the salvos being fired at point-blank range.

"Then don't come." Ruth's lips moved but her white, even teeth remained clamped together.

In response, my father's usually sunken chest expanded with his held breath. His face puffed up with inflated fury until his eyes bulged and the tiny hairs along his ropy neck stood straight out. Like certain animals when they're cornered, my father was making himself larger, to fill and dominate the space, but I doubted this opponent would be taken in by his trick. His voice was strained, a low, controlled rasp. "Sure, then you'll say I didn't cooperate and you'll turn it against me. Nosirree, Ruth Hoving, you give me something else to do."

"You must put aside your personal feelings about the church." Ruth warmed to her task, her cheeks glowing with battle lust. "You live in a community in which—"

"Don't give me that. You just find something for me that isn't inside a church." My father closed up his face and it was clear to me that in this at least, Roy's intransigence would be stronger than Ruth's determination to have her way.

I wanted to shake them until their teeth rattled, but they weren't my children and I was not responsible for them. The old yearning crept into my heart, for parents who would guide me through the maze, who would, by precept or example, help me to make my way, but I let it go.

My father had moved to the far end of the room, a thin, disheveled pariah too nearly the right size for the child's desk at which he sat. Ruth was off conferring with her cronies as I approached him; he flinched when I stooped to kiss his cheek.

"Why do you have to argue with her? Couldn't you wait and

phone her, instead of starting a public fight?" I pulled my chair closer to his so that he wouldn't have to raise his voice to answer me.

"You heard what she told me?" The muscles alongside his jaw bulged and a flush brightened his cheeks.

I wanted to run away but he turned to me, anguish in his eyes, and I was caught, against my will, by his need for an ally.

"She said if I was going to honor my commitment to be in her pageant, I'd have to go to rehearsals in the Sunday-school room of some damn church." He fairly spat out each word. "She knows I don't do that."

"Nobody's asking you to take Communion or even believe in God," I reminded him. "It's just a silly play."

His turtle-skin hands rubbed at his knee, the yellow, age-cracked fingernails rasping against his pants. He coughed, then asked, "Syrup done yet?"

I would go along with his need to seem normal. I shared it with him, and I knew better than to spend any more energy trying to convince Roy Stanton of something he'd set himself against. "Looks like it. I have to get started painting hives and—"

Full of smiles, Ruth sailed toward us. "I'm so glad you've come, dear. Oh, and Roy, I've been thinking. Right here, the Copake School is perfect for rehearsals. Bigger, easier to get to, good parking, don't you think?"

At least my father knew a peace offering when he heard one. His nod seemed to satisfy Ruth and signal an end to the skirmish. I wondered if either of them had learned anything; I doubted it.

"Sounds good to me," I said, girding myself against the hollow sound of my own voice mouthing inanities. "Excuse me, Ruth, I have to talk to Peter."

I was more forceful this time, not stopping, only nodding hello to people in my path. Peter looked so tired I wished I could soothe away the wrinkles on his forehead with a kiss. "Bad day?" I asked.

"Damn pipes were the wrong size." His frown deepened. "I had to go all the way into Poughkeepsie to get the right ones. What happened to *you*? You were even later than I was."

"Nothing important. I'll tell you later, after I figure out how to put you in a better mood," I whispered.

"Speaking of good moods," he whispered back, "did anyone ever tell you that reindeer socks are not sexy?"

"A whole lot more appealing than that dickey you wear." I ran my finger between his soft turtleneck and his even softer skin.

"Hey, you're the one who—" Peter stopped in midsentence.

I looked over my shoulder into the thoughtful face of Ben Yarnell, who had materialized from the crowd.

"That story about the minister," Ben said to Peter, as though he wasn't aware that he'd interrupted a private conversation, "got me thinking. Did it sound familiar to you? Put me in mind of old Ed Fitzhugh. Which made me think of Alicia. Which made me wonder whether anyone has thought to offer her a job on the bicentennial committee, something to get her out and with people again."

I doubted that being with people ever had been high on Alicia Fitzhugh's list of comforting things to do.

"Check with my mother or Marge about that," Peter suggested.

Ben nodded absently and headed into the crowd again. Peter's warm breath slid over my face, and I wished we were at Vixen Hill, forgetting for a while all the small and large half-resolved and still-mysterious questions. "Race you home," I offered.

"Loser has to grant the winner a wish," he countered, his face lighting with mischief and delight. Lovely man, he hugged me to him and then walked away, tossing a final remark over his shoulder as he went. "In fact, no contest. You're the winner. Be thinking of what you want."

The very notion sent waves of anticipation through me, and I followed Peter out the door to the steps of the school, happy to close the bustle and noise of the meeting behind me. Peter got to his van first and was headed down the road before I even reached my pickup.

Great fat snowflakes drifted through the moonlight so slowly they seemed to hang in the air on invisible threads, forming a curtain around me. The plows were out, and the sanders; the roads would be passable for a while, until the snow got small and mean and came down faster than the road crews could push it aside.

"Sarah!"

I whirled around and faced my father, and saw again, as I had the afternoon I'd fled his house, an accusation of betrayal in his eyes. We hadn't talked about that day, hadn't said Julia's name aloud since then. I picked my way over the icy walk, wondering if what I saw on his face was concern rather than anger, but I didn't want to take the time to find out now. Yet, as anxious as I was to be on my way, I couldn't pretend I hadn't heard him. "What is it, Dad?"

Snowflakes settled on his eyebrows and on the worn collar of his coat. "When am I gonna see you? You gonna come for Sunday breakfast?"

"You forgot—Saturday. I'll see you Saturday at six, at Peter's birthday party, right?"

At Ruth's house.

With both families pretending we were a jolly, close-knit group.

With the civilities maintaining a surface calm while the bubbles started rolling deep below, in preparation for the next eruption.

"Right. I remembered," my father mumbled as he turned and climbed into his truck.

The door slammed and I started to walk away, but I heard the squeak of the window being cranked down.

He stuck his head out the window. Against the black sky, with his breath steaming from his mouth, he was an apparition, a dragon of righteousness. "That harridan—she puts on her cloak of false piety and thinks God isn't watching. He sees her okay, she better learn that. And He metes out His punishment." His eyes burned with the flame of an anger that only my mother-in-law or the mention of Julia's name could fan into such brightness.

These great, extravagant, and insignificant dramas were tiresome to me, enervating to him, self-perpetuating.

How could a sensitive woman, one who tended a flower garden and painted watercolors, have married him? Or was it their marriage that turned Roy into the bitter man I knew?

March

Young queens, bred for resistance to disease and stress, produce more eggs, stronger pheromones to guide the colony's work force, and are beneficial to colony morale.
—*Everywoman's Guide to Beekeeping*, Revised Edition

Five

In the six years Peter and I had been married, we'd spent only one of his birthdays alone, the year Ruth went to Albany to lobby for money to fix the county's roads. She'd managed to extract proof of fealty by having a substitute birthday dinner four days later. I knew such obligations were part of the bargain when I married Peter; what I couldn't have predicted was that it would be Walter Hoving's measured conversation and long silences that made me comfortable on these occasions.

"Wonder what's keeping Roy," he said, handing me a brandy and pouring one for himself. In the lamplight, the brandy, Ruth's brass eagle above the fireplace, and Walter's blue eyes all glinted brightly.

"Taking care of some chore at the garage, I'd guess." My father was seldom on time; I was just as happy that he hadn't yet arrived.

Walter smiled and accepted my explanation without comment. I loved his solidity, yet he'd never felt unbending to me, and his laughter was seldom mocking. Men often say that they see in their mothers-in-law what their wives will become; Peter was, under the surface of his intensity, Walter's son. The resemblance was a shared dignity rather than anything physical, since no two men looked less alike. Where Peter was tall and dark and slender, Walter was stubby, pale, like an ear of corn that hadn't fully elongated or completely ripened.

"Wait till Roy and Clayton hear that Ruth wants to deck us out in knee britches for the pageant. Clayton's probably going to insist on a lollipop pocket in his shirt."

I couldn't keep back my smile at the picture of Walter, Clayton, and my father in wigs and balloon-sleeved shirts, wearing white stockings and pants that fastened below their knees.

"At least you gals can cover up, and in the kind of frilly dresses you don't get to wear around here these days." Walter leaned against the mantel, smiling along with me.

Before I could stop myself, without ever knowing it was coming, I heard myself say, "Did Julia Stanton like to wear frilly dresses?" To cover my own surprise, I swirled my brandy and watched the fire leap and flicker in the curve of the glass.

Walter's sturdy features didn't change, but his voice quavered, became a little sad, a little wistful. "Dresses, sure enough. She was partial to dresses. What she loved best, though, were pretty scarves."

"Scarves?" I prompted, eager to draw him out.

"I swear, she had a thousand. Flowered and plain, short and long, bright and dark. Wore a different one every day, practically. I always wondered whether it was her own idea or something her mother started when she was a little girl. We never did get to know her family really well. Her mother and father moved back to New York City as quick as they could, about four years after they moved up here. Julia was married to Roy by then." His smile broadened, deepening the dimple in his cheek. "One day, I guess she'd been married about a month, Julia invited Ruth and some other ladies, I don't remember who, to tea, all so proper, in the parlor. Lord, she couldn't have been more than twenty, bustling around pouring Lipton's from her fine china pot."

Just like a child playing house. Walter seemed much more charmed by the foibles of the young Julia than I was.

"And then she excuses herself and goes out into the kitchen and they hear plates clinking and such and then the oven door opening, and next thing you know there's a scream and a general commotion.

"Well, of course, Ruth rushes into the kitchen and there's Julia, sitting on a chair, sobbing into her apron and pointing to a pancakey thing on the floor. Took ten minutes to get Julia to say it was supposed to be bread. Thought it would rise in the oven."

This time I did laugh. A woman who dissolved into tears at no more provocation than an unrisen loaf of bread was impossible to take seriously.

"She wasn't to blame, you know," Walter said. "Her parents were odd ducks and they never did take the time to teach her anything, not even the most ordinary things. Why, she was so untutored she thought that all it took to clean a toilet was to flush it. That it cleaned itself each time." He chuckled.

"Thanks, Walter." I spread a thin layer of cheese on a cracker, just to have something to do while I chewed on this new information.

He looked as though he would ask the question I most wanted to avoid, about why after all this time I was inquiring after Julia, but he was distracted by Ben's old Volkswagen shuddering to a stop in the driveway, followed by a sleek gray Ferrari that pulled up behind my truck. Catherine Delaney stepped out, scooped up two brightly colored gift bags, and trailed close behind Ben on the path.

Maybe Catherine was Ruth's reminder to Peter that there were other, more suitable women he might have married. She certainly came closer to the ideal, according to everything Ruth had tried to change in me, and she appeared to get on with my mother-in-law with an ease we'd never shared and likely never would.

I looked down at my jeans and black wool sweater, at my reindeer socks. We made an interesting study in contrasts, Catherine Delaney and I.

"Something's bothering you, Sarah. You worried about your father?"

Walter's voice startled me; I'd forgotten he was in the room. I stepped closer to the fireplace and stared at the tongues of flame that licked the air. "A little. He usually remembers to call if he's going to be late."

"What made you—"

But before he could ask the question, everyone tumbled into the living room, laughing and chattering, bringing the scent of winter and snow with them. I said an awkward hello to Catherine, who wore plain black trousers and a lemon-yellow sweater with a strand of pearls at her neck. I was relieved that it wasn't quite the fashion ensemble I'd expected; still, she looked as though she'd *chosen*. Ben planted a quick, friendly kiss on my cheek, the tip of his nose cold as it brushed my overheated face. Walter got busy acting the host and pouring drinks and Ruth decreed that we'd give my father another half hour before we went ahead with dinner without him.

Ruth steered the conversation to the one topic we all had in common: the pageant. "From what I've seen of Ben's script, this is going to be a play audiences will remember." She patted his hand. "I *knew* you'd do a wonderful job."

"Why, ma'am," Ben said, affecting a southern-gentleman tone and fluttering his long lashes, "how you *do* go on."

"Oh, Ben, just take the compliment gracefully so I can move on to the next person." Ruth sounded as though his antics were wearing a little thin, but she wasn't angry—he was too good-natured.

"Oops. Blew that one, didn't I?" Ben grinned and looked around the circle of faces in mock concentration. "And the spotlight moves to"—he rose and pointed at each of us in turn—"our new friend, Miss Catherine Delaney. Tell us, Miss Delaney, how do you plan to prepare for your latest role, the dazzling Klaudia Weigelt?"

Catherine seemed startled but she recovered more quickly than I would have. Perhaps that poise was a result of her acting experience. Her smile looked relaxed enough until I noticed her restless fingers tracing patterns on the arm of the chair and realized that Ben had made her at least a little uncomfortable. Somehow, I liked her for that.

"Oh, I don't do much preparation, Mr. Yarnell," she said brightly. "I'm too susceptible to losing my own identity and being taken over by the character if I think about her too much. Occupational hazard."

An awkward hush fell over the room; I half expected Catherine to recite a soliloquy about depending on the kindness of strangers, but Ruth, as usual, took charge. "I do believe it's time to open Peter's gifts," she declared as she piled packages on the coffee table, ever watchful that her guests were happy.

"Sweets is his best present," Ben said, setting a square package wrapped in the Sunday comics atop the pile. "But this is in case you needed something else, good buddy."

Peter opened a book of Wyeth prints from Ben, a hand-knit, shawl-collared cardigan from Ruth and Walter, and an antique basket stuffed with thirty-three paper promises, one for each year, from me. I wished he would unfold one, just one, and not show it to anyone else so that we could share a moment of private anticipation, but he didn't; the stab of my disappointment took me by surprise.

"Mine's next." Catherine's teasing voice promised a treat.

Peter peeled back each bit of tape from the marbled paper, then stared wordlessly at a wood-framed eight-by-eight-inch canvas for too many long, silent minutes. Clearly he was moved by Catherine

Delaney's gift in a way he hadn't been by mine. I sat back on the sofa, away from him. Finally, he held the canvas up so that everyone else could look at it.

What I saw took my breath away. How wonderful it must be to have such talent. Two figures, a man and a woman in colonial dress, dominated the painting. They looked as though they might step into the room and ask for a hot toddy. The details—buttons, the cut of the woman's bodice, the shape of the man's collar—were as disturbing as they were extraordinary. Already, Stefan and Emily Schiller had acquired a too-tangible presence in my life. Or had Catherine painted a portrait of Stefan with Klaudia Weigelt?

My jaw tightened and a frown carved my forehead—these figures made me *angry*. And then I realized: it wasn't only the figures. Catherine was a painter, and I'd been wrapping her up with Julia Stanton in my mind. My relief made me feel generous, expansive toward Catherine. "It's a wonderful painting," I offered.

"Thanks." Her green eyes crinkled. "I wasn't sure how I'd research the costumes, but I found a great book in the Millerton library. I *love* libraries." Her own fervor made her laugh.

I was beginning to like her enough to regret that I'd nearly chased her away with my rudeness. "How's your hand?" I asked.

"Absolutely fine," she said, waving away the need for an apology. "No problem."

"Your hand?" Ben's reporter's gaze flitted from me to Catherine and then back again. Catherine's answer was an embarrassed shake of her head, and the topic was effectively closed.

When the conversation flagged, Walter told a sad little story about Alicia Fitzhugh going to the pharmacy to renew one of her husband's prescriptions. "Poor thing," he concluded, "she's at a loss without Edward to take care of. Been her whole life and now he's gone and she's all at loose ends. Doesn't know what to do with herself, I'd guess."

"Well, I know what to with *my*self. I've got two major jobs this month. One artist's studio on Wilkie Bridge Road," Peter said, the corners of his eyes lifting as he smiled at Catherine, "and a kitchen renovation I plan to start tomorrow if I can get the lady of the house to sign off on the plans."

"Can you really? That's wonderful!" We had talked for hours about the proper height for the counters, the placement of cabinets, the fact that I absolutely would not give up the eight-burner, three-oven monstrosity of a stove that took up the entire center of the room. And now it was really going to happen.

I jumped up and hugged him. "I like this—getting a present on *your* birthday."

"Your father promised to help me tear up the old linoleum tomorrow." Peter grinned.

"A kitchen transformation—what fun! Are you changing *everything*?" Catherine asked.

As Peter described the new cabinets and our plan to strip the floor and bleach the wide pine boards, Ruth bustled into the room, her white apron so bright against the light from the west windows that it hurt my eyes. "Dinner will be ready in a few minutes. Sarah, would you bring in the hors d'oeuvres tray?" She smiled at Catherine as if to apologize that she wasn't the chosen one, then marched into the kitchen.

I gritted my teeth; one thing Ruth couldn't complain about was that I'd never acted—or been treated—like a guest here. Ordinarily, I'd be pleased to be in the kitchen with her, trusted to perform some task in honor of the birthday of a man we both loved. I carried the tray to the kitchen and set it on the counter. Somehow, when I reached for the cracker box, my hand struck the basket; it fell to the floor, crumbs scattering everywhere, and for a startled moment I felt tears spring to my eyes.

Just like Julia, I thought, and the sound of her name in my head and the unwelcome comparison to her excessive emotions were enough to keep the tears from spilling over. "Sorry," I muttered. I got the broom and dustpan and swept the mess—minor, really, just a mound of crumbs no bigger than an anthill—and dumped it into the trash can.

Ruth reached over to take the cheese tray from my hands.

"Don't bother with that, Sarah. Two things. First, I'm afraid we're going to have to go ahead without your father. Walter couldn't reach him at home or at the garage." Her frown of disapproval was at odds with the concern in her voice. "And Sarah, dear, do you really think it's wise to be asking about your mother? After all these years? You know, I suppose, that Roy would be angry. But even more than that, one should leave the past alone. You have a life, a good one, with Peter and your bees. It would be much better for you to drop the whole thing." She took my hand. Hers, while not cold, felt very still, without tremor or even a discernible pulse.

My jaw clenched with the effort not to tell her to mind her own business and let me finally find out about mine. I didn't care whether the concern on her face was for me, for herself, or for her son, the boundary we shared. Damn her patronizing tone—she didn't know what I needed, hardly even knew *me* at all.

"Ruth, it's time for me to find out about Julia," I began. "I need to learn about her and about my own past. And my father already knows what I'm doing."

She let go of my hand and stepped back, her face a mask of serenity. "I see," she said, a musical lilt in her voice. "Will you take the rolls to the table while I finish up in here?"

I was dismissed.

My hands shook so badly the rolls nearly bounced onto the floor, but I would not, would *surely* not allow myself a repeat performance of Julia Stanton's silliness. I set the rolls on the table. Ruth had gone all out—her best drawn-thread linen, the holiday silver, and her fine white china with its slender gold band. Two pairs of candlesticks surrounded a low bowl filled with newly bloomed paper whites and pink freesias. Impressive—Ruth must have been anxious to assure our newcomer that she hadn't moved beyond civilization.

I just barely got through the rest of the evening, between Ben's bright chatter, Catherine's enthusiastic appreciation of the homey food, and Walter's long, gentle tale of taking down a barn and selling the weathered wood to an attorney for the walls of his city apartment. I made polite conversation and sang on key when the cake arrived. Finally, after the dishes were cleared, after Ben and Catherine said their good-byes, Peter and I were standing in our coats, the deep black sky tantalizing through the little arched window at the top of the door.

Ruth's lips brushed the air beside my face. "Remember what we talked about in the kitchen, my dear," she whispered against my cheek. "It's really the better way."

I'm only doing this for your own good.
This will hurt me more than it will hurt you.

No, Ruth, not quite.

"Thanks for dinner." I would not give her the satisfaction of a direct response, not on that topic. Walter came to the door and hugged me, and Peter and I carried the presents to his van.

Peter pulled the van door shut. The air was bitterly cold, but the van was new and the heater worked quickly and efficiently, unlike the temperamental thing in my old truck. The cocoon of the small space, just the two of us closed inside, was a gift after the strain of the party. Until Peter spoke. "That Catherine—she's so anxious to leave her old life behind. She got a phone call while I was taking measurements for the new windows. From some producer or her agent or something. Sounded like she was turning down a lot of money. She must really be into the simple life."

"Maybe she's just bored with acting." *Or else she's running away from something,* I thought, aware that I was feeling self-protective and a little peevish. I didn't want to give Peter the chance to ask if I'd been so quiet at dinner because of her presence. "I'm worried about Roy. He's never just not showed up before." He'd missed an appointment or two at the garage, but he'd never forgotten an occasion like a birthday dinner.

"Bad news travels fast, Sarah. We'd have a gotten a phone call if something happened. He probably just forgot. Let it go, okay?" His right hand, strong and graceful, lay on the seat between us.

I placed my own hand atop it, absorbing its warmth and settling into the slow quiet of the ride home. Peter hummed a tuneless song as he drove; when he stopped singing, our breath rose and fell in time to some absent metronome until he turned into the gravel drive of Vixen Hill Lodge.

"Wait," I said as he walked ahead. The stars shone like blooms of light in the night sky. Velvet quiet blanketed our hilltop, unbroken by voices or nocturnal movements. Peter bent his head and kissed me, a sweet, lingering kiss that warmed me from the inside.

"Paper promises. Anticipation isn't *really* the better part of an experience, you know." His kiss this time was more insistent.

I grabbed his hand and pulled him behind me, our boots crunching along the path to the back door.

"Hello, puppy." I flipped the light switch and reached down to scratch Prince's head; he pattered toward the living room, stopping at the doorway to see if I was following. When I didn't, he padded back to me and stuck his nose in my palm, the worried whine high in his throat a sound I wasn't used to hearing from him. Peter had disappeared into the bathroom. I followed Prince, little more than a low dark shape in the gloom as he led me toward the living room. A moan from the vicinity of the sofa startled me and I nearly tripped over the dog, who had gotten his legs tangled up in mine. But the moan was human, and I knelt to peer at the lump on the sofa.

It was my father.

Even in the dark, I could tell his slight form, his shoes spotted with grease, his stained green coveralls. No wonder Walter hadn't been able to reach him on the phone. He'd gone too far this time, working himself to exhaustion and passing out on my sofa in his mechanic's clothes, on my husband's birthday.

"Dad." Angry, I reached over and snapped on a light, taking a little mean pleasure in the way it would shock him.

His hands flew up to his eyes and the moan changed to a startled yelp. "Oh, Jesus, that hurts," he rasped.

"Go home, Dad. Go to sleep in your own bed." I leaned over to help him to his feet, hoping to avoid a war of words. He would try to keep me engaged in conversation, a meaningless argument about which neither of us cared.

"The belt. It was too late. . . ." He groaned again and twisted out of my grasp, mumbling incoherently, laughing as though he were telling himself an amusing story.

His coveralls had no belt—I was getting angrier with each syllable of nonsense. He was spoiling Peter's birthday and I wouldn't let that happen. The sooner I could get him into his own bed, the better we'd both feel, but I didn't know if I'd be able to manage it alone.

I touched my father's hand, determined to get him on his feet and moving, but I pulled back with a start. His skin was burning.

A feverish light glinted in his eyes; his lips were covered with a whitish dry scale. I bent close enough to see the big oily drops of sweat on his forehead. Shame flooded through me. He wasn't overworked. He was very sick, and his ramblings continued while I got him to swallow two aspirin and then pulled a blanket over him and went to the bedroom to explain to Peter, and to call Doc Verity.

Six

"You *have* to stay in bed, Dad. You heard Doc Verity. The flu is bad enough. You don't want it to turn into pneumonia. Then what would you do? Two or three days away from the garage now, that's better than a month or two later, right?"

Caught between the desire to make up for my abruptness the night before and the need to get on with my work, I glanced over at the poor, huddled figure seated beside me in the cab of my truck. My father's eyes were rimmed with red, the rest of his face the color of beeswax, and as bloodless. He sneezed in the glare of the sun and I wished that a bit of heat went along with the brightness; somehow the dampness of March seemed to be in my very bones and no amount of this hard light would do to dispel the chill.

The truck rattled along the macadam surface, jarring me with every bump and pothole. We passed a row of leafless maple trees as we headed toward Vixen Hill Road, and I fought a wave of dizziness induced by the flickering light.

My father coughed convulsively, his face turning red with the strain. Eyes closed, he shuddered, and then spat into his handkerchief. He tugged at his scarf, pulled it off, and opened the top button of his shirt. "Turn the damn heat down. It's too hot in here."

I had no heart for arguments. Even though the heater was set at the middle position and I was so cold I could barely keep my teeth from chattering wildly, I reached over and slid the control to "off."

I looked up again in time to see a low, gray blur whiz past us on the other side of the road. Catherine Delaney, in her Ferrari, was headed toward Copake; seated beside her, flushed and smiling, was Ruth Hoving. My mother-in-law was certainly providing Catherine with the stamp of public approval. Without it, an outsider might be tolerated in Taconic Hills but never really included. With Ruth's blessing, she'd earn the right to prove herself on her own merits, a test that would last for years before she was really a part of the community. Given her family background and manners, and Ruth's sponsorship, Catherine would pass handily.

Had someone taken Julia under her wing when her family moved to Taconic Hills? Julia Stanton and Catherine Delaney: just thinking about them, it seemed, had the effect of making my blood boil, for suddenly I was overcome with a rush of anger and I began to sweat. I made the turn up Vixen Hill Road and pulled into my father's drive. "Dad," I said, gently touching his arm.

He twitched, then opened his eyes. "Oh, Jeez, I feel bad." His voice was barely audible and his breath had a sweetish-sickly smell. I hurried around to help him down from the cab. I didn't like how flimsy his body felt, as though the wind or the rain could carry him away, as though he had begun to decompose.

Across the road, the surface of the pond ruffled lightly in a midday breeze; along its edge, a hint of buttery-yellow forsythia shone on the tips of a few slender twigs. I balanced the bag of groceries in one arm while I propped my father up with the other, then stopped to let both of us catch our breath.

"Easy steps, Dad. We'll be inside in a second. You'll feel better then."

As soon as I closed the door behind us, he started shivering. I helped him to the sofa and arranged the blankets around him, wishing I could give him some magic potion that would take away his misery.

When I returned from putting away the groceries, he was snoring, his head thrown back awkwardly against the cushions. I let myself out. There was nothing more for me to do here and the hives I'd been worried about last week still had to be checked.

To reach the hive site I had to go down a stretch of Vixen Hill Road I otherwise avoided. Something about the way the light dimmed in the shade of the tall pine trees, summer and winter, always plunging me into a sudden tunnel of shadow, made me uneasy as soon as I neared the windowless shed that marked the edge of my father's property, and lasted until I had driven past the stand of pines beyond the pond.

The air was no warmer when I parked in the turnout. My body ached at the thought of carrying the smoker and my hive tool past boulders and dying elms to the sparsely wooded rise of land on which the hives sat.

I wadded up a sheet of newspaper and stuffed it into the small firebox of the smoker, my fingers stiff and uncooperative. I lit a match and dropped it in. The flame went out; I tightened my grip on the smoker to keep from flinging it to the ground in frustration. Luckily, the next match worked. I lay several lengths of baling twine atop the burning paper and closed the lid, using the bellows attached to the smoker to force a few puffs of air over the twine to keep it smoldering. Then I set out up the boulder-strewn hill.

Ten steps. Ten times I had to lift my feet out of the mud. Each step an effort, as though my legs were weighted with lead. God, I was tired.

I could turn back, sit in my warm truck, wait until my energy returned.

And then I thought of Emily Schiller, trailing her heavy skirts, tending her bees even though she was weary after baking bread and making soap and sewing quilts—or was I mixing her life up with Klaudia Weigelt's and assigning to Emily the lot of a different woman?

I tugged the collar of my jacket up, little enough protection against the chill of the March sun, and plodded ahead to the crest of the small hill. Dizzy and out of breath, I lowered myself to a rock and lifted my face to catch what warmth I could, my head pounding and my chest tight. The hives were only a few steps away, but my apprehension at what I would find grew with each second. Nothing moved, a bad sign in weather warm enough for at least a few explorer bees to be out and scouting.

It was unavoidable: I had to open the hive. I pressed the bellows and puffed some gray, thick smoke across the top of the frame. Healthy bees would respond to the smoke and the suggestion of fire by descending in search of honey to eat in preparation for abandoning the hive. Clumsily, I pried off the top with the hive tool, its crowbar end fitting nicely between the lid and the body of the super. It stuck; the effort to remove it produced a fine slick of sweat on my face.

The lid finally came free and I looked down into the hive. The death scene below made me pull back in horror.

Two frames, which should have been glistening with neatly opened comb emptied of its stores by the resident colony, were instead filled cell by cell with the bodies of dead bees, heads caught in the torn openings in a frantic search for honey they'd never find, stolen by robber bees from a neighboring hive.

They had died from the cold and from a lack of food. I could hardly bear the sight of the black-and-yellow bodies, legs like random pencil markings trailing off in all directions, eyes unseeing, wings turning brittle. This death wasn't the result of a natural illness like foulbrood—this was more like murder. A mouse or a mole had gnawed a hole in the bottom of the hive box, exposing the bees to constant, debilitating cold that left them too weak to protect themselves. I doubted the predator was aware of the havoc he'd wrought, but it was murder, nevertheless.

Drenched in sweat, I replaced the hive cover.

And then I understood: I, too, was sick. Every muscle ached, my head pounded, and chills and profuse sweating took their turns to make me thoroughly miserable.

My legs and arms seemed in danger of stiffening with cold and exhaustion, but I finally made my way back down the hill and started the truck, my teeth clattering in my skull and my fingers feeling as though someone had pumped ice water through my veins. With great effort, I drove home.

Grateful for the sight of the weathervane atop my house, glad to see Peter's van in the driveway, I hurried inside, wanting nothing more than to fall into bed under the warmth of the down quilt. Even Prince, nuzzling my hand as I struggled out of my boots, was no match for the illness. I wanted to cry from weariness; Prince only tilted his head and watched me walk away from the warmth he offered.

The bedroom was dark, shades pulled to the windowsills. When I sneezed, a hot new pain knifed through my head and my throat. If this was how my father felt last night, no wonder he'd collapsed on our sofa.

"Oh, God, I feel awful. My whole body's on fire."

Peter. I focused my sore eyes on the shape in the center of the bed. He threw off the quilt, then sat up and pressed two fingers against his forehead. "Forget starting work on the kitchen," he mumbled.

My shiver wasn't only from the fever that coursed through my body. This illness had struck my father, Peter, and now me.

Stefan and Emily had to stop work on their new home for weeks when they were stricken with some illness. Influenza, I think . . .

The flu would delay the renovation of our kitchen, too, but I didn't want to believe that indicated a connection with some two-hundred-year-old epidemic.

I lay down in bed, my skin so sensitive from the fever I curled into a ball as far from Peter as I could.

It was two weeks before I felt strong enough to resume my activities. Peter and I were careful to eat well and to go to sleep early. Spring warmth crept into the winter sunshine, and being outside, even to tend to my hives, felt more like a restorative than like work. The bees were roused, too, by the promise of spring, and with the blooming of the daffodils my busy time was in full swing.

I had to feed my hives diluted honey water to supplement the meager pollen supply, medicate them, and check for signs of imminent swarming, but first I had to move three hives from Craryville to Vixen Hill. The Craryville bees had scared a farmer by trying to eat a pile of sawdust near his pole barn. Even after I explained to him that they sometimes do that early in the season before they have access to a good pollen supply, he threatened to take me to court if I didn't have them off his land within three days. I had run out of time; I was also out of the wire screening I needed to cover the hive entrance and keep the bees inside while they were being moved.

The hardware store in Copake bustled with customers preparing for their own spring chores. Nicky Dembowski, pale eyes staring past me and full mouth pursed into an unpleasant smile, shouldered a bag of potash and pretended not to see me. I waved at Ben Yarnell, who only nodded because he had a gallon of paint in each hand. Nearly everyone was smiling, sharing a delight that the solitude of winter, welcome when it first arrived, was over for a while.

"Hey, Sarah. That flu bug bit you, too, didn't it?" Marge Hoysradt, a pencil stuck behind her ear, turned from her perch on a ladder and looked down at me as she grabbed a fistful of elbow pipes from a carton. "Seems like half the county got hit. Or just about anyway."

"At least we're all on the other side of it now." I stepped back to let Clayton and Jeanie Boice pass, tripping over my own feet and bumping against a bin of tenpenny nails. A vision of all those nails scattered on the floor like so many breadcrumbs flashed before me, but I steadied myself and the bin in time to prevent a spill.

Marge winked and offered a knowing smile. "Everyone's still a little shaky. Peter looks awful pale and Walter and Roy both seem wobbly. And that new woman—what's her name; the blonde, you know, the one from the city?—she looks so skinny I want to take her home and feed her chocolate cake. Even offered, but she turned green and I knew she wasn't over it yet."

"Well, I'm completely recovered. Can you cut me two yards of fine screening?" The vulnerability of illness might be endlessly fascinating to some people but I preferred to move on.

Marge refused to let go of the topic, worrying it like a hound dog with a cornered raccoon. "You know, when Roy and you got sick, and Peter and Walter and that city—Catherine, that's her name— when Catherine got sick, too, I thought it was odd. Like Ben Yarnell's story about having to stop work on the Schiller house two hundred years ago. Looks like your kitchen renovation got held up from illness, too. A lot of folks with parts in that play got sick." She quirked an eyebrow and leaned closer to me. "And that following so soon after Ed Fitzhugh's death. Just like that Methodist minister who froze in the snow on his way to the Schiller wedding. You got to wonder, don't you?"

"Just a coincidence," I insisted. "Everyone in the play didn't get the flu. Doc Verity herself and lots of other people who aren't in the play *did* get sick."

Marge's smile evaporated; maybe I'd been more abrupt than I'd meant to be before she began talking about Stefan and Emily and the Methodist minister. As Marge started down the ladder I noticed Alicia Fitzhugh in the next aisle. Her face was drawn and tired. She grabbed a package of sandpaper and disappeared behind the shelves. I hadn't seen her since her husband's funeral.

Julia, she had said, and turned my world upside down. *Julia*, she had called me, and sent me careening into a search that had so far proved more frustrating than enlightening. Somehow, into the center of a world I'd chosen for its simplicity, two women had insinuated themselves, and without my permission, I'd been thrust into the lives of Emily Schiller and Julia Stanton.

I was brought back to my own life by the sound of Alicia Fitzhugh's voice on the other side of the metal shelves. "I need a vacuum tube," she said.

Marge and I looked at each other. What an odd request—nobody used vacuum tubes anymore. New technology had made them obsolete, and the store hadn't carried them in years.

"Yes, a vacuum tube. For my radio. I think one of the tubes is burned out," she said impatiently. If widowhood had changed her, it certainly hadn't added warmth to her voice.

Marge set the roll of screening on the counter and counted out my change. "Funny, when I get sick, all I can think of is I wish my mother was around to take care of me. Of course, Julia would . . ." Her mouth open, she sputtered to a stop.

Before February, I would have been too shocked to respond but now I smiled at her, trying to offer assurance that she hadn't just stepped off the edge of the world.

"You knew her, didn't you, Marge? Was she good with sick people?" I asked in the most matter-of-fact voice I could muster.

Marge raised her eyebrows, then answered in a rush of half-whispered words. "She wasn't trained at nursing, but she was real good at it with you. I remember, I came in once to talk to her about some weevils, they were getting in my garden mulch, and she solved the problem just like that. Anyway, there you were, sitting on the sofa, looking all pale, but with the biggest gosh-darn grin on your face. Blankets up to your chin, pillows all stuffed behind you. And Julia, there she was, behind a big cardboard box with a hole cut out of it, working these hand puppets and putting on a show for you."

I flushed with an unexpected memory of sitting on a pink brocade sofa sipping orange juice, wearing flannel pajamas with little bow buttons and yellow-and-blue bows printed on them, my feet in plastic-bottom slipper socks.

"And the puppets, they told you to eat your soup and drink your juice. And to take your medicine, which was in"—*a little yellow cup with a handle you could only put your finger through if you were four years old*—"a cup couldn't have been any bigger than a thimble. She made you forget it was medicine, made you forget you were sick. After I saw that, I thought it was a wonder you didn't pretend sickness, just to get treated so special."

How safe, how cared for that little girl must have felt. How terrifying to have that taken away on a whim. I bent down and retied my shoes so that no one could witness my struggle to regain control.

The residents of Taconic Hills suddenly had such a store of things to say about Julia Stanton. Did they keep her alive among them-

selves, barring only my father and me from this collective remembrance? I felt exposed, as though I'd caught friends, relatives, and
even distant acquaintances with a revealing photograph of me. I
didn't want to hear about Julia being a good mother. I was sorry
Marge had told me this story, but I knew by my response that her
memory was accurate.

So much the worse for me. Another piece of the erratic puzzle that
was Julia Stanton, and another person who knew that I'd broken the
silence.

"Thanks for the screening." I grabbed my package, turned, and
bumped into Alicia Fitzhugh, who stared at me for one frozen moment. Her pinched face contracted; she pivoted as though someone
had called her name and then scurried out the door, the sandpaper
still clutched in her hand.

Bumping into things.

That's what it felt like I'd been doing for months, in constant
collision with the ghost of my mother since the day of Edward Fitzhugh's funeral.

I drove out to Craryville with the radio turned up loud to banish
those thoughts, and made short work of securing the three hives,
lifting them with the farmer's grudging help into the back of the
truck. Then I sped toward home. Peter had promised to meet me at
the Vixen Hill site at four-thirty to help me unload; I was already
fifteen minutes late.

As I rounded the bend and neared the shed, its weathered, wide-
board walls dark and as blank as unseeing eyes, I slowed when I saw
my father. His body tense, he leaned against the fender of his truck.
How odd for him not be at the garage in the middle of the day—but
lately, a lot of things were odd. He signaled for me to pull over, and
I let the truck roll to a stop on the grass beyond the shed, bracing
myself against the force of his anger.

I approached him reluctantly; I was always uneasy here, in the
shadow of the rickety structure. It soaked up all the available light,
somehow, and transformed it into darkness. Hanging back, I peered
into the bucket beside him; it was filled with fine gray powder. "Hi,
Dad. What's in the bucket?"

"Ashes from the stove. To put on the strawberry bed next
month." He slammed the bucket down inside the shed, then whirled
around to face me. "Don't do it, Sarah. Stop right now."

He was trying to draw me into another drama, fueled by bitterness. I wanted no part of it. "Peter's waiting down the road for me, Dad. See you later."

"Don't give me that innocent act. Think you can go around asking about her without me knowing? Well, you're to stop. Right now. You'll be sorry if you keep on with this. You'll regret disobeying me, Sarah." Framed against the doorway of the shed, he was a vision of contained fury. His eyes blazed but the rest of his face was a stone mask.

The sky floated toward me in a dizzying spin. I backed away, then grabbed onto my own truth: the search for Julia was *my* business, no matter what he wanted.

Softly, I said, "Don't threaten me, Dad. It's not good for you to yell like that."

My calm seemed to goad him. "You're talking to everyone about her. Jeanie. Walter. Clayton. Marge. I know. I have my ways of knowing. You quit now. I'm telling you, Sarah, don't stir up evil. You'll wish to your dying day you didn't."

I had to make one more attempt. He knew why Julia left, knew better than anyone what she was like. "Can't you understand that I need to find out what really happened? Aren't you a little surprised that it took me this long to *try* to know? Help me out, Dad. Tell me about her."

"She was evil. That's all you need to know about her." He kicked the shed door shut, then flipped the hasp latch and stuck a twig through to secure it. "Stay clear of it, Sarah, or you'll be sorry."

April

Bees in a crowded hive may raise several queens. Before the nuptial flight, the virgin queen searches the hive for rival queens and murders them, and then flies out to mate with the drones.
                    —*Everywoman's Guide to Beekeeping,* Revised Edition

Seven

Nothing in my life happens in a straight line.

If my father's threats and Ruth's warnings to leave off the search for information about Julia only underscored my resolve to continue, the demands of work kept me too busy to do anything else for a while. The quest for Julia Stanton was delayed by a flurry of activity to make up for lost time on the Vixen Hill Lodge kitchen. Ben's script was completed, and Peter and I had decided that the only way we'd ever learn the lines was to start now and hope the damn thing stuck by September. But we had little time for memorizing lines. My bees and Peter's contracting commitments kept us busy and tired us out by evening; the beginning of every day we spent on renovation work.

Early morning sun streamed through the window, falling like a benediction on the gleaming stove. Peter and I worked to the accompaniment of the chattering swallows, who had begun serious nest building in the overhanging eaves beyond the window.

"Hand me that sponge, will you?" Peter, catlike on his hands and knees, squinted up at me. "Prince come home yet? What is it—three nights now? Could be a skunk ran into him and he's being considerate."

"He must have found a lady friend." Worried despite my cavalier words, I passed him the sponge and dipped my brush into the can, lifting a thick ribbon of heathery blue paint. "You memorize that scene with the fur trappers yet?"

"Catherine says if I just keep reading Stefan's lines over and over, eventually they'll stick. At least Ben's got these characters sounding like *people*. Makes it easier to remember the words." He bent to his careful brushing again, but I was still stuck on how his voice altered when he talked about Catherine.

Catherine: her arrival in Taconic Hills coincided with an important change in my life—the search for Julia and the public breaking of silence. And she was playing Klaudia Weigelt. *Hanky-panky,* Ben had so quaintly called it, between Klaudia and Stefan surely had nothing to do with Peter's loyalty, or the capacity of our marriage to survive the upheaval I was going through. My bond with Peter had history on its side, and I felt a rush of gratitude for the hours we spent working together; we knew each other's rhythms, felt good in each other's silences. It wouldn't do for Peter and me to narrow our world so that it contained only the two of us.

The telephone rang. I jumped, my paintbrush nearly trailing across the top of the stove as I reached for the receiver.

"Mrs. Hoving? Patsy McClosky. It's the bees. They're coming into the house." The voice was high, nervous, almost shrill. "Please. You've got to get them out of here."

It was one of the perverse laws of nature: complications arise only when you have too much to do. With so many hives, I'd had at least one swarm each spring for the past five years, but knowing that didn't make me feel any better. Why couldn't the bees have taken off for the woods, as last year's swarm had? At least the McCloskys lived just down the road, on the other side of Vixen Hill.

I tried to calm Patsy by speaking softly, deliberately. "Stay inside with the kids and don't worry. The bees won't bother you unless you panic. This happens all the time. When a hive gets crowded, they raise an extra queen and then they all gorge on honey and go out looking for a new home. Just leave them alone. I'll be right over."

"The noise . . . God, it's so loud. They sound angry. It's terrible!"

I knew exactly what she meant. Better to wade into a sea of hostile bees with as much protection as I could muster. I pulled on the white cotton jumpsuit, annoyed at the way its bulk slowed me and hindered easy movement, bothered that it made me look like a worker at a toxic dump site. I grabbed the rest of my equipment and took off in a roar of dust and frustration.

My irritation was sure to trip me up unless I could get hold of it—

but by the time I got to the McCloskys', it was all I could do to make sure my truck didn't run over the newly dug flower bed in the front yard. I parked in the rutted drive beside a battered station wagon. The old car was a fitting companion to the no-color bungalow that should have been repainted years ago.

I shoved my bee hat on and pulled the veil down, then got the smoker going, listening for buzzing, watching for evidence of a flight pattern.

Patsy McClosky stepped into the front yard as I pushed my hands into my gloves. She was a tidy young woman, thin and clean, sharp-featured, and I could tell by her pale face that she was terrified. She looked altogether too young to have a four-year-old son and an infant clinging to her, runny-nosed and wailing. Her freshness wouldn't last much longer—three years, five—before the hard realities of living poor in the country lined her face and bent her back.

"In here," was all she could say as she held the door open.

I followed her through a cramped, dark parlor into a smaller room that held a narrow cot and a crib, the feeling of shabby neatness undisturbed by the few toys on the uncarpeted floor.

Both children were crying and snuffling, but another, more distressing sound rose above their frightened whimpering: bees, loud and persistent, signaling to each other in their agitation.

"Mommy, I *hate* that noise!" The little boy wailed and stared at me, flinching as I moved toward the door. It was no wonder—between the bees and my getup, the scene was anything but reassuring.

"Come on, Michael, let's read a story in the living room." Calmly, the anxiety gone from her voice, Patsy reached up to the shelf for a book as the boy attached himself to her leg. "When Mrs. Hoving is finished, we'll go water the peas."

I left them to their activity and ran outside.

A sill board of one of the rear windows had come loose. Sun struck the outspread wing of a bee as she lit on the edge of the dangling board; her wings as she tucked them close to her furry body looked like crumpled parchment. Then she disappeared into a hole, swallowed up into the space between the siding and the interior wall. Their hairy bodies engorged with honey, a steady procession of worker bees wobbled toward the hole, led by younger, more slender scouts whose furious wing beats delivered directions to the site of the soon-to-be hive. Unless I did something about it, in a year Patsy

McClosky would have enough honey to bake a thousand cookies for her kids.

I puffed a cloud of black smoke into the hole. An angry buzz rose in protest and alarm. I worked carefully, trying to keep the smoke cool, hoping to convince the bees to abort their mission.

After a while the noise quieted. I pried off first one siding board and then another. Shaped like a fist, a knot of bees clung to the slender lath. Individual bees moved slowly, one or two of them stepping daintily along the edge of the upright toward the windowsill, others immediately taking up positions vacated by the few who flew away when the board was removed.

I had to make sure I got to the queen. Everything depended on her; the hive's existence was justified only by protecting her. If I couldn't find her, the only way to get rid of these bees would be to kill them chemically; a sharp sour taste rose in my throat at that thought. I directed smoke at the knot of bees. Only the top layer split off and flew in a confused pattern away from the wall. There was nothing for it but to reach in and pull them off.

As I extended my arm, a squeal of terror behind me nearly sent me lurching forward. Bees will attack a human intruder whose movements threaten them; my concentration had been shattered and that was dangerous. I whirled around to face Patsy McCloskey chasing after her four-year-old. I shot them an angry look, then thought better of it.

"Don't be afraid. It's all right." I knelt beside the boy, who pressed against Patsy's leg and shook his head as though to tell me it definitely was *not* all right with him.

I clenched my hand into a loose fist and extended my index finger, pretending it was flying through the air, nearer to Patsy, then over and around the little boy. The terror in his eyes changed to curiosity. I kept my finger circling and began talking quietly. "I—*buzz*—won't hurt you if you—*buzz*—don't hurt me. Pleazz, Michael, don't move so I don't get scared. You stay right here next to your—*buzz*—mother. I'm going to help Sarah move the beezzzz to a new home."

He giggled, and although the sound was high and strained, I was sure he'd let go of some of his fear. And as I watched him a momentary horror filled me.

Just like Julia, an inner voice said again. Just like the story Marge had told about the puppets and my medicine. I had no time to ponder the meaning, though. The longer I waited, the more established the bees would get.

Patsy laid her hand on her son's head, a gesture that touched me in its natural wisdom. I returned to the smoker and the wall and settled my uneven breath until I felt my true stillness return. Then I tugged on my gloves, reached between the boards, and scooped up a cluster of bees.

Luckily, my handful contained the queen. Her long, elegant body, yellow with three black stripes, marked her as different from the squat, honey-swollen bodies of the workers whose job it was to feed and protect her. She walked with stately dignity across my glove, her cadre hovering above her, but something was wrong. The hair on my neck prickled; the sixth sense I've always had about my bees told me I'd never get this swarm into the hive.

The beating whir of thousands of bees approaching over my shoulder was all the warning I needed. Suddenly my arm was covered with bees; dozens tried to crawl under the gauntlet of my gloves. A sharp, burning sting on my ankle startled me. They'd found the hole in my protective suit. And then, as though following orders from a single, powerful command center, the bees surrounded my hand and enclosed the queen, then took off, a shimmering river two feet above the ground.

At least they were gone from the McClosky house. They moved over a small patch of crabgrass lawn and slid up the trunk of an elm tree. The low branch, tented with caterpillar webbing, sagged with their weight. Then they headed for the woods that separated my house from Patsy's.

"I'm going to try to lure them into the hive box in my truck. I'll be back later to nail up those two boards, okay?" I was half running, unzipping the suit and pulling my arms out of the sleeves as I told her my plan.

"Thanks for coming so quick," she said. "Don't you bother. I can fix the siding." The child beside her was busy digging in the dirt with a small plastic shovel, the incident already stowed among the other bits of his past.

I stepped out of the cotton suit, tossed it in the back of the truck, and drove away, pursuing the swarm down an old fire road cleared years ago by the town. When the road dwindled to a narrow path overgrown with the stalky remains of last year's weeds, I parked the pickup and jumped out.

No bee sounds reached me; I looked high into the branches of trees and along the tops of bushes but I saw no sign of the swarm.

Jays chittered and argued and a tanager flitted by in an orange streak. A breeze rustled the layer of leaves that lay on the floor of the woods, bending the violets and columbines. In the distance, between two graceful birches that leaned toward each other, a honey-colored shape lay on the ground.

"Prince!" I shouted, and ran toward him. He didn't respond to my voice. His golden hair gleamed in the sun. I called out again and still he didn't move his head or get up to greet me. I shouted his name one more time, and my stomach turned and all the air went out of me.

Stunned, I stared at his unmoving body, none of my thoughts very clear, warning voices clanging in my head to produce a brilliant pain.

My curious, attentive, five-year-old Prince should have lived to a peaceful old age. I'd made him a bed beside the Ashley stove. I'd outfitted it with a faded cotton summer quilt and the leather slipper he'd stolen from Peter's closet. But Prince had been unwilling to put up with being housebound. He'd gone off at a joyful lope three days earlier, as though he had a mission to accomplish, and he hadn't come back. I never for a moment thought he was dead.

Dead. He had so much exploring to do. So much romping. *Dead.* My eyes filled with tears; I stumbled blindly to the truck. Breathless, I grabbed an old blanket from the back, then returned to the woods that bristled against the crest of the hill, to the spot where I'd left his body.

The wind swirled a dusting of dry leaves around me, breaking brown flakes free of the pile that had held them all through the winter. In the cool shade, a rime of ice covered the blackened organic debris beside the two trees. Small twigs clung to everything, looking like slender inchworms that had taken leave of their counting.

The unearthly quiet made my breathing seem like an intrusion. Through my tears, I tried to tell myself that death was nature's way of making room, but the words meant nothing.

I lay the blanket on the ground and slid Prince's lifeless body onto it, aching for all the times we'd never have together.

I lifted him in my arms, expecting to feel warmth, the rise and fall of his chest, aware only of how very heavy he was. I lay my cheek along the ridge of his haunch, pressing my face to the blanket to blot my tears as I made my way back to the truck.

He was stiff with cold and death, and I felt at once a futile anger and a sudden perplexity. What happened to *Prince,* to the quizzical eyes and the indulgent disapproval when I set his dish in the wrong place? This body in the woods was Prince's *body* but not *Prince.*

I was raised around animals: I should have had an easier time with death, but this wasn't an idea. This was Prince, and I would miss him terribly.

I knelt, bracing my knees to lower his body onto the bed of the truck.

Suddenly, with an awful, ripping sound, the blanket gave way. First one padded foot and then Prince's whole, cold body slipped out of my grasp and crashed onto the metal truck bed. I know I screamed in terror, unable to make sense of what I was looking at.

Only later—minutes, I think, rather than hours—when I stopped trembling, did I bend to examine the three holes, black with dried blood, that made a macabre, evenly spaced pattern on his chest. They weren't bullet holes but punctures. It was as though three sharp teeth, spaced too far apart, had pierced him. His pelt was matted and caked in neat, defined rings around the holes. Otherwise, he was unmarked.

A scene more powerful than any fantasy had a right to be leaped into my mind. I saw three sharp prongs stab the soft flesh of a man's chest, watched as three bright swelling bubbles of blood became scarlet rivulets. I heard screams rebounding from mossy walls, and then impenetrable silence and darkness. And I saw the starred cross, gleaming, winking at me in a lewd invitation that I didn't understand.

My legs buckled and a wave of numbness rolled over me. Somehow, I drove back to Vixen Hill Lodge.

Peter led me into the kitchen and sat me down and held my hand and listened while I told him about Prince. I had no answers to his questions.

"The only thing I can think of, Sarah, is that he got caught in some kind of animal trap."

In the quiet of the kitchen, I heard an echo of Ben's voice.

Stefan's dog never made it back from one of their missions.

No, no, no, I wanted to shout. He's mine, not Stefan's.

Not *Peter's,* I amended mutely.

Peter fed me soup and stole glances when he thought I wasn't looking. I didn't mention the cross, the screams, that half-formed image of punctured flesh. Marriage wasn't a sacred vow to share every thought and experience. This required some silence, until I knew how to place it in my life.

Eight

I dreamed about Prince that night, waking to a powerful memory of a dazzling sun and three bloody holes in his golden fur. The dream didn't stay with me beyond the next night's exhausted sleep. On the surface, my life appeared normal, even good.

Peter and I finished painting the kitchen and then he laid the new floor and put in the sink. Mornings exploded with sweet new life so vital that the dogwoods and lilacs soon burst into full flower. The air was charged with radiance; butterflies preened in the sun.

But something inside me recoiled from all that showy lushness and longed for containment. Small indoor tasks suddenly became attractive to me. One evening, after I'd read and reread the scene in Ben's script where Stefan and Emily accept the deed to their land, I found myself going through my bee magazines, cutting out articles for my files. Peter sat at the dining-room table, a stack of accounting papers on the highboy beside him as he recalculated figures he hoped would convince the bank to lend us more money to finish the kitchen work and start the renovation of the bathrooms.

I'd made a pot of tea and was about to pour a cup when the quiet was broken by the rumble of a car pulling up in the drive. A timid knock sounded on the front door. Regular visitors to Vixen Hill Lodge knew to go around to the kitchen. Half expecting Prince to come running and tangle himself in my feet, I opened the door to the tentative smile of Patsy McClosky.

"I'm sorry to come by so late. I just want to drop this off." She held out a piece of fabric, rolled into a cylinder and tied with a limp red ribbon.

"Please, come inside." My faced flushed with embarrassment; *I* should have brought *her* offerings and apologies, for the scare the swarming bees had caused her and her children. I tugged at the ribbon. A stunning embroidered likeness of my oak tree and the rock at the edge of the pond filled the center of a tiny oval. The small, even stitches flowed like fine paint on canvas; the fabric looked like it might fit into my empty cherrywood frame.

"Oh, Patsy, it's beautiful. Thank you. Please, come into the kitchen. I was about to have some tea. You know my husband, Peter, don't you?"

She nodded at him and smiled shyly, then took a backward step toward the door. "I just wanted to thank you for coming over so fast the other day. I didn't want Michael to know I was afraid. He'd pick it up and, well, I don't want him to be afraid."

"Wait, please. I want to give you a jar of honey, and I'd love some company." I steered her past Peter into the kitchen and poured two cups of tea. We sat down at the table. "No more bees?"

"Only in the lilacs where they belong." Despite the darkness, she glanced out the window in the direction of the pond. "I love that spot. I take walks up here sometimes. You don't mind, do you?"

"Not a bit—come up here anytime. Bring the kids, bring Grady, whatever." My words rang false; I was sounding like the benevolent lady of the manor and I didn't want her to think I was being condescending. "You're Mike Stewart's sister, aren't you?"

She nodded and sipped her tea.

"How is Mike? We went to school together."

Her mouth tightened into a thin, white line. "You didn't hear? About the trouble?"

"I've been real busy lately." I didn't tell her that I wasn't exactly a mainline stop on the town gossip circuit.

"I thought everyone knew by now. Tommy Hoysradt lost a whole shipment of milk. Something happened to the cooling mechanism of the tank. One thousand gallons, spoiled. And Grady . . ." She stared down at her hands. "Mike's the foreman, but he cut his leg last week on a silo chute, so Grady was helping out. Grady went to check the tank temperature at nine and then went out to do the rest of the chores. When he came back, couple of hours later, the thermometer read seventy degrees. All the milk was spoiled."

Cold prickles of sweat had formed on my palms while she was talking. *Gunther Meier, a worker on Stefan's farm, sent an entire shipment of spoiled milk to Albany.* At once, a question and my certain, chilling knowledge of its answer leaped into my mind. "You doing anything for the bicentennial?" I asked, circling around my real concern.

"I'm going to take a turn at the PTA booth on the day of the pageant. I hear you have a part in the play."

"Yes. I've never done anything like that before." I took a deep breath and sipped my tea, trying to sound casual. "And your husband, is he in the play?"

Her laugh made me feel a little better. "Grady? He hates it if he has to talk on the telephone, never mind say strange words in front of hundreds of other people."

Of course he wasn't in the pageant. I stroked the line of chain stitches that formed the top branch of the oak tree.

"The way Mike talks about it, I know Grady would die rather than have to say those words." And then her face went white and my breath caught; I wasn't safe yet.

"What is it, Patsy?" I knew what she would say, but in order for it to be true, *she* had to say it. I waited, a dry, hard lump growing in my throat.

"Mike. He's in the play. That farmhand, Gunther, the one whose milk spoiled when the Livingstons got mad and nearly took Stefan Schiller's land back, that's his role. How weird," she said.

I didn't think it was weird at all. I found it perversely predictable.

Peter's reaction was pretty much what I expected it would be.

"You surprise me, Sarah," he said, after Patsy had gone. "You're the last person I'd expect to hear such a theory from. You might as well start consulting astrologers or tea leaves or some other New Age, old-nonsense stuff. It isn't like you to imagine a mystical connection to the past." And then he turned back to his columns of numbers.

When I was eleven and the buds of my breasts began to grow, and downy hair appeared in places I had assumed would always be smooth, I realized that the differences between me and the adults in my life were measured by more than height, years, or responsibility. And so I watched, hoping to identify details and understand principles.

One night, I awoke to a flood of moonlight pouring onto my bed. In the exact center of that pool lay a tack, rusted and bent. I popped it in my mouth, gulped it down, and then swung my legs free of the covers. My bare feet on the cold floor sent a shiver though my body as I walked to the window and put my hand on the damp glass.

That hand looked as though it belonged to someone else. Not round and dimpled like a child's, these fingers had become longer, more slender. Shocked that my own hand could have changed without my noticing, and then, compounding its betrayal, could reach out for a tack and put it in my mouth, I crept back to bed. But sleep eluded me: I had swallowed a rusty tack and would surely die soon.

I spent the next week taking long walks with Queenie, asking my silent friend what to do, telling her, because I could tell no one else, about the fear that filled me like a train whistle. Her eyes held endless wisdom, and if I couldn't exactly understand, that hardly mattered because the world reflected in her gaze was a kind and sensible place. She seemed to be saying that strength and dignity would see me through, much to be preferred to thrashing about and wailing.

After two more weeks I realized that either I'd dreamed the tack on my bed or that it had already passed through my body, that I wasn't going to die—and that Queenie hadn't told me anything at all. It was me, Sarah, who had provided the necessary wisdom.

As long as I held fast to my own counsel, I'd arrive at the truth behind this series of disquieting coincidences. I simply hadn't yet discovered the logical explanation that would unlock the meaning of these odd parallels to the past.

The morning after Patsy McClosky's visit, as I was loading my truck with honey to deliver to my customers in the Berkshires, my father ambled across the yard toward me. A flood of anger and confusion swept over me; our last meeting had been charged with warnings that I'd regret talking about Julia.

My father was bitter, hard, and he could be vindictive. I'd willfully gone against his wishes—and I wondered if Prince's death had anything to do with those facts. I leaped up and grabbed a carton filled with honey jars, moving, lifting, adjusting, arranging, anything to keep from seeing the image of Prince, stiff and golden, lying on the leaves.

"Hey, Sarah, I brought these by for—" He coughed, a dry and painful sound.

I was deliberate about getting up and turning around; by the time I faced him, he'd returned his handkerchief to his pocket. "You okay?" I kept my voice even. My father didn't want my concern.

He nodded and held up a plastic bag of bones, bits of yellow fat and liverish-colored meat clinging to them. "Where do you want me to put these? In the refrigerator?"

My stomach lurched and I grabbed for the side of the truck.

"They're for Prince." My father frowned and shook the bag again. The bones knocked against each other wetly. "I saved them like always. You want me to put them inside?"

"That's fine. I've got to get going." How could I let myself imagine, even for a brief moment, that he was capable of being responsible for Prince's death? And yet I couldn't bring myself to tell him about it, even now.

Still in a daze, I sped off. My first stop was forty minutes away. The drive was just long enough for me to recover; I managed to engage my customers in talk about bees and flowers and Easter dinners, as they expected, and distract myself at the same time. The reprieve from my own questions was temporary, but I welcomed it, knowing that on the return trip, all my uncertainties would resurface insistently.

As I drove through Taconic Hills on the way back home, I noticed Ben Yarnell striding across the road toward the newspaper office, his blue knit tie flapping over his shoulder and a lopsided grin on his face. On impulse, I pulled into the parking area.

"Ben, wait up." I trotted toward him, already feeling a little foolish about what I wanted to ask.

"Hey, Sweets. How nice to have you running after me for a change. What can I do for you?" His dimples deepened and he stuck his hands into the pockets of his trousers.

"What do you know about the Hoysradt milk problem?" The sun blazed behind him and I raised my hand to shield my eyes. I trusted Ben to tell me the truth; I liked watching his earnest frown as he considered his reply.

"Only thing I heard was that Tommy lost a batch of milk because the cooling mechanism failed—or because Grady McClosky failed to check it at the right time, depending on who you talk to. But it's not news or anything, at least not yet. Why?"

Ben wasn't just having a conversation—he was waiting for our discussion to reveal its front-page potential. I smiled at the way both of us couldn't spend any measurable time without working. "Don't you think it's odd that three of the events in the Schiller saga have been repeated?"

He put his hand on my shoulder and leaned forward. "To what exactly, Sweets my dear, are you referring?"

It was my turn to frown. "Reverend Fitzhugh's death, the way everyone got the flu and had to stop work on our house, and now the spoiled milk. And the last two happened to the people playing those parts in the pageant." I didn't mention Prince and the similarity to Stefan's dog. It was too soon, too fresh, and I didn't want to turn his death into an artifact by putting it on display.

Ben released me and kicked at a seed pod. It split open, spilling tiny seeds onto the blacktop. "Now, that *is* an interesting phenomenon."

This was as good a time as I'd find to ask about the hint he'd dropped at the meeting. "Did you ever discover what happened to Klaudia Weigelt? I had the idea you had, from the way you were talking at the meeting the other night."

"Only a new way of looking at some old letters. Have you suddenly developed a burning interest in history, Sweets?" He winked and chuckled, knowing very well from our student days, when he was three years ahead of me in school and saved his old history notebooks to pass on to me, that a feel for the past wasn't one of my great talents.

"Just tell me."

"Nothing to tell. Except there's a hint that Stefan was miffed because Frau Emily did something to chase the fair Klaudia away. To where, or how, or why, or even if it's really true, you have to read between the lines and guess. Me, I'm willing to believe the lady made sure, one way or another, that her rival departed these verdant hills and never returned. But we won't tell anyone. Wouldn't want you to have to bear that black mark, my dearest Emily."

"Do you or don't you think these coincidences are odd?"

"Well, I don't believe in magic. Are you proposing, Sweets, that someone went and gave practically everyone in Columbia County the flu?"

My cheeks grew warm. "Okay, maybe I can't explain *how* or *why* or even if it's really true. But don't you think it's strange?"

Instead of answering, he closed one eye, folded his arms across his chest, and swiveled his head first to the left and then to the right.

"What are you doing?" I demanded, exasperated and embarrassed. "Are you waiting for a question you like better?"

"No, I'm making sure no one else can hear this." Ben waggled his eyebrows and whispered conspiratorially. "I think everything is strange. I also think nothing is strange, given the strangeness of everything. Your story won't sell papers, Sweets, although Lord knows I wish it would. Nobody's crying over Tommy's spoiled milk; they don't want to read about it, either. Unless you've discovered a cure for cancer, what you need is a little scandal, adultery, maybe a little embezzlement, some murder or arson. Even a smidgen of shameless political corruption would help. No scandal, no sale."

By the time he finished his speech, I was the one shifting uncomfortably.

"You better be prepared to make the front pages next month." He framed a square with his thumbs and forefingers and peered through it. "Yep. You, all dressed up as the magnificent Emily Schiller, heroine of Taconic Hills, rolling triumphant down Main Street on the bicentennial float of the Memorial Day parade—just about the most eye-catching front page we ever had. I can't wait, Sweets." He winked, saluted, and went on his way, leaving me standing alone as the sun ducked behind a cloud.

Ben was being adamantly dense—whatever he wasn't telling me, I'd just find out for myself, the same way he had. As I marched across the parking lot toward the Historical Society, my annoyance turned to anger. Both Peter and Ben, each in his own way, had discounted my concerns, but that didn't mean I would ignore the troubling questions that persisted and badgered me into paying attention.

The white and purple lilacs beside the stairs of the neat clapboard saltbox filled the air with their heady perfume. I flew up the front steps and peered into the lace-curtained window, then pushed open the front door. The hall was cool with a musty dampness; the low, pleasant hum of conversation—two women, from the sound of it—drifted in to me from the reading room.

Marge Hoysradt, seated on one side of a heavy maple trestle table, looked up and smiled as I entered the room. Spread out on the table were four looseleaf notebooks filled with plastic sleeves. Each sleeve held a letter written in black ink. As I leaned toward the table, it appeared that the handwriting in each notebook was different. The signature at the bottom of one of the pages leaped out at me. Emily Schiller.

"Hey, Marge," I said, "getting ready for the play?"

At the sound of my greeting, the other woman, whose smooth blond hair and slender shoulders were just barely visible above the top of her high-backed chair, swiveled her head.

"Catherine!" I said sharply, as though she had no business being here. "Aren't you worried about studying too hard for the pageant and losing your own identity?"

She smiled, her porcelain skin coloring. "Just doing a little reading. I know I told Ben that I don't do preparation, but I wanted to learn more about Klaudia. I think now I've got some insight into her."

"Help you with something, Sarah?" Marge tilted her head to wait for my reply.

"I guess I'm here for the same reason. I was hoping to learn a little about Emily Schiller from her letters." I sat down at the foot of the table.

Marge tapped the notebook nearest to Catherine. "These are them."

Catherine slid the binder toward me and flashed me another incandescent smile. "Enjoy," she said, scraping her chair back, standing, and gathering her purse in one fluid, connected motion. "Gotta go. Thanks, Marge. See you, Sarah." She waved, her fingers folding in one by one toward her palm, and was gone.

"Too much perfume." Marge wrinkled her nose and glanced at the empty chair. "But she has good manners."

I nodded and tried to smile and wondered why Catherine, who had said she wanted to learn more about *Klaudia,* had been reading *Emily's* letters.

"You go ahead, Sarah. I'll put these others away and then I have some filing to catch up on. I have to close up in fifteen minutes, though. Promised Helen I'd take her to the podiatrist in Hudson. Corns," she muttered as she slid the other notebooks onto the shelf and padded to the door, her crepe soles noiseless on the waxed floor.

It took a few minutes to get used to Emily's writing—capital letters appeared where I didn't expect them, and the difference between *s* and *f, g* and *z,* and *h* and *n* were especially hard for my eye to judge. I was distracted, too, thinking about Catherine. Occasionally, a blob of ink swallowed up a word or two, as though Emily had rested her pen on the page while she was considering what to say next. But gradually I slipped into her rhythms and I found myself smiling now and then or frowning in anger, in reflection of her feelings.

The first letter was addressed to *Dear Adele;* the opening line identified the recipient as her sister. Emily delighted in her bees, her herb garden, and in gathering flowers and spices to make potpourri. Her obvious pleasure practically spilled from the page as she described in loving detail how she had begun to harvest honey from the straw hives. I could almost see the feathery leaves and tight flower clusters of the yarrow and the blue-gray borage and hyssop in her garden, could almost smell the hard brown cloves with a scent as sharp as their dagger points.

But the tone changed when the subject turned to *John.* No last name—he was clearly in the inner circle, perhaps even the fiancé Ben had mentioned. *John told Father that Trenton is bound to be a hub of Commerce and that we should establish ourselves there. I will not be torn from my family and this lovely Land, no matter what the Council says.* The seeds of discord between Emily and John had been sown, and in the next letter, they blossomed into all-out rebellion. I could hardly blame her for wanting to stay in Taconic Hills, no matter the arguments favoring New Jersey.

Another reference to the wishes of the council and several lines about John and the picture came clear. Emily was being pressed to join John in a new venture, but she held firm. I felt a glow of achievement, as though I had somehow been part of her resistance. Ben hadn't shown this side of Emily in his script. I wished he had.

I glanced at my watch. Marge would be returning soon; I'd read five letters, all of them addressed to Emily's sister, Adele, none of them containing any mention of either Stefan Schiller or Klaudia Weigelt. I flipped a couple of pages, scanning the lines. There—the word *marry* caught my eye.

*I shan't be pledged to marry such a—*and the next few words became illegible. *The Council finds him to be a Thief,* she concluded. The rest of the letter spoke of a ball she had attended; a gleeful description of a pompous old man's wig and the cut of his britches ended the letter.

I flipped pages again; my jaw tightened with frustration. Finally, I came to a letter addressed to *My only Stefan.* My eye found the letter *K.,* a curlicued capital finished off with a stab of a period. Palms sweating, I started to read from the beginning.

"I'm sorry, Sarah, I have to close up. Helen and her poor feet, you know. That podiatrist works wonders." Marge stood behind me, her bosom rising and then falling with her labored breath.

"Five minutes?" I could come back another time, but I was so close to unlocking her secret.

"Oh, dear, I'm late already." She reached for the book. *"One minute, Sarah. Just one."*

I nodded and turned back to the letter, my eyes leaping over the lines until I reached the reference to K.

Therefore I must insist if we are to be wed that K. be informed with dispatch, she wrote. *If you chose to leave the task to me, I will strive for Clarity and Finality.*

Her words felt neither clear nor final to me, but two pages later, in another letter to *Dear Adele,* the missing bit of information jumped out at me.

Stefan and the Council have not said a word about K. and her hasty departure. For my part, I am certain she will never again disturb the tranquillity of these verdant hills.

Behind me, Marge coughed and shuffled papers. I closed the notebook and handed it to her.

"Catherine was taken by that last one, too," Marge said as she slid the notebook into its place on the shelf. "She read it through twice."

May

For all their generally docile nature, bees are more likely to sting their human neighbors when the weather is cool and cloudy, or when they think they are being attacked.
—*Everywoman's Guide to Beekeeping*, Revised Edition

Nine

With all my work in the bee yards, any thought of going back to the Historical Society to read the other notebooks was forgotten. I forgot, too, about the costumes Peter and I needed to make, borrow, or buy in time for the parade at the end of the month, until Ruth called to ask about their progress. She offered to make Peter's vest and knickers at the same time she did Walter's. I'd take care of my own, I told her, pleased not to mark her side of the ledger with a debt of gratitude from me. But I had attempted to sew about as often as Tom Hoysradt's cows tried to fly. Mrs. C. made whatever costumes I'd needed for school plays; once, after the old housekeeper had died, Jeanie had whipped up my sailor outfit for *South Pacific*, the senior play.

I hated imposing, but I couldn't think of anything else to do, and so when I stopped at the post office I asked Jeanie if she had time to help me with my costume.

A beaming smile lit her face. "It'll be fun. I never get to fuss with hoop skirts and ruffles." She continued to flip envelopes into their slots, seeming to know by feel whether the box was Hoving or Hoysradt, Diller or Delaney. "You get me eight yards of light cotton, a pale color, and two yards of white. You'll want to find some brass buckles for your shoes, too."

But two weeks and two fitting sessions later, as I stood in her Sunday-quiet living room for a final try-on, Jeanie puckered her face into a frown.

"Bad news," she said, unfolding billows of fabric to reveal the long, graceful lines of the dress. "Ruth stopped by after church this morning. Said we need lace on the sleeves. And she left this brooch for you to wear at your throat like so." She held a lovely cameo at the top button. I'd wear the pin but I'd just as soon leave the sleeves the way they were. I could hardly picture Emily Schiller doing her daily chores in sleeves dripping with lace; she would have disdained such foolishness.

"It'll have to do as is," I said firmly.

"Ruth had a book with her. A fancy dress really does need lace, and the committee's decided you and Peter should wear fancy clothes on the float. Nothing's open now unless you want to drive all the way into Hudson. And I leave tomorrow morning to visit my daughter in Rochester, and I won't be back until the night before the parade. There's time, if you can dig up two, three yards of lace by, let's say, four o'clock."

"I bet Julia Stanton had a collection of lace and took it with her when she left," I muttered, annoyed at the prospect of chasing around on an errand of Ruth's making.

Jeanie cocked her head. "Honey, don't do that to yourself. You'll only make yourself unhappy. It's not good for you."

Her words were familiar, an echo of Ruth's warning at Peter's birthday party. I imagined Ruth and Jeanie and Marge, huddled together around the butler's table in Ruth's living room, speculating on how much I'd learned about Julia, clucking in dismay that I might discover something *they* didn't know. But Jeanie's smile was so honest, so open—I shouldn't let my feelings about my mother-in-law spill over onto her.

"You're a marvel," I assured her with a hug, "and the dress is wonderful. I'll try to find some lace before you leave." I held out a pint jar of Sweets maple syrup. "This is for you to bring to your daughter, to remind her of what she's missing by living so far away."

"Can't you just take a favor without returning it?" Her eyes crinkled into a smile. She'd be disappointed and count me short on manners if I hadn't brought her something. I was only playing by the rules: we both knew she was going out of her way for me and if I didn't mark that with an offering of gratitude, I'd be thoughtless and no less beholden.

Lace, I thought sourly as I marched to my truck. I had never worn lace in my life. Well, that wasn't exactly right. One Halloween, long ago, I'd decided that Good Queen Bess was a perfect choice because she did as her royal heart desired. If Dad had stored that costume in the attic with the other remnants of Halloweens past, there was a chance I could avoid a drive into Hudson.

It was going to be one of those days, I knew it. Even the slightest achievement would be won only after a struggle. My father's truck wasn't in the driveway.

Sighing, resigned to this new delay, I dialed the garage. On the eighth ring, as I was about to hang up and drive into Hudson, my father answered with a grunt that meant he was surrounded by screws, gaskets, and filters and had just crawled out from under a piece of uncooperative, dysfunctional machinery.

"Quick question, Dad. You remember where you put those Halloween costumes Mrs. C. boxed up? I need the lace from one of them."

"Shoot, I can't keep track of every carton. I don't know." In the background, a country ballad twanged on the radio.

"Can I look for it? It'll save me a trip to Hudson." For all the good it would do me on a day like this, I still had to go through the motions.

"Suit yourself," he snapped. "Gotta go."

I hung up and crossed the dusty road to his house, battling the feeling that I was intruding on his privacy. I had his permission, after all. I trudged in dim light up the narrow stairs in search of lace.

The attic was hot and airless, the buzz of a lone fly careening against the rafters. As a child, I avoided coming up here if I could; the slanted ceiling made me feel jiggly, anxious to be outdoors. Still, I'd put up with the attic's closeness each fall and spring when we hauled down boxes of clothing for the new season. Mrs. C. and I made apple leather one October, grinding the fruit to a fine mash and spreading it out on waxed paper atop the clothing boxes until it turned dark, tacky-dry, and very sweet. Another year, we'd strung stalks of basil from Mrs. C.'s garden and hung them from the rafters until they were pale and crumbly.

I stepped around the Flexible Flyer I'd pretended was my spaceship as I screamed down Vixen Hill toward the pond, then maneuvered past an old chair draped with a sheet, and an ancient television with a round screen. Boards creaked beneath my feet. The air smelled like old banana skins and sour milk, mold and the pall of woodsmoke deep in the pores of the walls. I wiped a trickle of sweat from my forehead. All this for a piece of lace that I wasn't even sure existed; this was absurd. Damn Ruth for her last-minute pronouncements, anyway.

All six cartons were full of empty jars. I should have known.

The only other possibility was the leather-covered, wood-framed trunk I used to sit on while Mrs. C. bustled about. Hidden under a white sheet so thin it was nearly transparent, the trunk sat in the middle of the floor, under the peak of the roof. It was the only place an adult could stand without hunching. I pushed the sheet aside and lifted the heavy lid of the trunk; a thick, musty smell rolled out. The arms that locked the lid open were missing. I propped one side of the lid with a dusty wooden ruler; a motley collection of boots, scarves, mittens, and woollies stared back at me. I scooped them up and laid them on the floor. Piles of stuff remained: boxes, clothing, blankets.

As I brushed a fly away from my face, I heard footsteps on the stairs, light, quick, and uneven. Dad. Strange, he hadn't sounded like he was finished with his work when I spoke to him. A confrontation with him wasn't exactly my idea of the perfect way to change the direction of the morning: I wanted nothing more than to find the damn lace and be done with the whole enterprise.

"Hey, Sarah." His voice was wary, nervous. The penetrating smell of oil from his coveralls and his unwashed hands were evidence that he'd left in a hurry. "Find that lace?"

"Nope. I may have to go laceless." How good we were, my father and I, at not saying the important things. He hadn't mentioned Julia since that day at the shed, and I'd convinced myself he'd buried the incident behind a hastily built shield of hard work. I turned to take some more things out of the trunk but my father reached over and pulled my arm away.

"That Halloween stuff . . . I put it in a carton and moved it somewhere. It's not here, that's for sure." He yanked the ruler out and banged the lid shut. The ruddy blush on his cheeks deepened; he sat down heavily on the chest. "Wasn't sure what I was going to do with them, figured maybe to take 'em to the hospital for the sick kids, or give 'em to an orphanage or something. Where'd I put those cartons, anyway?"

He closed his eyes; his head rolled forward on the thin, wrinkled stalk of his neck. For a moment I thought he'd dozed off from exhaustion but his eyes flew open. "The shed. I must have put 'em in the shed. Wouldn't put 'em in the garage. No room in the damn garage. Try that stack of cartons in the shed.''

His speech was punctuated by the sound of the fly beating against the window, too tired or too blind with its own need to see the crack just inches from where it threw itself at the glass. I opened the window and pushed it outside. My father followed my movements with his dark, darting eyes, the rest of him still as a boulder.

I said good-bye and hurried downstairs. I'd go to the shed. I'd find the lace and avoid war with Ruth.

Glancing at the woods on the top of Vixen Hill, I thought about the swarm that had escaped and led me to Prince's body. I'd undertaken a vain search up the firebreaks and down the deer runs every day for weeks, hoping to find them, not succeeding. They were probably nearby; the thought made me uneasy. It was as though some part of me had gone wild, and the other, more civilized side would have to reckon with it later. I didn't mind for myself so much. The wildness meant a freedom I found seductive, but I didn't want anyone else to suffer the consequences, as Patsy McClosky had.

The shed looked gloomier than ever, its north wall furry with dark green moss. The late-spring afternoon had turned changeable; from a horizon that stretched blue and endless, a cloud would appear, whip up a fierce wind, and then blow over without leaving any mark of its passage. When I approached the shed, the cloud was building again in the west.

The metal latch glinted in a shaft of sunlight as I removed the stick, the same one my father had jammed in the day he'd delivered his warning. Standing in the sun, I felt cold. Lace couldn't be worth all this trouble, even to placate Ruth.

Shivering, I almost walked away. I couldn't remember going into the shed but I'd driven past it so many times, stopped to talk to my father beside it, strolled by it with Peter after dinner—it was foolish to be afraid of this collection of wood and nails and tin. I held my breath, pushed on the door, and stepped inside. Odd: I knew immediately how the interior would look, the half wall that divided the space lengthwise, the narrow shelf that ran along the wall to the left of the door.

A carpet of sun lit my way. On the shelf, as Dad said they would be, three boxes tilted in disarray. A sticky spiderweb caught the side of my face; my throat closed up as I brushed it away.

The first box held a single old blanket, the second a collection of pitted enamel saucepans and colanders that were candidates for hanging on the wall of some city person's weekend kitchen but not much else. The Halloween costumes had to be in the third box. But when I opened it, I found only a sorry assortment of bath towels, strings dangling from the side hems and all the color gone from repeated washings. My father had sent me on a fruitless chase.

I stuffed the towels back into the carton. As I did, the wind kicked up; the door slammed shut with a loud crack.

I stood in the center of the dirt floor, embraced by a damp and ancient darkness. Fragments of a scene flashed before me, brilliant and shattered, like the view through a kaleidoscope. *The cross. The three holes.* My mind was whirling, my senses reeling. I couldn't grab hold of any meaning. The scar on my arm throbbed as though it had been cut open by the silent screams that collided against each other in the gloom.

Then, as suddenly as it had swelled up, the wave of sounds and images subsided. I sat on the dirt floor and listened to the cry of a dove in the dust of the road just beyond the walls. A message was waiting for me here, in the darkness into which I had been plunged by the wind, if only I could understand it. The screams, the high, choked sound—they weren't mine, I knew that. And they weren't my father's.

My father.

Whatever had happened here, my father was part of it. I struggled to see past the years, beyond the darkness.

Those screams—were they Julia's? Why did I hear them now? Had I somehow become her, absorbing not only her behavior, as I had at Peter's birthday party and at Patsy McClosky's house, but her memories, too?

I lay down on the cold dirt and closed my eyes.

And as I did, I saw again a man's chest with three holes bubbling bright with blood. And saw the *crux stellata* outlined against white skin.

This time the images faded more quickly and more completely. I didn't want to wait for more, couldn't bear to bring the pictures into sharper focus. I sat up, wiped traces of dirt from my face and hands, brushed off my shirt and jeans.

I returned home without seeing the road at all, upset by what I'd heard and seen and anxious because I knew that wasn't all—there was more, and it was rank from being buried too long. The sight of my father moving my hand away, pulling the ruler out, planting himself on the closed lid of the trunk was burned into my brain.

Roy had sent me out of the attic because he was afraid I'd find something there. Instead, I'd made a different discovery, in the shed. I couldn't help my bitter laugh; I didn't even have any lace to show for all this.

I was weighed down with secrets and with the constant, nagging feeling that nothing was what it seemed. Peter must have assumed Julia was the reason for my preoccupation; he was undemanding and I sensed he was waiting for me to discuss it with him when I was ready. But it wasn't Julia—it was the shed, and I couldn't talk about that afternoon in any logical way. It was unlike anything I'd ever experienced, the feeling of being a blank screen for pictures that had no substance, sounds that evaporated when I reached out to touch them.

I wanted to crawl into bed and pull the covers over my head—but Ruth would surely come poking around and try to *fix* me as though I were a cup whose handle could be glued back on to make it as good as new. So I joined everyone else at my father's garage on Route 22, to help build the float for the Memorial Day parade—a replica of Stefan and Emily's first house on a six-foot-long flatbed.

Dad had cleaned up the place for the occasion, imposing a temporary suggestion of order on the clutter of his parts shelves. Pools of dark oil had been soaked up and now were only shadows on the concrete floor. Boxes of wiper blades were stacked neatly on a shelf, and all the stray pins and nuts and alligator clips had been swept from the work counters into glass jars. The din of hammering, sawing, shouting made me glad I hadn't found an excuse to stay away— working together felt good, as Ruth had known it would. We *were* a community, and it took all of us to make Taconic Hills.

Even Catherine Delaney.

"I meant to tell you the other day," she said as we scanned the printed roster to see what tasks we'd been assigned. "Sometimes the best way to understand the character you're playing is to figure out the impact she has on the people around her."

I thanked her for the advice—I'd neither asked for her help nor for an explanation of why she'd been reading Emily's letters—and then forced a smile as she tapped the page.

"Look, we're both working on the base of the float."

And so we were. We picked up our supplies from Walter and set to our tasks silently.

I was on my hands and knees beside Catherine, gluing bright green excelsior to a plywood sheet, when I heard a voice behind me.

"It's never going to be ready if you work with separate pieces of grass. Do it in handfuls. Nicky Dembowski will have that land sold, cleared, and developed before this float is finished." Ruth, regal in her navy-blue dress, failed to hide her exasperation. I didn't look up; if she said anything more to me, I couldn't guarantee that I'd react civilly.

"Interesting management technique," Catherine whispered as Ruth moved on to cast her eye—and her criticism—on someone else's efforts.

"Give her honey to cut her vinegar and she'd probably think it was an offering of gratitude," I said, reckless about talking that way in front of a stranger.

Catherine grinned and we resumed the tedious work. Soon, despite the inefficiency, the big flatbed began to look like a rolling replica of a crude cabin in a newly cleared crossroads.

Deeny Lambert stood back, cocked his head, closed one eye. "The facade is listing to the right," he proclaimed. "We need a boulder, something, to prop it up. If we don't, it could slide right off onto the street."

Whether or not he'd been sipping steadily from his silver flask, as was likely if it was past noon, Deeny still had a good sense of the straight and true.

A general flurry of activity followed his suggestion. Tom Hoysradt, Peter, and Deeny agreed to build the base of the boulder. Catherine said she'd cover it with papier-mâché, if she could get someone to help her; scanning the volunteers, she hopped down gracefully from the float and stood beside Alicia Fitzhugh. I hadn't seen her in a long while, since that day in the hardware store. She appeared less startled now, more comfortable with the bustle and disorder of the everyday world.

"Can you come on Friday night," Catherine said warmly, "to help with the boulder? I'll pick you up, if you like."

Alicia's impassive face glowed under the harsh garage lights; one fine wisp of pale hair escaped onto her neck, and her eyes, too, looked unfixed. "All right. But only after I finish working on the parish accounts," she said softly.

Ruth whispered something in Alicia's ear; the woman nodded, her expression more attentive, as though she'd just returned from a dream. "Friday will be fine."

Poor woman, Alicia seemed so easily distracted and confused. Since I'd first become aware of her odd lapses, I'd felt a gradual softening toward her, a protective impulse I doubted I'd ever act on to assure the widow that facing reality, whatever it was, would eventually be better than retreating into make-believe.

"What if it rains?" I asked Catherine. "I know the parade is three days off, but the newspapers say the weather's going to be cold and damp. Won't a papier-mâché boulder melt if it rains?"

"We'll build a canopy to keep it dry." Ruth seemed to be everywhere at once. She headed for Roy, who was fixing up a hitch to connect the float to the truck.

Clayton Boice stepped up to the platform and leaned down close to me. "Don't let her bother you," he said a little too loudly. "She's just concerned about this enterprise and that's how she covers it up. She's really a good heart, you know."

Appalled that my reaction to Ruth had been so easy for him to read, I squeezed his hand and then turned back to my work. Fortunately, the din of the hammers and Clayton's hearing problem made further conversation impossible.

"Hey, *watch* it!" Someone shouted a warning. I looked up to see Walter duck just in time to avoid getting smashed by a six-foot board. Deeny had hoisted the board onto his shoulder, lurched into an unsteady forward wobble, and then stopped in midmotion. Behind him, Grady McClosky, arms folded across his chest, glowered at Tommy Hoysradt, both of them oblivious to Deeny's board and to our attention. Tommy's eyes glittered with anger.

"I'm telling you," Grady said plaintively, "it's spooky."

"I don't put stock in that superstitious hog bleep. So what if Ed Fitzhugh died in the snow like some old Methodist minister did. Okay, so a whole bunch of people got the flu and stopped working on the Hoving kitchen. That's got nothing to do with it. You're trying to convince me that you weren't responsible for the milk spoiling and all I got to say to that is 'Bullshit.'"

Grady's face turned ashen. "You're wrong. I'm telling you I *know* I checked that milk. The damn thermostat was working when I went out to disk the field. That's a fact. Whatever happened in there, I have to think it has something to do with this damn story."

"Leave off, man. You *messed up*. Just admit it."

"I'm sorry you feel that way, Tom." Grady kept his voice soft, but it was clear he'd reached the end of his patience. He shrugged and started to walk away, then thought better of it. "Maybe someone wanted it to look like I screwed up. Me, I think it was supposed to happen to Mike and I happened to be there helping out. *He's* the one playing the part. Hell, I was just a stand-in for him that day. What if something's making history come back and haunt us? Making things happen now that happened back then—and to the people in the play."

I shrank back from the fear in his voice; I could add the fact of Prince's death to his list. The hush in the garage seemed filled with voices, Ben's, Ruth's, colliding against each other, careening into the walls. *Stefan's mother was bitten by a mad dog on the Fourth of July. . . . The lady made sure that her rival departed these verdant hills and never returned. . . . Stefan shot in a hunting accident . . . So long woodcutter and bye-bye Emily.* Dazed, I looked for Peter in the crowd but all I saw was a blur of faces without differentiation, without expression. Except for one.

"Grady McClosky, you stop talking nonsense."

Ruth stood, hands on hips, her features fixed in an indulgent smile. Her voice was calm, very nearly lighthearted, as though she were letting us all know that we ought to be able to judge from her tone alone that none of this was to be taken seriously.

"You think I can pretend there's no connection between the past and what's going on now? Well, that'll be wrong. I don't know how Tom's milk spoiled but it wasn't me caused it." As Grady's voice rose, we gathered closer until the place was wrapped in an eerie, pulsing silence.

"Don't be foolish, ain't nothin' can come back and make things happen two hundred years later." I recognized the speaker as the new school-bus driver, a putty-faced, potbellied fellow whose voice sounded too thin for his oversized body.

But Grady held his ground, his anger at the loss of his reputation apparently as strong as his fear of some unknown future. "Think about it, Ruth. Think about all the things that could happen if you keep going with the play."

Her face was stony as she drew herself straight and glared at Grady. "So you want to let Dembowski and his kind have an easy victory because you figure you have some ghost trailing around after you switching off cooling tanks? No, my friend, that doesn't make a bit of sense. I'd daresay Grady has scared one or two of you tonight with his . . . theories. If it wasn't for the fact that I've known him all his life, I'd wonder about the stability of a person who would talk such foolishness."

It was a nasty thing to say, in public and when he was vulnerable, but Ruth wasn't stopped for a second by that. She tilted her head and curled her mouth into a chill smile. "I know Grady's still upset and that's making him think a little, well, unclearly. There are no magic visitations from the past. There is no dark force making things happen to people in the play. And anyone who believes otherwise can just declare himself on the side of those who would let Taconic Hills become one big subdivision, and remove themselves from the play and the whole celebration." With decisive steps, chin high and fists clenched at her sides, she marched to the back of the room, where her flower-making supplies were neatly arrayed on the long table.

Grady flung his hammer down. It landed with an echoing crash on a pile of boards. "Not that I needed your permission, but I was about to say count me out." He whirled around and strode to the door. Patsy followed after him, throwing me a confused look of apology and apprehension as she went. The door slammed behind them.

For a second, no one else moved. Then everyone did, slowly, silently, returning with distracted expressions to the tasks they'd been working on before Deeny nearly whacked Walter with a board and before Grady McClosky voiced a theory that made terrible, chilling sense despite its improbability. I looked down, surprised to see a clump of excelsior still clutched between my fingers; my hands, where the nervous sweat came in contact with the artificial grass, were stained a bright, awful green.

As I knelt to resume my work, a young waitress who lived in the trailer down the road from Vixen Hill Lodge backed away from the float. "I've got three kids to think about." She said nothing else, and she, too, pivoted and headed for the door.

Ruth seized the silence. "Well, now, if that's all over, we have a float to build."

Ten

It poured the night before the parade. But the next morning, to everyone's surprise, golden sun streamed through every window, glinting from new-washed summer surfaces. I should have delighted in all that beauty, but the only significance to me was that the damn parade would go on as planned.

Cursing my own part in this—I had after all not been forced at gunpoint to take the role of Emily—I weighed the bulk of my costume in my hands, glaring at the long, cumbersome skirt. Hours—I'd agreed to spend hours in this contraption. The last time I'd worn a skirt, at Edward Fitzhugh's funeral, I'd felt odd enough. This was going to be a real challenge.

I slipped the dress from its hanger. A challenge—I could handle that. Make it until two in the afternoon? Of course I could. Maybe wearing this dress, with its spill of lace at the sleeves and the high-necked white bodice above a billow of a dove-gray skirt, would suit someone like Catherine. I'd get my pleasure from the knowledge that I could take it off at the end of the parade.

"We're going to be late." Peter's matter-of-fact voice carried from the bottom of the stairs.

"Be right down." I tugged the dress over my head, slid my arms into the sleeves, and fastened the tiny buttons, all eighteen of them, until I was ready to scream from the desire to do dervish turns around the room with my arms windmilling through space. Fine motor skills had never been my long suit.

I rummaged on the dresser for Ruth's brooch, pushing aside a hairbrush, two cotton bandannas, a package of moleskin, a tube of hand cream, and finally found it. When I looked in the mirror to put it on, the image looking back at me made my breath catch.

The woman in the mirror was resourceful, strong, wise; determination shone in her eyes. With my hair braided and then wrapped around my head the way Catherine had showed me, in clothes that were centuries old in design, the *gravity* of Emily Schiller struck me. Peter and I had been reading Ben's script aloud to each other, and we both felt less self-conscious than when we'd first tried it, but it wasn't until I put on these clothes that I really felt I could *become* Emily in the play.

Ruth's brooch cemented my connection to Emily Schiller. I could be the physical body in which her spirit was living out a continuing quest, searching for the completion that had eluded her in her life, attempting to fill an emptiness that had been passed to her by some keen and restless ancestor. A lace handkerchief tucked into my waistband would be the final right touch.

I pulled open my top drawer and dug through a scramble of white socks and moved aside the little sachet pillow. The handkerchief, neatly folded and never used, lay beneath the sachet, and when I held it up, a lovely perfume, a blend of flowers and spice, drifted up to me.

The blue-gray borage and hyssop . . . the hard brown cloves . . .

"Madam, your carriage awaits."

Startled out of my daydream, I turned to see Peter, transformed into a rather silly creature in pedal pushers and a wig, a sight that made me double over with laughter. "You look a little like Cher after a rough night," I said, still giggling.

He frowned. "That bad?"

My nod got only a shrug in response, so I hooked my arm in his. "Can't keep our public waiting," I said, nearly choking on my attempted solemnity. "I wonder if this is how Liz and Richard started."

Ours was the last float, the pièce de résistance of the parade. Forming the vanguard were three fire trucks from south county volunteer departments, stolidly bright in the midday sun, their metal gleaming and their painted surfaces richly carmine or chromium yellow. Behind them, the Taconic Hills Marching Band milled restlessly, the tuba player already tired and impatient, while a lanky young man with a glockenspiel tinkled a fanciful version of "Heartbreak Hotel."

Two VFW contingents clustered around a bunting-draped pink Cadillac convertible, vintage 1954; Brownies and Cub Scouts chattered in sweet, round-faced disorder. The mayors of Copake, Hillsdale, and Ancram, in the best tradition of politicians, would fill the remaining antique cars and wave to the crowd, and the whole thing would be over in forty minutes. We could all congratulate ourselves on having been good citizens and feel a moment of unalloyed good fortune that we'd ended up here and nowhere else, and that once again summer, which couldn't begin without the Memorial Day parade, was a-cumin in.

The night rain had washed the air clean, but the sun threatened to make my time in Emily's outfit a misery of heat and starch. Peter had his embarrassment to endure as well. Standing in front of the precarious cabin and its papier-mâché boulder, resting against a fence we prayed would stay upright until we reached the small grassy field where the cannon would be fired, we both had our burdens to bear.

"Hey, Emily, you look right fetching!"

Ben Yarnell leaned against an Ancram fire truck, arms folded across his chest, his ordinary chambray shirt and jeans an indecent contrast to the pre-Federal yardage draped around Peter and me. "And you too, Stefan. Mighty becoming," he drawled. He raised his camera, snapping away, circling and bending to get different perspectives, apparently determined to make good his threat to put me on the front page of the *Journal*.

Peter scowled. "You got your history confused, Yarnell. You sound like you're talking to Annie Oakley and Shane or something."

Before Ben could answer, the truck lurched and I grabbed for Peter's shoulder to keep from tumbling into the street. My heart hammered; I steadied myself and dredged up a smile for the crowd.

"Stars and Stripes" rang tinnily from the band; the parade was under way. Starting from the bridge near the site of the old Copake theater, the parade route circled around the village memorial clock, then rolled out past the bank to the concluding ceremonies overlooking the Roe-Jan River.

I was conscious of every face, of every stare and good-natured shriek of delight. Peter shrank back as though he wanted to crawl into the facade of the cabin and disappear, but after a while he relaxed and even seemed to enjoy the happy applause that broke out when the float rumbled into view. I was stirred and upset at the same time by the way people responded to us. Surely Emily would have shunned the spotlight, preferring instead to tend her garden or her bees. Or was it Klaudia who was a gardener? Or Julia? Suddenly everything was in a tangle; I had to hold on to *Sarah*.

"Smile," I urged Peter, determined to favor the part of me that enjoyed the spectacle of the float and these costumes and the panorama of faces, most of them as familiar to me as my own father's. Catherine Delaney, Ruth, and Deeny Lambert waved their encouragement to us. Half a block later, in a swirl of smiling faces that included Jeanie and Clayton Boice and Alicia Fitzhugh, my father appeared; a benign grin softened his features. Even he seemed to be caught up in the spirit of the day.

The cheering throng lined both sides of the street, waving miniature flags. The noise unleashed a pounding in my head, a cacophony of trailing echoes of the high school band, bits of its percussive energy crashing against the whoops of children and the cheers of their parents. The noise was nothing compared with the heat, though; my dress was far too hot to allow me to forget I was wearing the silly thing. I had endured worse, although at the moment I couldn't think exactly what. Whenever the float passed beneath a tree, I basked in the shade, grateful for the momentary respite.

As parades do, this one had its inexplicable fits and starts, and one of the short stops caused my heel to catch on my long skirt. I stumbled, reaching instinctively for the fence. Peter grabbed me before I sent us both tumbling to the street below. The truck jerked forward again and I fell into his arms.

Shrugging away from me, he pulled Ruth's brooch from my dress; the shaft was bent, the clasp broken. "You all right?"

I nodded and let him remove the pin. A spot of blood marked the froth of lace on my bodice; I shook my head dizzily.

"It won't stay on now." He recovered his balance and ducked as a kid with a water pistol sped by on a bicycle.

I clutched the pin in my hand. I'd have to hold it for the rest of the afternoon. In the distance, marchers at the head of the line had begun to disperse into the field. The scene resembled a Napoleonic epic, tiny figures spread out over a verdant meadow, swarming around the little picnic tables, the diminutive bandstand, the miniature cannon.

As we rolled forward, strains of "The 1812 Overture," the crowning achievement of the Taconic Hills band, drifted toward us. Nobody cared about the mixed historical reference—the music was timed so that when our float arrived, the cannon firing in the closing measures would mark the end of the activities. For me that would be a freedom signal. I'd get out of these unnatural clothes and the crowd would disperse, each of the four towns going off to chicken dinners or spaghetti suppers in their respective firehouses. Taconic Hills had voted for chicken this year; the firehouse, a mile out of town, had been decorated by the high school graduating class the night before.

Heedless of the sun, young children rode high on their father's shoulders, and older ones on bicycles circled the perimeter of the crowd. Strutting teens affected the latest markings of adolescence; grandparents sat chatting in circles on the grass.

This community might have its oddities; it wasn't immune to a certain inclination toward narrowness. But it was familiar and reliable and thrifty in its way of valuing the world, and I felt a surge of gratitude that my solitary activities were surrounded by these people. Even Ruth, working the crowd as she made her way toward the float, seemed like an essential institution, a strong-willed glue holding the fabric of the town together.

"Think anyone doesn't know about the bicentennial now?" I shouted to her above the rising music and applause.

"The float is marvelous. You two look wonderful." She beamed with pride. Her pleasure was infectious.

"Thanks, Mother." Peter took the pin from me, leaned down, and passed it to Ruth. "This broke—got Sarah in the process." He smiled when he said it and Ruth smiled back, then frowned as she examined the bent shaft.

"I had that brooch fixed just last week. Jeweler should have done a better job." She opened her purse, unzipped a compartment, and pushed aside an envelope with green, block-printed letters. A clear image—that same green ink, the same square bold printing on the envelopes from New York City that I'd tossed in the trash years ago —made me gasp.

Ruth, getting letters from Julia? I was dizzy with confusion. But before I could form a question, the float lurched forward again. Julia Stanton, writing to Ruth Hoving—why? My mind wouldn't fix on anything but that envelope in Ruth's purse. I'd never puzzle out an answer on my own. I'd have to confront Ruth to find out: doing that when I was at such an obvious disadvantage would only make things more muddled. I held on to Peter's shirt as though the contact would help me regain my composure.

"Have you seen Clayton?" Ruth's long fingers tucked an imaginary hair into place, and she lifted onto her toes, simultaneous movements that drew her thinner, straighter.

"Last I saw him," Peter shouted above the rising volume of the overture, "he was headed for the field. He was talking to Roy."

"Well, if you see him again—Clayton, that is—tell him that he's to be at the podium—oh, there he is. Clayton! Clayton!" She sailed off, her print dress trailing behind her in a cloud of chiffon, her hat bobbing with each determined step as she made for Clayton, whose britches, white shirt, and wire-rim glasses made him look more like a Ben Franklin impersonator than a forge foreman.

"There's my girl. Time for the cannon, Sarah," a voice behind me announced. My father's smile still hadn't faded. Ruth's bicentennial must have struck a new and sentimental chord in him.

"Having a good time, Dad?"

"Too hot and too noisy for comfort. But it's nice to see some patriotic spirit for a change. See you later at the firehouse." He turned and headed for the field.

As I watched him go, his words suddenly rang in my head.

Time for the cannon, he had said.

Arnold Peck, the forge foreman, was killed when a keg of gunpowder exploded at the forge.

The music built, faster, louder. I grabbed Peter's sleeve. "How do they fire the cannon?"

He frowned. "What do you mean?"

"Gunpowder. Do they use gunpowder to fire the cannon?" My fingers tightened around the billowing fabric.

"Of course. You load the front with something harmless, then put gunpowder in the touch hole and . . . Oh, God. Clayton—" With the float still rolling forward, Peter jumped down and sprinted off in the direction of the field.

I lifted the cumbersome skirt, cursing its fullness. Clayton Boice was playing the role of the forge foreman in the pageant—and the forge foreman had died in an explosion of gunpowder. I hopped off the float, nearly stumbled, and then stopped as a deafening concussion tore through the air.

The echoing boom was pierced by a terrible scream; general commotion followed. Most of the crowd converged on the field, others ran toward the paramedic vehicle. Cries of fear and confusion tore the air and then, except for the sound of a gurney clattering along the blacktop, all noise stopped.

Slowed by my skirts, I ran, hoping that I would wake from this fearful nightmare, one someone should have predicted, one I'd rejected because I wanted desperately to believe that there was no pattern, nothing making the people in Ruth's play relive their roles.

The sharp smell of gunpowder fouled the air. Several burly men, wigs askew and shirttails hanging out of their kneebritches, pushed the crowd aside.

"Let' em through, folks. Give 'em room to get by."

Hushed, the crowd parted. As I reached them, I saw the gurney and the blood, and heard the moans. Clayton Boice, his eyes closed and his face contorted, was being carried toward the ambulance. A bright red stain blossomed across the blanket that covered him.

A radio crackled behind the gurney. "Code four, stat," the voice said; they were taking Clayton to Columbia-Greene, the nearest trauma facility. A white-faced Jeanie, her eyes wild and uncomprehending, allowed Ruth to lead her toward the emergency vehicle and the paramedics who had formed a cordon around Clayton.

"He's done this so many times before," a voice beside me said, disbelieving. "He wouldn't have made a mistake. I saw him check the cannon. I *saw* it." Patsy McClosky held her younger son, her face confused, shocked.

"It'll take a while to find out what happened. Looks like Del Santo and Hamm are working on it." Peter pointed to the two sheriff's deputies, who had isolated several witnesses and were taking notes.

Ben's words rang again in my head. *Emily Schiller drowned trying to save a drowning neighbor.* How could I think about myself while Clayton Boice was hurtling along the roads, needles pumping life into him, experts hovering over him, everyone working to keep him from becoming the permanent victim of something. . . . But, dear God, of what?

The residents of Taconic Hills wandered aimlessly on the trampled field until Walter and Dan Lambert made an announcement: the firehouse chicken dinner would be held as planned. Carrying on as usual would allow Taconic Hills to presume that things would work out for the best.

But things were not normal, and no one mentioned Clayton or Jeanie, except when they couldn't help it, consumed by worry and fear, when they were mixing salt and pepper into the flour or cutting carrots for the salad and a question popped out.

"What if Clayton had taken that trip to Minnesota last week like he talked about?"

"Why didn't we think about this? We shouldn't have had the cannon firing this year, what with all the other . . ." The sentence drifted into unhappy silence.

We all had the same questions and none of the answers. Had the cannon been tampered with? Was it possible that it was set up to look like an accident? Would this have happened if the bicentennial pageant had been canceled? Harris Del Santo and Riley Hamm moved among us asking questions, the little paper flags in their lapels drooping sadly, their sheriff's department badges winking whenever they crossed under a light.

Ruth was ghostly white, jumpy, distracted, as she diced celery for the potato salad. Her distress was so uncharacteristic that if I didn't know better, I'd have thought she was ill. Mostly, no one wanted to talk. We kept ourselves busy, watching out the window near the back door, looking at the telephone every now and then in the hope that it would ring and the voice on the other end would tell us that the surgery had fixed Clayton up, he'd be right as rain and handing out lollipops in a week—two at the most.

But the telephone didn't ring.

The knot in my stomach seemed to grow around a kernel of fear and sadness, helped along by the nauseating smell of oil and rubber and food. The big yellow fire truck, gleaming in the yard to make room for the long tables that had been set up inside, kept watch over the scene.

Occasionally during that interminable evening, Peter would come over and stand beside me, for no reason choosing to move his napkin folding to where I was. I was grateful for his nearness. Someone put the radio on, someone else turned it off. And in this way, the chicken, salads, rolls, pies, and lemonade were prepared, the tables set, and the townspeople served, more families drifting in dazed and speechless, needing to be part of the watch. Three hours passed since Clayton Boice, a dear man who had the bad luck to be the volunteer artilleryman for the Memorial Day parade and the forge foreman in the pageant, had been injured.

In downcast twos and fours, the farmers and shopkeepers and their wives and children came in. The city people who would go back to their other lives tomorrow morning had filed in. It wasn't until Nick Dembowski and his wife stepped inside that I felt anything.

I wasn't the only one; everyone turned to stare at the two figures in the doorway. What arrogance! I couldn't believe it. If Nicky had been less greedy, Clayton would be all right. If Ruth hadn't insisted on this damned pageant . . .

Suddenly everyone was talking at once, some in whispers, others in a dark, muttering clatter.

"Go home, Dembowski," a voice from the back of the firehouse called.

Nicky and Andrea, facing the food servers, their backs to the room, went white and still. Confusion swept over Andrea's pretty face, defiance over Nicky's. Their salvation came from a most unlikely quarter.

"They're part of this town and they have a right to be here. They can join the vigil if they've a mind to." Ruth took up her tongs and placed a piece of chicken on each plate, then waved the Dembowskis down the line and turned to the crowd behind her. "Well? You all have totally taken leave of your manners. Stop staring at me."

She was amazing, this demanding and exasperating woman. Andrea smiled gratefully and moved toward me, her plate shaking a little in her hands.

"Coleslaw?" She'd come to my station and I had to serve her, but I didn't have to like her, and I wasn't obliged to make small talk.

"Thanks, Sarah. Sure." She tried to smile, but her face dissolved in consternation. "Any word?"

"No. They took him to Columbia-Greene Medical Center. All I know is that he's got a big hole missing from his middle somewhere. They were going to operate and then someone was supposed to call here."

The very second I finished my sentence, the phone rang. Peter was nearest the wall where the black instrument hung, and he reached out and held the receiver to his ear. Everyone stopped talking; spoons full of mashed potatoes poised above paper plates, cups were suspended halfway to mouths.

It was a very tiny change, an exhale that left Peter looking as though he'd been punched in the diaphragm. His face went white. He said something I couldn't make out and then he hung up.

Silence followed, an unbearable moment in which the collective will of the gathering worked on reversing what Peter was about to report. But we weren't strong enough, and he turned and said, "Clayton died ten minutes ago on the operating table. His heart stopped."

June

In the summer, bees are most benign since they are busily occupied satisfying the purpose for which they exist. Workers return to the hive slowly, legs heavy with pollen, deposit their treasure, and go out again in search of additional bounty.

—*Everywoman's Guide to Beekeeping,* Revised Edition

Eleven

Despite their attempts to be unobtrusive, Harris Del Santo and Riley Hamm, the sheriff's department men assigned to the lower part of the country, were everywhere, talking to everyone, constant reminders of the unanswered questions surrounding Clayton's death. The community was in shock, at the loss and at the way it had happened, and for days I went about my necessary business, adding supers to my beehives, stopping at the grocery store, always avoiding the post office, in a town of ghosts.

On the day of the funeral, Ruth requested we drive together and I agreed; our differences seemed meaningless in light of the bond of sorrow, and of compassion for Jeanie. This was a different occasion, no less a cause for speculation than Reverend Fitzhugh's death had been, but a time of far more genuine sadness for me. I even thought my father, his face lined with sorrow, would break his own restriction against churchgoing to attend Clayton's memorial service, but at the last minute he shook his head, slammed his hand hard against the steering wheel, and drove off in the direction of his garage. Ruth and I hardly exchanged ten words on the way to the funeral.

I sat on the hard pew, light pouring through the petals and the leaves of the lilies in the stained-glass window, buffeted by a storm of thoughts and images: Clayton applying peroxide and blowing on my cut knee after I fell off the climbing bars at school; Clayton at my wedding beaming as though he were a proud uncle; Clayton describing Julia Stanton's talent as an artist. And then the swirl expanded.

The picture of Julia, still out of focus but starting to take on definition. Ruth and my father warning me against continuing the search. Patsy McClosky's face when she told me about Grady and the spoiled milk. Prince.

I hardly heard a word of the service, but something in me changed as we gathered around Clayton's grave and watched his casket being lowered into the ground. I can't say what exactly or why, but I felt a cloud lift, taking with it a darkness that had obscured my vision and diminished my world. And now that I was thinking again, I felt, more than anything else, anger.

It wasn't true that everything was beyond my control. Maybe I didn't understand the parallels between the lives of the players in the pageant and the lives of the people who struggled to build Taconic Hills two hundred years before, and maybe I couldn't quite figure out how I felt about Catherine Delaney, but I *could* do something about one of the mysteries in my life.

I could learn more about Julia Stanton and I knew exactly where to start.

My father had sent me to the shed on a search for a piece of lace in order to get me out of the attic and, most particularly, to get me away from the chest. Like the shed, the chest was a receptacle for secrets: that was as certain in my mind as the fact of Clayton Boice's death, as real as the letter from Julia Stanton that I had glimpsed in Ruth's purse on Memorial Day.

Whatever was going on in Taconic Hills, whatever was making those centuries-old events play out in eerie similarity for so many of us in Ruth's bicentennial pageant, whatever had killed Clayton Boice, I knew suddenly and with great conviction I would not allow it to hurt me.

Ruth sat beside me in my truck on the way home from the funeral; I drove the familiar roads without paying much attention.

"Dear, you missed the turn." Ruth's voice was gentle but firm, touched with gravity, as though I'd just committed us both to a course that would have unnamed but dangerous consequences.

"Sorry," I muttered.

"Why don't you go up to Millers' and turn around in her driveway?"

And why don't you stop telling me the obvious? I wanted to shout. But I nodded and rolled to a turn in the shade of the tall pine tree, cut the wheel hard, and pulled back onto the road.

"Jeanie is a rock." Ruth fidgeted with the buttons on her dress. "It's a good thing she has so many friends and so many activities— they will surely be a comfort to her. She's that much better off than Alicia Fitzhugh."

I shuddered with the memory of that other funeral, the moment that had left me reeling with the shock of Alicia calling out my mother's name. And then I remembered the letter I'd seen in the bottom of Ruth's purse.

"The day of the parade, I didn't mean to spy, but when you opened your purse to put the broken pin away, I saw a letter."

Ruth's face, her profile all sharp lines and angles, showed nothing, not a flicker of recognition or even surprise.

"It looked like it was from Julia Stanton," I said finally.

"You're mistaken, dear. I don't have any letter from your mother." She spoke in the same matter-of-fact tone she'd used when she told me I'd missed the turn. I was convinced she was hiding something.

I gripped the wheel tighter. "Why are you lying to me? I saw it. A letter written in green ink. Block letters. That's her trademark. And it was on the bottom of your purse." My voice had risen and I was nearly panting.

"I'm sorry, dear, but whatever you saw, it wasn't a letter from your mother. Here, Sarah, don't miss the turn again."

I braked and the truck skidded, but we slid into her driveway. My head pounded with anger. I couldn't trust myself to speak; this woman was deceiving me, for reasons I didn't yet understand. If she really wanted to keep the truth hidden, simply asking, or insisting, or even badgering her would be useless. Ruth had decided to lie to me and nothing I could do would sway her.

"Sarah, Sarah. Everyone's in a state. Clayton's death is hard on all of us. Best to calm down, go on with your work, let time heal your wounds." She pushed opened the car door and swung her legs to the ground, but she seemed to be waiting for me to acknowledge the wisdom of her advice before she got out.

"Lying doesn't protect me, Ruth. All it does is keep you from having to do the hard work of explaining the truth." My hands gripped the steering wheel; I turned to face her, but she refused to meet my gaze.

She swiveled her head in my direction, smiled, and said, "We'll see you later. Thank you for the ride, dear." Then she closed the door gently. When I looked in my rearview mirror as I neared the bottom of her drive, she was still standing there, tall, straight, motionless.

My father would be at the garage until dark, and the knowledge made me dizzy. If Ruth insisted on denying that she'd been carrying a letter from my mother, if she and my father thought they could threaten or cajole me into abandoning the search for Julia Stanton, then they didn't know who they were dealing with. My father might have thought I didn't notice him steering me away from the chest in the attic. He might also expect that I wouldn't sneak into his house to continue my search, but on both counts he'd be wrong.

I pushed open the door and called out, knowing that no one would be inside. I had, after all, watched him drive away this morning, bound for work; he'd be gone for hours.

Every board creaked under my weight, and I set my feet down carefully to keep from making noise until I realized that I'd be better off just *doing* it and getting out of there. I ran up the stairs to the attic. At last—I *knew* I was about to discover something about Julia that would help free me from the need to blame her, or at least deprive my anger of its bitterness.

I propped up the trunk lid with the ruler and then scooped out the top layer of old winter paraphernalia and laid the heap on the floor. The heat pressed down on me, my heart pounded, but I went on.

Two white jeweler's boxes and a larger box secured with a faded blue ribbon lay under a white-and-gold crocheted afghan. This was what I was looking for, I was certain. They'd once belonged in Julia Stanton's world; I was about to let them into mine.

I opened the first box. Inside, on a bed of cotton, lay a single earring.

The silver filigree was finely detailed, surrounding a blue stone with an opaque center. Just touching the curved wire made me shudder. This was the part that went through the pierced hole in her ear, had actually hung there in intimate connection with her body. Perhaps she wore her hair pulled back, wispy tendrils escaping along her neck. The earring would have swayed as she listened to music in church, maybe, or at a party; this was too ornate a piece to be worn for everyday.

I was running a movie in my head. Worse, the movie was sentimental, but trying to shut it off did no good, and it played on in the background of my mind as I closed that box and opened the next one, and fingered the fine patterns of a lace-edged handkerchief.

Folded inside, a little metal shoe from a Monopoly game and a small, beautifully carved wooden flower rested against the white fabric, glowing with attic heat and setting off new stories in my imagination.

My father had saved these particular items because they meant something to him. *The flower?* Had there been a picnic in which he'd given her this intricately carved blossom? Had they embraced on a hill, clouds scudding behind them as they pledged eternal love? And this game piece, so familiar from my childhood—it must have come from a different set, and must surely figure in a memory my father wanted to preserve in its original shape. I held the tiny flower in the palm of my hand, hoping to understand its significance, knowing I'd have to return it but needing it near me. Exhilaration bubbled up in me.

The last box was wider than the other two but no higher, and I lifted the lid expecting nothing more than a tea towel or a pair of gloves.

The yellowing sheet on the top of a half-inch stack of paper was covered with words written in green ink. Julia's familiar block letters filled the page.

I touched it, then shrank back, snared in the knowledge that I was about to violate every principle of privacy and trust I'd professed to endorse. This wasn't like going to the Historical Society and reading Emily Schiller's letters. An old question formed: Would you do this if someone were watching you? And the unfamiliar answer came just as quickly: *No one is watching.*

I held the paper, letting my skin tell me what it would say, holding it to my nose and breathing in the very faintest hint of rose petals.

And then I unfolded the sheet, trying to keep my eyes from devouring it in a single sweep, forcing myself to look at each character slowly.

It was a letter to my father, dated a month before their marriage, all about a party in New York City, with a few polite questions about the health of Roy's mother, ending with a brief description of a sketch Julia had done the day before.

I'm afraid I don't like the straight lines and sharp edges of the city, the last line read. She wasn't very original with words; her observations of the party were banal and uninspired, and focused more on the size of the ham and the variety of pies than on the people.

Even here, she gave me nothing of herself. For all that these letters added to my knowledge of her, she might have been a stick. I felt a pang of disappointment as I folded the paper and returned it to the pile. Somewhere in these letters, some event in her past—I'd find a good reason to cut her out of my heart once and for all, or an excuse to allow myself to love her.

Mornings, I have to watch Aunt Holly's twins, she said in another letter, *but I have afternoons to sketch.* Even then, it seemed, children weren't her cup of tea.

She wrote about wanting to go to the Sorbonne, and in that dream I detected a flicker of passion, but soon the subject turned to their wedding plans, and the words became superficial again, reverting to the cool and distant feel of all the other letters. Apparently, their courtship didn't exactly crackle with electricity. From the evidence of her own words, Julia seemed incapable of that.

My father might have deprived me of my past by not talking about her, but imagining Julia wasn't very satisfying either. Yet he had kept these letters all these years, and they had either fueled his hate or fanned his love. I clenched my fists to keep from balling the paper into tight, ugly wads.

What I'd discovered was hardly worth the risk of sneaking up here. I looked out the window—the scene below was as still as a painting, no telltale signs of dust kicked up by an approaching vehicle. Across the alfalfa field, three figures, an adult and two small children, made their way toward East Taconic Road. Patsy McClosky and her kids, I decided from the swing of the woman's hips and the size of the children, walking along the bank of the stream, stopping occasionally to examine something. I was pleased that she'd taken me at my word about using the land.

Two more letters—I might as well finish up and get out of here. I scanned the next one with resignation, but as soon as I unfolded the last letter, the skin on my hands prickled, as though the paper were on fire. This was different from the others. For one thing, two inches were torn off the bottom, and the date alone was enough to make my breath quicken. This letter was written seven years after she'd left. I could hardly keep the paper still in my hands. The message was four lines long and by the time I'd read it for the second time, I'd memorized it.

Dear Roy, it began, as all the others had. *I hope you and Sarah are well. I am moving to Pearl River next month when I marry Lawrence*

Travis. I want you to have my new address. You can reach me there from now on.

You can reach me there . . . Had Roy and Julia kept in touch? Then it was only me she'd refused to have contact with. But I'd rejected her advances—those unopened letters I'd thrown away must have been written at about the same time as this one. If only I could go back and make that stubborn child open just one of those envelopes.

Pearl River. Seventy-five miles away, on the other side of the Hudson. If she hadn't moved since then, Julia Stanton was close enough for me to drive down to see her in between lunch and dinner on any ordinary day—except she wasn't Julia Stanton anymore.

Julia *Travis* might even have another family. After all, she had remarried eighteen years ago; she would have been in her thirties, not too old to bear children.

Why did she give me up and start over with other children?

I pictured a comfortable neighborhood of older homes, small but well kept with yards edged by large, graceful trees providing leafy shade. Her house would be brick, with a side chimney and a box hedge lining the curved walk to the front entrance. I imagined a station wagon pulling into the driveway, saw three doors fly open. From the rear door, a long-legged, titian-haired girl in cutoff shorts and a big white T-shirt hopped out and ran to the front door. A gangly, frowning boy of about sixteen got out on the passenger side in front, his arms loaded with packages.

I could hardly breathe and my heart was racing, but the pictures crowded in. A woman, tall, slender, her long, light brown hair caught up in an elastic tie, emerged from the driver's side of the car. She moved with a composure that was close to serenity, seeming to glide rather than walk.

Everything in my daydream was filtered through gold light, and it all moved slowly, slowly, so that details were burned into my mind's eye. I saw her wrist, bony but well formed, encircled by a silver bracelet. The boy's sneakers were untied, his laces frayed. As he moved toward the walk, a small paper bag fell from the pile he was carrying, but he didn't notice.

I was unaware of any feelings I attached to the imagined picture. I was a recorder, not an interpreter.

Until the next frame of my fantasy, when she spoke.

"You forgot to shut your door."

She smiled as she said it, without rebuke and without condescension. But her voice made me hurt inside. It was honey, turned to sound—and I remembered how it had soothed me and hushed me and sung to me.

What would I say if I were on that street? *Hello, I don't want to disturb your new life, I just want you to explain why you left me. Then I'll go back where I came from.* Businesslike, a request for information and an admission of my intended limits.

I could no more approach the woman in my fantasy than I could undo Clayton's death. She had chosen, and it hadn't been me.

The letter slipped out of my hand and drifted toward the floor. I leaned forward to pick it up—and heard the front door open, then close with a slam.

Instantly, a slick of fine sweat covered my body. I should have been safe. My father shouldn't be home yet. It was too early. Unless something had happened at the garage, some quirk, some accident.

I didn't dare move to look out the window. It could only be my father. His footsteps, silent as he passed through the carpeted living room, sounded loud, sharp as he proceeded to the back of the house.

Drawers slammed shut. More footsteps, pounding across the kitchen floor.

Panting, I laid everything back in the chest, trying to remember precisely where each box had been in relation to the others. Nothing looked right. I couldn't get the picture to form in my mind. The hinge of the chest lid creaked like the door to a castle keep. I lowered it all the way, then tiptoed to the cartons on the other side of the attic, as far away from the chest as I could get.

Centuries ground slowly on, and I ceased to have clear thoughts. When I looked at my watch, three minutes had gone by.

Maybe I should run down the stairs, make up an excuse for being in the house. I'd seen smoke and I came to investigate. I'd heard a noise. No, exposing myself was a needless risk. Dad was certain to leave again soon to go back to the garage. It was only two in the afternoon.

A door slammed in the kitchen; a loud curse rattled through the house. He was looking for something, stomping around, angry. His footsteps rattled the stairs, and I held my breath.

"Sarah!" With fierce eyes, he stared at the wooden chest, then back at me. "What the hell are you doing?"

I retreated as he approached me, his nostrils flaring and his body quivering. He grabbed my wrist in a viselike grip; I smelled the thick, brownish odor of oil and metal. "I was—Dad, you're hurting me."

We both looked down at his fingers digging into my flesh; his expression changed to horrified regret and he released my arm. I could say anything now, it hardly mattered, but I had to say something.

"Clayton's picture, the one from the yearbook. I was looking for the yearbook. I wanted a picture of him and that was the only one I could think of." As the rush of lies spilled out, I maneuvered toward the door. My wrist burned where he'd grabbed me.

"Oh, Sarah, I'm so sorry. Oh, God, forgive me, I didn't mean to hurt you." He caught his breath in a sob, then covered his face with his knobby, grease-stained hands.

For a second I almost let myself believe that it was *my* lie that had caused *him* pain, but I'd known well enough and for a very long time that it was his bitterness that had so warped him that he could act this way. I would not be blamed, not even silently and by myself.

"I'll be all right, Dad," I said. My fingers closed around a small hard object in my pocket. The flower—I'd forgotten to put it back.

"I've lost my new torque wrench," he said to the air, as though in answer to a question nobody had asked.

I didn't begin to recite the list of the things I'd lost. Instead, I went to the shade of the oak tree near the pond, to think or to forget, whichever I could manage.

Twelve

Even the venerable old protector of my childhood had no comfort to offer me. The bark was ridged with sharp edges, the ground strewn with burrs. I huddled under its branches, numb, still, and unaware of Peter walking across the grass until he sat down beside me, stirring the hot air enough to startle me.

"You were sure far away." He kissed me, then screwed up his nose. "And here I thought I was the one with a reason to feel bad. Donahue says our credit is overextended. He won't give us any money for renovation until more of the first loan's paid off. He didn't care that three clients owe me thousands of dollars. Bottom line, he said. Banks have to toe the bottom line. So no more work on the old barn for now."

Vixen Hill Lodge seemed like such a minor concern, one that would be there, unchanged, even if we let it go for a while. Before I could think of some response, Peter put his arm around my shoulders. His touch was so unexpected my eyes filled with tears. I blinked them back, and wiped at my face with cold hands.

"I've been waiting for you to do that. It's okay to cry about Clayton's death, Sarah."

He drew me closer, but I pulled back.

"That's only part of it. I need to talk to you, Peter."

He frowned, then nodded. "Sure. We're not supposed to be at my mother's for another hour, hour and a half. Let's drive over to Bash Bish Falls."

"Your mother's? Dinner." I got to my feet, brushing leaves and dirt from the seat of my jeans, and walked toward the van. "I'd forgotten."

"We're supposed be at the house at six. What's going on?"

I didn't answer until we were both seated in the van and on our way down the road. "Let's wait until we get to the falls. It's only ten minutes away. Tell me something, anything, about your day, about the work you're doing."

"What is this, Sarah? You look pale."

"Please, let's wait until we get to the falls. Tell me about your meeting with Donahue."

And he did, talking hesitantly, looking at me every few seconds while I tried to keep my shoulders loose and my mind aware that I was sitting beside my husband. Only three other cars, spaced far apart, were in the parking lot when we drove up. I hopped down and kicked at small pebbles, empty of all thought as I waited for Peter to get his canteen from the back of the van.

"Prepared for anything now." He slipped his fingers through mine and we set out up the wide dirt path. Leafy overhang sent dappled shadows raining down on us; the stream to our right gurgled icily downhill.

We walked in silence half the distance to the falls, the noise swelling as we approached the cascade. A couple on their way down smiled at us, and I forced myself to smile back. He was tall, thin, with the same reddish hair as the girl in the scene I'd imagined—*my sister:* words I'd never before thought.

"So?"

Startled, I turned to Peter. "So what?"

"So what's taking you away from me, Sarah? It's more than Clayton's death, more than Prince. Are you worried about the pageant? You aren't thinking about quitting, are you?"

"No. I won't be chased off. Whatever's going on, I won't cut and run. Maybe Dembowski is desperate and he thinks Ruth's idea is a terrible threat, so he's trying to scare everyone away. I don't know, but I'm not going to be run off."

"Dembowski was in Hudson when Clayton was killed. Several people have vouched for that." We'd heard that Hamm and Del Santo were satisfied that Nick Dembowski was far away from the Memorial Day parade, from early in the morning until his appearance at the firehouse. But Nicky didn't have to be there at the actual moment of Clayton's death for him to be responsible, I thought stubbornly.

Neither of us spoke. Finally, we reached the rocks beside the catch pool of the falls. The roar and the mist crashed around us, but instead of calming me as it always had in the past, the rush of water plummeting down the fifty-foot drop added to my agitation.

"What would you do with my bees if something happened to me?"

"Happened to you? What would happen to you?" Peter's voice was light with amusement.

I shrugged, brushing away a fleeting thought of Emily Schiller and the woodcutter. "If I got sick again, at a time when there was work to be done—medication, checking water supplies, getting ready for winter. You know."

"What I know," Peter said, "is that you're one of the healthiest people around, and this line of talk bothers me."

The roar of the falls pounded in my ears. "I read about a custom among beekeepers. Promise me you'll do it."

"Tell me what it is first." Peter seemed confused by the turn the conversation had taken.

"You must be my messenger. Every beekeeper needs a messenger. When a beekeeper dies, the messenger must go to each hive and knock three times and, after each knock, tell the bees about the keeper's death. Three knocks, three tellings. If you don't, they'll fly away. Maybe go wild and attack people. If you *do,* then they'll stay in the hive until you can find someone to take care of them."

Peter erupted with anger. "You're being ridiculous, Sarah. Why are you talking about this now? Something happened, something you're not telling me. I want to know what's going on."

"Promise you'll be my messenger."

Peter rolled his eyes. "Okay, all right. Now, *tell* me."

The chill spray of the water dampened everything; I needed to tell Peter what had happened in the attic before my inner cold turned to numbness again.

"I read some old letters Julia wrote to my father."

He didn't move, except for a tightening of the muscles around his mouth. "What do you mean? Where were they?"

"In his attic. In that big wooden chest, in a box with some other things. That's not all. I saw a letter I know was from Julia in your mother's purse, but when I asked her, she denied having it."

"The letters—what did they say?"

"Oh, they told me plenty. That she's a person who doesn't have strong feelings, doesn't much like children—and she married someone named Lawrence Travis eighteen years ago. Or planned to, anyway." I closed my eyes and shook my head again. "I don't understand, Peter. What's the big deal? Even then, people had affairs and remarried. Why all the secrecy, all the exaggeration? There's got to be more to it. It doesn't make sense."

Peter put his arms around me and held me to him; I felt his closeness and his body heat, heard only the silence in my head and the roar of the falls. He let me go and looked hard into my eyes.

"What would make you happy, Sarah? What do you want?"

I could only lift one corner of my mouth into a smile. "I'd return to January and start over. I'd skip February entirely and move on to a different March." Ruth and my father had been right, after all. The past that I'd uncovered had brought nothing but pain.

"If Roy has gone to all this trouble to keep me from a woman whose main sins were that she wrote boring letters and had an affair that led to their divorce and her remarriage, and if your mother has agreed with him that I should be shielded from that, and if *my* mother hasn't kept connected to me, then more than anything else the situation is pathetic. Just plain sad that they all reacted so extremely."

A bright and cleansing anger had finally broken through, and for a moment I felt a kinship to my father. But I wouldn't let myself be consumed by hate, as he was. I could make a situation not of my own doing the centerpiece of my life, as he had for nearly a quarter of a century, or I could reclaim the right to chose my own path and go forward.

"Then there's probably more that you don't know yet," Peter said after a while. He took my hand, shaded his eyes with his other hand, and looked up. The rocks were heaped together as though a giant child had thrown them carelessly into a pile at the top of the falls. "Look. Think he's going to make it?"

I followed his gaze. A figure hugged the outcropping just below the summit, a young man in denim shorts, a T-shirt, and sneakers, a green-and-white bandanna around his head. Clinging with both hands to rocks above him, he lifted one leg and explored for a foothold; the wandering foot came down. As he shifted his weight, the rock seemed to explode and crash down into the cascade of water.

I choked back a scream. A flashing image of his body crashing into the pool, held under by the force of the tumbling water, faded as quickly as it formed. The boy swung by his handhold; with grace and sureness he found first one then another safe spot to put his feet. Finally, when I could speak again, I said to Peter, "Let's get out of here. I can't stand to watch him."

Partway down the path to the parking lot, Peter stopped abruptly and turned to me. "Beekeepers aren't supposed to take summer vacations, I know, but I'd like us to go away. Three or four days. Just to break the mood. What do you think about Cape Cod? Lobsters and sunsets and long walks on the dunes? I can rearrange my schedule."

His voice was gentle; was I behaving so inexplicably that he feared for my sanity?

"I won't run away from my own life. Really, I'm fine. Reading those letters—maybe I didn't understand everything, it hardly matters, but at least I'm sure of one thing. Whatever her reasons, Julia's not going to waltz back into my life and repent her errant maternal ways. She's gone on, and I have to, too."

Peter wasn't satisfied, not completely. "One day, then. We'll go on a picnic to that pond in Hillsdale, on the Hotaling property. They said we could use it while they're in Colorado."

I agreed because I could think of no reason not to, and we drove to Ruth and Walter's house planning the picnic menu, agreeing tacitly to postpone further discussion of Julia. The long, shadowed afternoon had slipped toward twilight, and a breeze blew in through the van window, bringing with it the scent of new-cut grass and of the first sweet honeysuckle. I was reminded of the years before, when those smells had been enough by themselves to make me feel peaceful.

Gradually, as we neared the Hoving house, my calm returned. I wouldn't let anyone jeopardize my marriage or my well-being, not Julia, not Ruth, and certainly not Emily Schiller or Klaudia Weigelt. They were outside of me, and I couldn't control what they did.

Two Adirondack chairs, their straight backs and sloping seats newly painted white, broke the green expanse of lawn below the big house. If only I could sit alone in one of those chairs and watch the swallows swoop over the hills . . . Sighing, I slid out of the van and followed Peter across the flagstone steps to the side door.

"Hey, Dad, we're here," Peter hollered through the screen door, and an answering shout echoed from the depths of the house. We stepped inside. The mud room was the coolest part of the house in summer; the chill, damp air seemed like a lake bottom, slightly green and slippery. The kitchen beyond was also protected from the heat, but the smell here was of strawberries, sharp and sugary. On the counter, gleaming with ruby lights, were two dozen pints of preserves. Ruth had certainly been busy.

"There you are. You two look cool as frogs' bellies." Walter, his pressed pants and white shirt spotless, appeared in the doorway. He held my shoulders and kissed me, then patted Peter's back. "Can you wait a minute before we go out to the barn to check out that old inkwell? I want to hear what your mother has to say. She'll be right down. She was talking to Riley Hamm on the telephone."

At the sound of the deputy's name, a shiver of recognition rippled through me: something important was being discussed upstairs.

"They got the report back?" Peter's eagerness to hear about the police report was shared by everyone in town. Riley had been promising new information as soon as the state police got done examining the cannon, but the talk was that no matter what the report showed, it would never really be conclusive. Tampering might be obvious or it might look accidental.

"Now, I don't know. The phone rang just as you hollered up, so I didn't hear everything. There's your mother now."

We all turned expectantly to the hall. With the light behind her, Ruth looked like a shadow. The slump of her shoulders warned that something was amiss, but as she stepped into the kitchen her posture straightened and she smoothed the waistband of her skirt.

"Iced tea?" she asked brightly, transformed instantly by my presence into the good hostess.

Peter kissed her lightly. "What did Riley have to say, Mother? What did they find out?"

A flicker of pain crossed her face, and I felt momentary sympathy for her struggle to make the world familiar again. "He wouldn't tell me over the phone. He's coming by in half an hour."

"You mean he didn't give you any—"

"Sugar?" she asked. "You take sugar in your iced tea, don't you, dear?" She smiled at me as though she hadn't heard Peter's question.

"Why don't we let the gals have their tea in private while you and I go see about that inkwell?" Walter hooked his arm through Peter's.

Peter tossed a questioning look at me; I nodded. Ruth was the last person with whom I wanted to be alone, but I was determined to give the appearance that things were normal, fine.

Peter and Walter went off in the direction of the barn; Ruth and I took our sweating glasses, decorated with the inevitable mint leaves, to the Adirondack chairs. We sat without exchanging words or glances until Ruth leaned toward me. She reached up, tucked a stray hair behind her ears, and looked directly into my eyes.

"I've been thinking about a lot of things, Sarah, especially your asking about Julia. And I've decided I was wrong to keep the truth from you." She took a breath that lifted her bosom; I didn't see her exhale. "Yes, that was a letter from Julia you saw. She hadn't heard from me in so long she got worried. You see, I've been writing to her four or five times a year, to let her know how you're doing. But what with the preparations for the—"

"Four times a year? A hundred letters?" My stomach clenched, as though someone had punched me. A sharp pain shot along the side of my head. "How dare you spy on me! Lying is bad enough, but this goes further than my wildest imagining."

I was *not* going to swallow my anger this time. She was my husband's mother and she was a self-anointed town sage. That didn't give her license to betray me. "You can't go around acting like the secret police. What makes you think you know what's important to me or how I feel? Who gave you the right to pass off your opinions about me as fact and then write them down for *her?*"

Ruth paled but she didn't flinch. Even now, knowing what I do, I have to give her credit for taking my verbal blows without backing away.

"Sarah, dear, I knew you'd be upset. Let me explain."

In answer, I got up and started for the barn.

"Wait. Please."

It was her tone that got to me. I wasn't sure I'd heard concern before from Ruth, at least not directed to me. I couldn't trust myself to speak, but I did turn and face her.

She rose from her chair and walked to me. "I understand. I know you're angry, but we've been trying to protect you, dear. Now, for the same reason, it's time for you to know."

"We? What *we* is that?" The idea of the unholy alliance of Ruth and Roy rocked me, but that seemed to be her meaning.

"Listen for a moment. You've been spared for so long we thought things could go on like that forever. It's different now. You *want* to know. You've been searching. And it's not fair to keep it from you."

"What are you talking about?" Earlier, she'd denied having a letter from Julia, and now here was Ruth, about to share secrets she'd been keeping for a very long time. I didn't like dangling from the end of her precarious thread and swaying and jerking whenever she decided to move.

"What's wrong, my dear? I thought you wanted to know about her. Your father doesn't think it's a good idea, but—"

"My father? Do you and Roy get together to decide just how much little Sarah should be told? I'm sorry, Ruth, but I won't be part of your game, whatever it is."

"I believe that when you know what I have to tell you, it will make things clearer."

A thousand questions flew around me again, but it was oddly soothing to hear her voice. The anger that had coursed through me subsided a little as she led me back to the chairs. I shrank from the feel of her hand on my arm.

"I'm ready to tell you why she left. But only if you're ready, too. Do you want to know?"

Mesmerized by the dark, expanded iris of her eye, I nodded.

"Only a few people know about it. Walter, of course, and Dan Lambert. And Jeanie." She paused, not saying that there was one less witness now that Clayton was gone, but thinking it, I was sure. "The town speculated, there was lots of talk, but no one else had the facts. Julia had an affair with another man."

"I know," I said quietly, glad that I'd gone ahead and read *all* the letters so that I didn't have to learn about my mother's past for the first time from Ruth, glad to be hardened to the history so that my first shock had been private and not for her viewing pleasure. I folded my hands in my lap. Soon I would be able to let go of Julia Stanton. Perhaps, in time, I'd stop being angry at Ruth, too.

"Oh, Sarah, my dear girl." Ruth reached for my hand, tears shining in her eyes. "I didn't want to pain you like that. But you have the right to know. I'm surprised, frankly, that your father told you."

"He didn't," I said, and her face dissolved into questions I had no desire to answer. I had a more difficult task: to bury thoughts of my mother as finally as we had buried Clayton Boice. "I'll be all right. Don't worry about me."

"But if Roy didn't tell you, how—"

Before she could finish her sentence, and before I could ask Ruth *my* question, Riley Hamm's Bronco screeched to a stop in the driveway. One of those thin men who walk as though each joint is hinged, the sheriff's deputy straightened his limbs and then bore down on us with a gait that signaled trouble. Peter and Walter emerged from the barn at the same time, talking earnestly and heading toward the chairs where Ruth and I, the center of the double storm rolling toward us, sat and waited.

"Someone jammed rocks and mud and a piece of leather into the damn cannon. Way back, pushed it in, then wedged it with a pot lid. Goddamn—a *pot* lid! Looked like a false back to someone who couldn't see too good. When Clayton loaded that fake ball, he never even knew." Riley spoke through gritted teeth.

The wind lifted the down-pointing fingers of the willow and trailed them into the stream beyond the lawn. A bird sang a self-congratulatory trill. Clayton had been murdered.

"Someone did it on purpose?" Peter said what none of the rest of us dared.

"No question. Even if Clayton checked, with his cataracts . . ." Riley reached down and yanked a stalk of timothy from the lawn, running its slender length through his fingers. He looked bent today, worn out by the news he was delivering. I'd seen Riley pretend not see a woman being beaten by her husband in Trotta's parking lot; his expression then had been too close to pleasure for me to have any illusions about his gentleness, but he seemed touched by emotion now.

Ruth hadn't moved from the chair. She examined Riley coolly. "You have no suspects, is that right?" Hardly waiting for his nod, she went on. "But you think it has something to do with the bicentennial. And you want to put on extra protection for the other people in the pageant, like Peter and Sarah and Catherine Delaney and all the bit players and Margaret Kimball, because of your concern."

Riley's sputtering was almost comical. "Hold on, now. I never said nothing about protection. Yes, that's one of the possibilities. Even a blind man could see the play *might* be connected somehow. We got folks looking into Dembowski's activities, and a couple other things. But I came here to ask you to consider canceling that play. Thing I'm worried about now is the Fourth of July."

And Stefan's mother, good woman though she was, was bitten by a dog during a Fourth of July celebration and she died of rabies. Margaret Kimball, tall, dark-haired, a criminal lawyer with a practice on the Upper East Side of Manhattan, was playing Stefan's mother in the pageant. Or did *Ruth* qualify as Stefan's mother? My mother-in-law's wary, appraising look told me she was a couple of steps ahead of both Riley and me.

"You know, we've lost touch with some old traditions here in Taconic Hills and I'd like to see them restored. When I was a child, every Fourth we'd have a wonderful celebration, everyone in the village. Families would get together and have a daylong picnic, one year on the Hotaling farm, next year in one of the Kronenburg fields, year after that in a Lambert backyard, until everyone had their turn. We'd all bring a dish to share. There were gallons of iced tea and beer, huge watermelons. People felt part of a community. That's what we need now. So I'm going to restore the tradition. I'm going to have a good old-fashioned clambake right here, on the Fourth of July, and everyone in Taconic Hills is invited." She smiled brightly at the lean and scowling deputy. "Even you, Riley, even though you live in Ancramdale."

Walter's wide-eyed surprise was answer enough to my question about when this plan had been hatched.

"You're having a clambake?" Riley's raised eyebrows peaked in upside down V's over his washed-out blue eyes.

"Folks'll bring salads and desserts, I'll get Tommy to cut some early sweet corn, and maybe Ike Kronenburg will butcher some chickens. I'll provide the clams and mussels from Long Island, and a keg of beer and a pit."

Walter got caught in the spirit of her plan. "Night before, we used to dig a big pit, fill it with huge rocks—boulders, really—and then sand and firewood. Next morning we'd get up early, in the dark, to start the fire and get it burning just right. Put in potatoes, then chicken, then a layer of corn, and finally the mollusks. Covered it with wet burlap and cornhusks and let it cook away. You could smell it all day—by the time you got to eating, it was about the best thing ever."

"We're going to make memories that are as good as Walter's," Ruth said decisively as she got to her feet. "We need some extra healing now and Clayton wouldn't think it disrespectful if we did this clambake in his honor, kind of like a giant wake, everyone coming together to prove our resolve."

Riley harrumphed and shook his head. "I'll come, but only in my official capacity. There's too much opportunity for mischief. You're providing *someone*—I don't know who but *someone*—with a clear target. I wish to hell you'd call off the whole thing, but I never did know anyone to convince you to do contrary to your own wishes."

"I'm glad you're going to be there. Bring Ellie and the kids. And bring your dog, Riley," Ruth added for good measure. "I'm making it a point to tell everyone to bring their dogs."

July

Securing the primary honey flow, which in many parts of the north-east is associated with alfalfa, requires hard work more than it does good judgement.

—*Everywoman's Guide to Beekeeping,* Revised Edition

Thirteen

"This will be the most time we've spent apart in six years." Peter's skin still smelled of soap from his shower; a drop of water slid down his neck from his wet hair.

"You drive carefully, okay, and don't let Deeny behind the wheel if he's been drinking. I know it's an honor for you to be chosen to go get the clams. I just wish you didn't have to do all that driving." I smiled up at the truck and waved at Deeny. He grinned and flashed a two-fingered salute against the bill of his Mets cap.

"Change your mind, Sarah. Come with us. We could take a moonlight walk on the beach."

"Deeny likes beaches." I tried to laugh, to show Peter I was making a joke. "Besides, I have go to sleep early tonight."

"Not that that's any different than the past, oh, twelve, fourteen nights." Peter's voice had an edge, of scorn or exasperation, I couldn't tell.

I tried to remember beyond the last two nights but the time all ran together in my mind. "Well, I work hard and I need my rest."

"Work? What you're working on is not feeling hurt anymore. About your mother. And about *my* mother. And you're doing such a good job I don't think you feel anything right now. You know, maybe a little disorder, a little bit of wallowing would be good for you. Scream, shout, tear your hair—"

"Beat my breast? Come on, Peter, when's the last time, when's the *first* time you saw me behave like that?"

"My point exactly. You're all closed up, Sarah."

I wasn't, not really. But letting the idea of Julia Stanton into my life had made me vulnerable again. I'd been working hard at putting aside the mess of Julia's past and my own, but I needed more time so I could finish the job of destroying the disturbing feelings. Just a little more time, that's all, and then it would be behind me, over, out of my way. Julia Stanton had traded a life she didn't want for one more to her liking. And now *I* was giving *her* up, finally.

But it was taking time, time that I'd stolen from Peter.

"Are you feeling neglected?" I asked, a bit of teasing in my voice. "I promise, when you get back, I'll start asking about your work again. I can't go with you anyway. I'm taking the first watch at the clambake fire. Five o'clock in the morning—God! This event is so . . . orchestrated. That's what's making me tired." I frowned and shook my head. "Sorry. I guess I have been preoccupied."

"Well, maybe you can shake it while I'm gone." He sounded unconvinced. He swung his overnight bag into the truck; Deeny stared out across the horizon, giving us privacy we didn't need.

I nodded absently and waved. Peter climbed into the cab, slammed the door, and Deeny pulled away, heading for East Taconic Road. The truck receded into the dust-filled distance. By the time the air cleared I recognized a feeling I'd never known before. *Alone:* I was going to be alone in my rambling old barn of a house through an entire night. A flicker of excitement lapped at the cold, numb core of me in anticipation of this adventure.

I took my time preparing a salad. The rhythm of chopping parsley soothed me; I sliced cucumbers paper-thin, smiling with pleasure as the setting sun glinted off the shining porcelain face of the stove. I grated a carrot until I was in danger of cutting my fingers on the sharp edges of the grater. I reached to the top shelf of the pantry and pulled down a dusty can of chick peas—Peter hated chick peas in his salad. I squeezed a whole lemon into the bowl and left both pulpy halves on the counter. Jewels of light twinkled from the beveled-glass cabinet fronts and sparkled off the facets of the crystal goblets, wedding presents we'd used only four times.

I had gone so quickly from my father's house to my husband's, with only my four years of college dormitories in between. I had never, not once, spent a single night alone, had never experienced this delicious freedom. It would do both of us good to have a night apart. The timing couldn't be better: Peter's concern had begun to feel oppressive lately. The more he worried, the more I retreated. I couldn't help thinking I'd gotten the better of the deal tonight. I sat at the kitchen table and ate my salad and waited for dark to fall.

A black, star-strewn sky splashed through the window when my alarm went off.

I liked waking in the dark and sitting up in bed, covers up to my chin, listening to the sleeping world. I sang an old Beatles tune as I pulled on my jeans and sweatshirt; amazing what the simple fact of Peter not being home had liberated in me. I never knew I liked falling asleep with the radio on.

The kitchen still smelled of lemons. I tossed the leftover rinds into the trash and filled a glass with orange juice and sat down to look out over the pond at the oak tree and the hills beyond. Since I'd awakened, the sky had gone from ink black to a deep, Prussian blue. In the quiet of my kitchen, I wondered how many dark nights Emily Schiller had seen, transformed by the sunrise to a day filled with chores.

She must have known the dark, but only briefly, as the boundary on either end of a long workday. And she, too, must have had little opportunity to be alone. Poor thing, perhaps she'd never felt this sweet freedom.

I could float through the day on these good feelings, never having to touch the ground. Patsy McClosky's delicate embroidery glowed in the reflected light of the gas jet under the kettle; Peter's antique baskets, hanging above the stove, cast strange shadows on the ceiling. I glanced at my watch—no time for coffee. I had enjoyed my morning and my kitchen too long. Ben Yarnell had been waiting for me in the meadow below Ruth and Walter's house for ten minutes. I turned off the gas and set the cup back on the shelf.

I grabbed a jacket and stepped outside onto the dewy grass, glancing back at the kitchen window, now dark. Along the road, the silhouettes of houses, barns, and trees stood stark against the navy-blue sky. Fog clung to the ground, creeping up the trunks of trees and insinuating its way around the corners of buildings, making me feel as though I were driving into an impressionist painting. Two cat's-eyes of light from a farmhouse kitchen window cut the dark as I drove on toward Ruth's yard—Tommy Hoysradt, stoking on coffee to get him through morning milking. The kitchen lights blazed in

Ruth's house, too, but I drove directly to the clambake area. Ben was already there, his back to me, his car parked under a maple tree.

The thick mist, like plumes of breath from an invisible creature roaming the hills, swirled knee-deep along the lawn. In the hazy half-light, Ben's face looked different this morning, softer perhaps, and sadder. All its parts were the same; maybe what had changed was me.

I poured myself coffee from Ben's proffered thermos. He touched my shoulder and pointed to the hills in the east. A blaze of orange licked at the dark line of the horizon, and as we watched, the color spread upward, paled, turned golden as the disk of the sun pushed its way above the hill.

Wordlessly, Ben and I each struck a match, the crisp flare and the sulfury smell a reminder that we had work to do. The four-by-six-foot pit, four feet deep and half-filled with rocks and sand, was covered by a neat lattice of firewood. Pine shavings from Dad's work-room were stuffed in the spaces. In seconds, flame reached toward our faces; we stepped out of the way of the heat.

Crackling sounds in the brush behind us competed with the snap and hiss of the fire, and I turned in the direction of the noise. A large, mottled dog, sharp teeth hanging over a purplish bottom lip, lowered his head and growled as he advanced on us.

"Damn!" Ben's jaws clenched. "Go home, Twinkie."

"Twinkie?" Laughing, I sat down on the heavy log someone had rolled to the pit area. What a whimsical name for such a menacing animal. "I didn't know you had a dog."

"I don't. He's Tommy Hoysradt's. Harmless. But today's not the day for dogs, don't you think?" He stamped his feet, then marched toward the animal, who held his ground. "Shoo. Go home. Go scare a squirrel."

"No one's here yet but you and me. He can't bother anything."

Ben whirled around, his eyes seeking mine. A shadow of stubble along his jaw and on his chin made his face appear thinner, but it was his eyes, fiery one second and then cool the next, that held my attention.

"He can bother *me*," Ben said finally. He walked to the log and sat beside me, his long legs stretching toward the fire.

I focused on the frayed shoelaces in his boots, aware that his shoulder had touched mine and then pulled away as though the contact had scorched him. "What can Twinkie possibly do to bother you?"

"He's distracting me."

"From your fire-tending duties?" Was Ben thinking about the play, about rabies, and the other similarities to the Schiller story? Was he, too, worried about Ruth?

"Look at me, Sweets."

I frowned and turned toward him. "What's going on, Ben?"

"I want you to see my face."

I laughed, partly from nervous incomprehension. "I do believe it's a face I've seen before."

But as soon as I said it, I realized that I hadn't. Not this face, at once troubled and wise, without any of its cynical playfulness.

"Good. You did see. Because this is a face with secrets and I want to share one of them. I'm not even going to give you a chance to tell me that you don't want to hear it. I love you, Sweets, always have since you showed me the cocoons you kept in your room when you were ten. Remember? I used to mow your father's lawn—I was thirteen and saving for a ten-speed. Independent sucker, even then. You had dozens of cocoons, on sticks in mayonnaise jars. I kept dreaming of you waking up in the middle of the night.

"The moonlight did it. In my fantasy, I saw it reaching out to each chrysalis and waking the butterflies, and the butterflies stroked your face with their velvet wings. All those butterflies hovering over your bed—they had amazing markings, iridescent blue stars, burnt-orange ovals, yellows, greens. They lit on your hands and your eyes like little kisses."

I was hardly breathing now, not thinking at all.

"I know it's a burden for you to hear it, and I know you're a married woman, and part of what I love about you is that you'll honor that. What I want you to understand is that if anything should happen between you and Peter, I'm ready to offer whatever you need. Comfort. Friendship. My lifetime of watching over you. Whatever you need."

Perfect timing, Ben Yarnell, I thought. *Just when I'm practicing the art of being alone. And I don't need watching over, thank you.* I wanted to say something but my throat had closed up partway through his speech. I wondered if Emily Schiller had ever been in such a situation. What would *she* have said?

"Well, you didn't leap into my arms and say 'Me too,' but I only figured there was maybe a one-in-eighty-six chance that you'd do that. Don't worry. I won't ever say anything like this again. Things around here have been so—I don't know, so intense—I just had to say it." He got up and stacked more wood on the fire, keeping his back to me.

He shouldn't have told me. I could have gone my whole life not knowing, and everything would have been simpler. I wasn't responsible for what he felt, after all. I'd never given him cause to expect anything more than friendship.

And then a cold shiver chased a new thought into my sluggish brain. Was this how it started with Julia—an innocent woman until someone made an unexpected and intriguing declaration? Could I deny Ben's confession intrigued me?

The morning air was cool on my face; only my feet, pointed toward the fire, were warm. Regret stirred in me, a dim recognition that after this morning my friendship with Ben would never be the same.

"Don't be mad, Sweets," he said when he turned around, his face red from the fire. "I'll keep talking sassy to you in public and no one will know and pretty soon even *you* will forget."

The dog reappeared, pacing on the other side of the fire, his white teeth burnished by reflected flame. I tossed a pebble at his feet, but the animal didn't twitch.

The screen door at the side of Ruth's house creaked and someone stepped into the cool morning, standing between the two low tubs of geraniums beside the door. An unfamiliar protectiveness for my mother-in-law surged through me. Her attempts at controlling my life and Peter's aside, dying of rabies—or even having to endure the cure—wasn't a fate even she had earned.

"Shoo, you ugly mongrel." I jumped up and stomped toward the restless dog.

"Didn't think you'd take my declaration *that* badly." Ben picked up a handful of pebbles, tossed them closer to the animal this time. "I'm ugly maybe, but my mama would sure be pained at the mongrel part."

"You're not ugly, Ben. You've got terrible timing, though."

He shrugged.

Ruth marched down the broad lawn, one hand holding on to a floppy straw gardening hat that threatened to blow off. She was a hundred yards away, striding purposefully toward the fire, apparently unaware of the animal. Twinkie wanted her attention; he advanced toward her, head low and haunches tensed. Over the crackling of the fire, his throaty growl was like the overture to a dreadful rampage.

But he was no match for Ruth.

"Get out my way, you snarling cur." Without breaking stride, she grabbed a stick from the woodpile and brandished it like a sword, slicing the air above the dog's ear. "Stop scaring my guests. Scat! Git!"

The dog cantered to the center of the lawn, turned to check Ruth out, and then trotted away down the drive. When he left, I breathed easier, certain that all reason to dread the day was going with him. I wanted it to be so, and I let it be, convinced that the crisis had been met and averted.

"Well, now that we're alone," she began with a smile, her cheeks flushed but her face otherwise composed, "you two can give me an update. Everything going as planned?"

"Flame's burning pretty bright." Ben looked at me out of the corner of his eye. "Nobody's come along to throw cold water on it yet."

I shifted uncomfortably. He'd taken my silence to mean that I was keeping a possibility open between us, when I'd intended no such thing. Or had I? I hardly knew what I meant these days. Maybe I needed to play out a repeat of Julia's life so that I could understand her. Perhaps some true and complete inner knowledge wouldn't come to me until I'd relived her actions. But how could I, being childless, being happy, being fixed on maintaining what was good in my life?

Ben's voice sparkled with mischief. "Sweets here is keeping the flame burning just fine. What's in the basket, Ruth?"

"Seeing that dog, I nearly forgot. These are for the fire tenders, for energy." When she unwrapped the blue-and-white-checked napkin that covered the basket, a wonderful, rich aroma rose from her blueberry muffins, reminding me that I hadn't eaten breakfast. She set the basket on the log. "I'm going inside. If you all need anything, just come up to the house. Peter and Deeny called a bit ago from the road. They should be here in three, four hours. I told him you were doing fine, Sarah. You are, aren't you?"

I flushed with annoyance; if Ruth had come to get me when Peter called, I might have averted the scene with Ben altogether. I nodded, and forced a smile.

"Sweets was a little upset by Twinkie messing around here, that's all. She'll be all right." Ben snaked an arm around my shoulder and smiled down at me, the very picture of a brotherly friend. "Dog didn't reckon on you, Ruth."

"Neither did Nicky Dembowski," she said curtly as she swept away again toward the driveway and the battered red truck that had just rolled to a stop. "There's Marge with the potatoes. I'm going to give her a hand."

A hundred feet behind Marge's truck, Twinkie, now joined by a wiry brown-and-white mutt and a shaggy collie, yapped and circled each other. Any other time, these animals would have been part of the scene, expected, unnoticed, but today I knew I'd be looking up to check their whereabouts every few minutes.

"Ruth's loving it." Ben caught me following the canine trio with my gaze. "If no dogs showed up, she'd have gone out and rounded up a couple, just to make sure everyone got the message."

"When is Margaret Kimball coming?" I couldn't have been the only one to consider that "Stefan's mother" had at least one other interpretation in the current scheme of things.

Ben shook his head. "Didn't you hear? Her secretary called last night with regrets. Something about Margaret's car broke down and the mechanic won't be back until after the holiday and she couldn't find a single goddamn rental car in all of New York City over the holiday weekend and she's sorry, she doesn't want it to look like she's avoiding anything but she's not coming. Serve her right if a big old Manhattan Doberman came up and took a chunk out of her."

"Nobody deserves that," I said quietly. "If there's going to be a parallel, Margaret's defection leaves Ruth in a prime position, doesn't it? To be bitten by a dog, to get rabies. To be the next victim of these replays."

"Don't you see, Sweets? That's what this is all about—proving once and for all that no such thing is going to happen."

Ben got busy restacking the wood, a job that didn't need doing, and soon a flurry of activity took our attention. The Hoysradt family brought two dozen sawhorses and set up plywood sheets to make tables, enough for at least a hundred people. Ruth expected the whole village, except for the folks who were too old, too ornery, or already committed to go to their jobs or to family gatherings elsewhere. Dan Lambert brought stacks of paper plates and cups, plastic eating utensils, napkins. The cooling chest for salads set up under the tree was filling quickly with bowls of all sizes. Cars and trucks came and went all morning, each one greeted by the trio of dogs barking and chasing the spinning wheels up the long drive from the road.

After a while I hardly heard them anymore, and I actually let fifteen minutes go by without looking for them. Then Ike Kronenburg came by with the chickens; that was the signal that Ben and I were finished with our watch.

"You all go rest up for a while," Ike said in his best cowboy drawl, "and Walter and I'll make sure the potatoes and chickens don't burn. Where'd you put the burlap sacks?"

Before I could answer, the air was split by a scream. In the grassy verge along the driveway, a small child stood frozen beside the tulip bed. The dogs prowled in front of him, barking, moving with tantalizing slowness.

Except for the fire and the furious snapping of the dogs, each one prodding the other to a higher pitch, a frightened silence descended. Then Ruth, stick in hand, started for the driveway, yelling and stamping with each step.

Why didn't someone stop her? But she kept on, shouting as she went.

"Git, you curs! Leave that boy alone. Shoo! Scat! Go on now, before I make you sorry you showed your ugly faces around here." Her stick slashed the air. Twinkie, the leader, backed off first. The other two stood staring Ruth down. She didn't flinch but kept advancing on them; they gave one last growl, then turned and trotted off toward the woods.

The crowd broke into cheers and applause.

The consternation on Ruth's face was plain, even from where I stood. She went directly to the child, knelt, and gentled him for a few seconds. Relieved, everyone resumed whatever they had been doing, an open acknowledgment that the danger had passed. But I couldn't make my fingers uncurl from tight, balled fists. I needed time out to recover, and my sooty, dirt-stained clothing gave me the perfect excuse.

"I'm going home to shower and change," I told Ike, who had regained some of his color. "I feel charbroiled myself. I'll be back in under an hour."

"I'll keep an eye on Ruth for you," he said agreeably.

The shower, long, hot, and enveloping, washed away some of my tension, but I was sad to discover that in the light of day, some of the magic of being alone had gone, too. I dried myself with Peter's towel, opened his side of the closet, and breathed in the familiar smells. I put on shorts and a white shirt, and tied my hair up with a red ribbon, and went down into the kitchen tŏ spend a few calm minutes before I rejoined the hubbub of the clambake.

I did love this room—and I loved it in part because Peter and I had made the decisions together, had worked side by side, had each brought something to the whole. I ran my hand along the stove, straightened the oval frame of the embroidery, looked at the clock.

It was noon: Peter had been away nearly twenty-four hours. It seemed as though a week's worth of changes had happened in that short time, but when I tried to tick them off, I realized that despite a few dramatic moments, things were pretty much the same.

It was time to go back to the clambake, to wait for Peter to return, to find out whether things were also *pretty much* the same for him.

Cars and pickups lined the lower field. The party had tripled in size. The sounds of joyful shouting and laughter drew me toward the center of the crowd.

Peter had taken my place beside Ben near the pit. Seeing them together like that, two friends all their lives, I wondered at Ben, and how I had been so blind to his feelings. I wanted to rush up to Peter and hold him and share a long kiss to close the recent distance between us, but I wouldn't, not in public, not with Ben standing there.

"Sarah!" Peter shielded his eyes with one hand and waved to me with the other. Whatever the time apart had done for me, it looked like it had done him some good, too. His smile was unstrained, his shoulders no longer tense; even the fine worry lines around his eyes seemed to have melted away.

I threaded my way toward the pit past laughing, chattering knots of people. Peter gave me a peck on the cheek, then pointed to two bushels. "Beauties! We've got hundreds of these gorgeous beauties and we're just about to put them on the fire. Look."

He pried the staples from the wooden lid of one of the bushels; ivory-and-gray clams, stacked like so many stones to be worked into a mosaic, glistened in the sun. I could almost feel silky sand between my toes, taste dried salt on my lips.

"Well, Sweets, you look like a different person since our morning chores." Ben grinned at me from across the pit.

"Same old," I answered, wondering if every conversation with him from now on would be filled with double meanings that only we would understand, a kind of weird intimacy he'd imposed on me by telling me his feelings.

A child's ball came rolling toward us; Peter bent, scooped it up, and tossed it in the direction of the group of toddlers corralled by their parents into a neat circle. I waved to my father, who had arrived while I was at Vixen Hill. Dad looked at his ease as he presided over the iced-tea pitcher, ceremoniously handing a glass to a smiling Catherine Delancy. Grady and Patsy McClosky and the Dembowskis were conspicuously absent; otherwise, everyone seemed to be here, and having a good time.

"Time to put the clams on. This is where the art comes in: the timing." Walter flushed with excitement as he poked at the wet burlap with gloved hands, then pushed aside a few sweetish-smelling cornhusks, blackened here and there where they'd touched a burning coal. A cloud of fragrant steam rose; Walter replaced the burlap and cornhusks, then reached for a flat shovel and lowered several dozen clams to form the last layer. He repeated the process until the bushels were empty, then arranged a final covering of cornhusks and burlap back over everything. "Thirty minutes and we'll be digging into the best food you ever tasted."

Deeny, who had been wandering the edges of the crowd, made his way to the group gathered around the fire. "Anyone see Ruth? She said she wanted to play softball. We're gonna choose up teams in a second. We need outfielders and someone to play first base." He looked meaningfully at Ben.

"Lord knows, I'm the right man for the job, what with all my Lions Club experience. I'd like to, old buddy, but if I don't go home right now and shower off this smoke, I'll feel more like something fit to be served with barbecue sauce than to eat it." He smiled at me as he turned to go. "Keep the fire burning, Sweets."

"How about if I take right field and Ike plays first," Peter offered. "My mother went to pick up Mrs. Shook and get some more ice. She'll be back in ten minutes, maybe sooner. When she gets here, I'll give her my spot."

The small group trotted off to the flat field fifty yards from the picnic area and, amid much shouting and hooting, played two noisy innings of friendly baseball.

"What's the score?" Doc Verity leaned her nearly six-foot sturdy frame closer to hear my answer.

"Eight," I replied, grinning.

"Eight to what?" She gave me one of her you-can't-fool-me looks. "Can't have a score that's just eight."

"I don't think anyone's counting. Loose rules today."

Her green eyes almost disappeared into the wrinkles of her smile. As we watched from the shade of the tall maple tree, a small blond figure appeared at the edge of the field; when I squinted, I realized it was Alicia Fitzhugh and not Catherine Delaney. She watched for two pitches, then wandered away again, her place taken up by three dark-haired, giggling girls in matching sundresses.

Suddenly the softball game degenerated into raucous laughter. A pitch by Deeny Lambert sailed right past the catcher and landed in the center of a bowl of pickled beets, tipped it over, and nearly caused a chain reaction that might have been disastrous—macaroni toppling into coleslaw knocking over three-bean salad until the whole table was awash in spilled food—if Catherine Delaney hadn't reached out and caught the bowl.

"Good save, Delaney!" Deeny shouted as he ran toward the table.

Catherine shuddered as she swiped at the magenta stain on her white shirt and white shorts, dabbing at the thick red ribbons of juice that ran down her legs. "Good thing I live only two miles away," she said, tossing the ball back to Deeny and trotting toward the makeshift parking lot Walter had set up in the grass at the foot of the drive. "I'll be back before the inning's over."

This clambake, like so many other all-day affairs, was becoming a party of departures and arrivals.

"Sure looked like blood on that girl," Doc Verity said, her mouth pursing. "You talk to Jeanie yet today? She could use a little distracting, I'd say." She nodded with her jutting jaw to the table under the willow tree.

Jeanie Boice and Alicia Fitzhugh stood chatting in the shade; it was so odd to see the two widows together, to see Jeanie without Clayton at a town event. Jeanie looked as though she could use not only distracting but a little rescuing as well. I made toward them, hoping I'd know what to say.

Alicia, her face impassive, held Jeanie's hand in hers; as soon as she noticed me, she muttered something about having to go home to get a pan of corn bread she'd left on her kitchen counter. She hurried past me without so much as a nod in my direction. I was just as happy not to have to talk to her, glad not to have her and the reminder of Julia Stanton so inescapably close to my attention.

"Hello, Sarah. You look all fresh and pretty." Jeanie hugged me, her powdery, lavender-scented skin smooth and cool. The deep circles ringing her eyes were the only sign of her true emotional state. Even in mourning, she reached out to say something complimentary to me, her habit of pleasantness unshakably deep.

"Looks like the weather's going to cooperate for our little gathering." I smiled at the blue sky. "How've you been?"

"I'm doing all right. I'm going back to work next week. That'll be good for me." She stared into the distance, touched my shoulder lightly as though she were dubbing me into a mysterious peerage, and then walked off toward Helen and Marge.

I wish I could bring him back for you, I thought as the smell from the pit wafted to me on a gentle breeze and drew me down the hill.

"Now, boss?" I leaned over and inhaled the rich, strong aromas, briny, earthy, and laced with garlic and barbecue sauce.

Walter nodded, his face flushed with enthusiasm. "It's ready. I have to wait for Ruth, though. Wouldn't think of unveiling all this majesty without her." He shaded his eyes with his hand and waved a high sign into the crowd. Striding up the drive with two boys in her wake, each with their own bag of ice cubes, Ruth made for the big barrel. She supervised the dumping of the ice cubes—the boys whooped at the clatter—and then leaned to whisper in a little girl's ear.

Beaming, the girl accepted a metal triangle Ruth pulled from her pocket and clanged the striker energetically until all conversation stopped.

In twos and fours, people converged on the pit. I noticed Peter hanging back at the edge of the crowd, his face glowing with a sheen of sweat, his mouth curved into a satisfied smile. He leaned over to say something to Catherine, who erupted in appreciative laughter and wagged a finger at him.

"You ready for this?" Deeny stood in front of me, cutting off my view. By the time I managed an answer, everyone had gathered around the pit. Catherine came up beside Ruth; I didn't see Peter anywhere. No one paid the slightest attention by now to the dogs, who maintained a civil distance at the foot of the drive. With a ceremonial flourish, Ruth folded her hands in front of her and waited for the proper, respectful silence.

"Now, I know you're all anxious to get to the great treats we have in store. But before we do, I want to offer grace. If you'd all take the hand of your neighbor . . ."

The muttering from the rear could only be my father. I held my breath as he stepped out of the circle and headed for the willow. Each of my hands was lifted gently; on my right stood a shy and pretty girl of about thirteen, a happy grin on her chubby face, and on my left, Ben Yarnell. His fingers closed firmly around mine. I couldn't very well pull away. I finally spotted Peter across the circle from me, eyes cast to the ground, between Doc Verity and Deeny Lambert.

"Good. We thank you, Lord, for the plenty of this meal, for the life-giving sun and rain, for this planet we gratefully share with the birds and animals and fishes, and for all these good neighbors who work so hard to preserve our community. And we thank you for showing Stefan and Emily Schiller to our little place on your bountiful earth."

The murmured "amens" were followed by a lusty "Let's eat!" from Deeny. Walter peeled back the burlap, lifted the layer of cornhusks, and started heaping plates high. The spirit of the day was contagious. Cameras recorded smiles and hugs and laden plates; praise for Ruth and her splendid event slipped from one person to the next.

"Aren't you going to get some goodies?" Peter leaned down and kissed my hair, balancing a loaded plate. "Come on, get some food and meet me by the willow."

I watched him walk away; I couldn't let myself be angry because he'd spoken to Catherine Delaney. I grabbed a plate and some food and made my way to the small group sprawled on the grass beside the willow.

From the glazed and satisfied looks on their faces and their glistening chins, they had already done justice to their first round of food. I started with a clam; it was sweet and tasted like the sea, a little chewy, delicious.

"God, that's utterly wonderful." Catherine leaned back, practically purring with pleasure, like a cat who'd just nicked a choice salmon fillet from the market counter. "My New York friends would kill for a food experience like this."

Ben's rich laughter roared out over the circle; he set his fork, still brimming with coleslaw, on his plate. "A *food experience?* No wonder the restaurants down there charge so much. You're not just eating—you're having a whole experience."

I bit into the corn; hot, sugary juice spurted between my teeth, filling my mouth with the golden taste of corn picked half an hour before it was cooked. Then I tried the chicken; spicy, smoky, and perfectly tender. Peter leaned over and dabbed at some barbecue sauce that ran down my arm.

Deeny and Nancy Lambert, Ben, Catherine, and Peter kept up a stream of jokes and banter; I ate and watched and listened. Deliciously tickled by all the excess, my jealousy quickly fading, I wished that Peter and I were at home alone with all these sensory delights. His sideways glance told me that he'd read my mind.

"Shall we hide some of this bounty and bring it home for later?" His breath smelled of garlic and clams and tomato.

"Sounds like a deal to me." I kissed him, our mouths slippery from the butter we'd slathered on the corn. "Whoops! There are disadvantages, you see."

Suddenly heads turned. The chattering, laughing groups on the lawn fell silent. *The dogs—something must be happening with the dogs.* Peter got to his feet first and ran toward the shrubs, where I'd last seen the three dogs. But Ruth was sitting calmly at the long table, not an animal in sight. Then I saw the lights atop the Bronco that had skidded to a stop at the end of the gravel drive.

"It's Riley Hamm," Ben said.

"That's a pretty dramatic entrance for a down-home clambake." I wiped my greasy hands on the remains of a napkin.

The crowd parted and I saw Riley pointing to someone. It was Peter.

I pushed to a standing position and started toward the driveway, my pace accelerating with each step until I was running full out. From off in the distance, the claxon call of the Taconic Hills emergency signal bleated wildly, like a summons to arms from some faraway parapet. I was almost at the edge of the crowd when I saw the horror on Peter's white face as he turned around.

"It's Vixen Hill Lodge," he said. "It's on fire, Sarah."

Fourteen

The crowd exploded into action. Plates were tossed aside; people rushed to their cars and trucks, shouting commands, grabbing keys and roaring off. The volunteer fire department sprinted into action. Peter drove off beside Deeny in the first cluster of cars. The rescue squad, following protocol, let them leave first, then raced to their own vehicles.

Walter grabbed my arm as I started toward my truck. "Be better to let those who can do something get their cars out first."

"Please, Walter, let me go." *My house. My old barn.* I pulled away, my skin prickling with anger and frustration.

Ruth came up and tried to tell me to sit down, but before she finished, I was pounding down the hill to my truck. I tore across the two miles of back roads to our house, my fingers white, my jaw clamped tight. As I turned onto East Taconic Road, heavy gray smoke billowed up from the trees, filling the air with the smell of destruction.

When I pulled into Vixen Hill Road, the sight of flames devouring the west roof woke me out of my stupor. *A fire burned the whole thing to the ground, and Emily and Stefan had to start again.*

"It's the kitchen," I groaned aloud. "Our beautiful new kitchen."

The pumper truck had already pulled onto the lawn; three black-slickered men wrestled the spray of water from the huge hose toward the flames. Three others checked the water intake from the pond. An ambulance and a state trooper's sedan sat across the road, the static from their communication systems crackling, radio voices calling for their attention.

Dazed, I tried to stay out of the way. My jaw tightened each time I heard the crack of another roof timber crashing into the kitchen. What could I do? I wanted to grab a hose, pull an extinguisher from the truck, stomp on the greedy fingers of flame that now reached from the window to the outer wall.

I must have stumbled closer to the wall; I watched with fascination as the white paint started blistering and bubbling, as though the house were erupting with a horribly disfiguring disease. The heat made me dizzy.

"Sarah, stand back!" Deeny lunged at me and shoved me out of the way as the window exploded, shards of glass slicing toward us in vicious arcs, too fast for us to move out of the way. Miraculously, most of the larger pieces fell to the ground a few feet from us, tinkling like delicate chimes as they collided into each other.

When I looked down, I saw my own hand, bleeding onto my clean blouse.

"You all right?" Deeny waited until I nodded. "Okay, that was probably the propane line going. You have any volatile chemicals we should know about in the house, gasoline or something like that?"

"I don't think so, but I'm not sure."

"Any chemicals that might be toxic? New carpeting in that part of the house?"

My mind sped through the kitchen, the dining room, looking for chemicals, seeing only the new cabinets, the stove we'd just restored, our beautiful new floor. I shook my head.

Deeny nodded and raced back to the house. The kitchen roof was gone, but the flames seemed to have ebbed, and the absence of those horrible crashing sounds made my heart lift.

Peter appeared beside me, his drawn face stained with soot, and when I pointed to the weathervane, spinning in a current of hot air, he snapped: "You couldn't have left the gas on?"

My voice seemed to have deserted me. I shook my head again.

He was going over in his mind what I was sifting through in my own: How could this have happened? "Maybe there was a short. From my electrical work. Hell of an advertisement. Shit, Sarah, our house is burning up."

He turned away and wiped at his eyes; I reached out for him, knowing that this was not an accident of wiring, not an accident at all. But this time he pulled away, drawn by the devouring flames.

Deeny rushed around to the front of the house and stopped when he saw us. "The kitchen and the dining room are goners but I think we're going to save the rest of the house. We've got most of it contained; we gotta check for live hot spots. Sit tight."

"Thanks, Deeny." Peter's raw voice faded. "How? How could this have happened?"

And again I didn't tell him, because I couldn't bring myself to say what I believed—it made no sense that some part of the past was reaching forward to wreak this havoc, reproducing the events in Stefan and Emily's lives.

Only one person would benefit from scaring away the actors in the play. Was Nicky Dembowski so anxious to stop Ruth, so desperate for the deal to go through with the developers?

Deeny and Ike Kronenburg staggered onto the lawn and sat in the shade of my tree: the sight of their soot-blackened faces shook me. These good people, working so hard to save my home, were hot and thirsty and tired. I ran across the road and made up a pitcher of ice water in my father's kitchen and put a full glass in every outstretched hand. With each glass I got a progress report.

"Roof's collapsed onto the cabinets."

"Stove looks like someone took a hammer to it in a couple of places where a beam fell on it, but it might be savable."

"Nothing left of the dining room but a pile of ashes."

"Sarah—" Peter said beside me.

"Looks like we won't have to fight over the old highboy anymore," I said lightly. And with that, I buried my head in his shoulder and held on to him as though I was afraid one of us would turn powdery and gray and blow away in the slightest wind.

Fifteen

Peter and I spent the night on the narrow single bed in my old room in my father's house, the blank and silent darkness a refuge from the consuming fury of the fire. At dawn, unrested and silent, we walked beside each other through the trampled grass to survey the remains of Vixen Hill Lodge.

Only a blackened scar marked the place where the kitchen and dining room used to stand. We moved through the gutted rooms without speaking; sagging metal electrical conduits and twisted pipes poked out of the waterlogged ash. A wave of nausea attacked me with every breath—the foul, fishy stink of newly burned wood permeated the air, malevolent, mocking. Water had ruined every-thing in the upstairs bedrooms. Ashes covered every surface. All in all, Peter said, we were lucky that the volunteers got to Vixen Hill so quickly; fifteen more minutes and the rest of the building might have been lost. If the suppliers cooperated and if he could organize a couple of work parties, he assured me tonelessly, the house might be habitable again in about a month. Meanwhile we'd stay at my father's. We didn't want to be any farther from our sad old barn than we had to be.

At the end of that day, I fell into a deep, dreamless stupor, but even in my sleep, I smelled the fire's charred remains. When I awoke, I found myself curled in a corner of the bed, unable to bear the touch of Peter even accidentally brushing against me, while he, in his need for comfort and reassurance, moved closer and closer.

After two nights, I took a blanket and my pillow and slept on the floor.

And then, finally, three weeks later, after the debris had been cleared away and the outer walls rebuilt, we returned to Vixen Hill Lodge. I awoke that first morning feeling that the smoke had cleared at last, and that I was ready to reconnect with Peter. He was sitting on the sofa, unshaven and unmoving, a cup of coffee in his hand and his eyes staring out vacantly over the hazy landscape framed by the window. I poured myself coffee.

"Where'd this come from?" I held up an electric percolator.

"Catherine brought it by when you were out yesterday. She said she's got two others and that we should keep it as long as we like." He continued to stare out the window.

I set Catherine's percolator on the table and sat down beside him. "I'm back," I said quietly.

Peter didn't look at me.

"And I'm sorry. It's been hard on you, I know. It's been difficult for me, too. We're so different, Peter. When I'm upset or afraid, I go inside myself to keep other people from knowing how I feel."

"Even me?" He sounded hurt, as though the behavior I'd learned long, long ago and had fallen back on so often these last few months was an insult deliberately directed at him. "I can understand not wanting to have to answer other people's questions, Sarah, but why keep yourself away from *me*?"

"It's not you. It's what I do. You reach for me, you can see the comfort in that contact, you can see the strength in the connection. I wish I could, too. I mean, I can see it but I can't *do* it, I don't think of it, I only think of crawling away so that no one can see me, so that I can find my strength and come back out and face the situation." The curve of his shoulder was smooth and warm to my touch.

The birds argued in the shade of the butternut; a tractor chugged down the road, kicking up puffs of dust behind it as it churned the top layer of the dirt road. Strange, to see the world again, to hear the everyday sounds of it. I felt like a newcomer in an exotic and wonderful country.

And I realized that bad as the fire had been, it might have been worse. "At least our house didn't burn completely."

"Now you're completely convinced there's a parallel between your life and Emily Schiller's." There was no challenge in his voice, only a sigh of exasperation.

"Each thing by itself is an odd coincidence. Ministers dying in the snow. Spoiled-milk shipments. Us getting the flu. The way Prince died. Clayton . . ." The words caught against a lump in my throat. "And now this. You can't ignore the pattern anymore, Peter."

What I left unsaid troubled me as much as all that long and terrible list. What was out there waiting for us, tomorrow, next week? When would this end?

I couldn't help thinking that if I'd never made the decision to learn more about Julia, Taconic Hills would be unscarred. But that made no rational sense at all, and so I said nothing.

"I don't have to ignore it," he said. "I just don't see anything mysterious here. You don't hear Catherine going around worrying about being attacked by fur traders or something."

Catherine again.

"If some force is making the legend come true," he continued, "then wouldn't my mother or Margaret Kimball have been bitten by a dog? For sure that scrawny chicken of an insurance investigator didn't say the house burned because of *history*."

A gaunt man with splotchy cheeks and an annoying habit of clearing his throat at the end of every sentence, the adjuster had picked over the site for days, his clipboard, hard hat, and camera practically attached to him. It had been a relief, when he finally told us he was finished, not to see him stooped over the charred debris of our house.

"God, what a creep. He's so *sure* it was one of the baskets above the stove—but I didn't leave the gas on, I *know* it."

"I believe you. So that means someone else did." Peter's mouth turned down in disdain. "It's obvious—someone's trying to scare people away. Only one big winner if the bicentennial's called off. So what if Dembowski was at Lake George with his family. He could have hired someone to set the fire." Peter's face got red and he clutched the fringe of the Indian blanket. "Of course, there's always the anonymous call about that woman out back behind the kitchen."

"I told Riley. I came back to change my clothes after I finished my chore at the clambake. When the damn roof was crashing in—I told him right then." I slumped further into the sofa. "I'm the mysterious woman in the anonymous telephone tip. You know, anyone could have driven here and back—everyone was leaving to get ice or to change their clothes or to pick someone up. Every single person in Taconic Hills had the opportunity to set fire to Vixen Hill Lodge. Even you, on your way back with Deeny or something. Everyone."

Peter rolled his eyes and shook his head. "Ben's the one who'd know if Hamm and Del Santo found out anything else. I wonder why he hasn't called." Peter stared at the telephone. "Maybe he did, and then gave up when we didn't answer."

I didn't want to talk to Ben Yarnell, or hear the concern in his voice. The silence stretched on; if Peter was going to mock me for suggesting that history was repeating itself, I might as well lay out the other nagging thoughts that had disturbed me. "Remember how Catherine said a role can take you over? I don't think she meant this way, but what if everyone in the pageant is involved in a mass delusion? Maybe these things are happening because we sense we have to correct a terrible wrong committed in the past."

"Mass hysteria, like the Salem witch-hunts? You're talking nonsense, Sarah."

His dismissal was almost more than I could bear. We were driving each other away, and I couldn't bear feeling isolated anymore. "Hold me, Peter, please."

He sat up straight and pressed his body to the back of the sofa. "You're really pretty good at turning it on when it suits you, aren't you?"

I stiffened at his words; I understood and I had no answer.

Angrily, he pushed his cup away. "Sorry," he said finally. "I've gotten so used to being shut out, I wanted you to feel that emptiness. I don't mean it, Sarah. Come here."

He opened his arms to me and I fit myself inside, welcomed by his warmth. When he let me go, I pressed closer and cupped his smooth cheek with my hand and touched his mouth with my lips. We made a slow circle of love around ourselves and joined together again.

"Two cancellations," Peter said through gritted teeth that evening as he wiped a trickle of sweat from his neck. The July night was stifling. "Small jobs, nothing that's going to hurt us too much financially. But I can't stand the feeling that it's no coincidence. This is part of some whispering campaign. I walked into the diner in Hillsdale—it was weird. Everyone stopped talking, just stopped dead."

He cut a continuous, curling strip of apple peel with a small silver

knife, concentrating with an urgency that made him hiss with annoyance when the peel dropped onto the floor.

"My father says the thing to do is go public, maybe ask Ben to run
a story. I don't know. . . ." His voice trailed off. "Nobody's made
a formal accusation, not to my face, but they seem to think I've got a
black cloud of disaster hovering over me."

"Maybe it feels worse than it is. The cancellations are in Chatham,
half the county away. Nothing's changed down here, has it?"

Peter shook his head and put the apple down uneaten. "But people are talking, I know. Jim Slocum told me he nearly got into a fight
with two teachers who used to work with Clayton. Okay, people are
afraid. Something's going on, and since they can't explain what happened—why Tommy's milk spoiled, Clayton's death, and now the
fire—they're making up explanations. If I defend myself without being accused, I'll be keeping the rumor alive. If I don't, the gossip
might get totally out of hand."

He swallowed twice, hard, before he spoke again.

"It's not going to get any cooler if I wait around here. I'd better
get to work on those estimates," he said, "as long as I still have the
possibility of work to do."

Peter was right about one thing: Ben Yarnell was the most likely
person to know whether Riley Hamm and Harris Del Santo or even
the insurance investigator had discovered some bit of news we hadn't
yet heard. According to Ben's criterion, this story qualified as news.
For Peter's sake, to see if I could find out about the rumors, I'd go
see Ben.

In the month since the fire, I had been in hiding at Vixen Hill and
now it felt odd to see cars and trucks and people moving about in the
daylight. The ground beneath my feet was springy and the air
smelled of cut grass; if I'd been paying attention, I would have heard
the tractors as they went about second haying. Now, as proof that
I'd missed several weeks, the giant rolls of hay lay in the fields like
huge *bûches de Noël* as I drove down East Taconic Road and into
town, to Ben's office.

The firehouse noon whistle blew as I swung into the lot beside the
newspaper office. Cindy, the receptionist at the *Journal,* was already
heading for her car. Ben would be alone in the office. If I'd thought
about it before I came into town, I'd have realized my timing might

appear intentional to someone who was looking for signs, as Ben might be.

Better to take care of the Ancram hives first and come back when Cindy was in the office. Ben needn't think I was making some sort of gesture. But while I was deciding what to do next, the door to the *Journal* office flew open and Ben appeared, waving a paper in Cindy's direction. He trotted to her car, handed her an envelope, and then turned on his heels. When he saw me, he grinned and folded his arms across his chest. "Hey, Sweets. I hear the restoration is coming along. How are you doing?"

"I'm okay. The smell's going to hang around a long time, but the house is almost whole again. You have a minute?" So much the better if we could do our talking out here . . . but Ben didn't share that opinion.

"Come on in to my office. I'm on telephone duty while Cindy's off for lunch. I was going to call you later." He didn't wait to see if I was following but instead pushed the door open and strode inside.

The cool of the hallway startled me. Surely the great bumps of gooseflesh sprang up on my arms because I wasn't used to air-conditioning. Ben's office, though, wasn't so frigid. A green-shaded banker's lamp cast a citrusy light on the welter of paper on his desk and on the mustard jar stuffed with pencils, points up like bayonets ready for the next battle.

"You first," he said, plopping down in his battered swivel chair.

I moved aside a stack of newspapers that sprawled across the old church pew, the only other chair in the room, and sat down.

Ben propped his feet on the metal desk and laced his fingers behind his head. The heels of his loafers were worn down on the outside edge, the soles darkened and pitted from walking on blacktop and gravel. Red socks stuck out beneath the cuff of his pants. I'd never thought about it before: Ben always wore red socks.

"What do you know about the fire, Ben? What have you heard?" I studied the photographs behind him: the post office buried in snow after a blizzard; a shiny-faced teenager being crowned Miss Apple Harvest; Jimmy Carter waving from the front door of the general store. I turned my gaze back to him. His expression, neutral at first, softened into a hint of a smile.

"Should I answer as a friend, as an editor, or as an occasional fly on the wall in the precincts of Taconic Hills?"

"I can't imagine the answers would be any different." He was confusing me; I'd asked such a simple question, I thought. I had no patience for his games today. Maybe this was his way of maintaining the old, joking relationship, as he'd promised. "Just answer the question straight. This is very hard for me, Ben, and I'd appreciate your help."

The smile faded; his forehead knitted into a deep, solemn frown. Finally, he reached into a drawer and pulled out a folder and tossed it onto the desk.

"Eighteen letters. Two thirds say an investigation into the causes of the fire should focus on Nick Dembowski and that he should have the book thrown at him." He looked away from me and stared grimly at the unopened folder. Outside, a milk truck roared by, heading for the processing plant.

"And the others?" I prompted, doing some quick arithmetic. What kind of consensus could six people have reached that didn't have to do with Nicky?

"The others suggest that you and Peter needed insurance money to finish the renovations on your house."

His words clanged in my head, banging around without meaning. It wasn't possible that I'd understood him. He couldn't be saying that people I had known all my life would think me or Peter capable of such behavior.

"*Six* letters?" The chair felt hard against my back; I leaned forward. "Who from?"

With a crooked grin, Ben laid a hand atop the folder. "Nick Dembowski and five of his friends and relatives."

I realized I hadn't been breathing. "What are you going to do with them?" I demanded.

Ben rolled a pencil between his thumb and forefinger. "Haven't decided. Seems like if I print one side, I have to print the other. If I print none of them, that's managing the news."

"No, it isn't. That's managing the letters to the editor. Are any of those letters significant? Do they reveal any new facts?"

"No," he admitted, "but they do bring up questions that nobody's been willing to say out loud."

"And so would a letter accusing the governor of participating in satanic rites, but you wouldn't print that unless you had some real proof, right?"

"Whoa, take it easy, Sweets. I never said I was going to print them. I wanted you to know about it, though, because if Dembow-ski is organizing this disinformation campaign so quickly, he's going to find other places to be heard. He's going to use the jungle drums to get a good rumor going and that could be truly damaging to you and Peter."

"Do you think anyone will really believe his nonsense? We just finished work on the kitchen a couple of months ago. It would be ridiculous to—"

"The insurance investigator might believe it," Ben said steadily. "There's that call about a woman seen near your house a while before the fire. And you did go home to shower, you said, after our fire-tending watch was up."

"People were coming and going all day, even you." I sat back in my chair, wondering how much more I'd have to go through until life returned to normal . . . if it ever would. "It's not nearly over, is it?"

"Can't promise how it's going to shake out, but I do agree there's a lot more rocking and rolling before the dance is done. Town's going to take sides about the development, that was inevitable. But now they're going to try to lay blame for the fire—and in some quarters it's going to get tied to the Schiller story and to Clayton's death."

The full impact of his words hit me. If Nicky Dembowski was going to accuse Peter and me, his strategy would be to say we set up certain events to make it appear that some mysterious force was at work. And one of those parallels was Clayton's death. My stomach churned and my hands turned icy.

It was too much: the threats, the near disasters, the deaths. The unexplained pieces of three puzzles, one of them two centuries old, another that happened more than twenty years ago, and the chaos of the present. And now the censure of the people I'd lived beside all my life.

I was tired, so tired.

"Hey, Sweets, it's hard, but hang in. Things are bound to change."

I didn't know if I could handle more change in Taconic Hills. I could go away, find a piece of land in West Virginia, maybe even Canada. Start again, where no one knew me . . .

Just like Julia.

No, that wasn't my answer. I had to see Jeanie right away, though, before anyone else talked to her. I'd deal with the rest of it when the time came, but I needed Jeanie's understanding now, her confirmation that no matter what anyone said, she knew Peter and I didn't do anything to hurt Clayton.

Sixteen

Ike Kronenburg, his hands in his back pockets, leaned against the post office counter, a grin on his lean, lined face and his country twang sharp. He was all wound up, involved in a tale about his latest haircut—how he'd fallen asleep in the barber chair, how the barber had kept trying to get Ike's sideburns even like someone snitching forkfuls of pie until there was nothing left. Ike hardly blinked when I walked in; Jeanie just reached around and grabbed the mail from my slot and set it on the counter.

Her smile seemed real, but her eyes never met mine. She nodded but her gaze was still fixed on Ike. I'd have to find another time, perhaps when Jeanie was at home and not in this setting where she belonged to everyone, to make sure she understood that Peter and I weren't responsible for the fire or the spoiled milk or the cannon accident.

"See you, Jeanie. You take care." I clutched my mail with both hands. Jeanie only nodded.

Confused and upset, I turned to leave and found myself nose to nose with Nicky and Andrea Dembowski. I started to back away, to ignore them completely, but Andrea's fatuous smile and chirpy hello cut the last, tenuous thread of my self-restraint.

"Can I talk to you outside, Nick?" I said through my clenched teeth.

What he might have meant to be a smile turned into a smirk. He pursed his mouth and pushed on the screen door, holding it open for me as though he were proving what good manners he had, even when faced with a half-crazed woman. I stepped past him onto the porch, close enough to nearly choke on his piney cologne; he lingered behind. "I'll be in in a minute. Get the mail, Andrea, and a roll of stamps." He let the door slam, then turned and pushed it open again. "No flowers. I don't want stamps with damn flowers on them."

If that display had been meant to impress me, Nicky Dembowski was dumber than I thought.

"Stop spreading rumors, Nicky. You're telling lies about our fire. You're making up stories about me and my family, and I swear to God I'll make sure you lose everything, not only this land sale, if you keep it up." The heat of my anger sent a flush up from my neck to the top of my scalp; I was trembling with rage. I hadn't realized until I stood face-to-face with Nick Dembowski how satisfying it could be to imagine hitting another human being, hard.

But Nicky was enjoying himself. His oily smile oozed across his face. "Sarah, do you hear what you're saying? Threats. That's not nice. The lady doth protest too much, is that what you want people to think? Back off, kiddo. Nothing personal. Ruth Hoving set the rules for this fight, and I'm just playing by them." He reached out and chucked me under the chin. "Having fun yet, are you?"

"Don't touch me, Nicky. Don't ever touch me again," I snapped before I ran down the steps, pounding along the side of the road until I reached my truck. My chest heaved with every breath; I waited inside the cab until the white heat of my anger cooled enough for me to see clearly. Then I drove to Vixen Hill, to get what I needed for the afternoon's work at the Ancram hives, talking to myself so that I could calm down. By the time I reached East Taconic Road, I was breathing normally again.

Annoyed at how vulnerable I'd let myself become, I started to load empty supers into the truck; heat mirages shimmered above the road and over the pond. I had stacked only three in the bed of the truck when Catherine Delaney's car rolled to a stop in the driveway. She looked years younger than when she first came to Columbia County; her hair was pulled back into a youthful ponytail, her face was free of makeup and of the tired, puffy grayness that the makeup had only covered. She glowed with health and energy; it made her even prettier.

She looked up at me and then down at the supers. "Need a hand?

I was concentrating so hard on a tiny canvas, it began to feel like I'd go blind and start talking to myself if I didn't get out of my studio."

"Sure. I never turn down an offer of help. Here," I said, "pass those up to me, one at a time. What are you working on? What painting, I mean."

We chatted for a while about the minutiae of nature—rose hips and the configuration of peas in early pods and the way blossoms browned from the ends in toward the zucchini that were beginning to be the bane of every gardener's existence. We talked about Queen Anne's lace and the wings of flies and the eyes of Japanese beetles and then we came to a long pause in the conversation.

"You feeling okay about the lines you have to say for the play?" She leaned against the truck, her throat glistening with sweat.

"The lines are fine. I practically recite them in my sleep these days, to keep myself from dreaming. What terrifies me is the thought of saying them and actually *moving* at the same time."

She flashed a warm smile. "We'll have dress rehearsals. You'll see— it's easier to do than it is to think about. Listen, maybe this will help you. Two acting principles I learned when I was a student. First, it's not what you say, it's what you're thinking. Keeps the irony alive, you see. And then, the one that may really help you: Be physical and don't act in your head. It's fun, once you get into it."

"Maybe for you." And maybe it's easier if you're not wondering all the time whether you—or someone who's threatening you—will be the next victim. "What if I drop the pitcher in the wedding scene? God, imagine what it would be like with all that broken crockery on the stage."

Catherine laughed and flipped her ponytail off her shoulder. "I see I'm going to have to tell you the one acting secret I've always hoarded for myself. I'm sure it gives me an edge, so I've never shared it with anyone. My first acting coach told it to me—and I'll tell it to you only if you promise not to repeat it. Promise?"

I nodded; this was fun, like schoolgirls sharing a secret.

"Okay, here it is." She leaned closer, and her spicy perfume, the one she'd been wearing that day when she'd burned her hand on the hot maple syrup, hung in the air. "Know your props as well as you know your own underwear."

"If I think about *that* advice," I said, hardly able to speak through my giggles, "I'm afraid I'll laugh in the middle of some terribly serious moment."

Her eyes sparkled. "And then you'll be all relaxed and everything will be peachy."

I realized all at once that while we were talking about acting, she hadn't shown a bit of the tenseness she claimed drove her out of her house. But Catherine Delaney had been a professional actress; I wondered if it were as easy to cover over one's own feelings as it was to assume someone else's.

"You feeling better now?" I asked casually as I did a mental check of the equipment in the truck.

She leaned against the front fender, her eyes on her tennis shoes and her mouth drawn down. "That was mostly an excuse. I came over to see how you were doing. And I realized that I don't know you well enough to know. You seem okay, but I can't really tell."

"You mean, since the fire?" I shrugged. "It's been hard but life is getting back to normal; the work helps and the fact that all the burned stuff has been carted away helps even more."

"Well, yes, the fire, but that's not all I meant."

I frowned. And then I understood: Even Catherine, a stranger in town until Ruth took her under her wing, had heard the talk about the insurance money and the speculations about the fire's origins. "What else are you talking about?"

"Ah, Sarah, you know about the rumors by now, surely." She knelt to pull a pebble out of the tread on the bottom of her sneakers; her golden hair obscured her face. "What are you going to do about it?"

"Do? Anything we do now will be seen as damage control and that's all."

"Can you hear your phone out here?" Her wide blue eyes stared up at me again.

I frowned. "No. I keep the ringer turned down on purpose. If someone really wants to talk to me, they'll call back when I'm home. Is there something you haven't said? Something you came up here to tell me or ask me?"

"Then you haven't gotten the message that Ruth's called an emergency meeting tonight at the Copake School. When I pressed her, she said the oddest thing. Something like 'Nobody's best interests are being served by this pageant anymore.' She asked me not to tell anyone she said it, but I'm worried. I've finally found a home, a place to be myself. I *love* it here. I *hate* the idea of the developers getting a foothold. I don't want to see this effort to stop Dembowski fall apart."

"Do you mean you think Ruth's going to pull out?" I couldn't believe it. She wouldn't call off the bicentennial, surrender and let Dembowski win this battle.

Catherine ran her fingers along the gold chain at her throat. "Now, this is my guess, but I'd bet she doesn't want to take the chance of anything else happening. Clayton's death, the fire—it's gotten to her. She's going to announce she's calling off the pageant."

"I never wanted to do it in the first place, but throwing it away now would be letting them, whoever they are, bully us all."

Catherine paced the gravel drive, catlike, small, ready to spring, her fingers tracing restless patterns on the seams of her shirt. "Won't you let Ruth sacrifice the play in order to protect you?"

"I'll protect myself. I don't want to run away from this. I don't want anyone to be tempted to say I encouraged canceling this play because I was afraid, or worse, because I had something to hide. No, I can't let her do it."

Her face brightened. "Good, I was hoping you'd feel that way. Because I think, if I can figure out the right things to say, I can persuade Ruth and the others to go on. What do you think?"

How did it happen that this woman who had been a stranger just a few months ago cared so very much that she was willing to put up a public fight to continue with this bicentennial celebration? "Good luck trying to convince Ruth of anything."

She looked at me coolly. "Peter seems to think I should do it."

Klaudia dropped from sight—no one's sure what became of her— and Stefan married Emily shortly afterward. If I could have made Catherine disappear at that moment, I would have done it without a qualm.

"When did you see Peter?" I asked.

She looked shocked by the accusation in my voice, but I didn't trust myself to say anything. How could I judge whether someone who had been paid to cry and laugh and scowl on cue was giving me her true feelings?

Her voice was clear, without hesitation. "He stopped at my house before I came out here today. He was dropping off some boards and nails and things. For when he starts work on the skylight."

"So Peter told you he wants to convince his mother and everyone else that we should go on with the play?" I heard myself continue the discussion, as though we were talking about how many carrots to plant in the garden.

"Sarah, you can't think . . ." She shook her head. "You can do anything you want to. You're the one who's been through this fire business. Now, to make it worse, there's all the talk. . . ."

What, exactly, was Catherine Delaney's stake in this? I didn't like the way she was playing so chummy with me all of a sudden.

"Listen, I have to get these supers out to my hives. If you figure out how to convince everyone to go on, I'll go along with the idea that we should still do the pageant." I pulled myself into the cab of my truck and turned the key.

"Fine," she said, her expression no longer startled. She held on to the door handle of her Ferrari and smiled at me coldly. "You call when you feel like company. I'll be waiting to hear from you."

And I'll be waiting for the sap to run in July, I thought angrily.

Seventeen

My hives had produced such an abundance of honey that I worked for six hot hours without rest, every part of me slippery with sweat. When I returned to Vixen Hill, I gave in to the lure of temporary relief and shucked my jeans and shirt and spent fifteen minutes floating and bobbing in the lukewarm water of the pond. The algae had been blown to the north end of the pond earlier in the week by a kind wind. Water striders made their long-legged way across the surface; except for a few twigs and leaves, the water was clear and inviting.

The dunking cooled my body but my mind was still charged with overheated images, and it would be a while before they left me alone, I knew. Over a supper of cold vegetables and bread, Peter informed me that another client had canceled. Yes, he said impassively, he had talked to his mother, but their conversation had been frustrating because she wouldn't tell him anything. Too tired and too confused for a confrontation, I didn't bother to mention Catherine's name.

Even during the drive to the Copake School, I found myself preferring the tense silence to a discussion that might touch on topics I wasn't ready to explore.

Eighty people, grumbling a litany of weather-related complaints, had crammed in to the high-ceilinged room, generating enough extra heat in the humid night to make the space hellish. I was sticky, cranky, and wary, watching for evidence that one or another of our neighbors might be blaming Peter and me for our fire, and for other imagined crimes. I had never known anything but the regard of the people in this community; if they didn't understand me, at least they respected me. That was the pact I'd grown up with, and I didn't know how I'd get through any change in that treatment.

For some of our neighbors who milled about the stifling room, Peter and I were clearly tainted goods. It was almost comical, the way they backtracked as soon as they saw us. Most, though, came right up to us and offered their support, in ways only a practiced ear could recognize.

"Big sale on cut oak over to Millerton," Clarence Dunlop told Peter.

"You going to enter your syrup in the fair again this year?" Lillie Gerber asked me.

"We got that new John McPhee book in the other day," Dick Mueller told us. "I'll put a copy aside for you, if you want it."

"Too hot for all these bodies in this space, don't you think?" Nancy Lambert asked, dabbing at her forehead with a damp handkerchief.

What they were really saying was that we were still part of Taconic Hills, and they didn't believe any bit of the vicious rumors. I responded to each as graciously as I could, and restrained the impulse to hug them and say thank you.

My father and Deeny Lambert came in; Catherine followed soon after, looking cool and demure in her sapphire-and-white sundress. Ben moved from group to group, chatting and glad-handing and finally making his way to where Peter and I sat.

"Can you give a starving reporter a hint about what's going on here? Ruth's announcement—did you get to preview it?"

"You really think if she wouldn't tell you, you're going to get *me* to say anything?" Peter smiled up at Ben. Perhaps only I recognized the shadow of uneasiness in his voice. "I mean, even if I did know, which I don't."

"I surely have to take your word for it, because you're a man who wouldn't hold out on a friend, right, Hoving?" Ben made himself comfortable in the chair next to Peter; it confused me to see them together, to know that Ben and I shared secrets that we'd kept from Peter. They started discussing the time and place of the next poker game, but a rapping on the big desk at the front of the room interrupted them.

"Ladies and gentlemen, I appreciate your coming tonight, and I do apologize for the heat," Ruth began, as though she was in charge of determining the temperature as well as everything else. Her apricot-colored blouse and pale flowered skirt looked almost festive; her smile was serene. By the time she finished her welcome and took a sip of water from the glass on the desk, people were in their seats and quiet. "This building's been closed and the heat's been accumulating all summer. I'm afraid we'll all cook if we stay in here much longer. The only sensible thing is to hold the meeting outside, so if you'll gather around the front steps, I promise we'll all be more comfortable."

She could have saved us fifteen sweltering minutes by making that announcement earlier. A flicker of suspicion lit a corner of my mind: By waiting until *she'd* convened the meeting, Ruth ensured that everyone knew precisely who was calling the shots, and she got to stretch out her buildup and draw the curiosity of the crowd a notch or two higher while we waited to shuffle outside.

Deeny was the first to stand. "Sounds like a good idea to me," he said heartily. "Anyone object?"

But no one did, and in slow motion we filed out of the old school-house. The night air had turned a little cooler; in the haze, the stars seemed like they'd been daubed onto the darkness with a cottonball. Crickets reported the temperature; fireflies, tired from doing half the summer's work, blinked in desultory brightness out beyond the trees. The grass was dewy but no one seemed to mind trading heat for dampness; we formed a half circle facing the front steps and waited for the business to begin. The green enamel hood of the light above the doorway quickly became the prime target of a squadron of moths. Ruth stood in the light, her face composed and her flowered skirt clinging damply to her legs.

"I'll try to make this as brief as possible so that you all can go home. I don't have to go over everything that's happened in the past few months. It has been a curious, difficult time, a *sad* time for this community. We've accomplished something important—we've proven to ourselves and to anyone who might be watching that the hamlet of Taconic Hills has something worth preserving, a way of life dependent on the goodness of nature and neighbors."

A round of mild applause followed that statement. I joined; her speech was almost eloquent, admirably positive, and thoroughly political. She peered into the crowd; I knew she couldn't gauge our reactions because we were all shrouded in blackness, our bodies only dark, small shapes among the darker trees. An otherworldly hush made the scene even bleaker, and I half expected sulfurous vapors to swirl about us. I swatted at a mosquito on my arm and shuddered when I took my hand away, feeling rather than seeing the spot of blood.

"It appears that the bicentennial celebration is causing more problems than it's solving. Many of you have expressed concern for the safety of the participants in our pageant. A lot of people have grown uncomfortable and that's made me think long and hard, and here's what I conclude. Our purpose has already been served. We've brought attention to the threat of a large, high-density development. That was, after all, our goal."

"My goal," whispered Catherine as she blotted her damp upper lip with her hand, "is to sit in a tub of cool water until October."

Deeny nodded. "Or lock myself in an air-conditioned movie theater and eat popcorn and drink soda. It wouldn't matter what's playing."

"And so I suggest," Ruth said from her spotlight on the steps, "that we call off the pageant and—"

"Wait!"

Catherine was on her feet before I realized what was happening. Everyone turned to look at her; even Ruth, standing in that strange light on the cement steps, stopped her speech and stared.

"You want to say something, Catherine? Come up here, my dear, so that you're not just a voice crying out in the darkness."

Ruth, waxing not only poetic, but solicitous, too. She seemed to undergo all sorts of transformations when Catherine was around. I moved a little closer to Peter, needing to be near him despite the clammy heat.

Catherine stood next to Ruth in the pool of light, the very picture of innocence with her hair pulled up in a ponytail, her pretty dress only a little wilted. "I wanted to stop you before you said something I don't want to hear. I'm just getting to know this community, and some of you don't know me very well yet. Being an outsider gives me one advantage: I can see very clearly what we have here. I want to be part of it—part of the neighborliness, part of the respect for each other's privacy, part of the pact to take care of the land. And it seems to me that we must go on with the plans for the bicentennial, if we're going to preserve all that is precious about Taconic Hills."

The audience clapped politely, waiting for a sign from Ruth before they went along with this outlander; Catherine was charming but she wasn't one of us. If I had been up there saying the same things, they'd be on their collective feet, cheering and stomping. Then again, maybe not. After the fire and the ugly innuendos that had followed, I wasn't exempt from suspicion these days. I hated whatever had brought that change to Taconic Hills; it might just as well have been Dembowski's damn high-density housing, for the way it had altered the community.

"Thank you, dear." Ruth smiled and patted Catherine's arm. "But I do think we've got to consider everyone's safety, and weigh the benefits against the costs."

"The girl is right," someone called out. "We can't give in now."

"Dembowski can't intimidate us. We can't let him do that!" This time the voice stirred a chorus of shouts. The gleam in Ruth's eye brightened; then she composed her face and stepped forward again.

And suddenly I realized what we had just witnessed. Had no one else seen it, too? Ruth Hoving had engineered this surge of support. It had been a terrible risk; shrewdly, she had played a little negative psychology, to marshal the town to the rescue of her project, to make people feel as though *they* had convinced *her* to go on with the play.

By now, the crowd was on its feet and moving toward the steps, chanting, smiling, clapping. Revival-meeting fervor swept through the oppressive night air, and I half expected a rousing rendition of "She's Got the Whole World in Her Hands" to burst out at any moment.

"You don't think there's any danger in proceeding with the pageant?" Ruth asked.

A huge "NO" swelled the air.

"And you're willing to put aside the differences that have arisen since we started work on this production, because you think it's necessary to save Taconic Hills?"

"Getting them all worked up, isn't she?" the voice beside me muttered. When I focused on my father's face, I could see the tight slash of his mouth forming around his words. "Knew all along what was going to happen here tonight. Always shoving things down someone's throat, forcing them to do what she wants them to and then making 'em think it's a good idea."

Peter, on my right, leaned forward to glare at my father, but Roy

Stanton was in the throes of a passionate hate that frightened me in its intensity.

"Dad, come take a walk with me, okay?" Uneasily, I stood up and reached a hand down to help my father to his feet, but his stare burned right through me.

"Playing God all her goddamn life." He shook his head, his lips working soundlessly. "I'm all right, Sarah. Sit down."

Relieved, I turned my attention back to the steps; Marge Hoysradt threw her arms around Ruth. Ruth dabbed at her eyes. Clearly, I'd missed a touching moment, at least one that was meant to look that way. Ruth folded her hands in front of her and addressed us again.

"Please, please," she said, her voice barely loud enough for the crowd to hear. "Let me understand. Everyone here thinks we should go on with the bicentennial activities as planned?"

The crowd roared its assent.

Ruth's glowing eyes swept over the assembly. "Then we will."

My mother-in-law and Catherine had made certain that the reenactment of Stefan and Emily Schiller's lives—and Klaudia Weigelt's—would go on as planned. Were they working so hard to ensure the pageant's continuation despite the disastrous parallels or because of them? Ben had his own reasons for wanting the show to go on, but pride of authorship might be only a minor factor in some larger scheme. To increase newspaper circulation? To somehow contribute to a disintegration of my relationship with Peter?

Nicky Dembowski had a host of company on the list of people who might benefit from a not-so-instant replay of the historical events. For me, that was at least as worrisome as the notion of a mysterious force, a karma, a delusional mass compulsion.

In any case, I felt alone now.

Beaming, Ruth raised a hand, looking for all the world like a prelate about to offer a blessing to a gathering of supplicants. "Thank you, every one of you, for this tremendous show of support for our beloved Taconic Hills."

Her timing was impeccable. With her last syllable, the western sky lit up, far across the Hudson, trees silhouetted in the eerie illumination of the sheet lightning. Ruth stepped down into the darkness, the crowd still cheering as another flash from the sky lit their way to their trucks and cars.

If we were lucky, a storm would move in before morning and the heat would lift. I wondered if Ruth had engineered that, too.

August

Bees have the advantage of an elaborate chemical communication system of scents, carried in pheromones and made up of at least fifty distinct substances, including the alarm odor secreted by a bee's stinger to call other bees to her aid.

—*Everywoman's Guide to Beekeeping,* Revised Edition

Eighteen

In spite of the lightning, there was no storm and the weather didn't change.

Nothing, it seemed, had changed. Dembowski didn't cancel his bid to developers; Ruth didn't call off the bicentennial; Roy didn't stop muttering about Ruth's maneuverings; and I couldn't get the crowd of concerns out of my mind. But the whispering campaign slowed down, or at least went so far underground that Peter and I could pretend we didn't feel its effects. I was still aware of Emily Schiller's presence in my life, and of the shadow of Julia Stanton, but I pushed them both into a dark corner, knowing it wouldn't be long before they were center stage again, grateful for a period of quiet, however brief.

The bees were happy; the clover was in a second blooming and wildflowers carpeted the hills and fields. The bees worked hard to keep themselves cool, and they replenished their energy with a temporarily endless supply of pollen, becoming as single-minded and as docile as they'd be all year.

Dark came a little earlier; summer colors faded from the constant, oppressive heat.

I was hanging wash on the line one afternoon when I heard a child's scream.

"The bees! Mommy, they're back!"

I froze; time slowed and a light as brilliant as a magnesium flare burst over everything.

I dropped the shirt, knocked over the bag of clothespins, and whirled in direction of the horrified noise. Patsy McClosky's older child pounded across the field on the far side of the pond. Even from here, I could make out the cloud pursuing him. *Bees. The wild swarm.* He screamed again, and I broke free of my paralysis. With a horror I felt in my arms and legs and most especially in my throat, deep inside, I saw that he was headed for the pond, running hard and so propelled by fear that he surely had no sense of where he was going.

His course was fixed and he would splash into the water before I could veer around the pond and scoop him up.

If only I could close the three hundred yards between us without scrambling around the boulder and dashing over the bridge and up a rock-strewn incline . . . but that was the only way, short of diving into the pond.

So long woodcutter and bye-bye Emily. I couldn't do it.

I couldn't go into that water.

Couldn't.

The boy's scream reached a new pitch and he slapped frantically at his face. The first of the bees had gotten him. I pounded forward and, to my horror, knew in an instant what would happen next.

Before I could fight the tightening of my throat at the thought of Emily Schiller, the weight of her heavy dress descended on me as he plunged headlong into the water. The bees hovered above his little yellow head and I was at the edge of the pond, kicking off my shoes, diving in, hitting the cold water, gasping for breath.

The boy floundered on the surface. Water flooded into my eyes. I saw him go down, breathless, soundless, and I swam harder, my jeans tugging at the lower half of my body. My legs seized up as though bands of steel had tightened around them.

Swim! I ordered myself. I reached the thrashing surface, gulping for air. The child swung his arms and his legs wildly, smashing me in the midsection and knocking all the air out of me.

Keep his head up.

I grabbed him under the chin. His body fought me but I was not going to let him go, not going to let him drown.

Not going to drown myself.

One arm working, the other holding him up, I made it to the shore.

"Michael! Oh, God, Michael!" Patsy sobbed and held on to her son's shoulders as he retched and a stream of scummy water spewed from his mouth.

My stomach heaved and I turned away, unable to reach the tree in time to conceal my own vomiting. I let it come, hot and afraid and angry, pouring from me. And then it was over.

"Michael, what happened?" Patsy held both her children in her arms, sitting on the grass, rocking back and forth, her lips in her son's hair, her face bone white. "You were supposed to stay on the road."

The boy, his color returning, sniffed and then snuck a look up at me. "I was throwing rocks at the water tree. It's a dead old tree. It's"— his little features screwed up in concentration — "a stunt. Right, Mommy, when you cut a tree partway down? It gets full of water. I threw a rock and I guess I hit their house."

"A stump," Patsy said as she brushed the hair back from his smooth forehead.

At the memory of what happened next, his little face dissolved and he started wailing all over again. His body quivered with the insult of it all. I took the baby from Patsy, and she folded her son into her arms, shushing him, stroking his hair, holding his body close to hers as though she could absorb some of his pain.

Two angry red welts had sprung up on his face; I leaned forward, the baby fitting just right on my hip, and scooped up a handful of mud. I knelt beside him as Patsy kept stroking him.

"I'm going to pull out the bee stingers with my fingers, Michael. It won't hurt, I promise. If I don't do it, it's like you're wearing a sign that says 'bee enemy here.' Then I'm going to put this mud on your face to make it feel better. Like a Halloween mask." That was as distracting as I could get this time; I had no heart for games. If I hadn't been around, the boy might have drowned, because of my wild bees.

And if I hadn't been paralyzed by thoughts of Emily Schiller, I might have gotten to him sooner.

The thought started a trembling in my arms and legs.

But I did get to him, and he didn't drown and *I* didn't drown. Maybe this meant that the spell was broken, that the reason to fear a force that reached forward from the past to touch Taconic Hills had finally disintegrated. Maybe we did share some experiences, Emily Schiller and I, but the differences were significant as well.

"Come on, you guys." I was eager to offer Patsy and her kids any comfort within my means; Emily, I thought smugly, wouldn't have been able to drive them home. "It's been a hard afternoon. Jump into my truck. I bet you don't really feel like walking home."

Patsy was too wrung out to object. Her face still chalky, she clutched her son as though he'd disappear if she let go of him.

My jeans and shirt were plastered to my body; small pieces of pond scum, green and slimy, clung to my arm, and my body was racked with chills.

Had I been released from my bond to Emily Schiller by replaying her story with a different ending, or was I simply trading that part of her life for another? I shoved thoughts of Catherine Delaney out of my mind and clung to the hope that I'd beaten the curse as I drove Patsy and her children home.

Nineteen

"You look different," Peter said that evening as we took our places in search of a cool breeze. I lay in the hammock between the butternut and a maple; Peter sat cross-legged in the grass beside me. "Less agitated, but also more, I don't know, more wary, as if you're looking out for something around every corner."

I did feel watchful, but being careful seemed only sensible. "I need to stay ready for whatever's coming. It's not over." I pushed off against the grass with my foot, but the gentle motion did nothing for me. I pushed harder, swung out a little further.

A spiderweb brushed the side of my face. I swallowed the scream in my throat and fought, silently, against an onslaught of the images that I'd seen and heard in the shed.

"Something just happened. Something on your face, it's gone tight again, Sarah." Peter towered over me, peering down into the hammock, his blue eyes swimming with questions.

"Nothing," I lied, regretting my inability to tell him, even now, about the shed, "there's nothing going on. I'm just tired, that's all."

Jeanie's house, on the edge of town, was shaded on three sides by fruit trees and a stand of pines, and bordered on the south by her flower garden. Crimson and yellow marigolds, the first richly colored dahlias, and a profusion of blood-red geraniums waved in the breeze. The stone walk still gleamed with water; Jeanie had been out with her hose. But the porch was empty and the windows dark. I knocked on the screen-door frame and called her name.

"Sarah? I'll be right out. I'll get us some iced tea," she called from the somber depths of the house.

I was glad not to go inside, glad not to see whether Clayton's certificate of merit, his bowling trophies, his drawings collected over decades of working with kids in the Taconic Hills schools were still on the walls and on the mantel and all over the house. I was glad not to notice whether the lollipop jar was full or empty.

I sat on the slatted seat of the rocker and looked out over the stillness of the late-summer twilight. The sky turned from hazy blue-gray to shot silver, streaks of pink and melon-colored wisps of clouds emerging from the haze. A calm settled over me; at last, I would know. I felt that with a certainty.

"Heard you're something of a hero. Or should I say heroine?" Jeanie's voice, even in jest, was softer than it used to be, a change that had occurred after Clayton's death.

"I'm glad I was home, and that I heard him. It's a good thing I was close enough to get to him in time." I sipped the tea, cold and lemony, then looked into Jeanie's face. "I want you to know I miss Clayton and I'm sorry, so sorry about what happened. There's been a lot of talk since the fire that maybe Peter and I—"

"Now, you stop, Sarah." Jeanie didn't move, didn't touch me, but her voice was warm and insistent. "I never for a minute, not for a second, thought there was anything to that talk more than Nicky Dembowski stirring up discord. You're not to even think about it again, hear?"

I nodded and kept myself from jumping up and hugging her. We sat in the twilight a while longer, until I realized I had no idle conversation to make. If I waited, I might lose my courage.

"I need your help with something, Jeanie, something more important than costumes and ruffles. But I'll understand if you can't give it. All you have to do is say so. It won't change the way I feel about you."

Her mystified frown told me that I'd already made a muddle of it with my apologetic preamble instead of going directly to the topic. She smoothed her face and smiled and nodded.

"You ask and I'll tell if I can do it. You know I will if it's possible." She took my hand. Hers was damp, fleshy. "Ask, honey."

"What happened in the shed out past Vixen Hill pond?"

Her eyes closed and the glass of tea in her hand tilted. "I knew it would be about Julia," she murmured. "I knew you were going to ask about her. I never did agree that it should be kept from you."

So she *did* know.

Who else had kept secrets from me?

I waited quietly, hoping that she would go on without my prompting, so that she wouldn't feel pressured into something she didn't want to do. A tawny cat stalked invisible prey in the privet hedge, a snarl starting high in its throat. Long, lacy shadows of the cherry and plum trees spilled over the porch. And finally, Jeanie began again, and I sat still in my chair, listening to her tell my story.

"You were such an energetic child, always wanting to explore, always trying to find out how things worked and what made the world turn. You could take apart a person's kitchen in record time, before you could walk. Your mother brought you by one day and she wanted to hold you on her lap but you squirmed and wriggled so she put you on the floor. The only things you could reach were my pots and pans, nothing that could hurt you or that you could hurt. But still, it didn't take you more than five minutes to have everything on the floor. You tried to fit saucepans into stockpots, turned them on their sides, banged on them with your little hand.

"Well, that's just to say that you were always busy, always going into things that interested you. And it didn't stop when you got older, although I can't say where you got all that fearlessness from. Julia was such a, well, an observant person. Got it, she said once, from watching how other people behaved so she could see how a thing was done. Trying to fit in here, coming at such a sensitive time in her life to this town, middle of high school when people have such strong lines of friendship and connection already established. And here not being the easiest place in the world for a stranger. All that old Yankee reluctance to believe anything but centuries of proof about the acceptability of someone, that hangs on."

She leaned back in her chair, took a sip of her iced tea, squinted into the twilight.

"Anyway, one day, it was spring and your father had been on his own at the garage for, let's see, a year it must have been. You liked to go with him if he had to fix a piece of equipment at someone's farm, and he liked taking you along. One day he was working in the garage and things were slow, so when he got a call from Harold Slocum that his old International Harvester had just given up and died, Roy went off to the Slocum field, out just north and east of Vixen Hill pond, to see what he could do. You know how cheap Harold is. He was determined to keep that tractor going for another two or three years.

"You went with Roy, like always, and you must have got to climbing on the harrow disks still hooked up to the back of the tractor. Roy was busy checking out some part or other and you slipped and fell, cut your arm pretty badly."

I looked down at the white scar on the fleshy part of my forearm leaping out even whiter, a map of long-ago events. I remembered how my fingers had tightened over that scar involuntarily when I first saw the starred cross in Ruth's living room, how my arm throbbed when the door to the shed slammed me into contact with my own past.

"Roy didn't know what to do, you bleeding and howling." She frowned. "You understand, part of this is what he said, part of this is what I heard from Ruth, and part is what Julia tells, not any of it, well, not much of it anyway, from what I know by my own eyes and ears.

"Well, he scooped you up and started to take you back to the house, but then he changed his mind. Says he remembered he kept a first-aid kit in that shed, the one up past the pond, for just this reason, for if someone got hurt while they were working in the field, or maybe he used to fix things out there on his own time, I'm not sure about all that.

"Roy drove like mad, parked, and carried you with him to the shed. Says he never noticed that the lock wasn't in place because you were crying so hard. He set you down on a stack of boards and told you not to move. Then he went to the pump outside, the one still connected to a well that must have been drilled a hundred years ago, to get water to wash off your arm.

"While he was gone, it couldn't have taken him more than two or three minutes to get the bucket and start the pump going, but you were already off and exploring.

"You must have hopped down from those boards and gone looking around, and when you turned behind that divider wall . . ." She looked down into her glass and stopped rocking.

The darkness was falling tighter now, pressing down on me. I couldn't bear waiting; my arm ached where the scar gleamed white and ropy.

"It was your screams brought him running. You must have been frightened at the sight, not expecting to see anyone back there in the shed. You had come upon your mother and her lover, both naked, terrified, hiding behind the divider wall.

"You know how Roy can get angry and make it seem like he doesn't hardly care? How he won't lose his temper and get into a real good rage? Well, it wasn't always like that. He picked up the hay fork leaning on the wall and stuck it in the man's chest, told him he'd kill him if he didn't leave Taconic Hills at once."

Prince . . . the three holes. I felt faint from the thought of my father and a pitchfork and the damage he'd wrought.

Jeanie leaned toward me and I realized that night had fallen around us as she had spoken. I could barely see the expression on her face. The hills beyond were undefined shapes ridging the horizon; it seemed right that this story be told in the dark, right that I not be able to see what lay in the endless void beyond the porch.

"How do you know all this, Jeanie? It doesn't sound like the kind of thing Roy would tell on himself."

"No, it wasn't Roy. Do you know that your father used to drink a lot? Now, you probably can't remember ever seeing him take a drink because that changed that day. But he'd been drinking since morning, which may account for how he forgot to pay attention to you so that you got hurt. And it probably explains why he was so hair-trigger close to violence. Does that to some men, you know.

"Anyway, what happened next is a little confusing. Somehow, Roy got you to Doc Verity's and she stitched you up, but by the time that was done, your mother was gone. Just plain gone. Never took one thing with her but her savings passbook and maybe one or two items of clothing.

"Roy calmed down eventually but he insisted that nobody ever say her name to him or to you, either. He swore off alcohol and set about denying that such a person as Julia Stanton ever existed. So that's what the shed meant. Only the four people in that shed ever did know what happened there—and you seemed to have developed amnesia about it practically right away. A blessing, I said, even back then when some folks supposed it would be better for you to talk about it."

Her story had to be true.

Jeanie wouldn't invent such a tale.

But where was my memory of it? Even now, even after she had told me how to fit together those pieces I'd retrieved—the screams, the three holes, the spiderwebs—I still couldn't make it run from the beginning through to an ending, the way a story should go.

Amazing, the human capacity to forget, to shove into dark corners what you needed to keep secret from yourself. Could it have been worse to know this than it was to wonder why Julia left?

Even when I assumed that what Jeanie had told me was true, I felt a lack of completion. Something was still missing. Jeanie had chosen not to—or had been unable to—give it all back to me.

"I have questions," I began, "only I'm not sure what they all are. It's hard to know where to begin. Maybe after I go home and think about it some more, I'll know what I want to ask. Do you mind if I call you again when I do?"

A moth banged against the screen door and Jeanie sighed. "I don't know yet if I did right by telling you this. I've gotten to be a strange old widow, Sarah, even in this short time, and I now believe that things shouldn't remain unsaid. The good that Clayton and I had together came from telling each other almost everything." Her voice caught. "It's the almosts that hurt now. So, yes, ask me. I hope knowing eases your heart in some way."

That was all the permission I needed. "Julia left because she got caught having an affair with another man. But what did that have to do with me? Divorces happen and mothers don't have to give up their children, didn't even then, because of infidelities. Why didn't she take me along?"

Jeanie's long silence was broken by the forlorn honk of a goose overhead, the first of the season. "I can't answer that, honey. From what I heard, she was terrified of your father and the threats he made. He's the one who knows the rest."

"So she went off and married this guy and forgot about her child." I couldn't fit that into my pieced-together picture of Julia Stanton, not just because it was my old pain, but because it was at odds with what I'd found out about her. She could be soft, caring, gentle. She had tried to mold herself into a model homemaker; she went out of her way to help people with their gardens. How could she walk away from me, her only child?

Jeanie didn't say anything, and I wondered what the look on her face meant. She was puzzling something out, worried about how or whether to tell me whatever it was.

"I'm sure I *will* have questions, but I'd better stop for now and get used to this. Thanks again, Jeanie. I know this has been hard on you."

"Not so very," she said softly. "Like I said, Sarah, it's clear to me now that things unsaid can hurt a person."

I drove back to Vixen Hill Lodge, lost in thought. A strong magnet pull seemed to draw me to the shed, but I fought the impulse. What would it serve to go there? It frightened me to think about that place, even more now than before I knew its awful history.

In the dark, I kicked off my shoes and walked to the oak tree, trying to concentrate on the velvety carpet of grass, on the sweet scent of the honeysuckle, on the way the light from Dad's workroom across the road reflected from the pond.

It was no good. I couldn't connect to the present and I didn't understand this new past Jeanie had given me. I sat down and stared out across the still water. With my back against the tree, intentionally facing away from the shed, I closed my eyes, hoping that new images would appear to help me remember more of that day that had altered my life irrevocably.

But they didn't. I couldn't remember words or faces, not even my father's. Jeanie had named some of the elements I'd recognized earlier and explained how they figured in the events that changed my life. And now I understood why I held on to my scar that first day at Ruth's house when I saw the *crux stellata*. That cross; I wondered why Jeanie hadn't mentioned it.

I had done quite a masterful job of hiding that day from myself. Why?

Why had I pushed it down so deeply? Because Roy had poked someone in the chest and made him bleed? Because of the trauma of seeing my mother naked with another man? That couldn't have meant all that much to me, a four-year-old with a curiosity about everything. Because of the blazing fury of my father's rage? It didn't make sense, even now, even knowing what I did, that the events of that day added up to a need to blot it completely from my memory. And the forgetting had happened immediately, not over time, according to Jean.

When I uncovered the pieces still missing from my understanding, would I be happier, wiser? Would my life be better?

Twenty

"I agree, there's got to be more to it." Peter measured my intention with his eyes while his hands remained unnaturally still in his lap. "What will you do?"

"I have to start with my father. In a funny way, I owe it to him to hear his story first. He stayed with me. *He* bound his life to mine with all the everyday business of raising a child."

It had taken me only part of the afternoon, sitting beneath the oak tree, staring at the pond, to realize that truth, and that knowledge had softened the obdurate need to keep my father at a distance.

"What I want to avoid," I continued, "is getting him all mad at Jeanie."

"You do have to say she told you, I guess." Peter shook his head. "I'm glad it wasn't my mother. Wouldn't exactly have been in the best interests of family harmony if you had to tell him his archenemy had spilled his secrets."

"Then he'd really be furious." And maybe then, if I saw his face contorted with anger, I'd remember. But even if provoking him was the best way to recollect the missing fragments of my childhood, I wouldn't do that, not consciously and with a hidden end in mind.

"Watch out you don't make yourself numb again, Sarah. Don't start acting as though you don't have any feelings about it all." He took my hand in his. "Don't close me away. And don't work so hard keeping it in. It's destructive."

A great unraveling began as he spoke. I *was* reluctant to show my feelings, but that wasn't only because of my natural reserve or an inner delicacy that kept me from displaying my messier, more primitive feelings. I had learned something terrible about the need to keep quiet.

After all, look what happened if you were four years old and screamed at the sight of your mother and her lover.

In that single lesson, learned in one long-repressed afternoon, I had come to regard my own emotions as dangerous, as having life-altering power. I had screamed; I had cried; because of that, Julia was gone from my life.

"I'm trying, Peter, I'm honest-to-God trying not to close off my feelings. But it seems like nothing's there right now. The one thing I know is that I want to be close to you. Let's take our sleeping bags out onto the grass in the back."

And we did, lying silently, only our fingers touching. We watched the sky, searching for meteors, pointing out shooting stars and the steady, stately progression of satellites monitoring the darkness. We heard the owl that lived in the woods halfway up the hills begin his nightly patrol of sound. And nothing changed and nothing became clearer but at least I had Peter beside me and part of my world was what I expected it to be.

In the morning, a rain fell and the sky remained pale yellow, hardly any blue or even gray in it, reminding me of the way the sky had looked when Dad and I visited an uncle in Illinois one year and a tornado had rampaged through the countryside. I hadn't thought about that uncle for years.

Uncle Sam. He used to kiss my eyelids whenever I said good-bye. He had a great glass jar in which he kept small white bones, and he'd shake out a handful and ask me questions. Did I think the pieces in his hand belonged to the same animal? What part of the animal was this bone from? Where did I think an animal with bones like this lived? After a while I could fashion replies that made sense, because after each one that didn't, he'd tell the true answer and the reason for it. By the time we left, after just four days, I'd learned about kangaroo rats, squirrels, crows, moles, and weasels. And I'd discovered that the process of understanding a whole thing sometimes begins with the only parts you have available, and that it's possible to build a wrong picture based on those pieces.

I needed to find out whether the pieces I had and the meaning I'd assigned to them were a sufficient basis for creating an accurate picture of the past. And so I drove to the garage, to talk to my father.

"Slow! Back it up *slow!*" my father shouted, and then added, under his breath, "You pea-brained shitkicker."

Deeny Lambert rolled his pickup forward five feet, then back again until the rear wheels found the grooves of the lift. "This good?"

My father jerked his head back, a wordless instruction to continue backing up, which Deeny did. He got out, cocked his hip, and waited while my father punched the button to raise the lift, walked all around, peered underneath, and finally pronounced the situation okay.

"Hour. Maybe two at most. If you're not here by six, I'll leave it around to the side. Pretty simple brake job." Dad took a rag out of his pocket and ran it along the axle. "Oughtn't let it get so gunked up, boy. It's not good for the joints."

"Thanks, Roy. I'll be back before six. See you, Sarah." Deeny saluted and strode off down the street into the sunshine.

The radio blared out a country song about a man who longed for his wife to ask him where he went when he was out at night. My father got out pans and tools and began draining the oil and muttering about preventive maintenance, oblivious to my presence. I had somehow expected him to have anticipated this visit, but he hadn't. He was too engrossed in his everyday angers, his shortsighted hostilities. And he was working, one of those tactics for avoiding feelings he'd surely passed on to me. We shared the need to be engaged in activities that produced results. Something—anything—that transformed the material world and kept you from thinking too much about subjects you wanted desperately to avoid.

"I need to talk to you, Dad."

"Go ahead, talk. Shit, I wish he hadn't messed with this before he brought it in." My father stood in front of the toolbox, his gaze checking and measuring and deciding which was the right tool for the job.

"Dad. I don't want to talk to you while you're working. It's important. It's about . . ." Again, as I had when the subject first came up, I hesitated over what to call her. "Julia. I have some things I want to ask you."

He picked up a wrench and tightened it around a lug nut, grunting, sweat beading his forehead. He left the wrench hanging and stomped off to the tall metal shelves, which had worked their way back to their usual state of sprawling disarray. He hunted through old, ripped cartons and jars overflowing with parts, muttering as he pushed aside gaskets and half-filled plastic bottles of thick, brown fluid. His shoulders got tighter, his face redder as he rummaged through the shelves.

He might pretend not to hear me for a while, but I wouldn't wait for his attention for another twenty-four years, not even for another twenty-four minutes.

"Dad." I reached over and took both his hands in mine. His face under all the streaks of grease went white and his eyes burned with violation. But he didn't pull away. His chest heaved and his breath, quick and hot, flared in his nostrils.

"I got work to do," he said.

"What happened in the shed? The day I cut my arm. I know some of it, but not all." I let go of his hands and stepped back, giving him room to breathe, to move, but I didn't let his gaze slip from mine. He needed to understand the true depth of my resolve.

"Who you been talking to? I know. That manipulative, scheming—"

"No, Dad. I didn't talk to Ruth. I didn't want to hear it from her. But I knew something had happened in the shed. Remember the day you sent me there for the lace? Well, I had the first glimmer of a memory then, but I couldn't get any more of it, so this afternoon I asked Jeanie Boice. You can't be mad at her, Dad. She told me part of the story and then said I should go to you for the rest."

I watched his face for signs but saw none. Then, as if he'd known all along it would come to this, he pulled an oil-stained rag from his back pocket, set it down on the shelf, and turned stiffly to face me again, his hands balled into fists.

"Whatever Jeanie told you, I'm sure she was right. She's not one to add things or leave them out. It's not something I'm real proud of. Happened a long time ago and it changed everyone's life, but at the time it was all I could do not to kill them both. I guess between the half bottle of whiskey I'd already had and my state over your arm being cut and it being my fault and all, I was near to crazed to start.

"So when you screamed, I was primed for something terrible happening to you. But I wasn't ready for what I saw. Even now, I don't know how I got hold of that pitchfork. Your mother and her pious ways, always wearing that cross he gave her. That was all she had on."

He stood like a winter tree, still and bare to his soul.

I heard a car horn outside on the street somewhere, realized that the everyday world beyond these walls was going on about its business, creating its own history as mine was being revised.

"Evil," he said flatly. "She was an evil spirit cloaked in all that begood activity. She was corrupt, and he was part of it. May they both burn."

"What was it like before? Did you know something was wrong? Could you tell she was unhappy?" I wasn't some outside observer, prying and poking among the rubble of his past. "Please, Dad. I want to hear this from you, not from someone else."

He raised his eyebrows at that thought. Then his face got distant and hard, his mouth setting into a rigid slash pressed tight against yellowing teeth. "You don't really, you know. You don't want to know how she'd complain all the time about being stuck here in the middle of nowhere with a little kid. No chance to go to Paris. No painter's gallery coming after her to show her foolish little pictures of flowers. Nobody who knew anything at all about style, and nobody who would tell her the real news of the town, the gossip, because she was an outsider. And most of all, a husband with dirty hands. Who'd she *think* she was marrying—the Duke of goddamn Windsor?"

His was a negative variation of the vivid portrait Walter, Jeanie, Clayton, and Marge had created, the subject of *his* painting all turned in on herself, self-deluded, self-obsessed. It wasn't the details so much as a discrepancy of attitudes. I was confounded by the fact that these particular pieces added up to a need to banish her completely, as though she'd never existed. I was proof that she had.

"Dad, listen to me. Don't yell at me. Just listen all the way through."

He didn't speak or even move his head; I went on. "What you're telling me must have been painful for you, I can see that. But we're not talking about ancient times. People had affairs, people got divorced, people got remarried. Why do you insist that nobody talk about her? You make it so dramatic, and it keeps you from going on with your life." His eyes narrowed; he seemed about to say something, but he nodded, perhaps in remembrance, and he honored his pledge not to interrupt.

"It's time for you to tell me the truth. You kept it secret and hidden—and it became something rotten in my life. It got to festering inside me. If only you'd told me about her mistake . . . It would have been so much easier for me."

"Her *mistake!*" He howled with indignity. "It was a sign of evil. She couldn't stay."

Why should I try to convince this stubborn man there might be another way to look at the past? Still, I had to finally tell the truth as I understood it. "It was a sign of *weakness.* At least she married him."

His words hissed between his teeth. "What's that supposed to mean? Edward Fitzhugh lived out the rest of his life right here in Taconic Hills."

I reeled. *Edward Fitzhugh?*

The room went dark and cold; I reached out to steady myself, and my hand touched the rough concrete wall.

My father handed me a paper cup of water. "Drink this. You okay?" he asked softly.

I nodded and sipped the water, and finally found my voice again. "I thought she married the man—somebody Travis—and they went to live in Pearl River."

"She *did* marry Lawrence Travis. She still *does* live there. I guess now you can understand why I didn't tell anyone about finding the body."

Two hours away. Seventy-five miles down the road. Close enough to see at lunchtime and still be back before dinner. And then his words rang in my head. *Finding the body.* He was still talking.

"Everything's coming out of the darkness all at once. You might as well know the whole of it. I couldn't tell anyone about finding him, fool that he was. Out in the middle of the field. Already dead when I found him, but if I'd called Riley Hamm like I would have if it had been anyone else in that sorry pile of snow, he'd find out about Fitzhugh and Julia, if he doesn't know already. They'd think I killed him. So I moved the bathrobe belt to make sure his body didn't stay there till the thaw, and then went straight home. No one else knows, Sarah. Ruth keeps looking at me like she wants to accuse me, but, hell, that's nothing new. I swear I didn't do nothing to the right and goddamn righteous Reverend Edward Fitzhugh except put three holes in the skin of his chest with a pitchfork twenty-five years ago."

Twenty-one

Did this handful of bones come from the same animal?

Fitting together what Jeanie and my father had told me produced a skeleton without a spine, great gaps and missing pieces where structural supports should be. I couldn't make sense of all the new information.

Edward Fitzhugh. My mother's lover, my father's rival. I spent the next several days in a fog of half-remembered scenes, trying to focus on a scrap of conversation, a glimpse of expression that I might have experienced personally of the man, but the myth surrounding him was all I could grab.

I went to the *Journal* office and made up some story for Cindy about researching the history of the Taconic Hills Methodist Church for a press release about the bicentennial; she let me pore through brittle, faded back issues until I found a couple of pictures of Fitzhugh officiating at a wedding or conducting Bible-study class.

He was tall, thin, severe, with eyes that met the camera straight on with a burning challenge. His picture reminded me of my father, in a way; the fire he exuded was as intense as Roy Stanton's inner heat. The difference was that while Roy's eyes spoke of secrets and suspicion, Edward Fitzhugh's were confident and passionate.

I helped Cindy return the old newspapers to their metal storage drawers and left, only a little closer to understanding Julia, or Edward Fitzhugh, or my father.

·   ·   ·   ·

I worked long days, adding new supers to my hives. It was the kind of labor that usually left me awash in the empty bliss of a physical fatigue that required only a healthy meal and a good night's sleep to restore me and to prepare me for the next day. Instead, I found myself dragging out of bed in the mornings, slogging through the daytime hours barely able to keep up with the demands of my work. Nothing soothed the weariness or the unrest. Always, the questions returned to the single one I'd formed at the beginning: Why had Julia Stanton left me behind?

"I can't go," I told Peter flatly as we lay in bed looking out the window at the stars against the moonless sky. "I'll call your mother in the morning and tell her I'm too busy, that I'm sorry but I'll have to miss the meeting."

His warm, smooth hand found my shoulder; he stroked my skin as though he were calming an agitated child. "You do what's necessary to take care of yourself, Sarah. I don't want you getting sick. She'll understand."

I was glad he couldn't see my face. Ruth, understand that some-one might not want to go to a meeting of the bicentennial commit-tee? But her approval wasn't my concern right now. She could think what she liked.

"You want me to stay here with you?" His heart beat rhythmically against the back of my hand, and its steadiness comforted me. Far off, a dog howled in the night, the sound trailing into uncertain silence.

"No, you go ahead. They won't miss me. You tell your mother that I'll keep my promise to be in the play, and that I'm still going to donate the honey and maple syrup. It's just . . ."

What? When I tried to talk about it, the only words I could dredge up sounded as though I had been sucked under by a petulant insis-tence on my right not to be abandoned by a mother who had other things to do with her life.

I couldn't let that childish feeling rule my life.

I felt as though someone had flipped on the light in a dark room. "I changed my mind, Peter. I'll be there. I'm going to the meet-ing."

"Good," he said with a smile in his voice, "because you've re-membered it wrong. It's not a meeting. This is our big dress re-hearsal."

I groaned. Part of me had been hoping to delay indefinitely having to put on that costume and say my lines in front of an audience. And another part had kept a wary eye on the calendar, and on the approaching Labor Day holiday, two weeks away. The pageant would be over then. Taconic Hills would be safe again, I was sure, after the performance.

I'd forgotten how it was to put on the long flowing skirt and tight bodice and feel instantly connected to a woman whose life, in many important ways, resembled my own. As she had on the morning of the parade, Emily Schiller took up residence within me and transformed me into herself. I was lifted into a state of gracefulness, compelled by the volume of fabric I was wearing to move more slowly. It was so easy to become her. Would that have been true if I were playing Klaudia Weigelt?

Klaudia. I hadn't spoken to Catherine since the evening of the meeting in the Copake School yard. If I had abandoned the seeds of our friendship to an early, arid death, it was, in a way, better for her. Whatever Emily had done to hasten the departure of her husband's blond friend, maybe I could avoid playing out that part of the story. All too well I recognized Emily's desire to have the beautiful Klaudia out of the way, even if I suspected she might have been too heavy-handed in her method.

As I turned to leave I saw the delicately carved blossom my father had given Julia on its place on the lace doily beneath my mirror. And I saw again the woman in the glass. She smiled at me. *They haven't gotten us yet. We're not going to let them this time, either,* she assured me.

The natural bowl, formed by aeons of wind and water and mysterious earth movements and then manicured by Ike Kronenburg into the perfect performance site for a pageant, was ringed by hickory and old apple trees on the west and by pines on the southern and eastern boundaries. The north end of the field, where it flattened into a mesa rich with alfalfa, was to be a parking lot for the bicentennial festivities.

In the meadow, too, music and crafts tents and food booths would be set up, access to be controlled by ticket takers at the bottom of the dirt road. Today the only guards were a pair of doves, powdering themselves fitfully with pale dust, settling into the shadows again to sound their lament when a car had passed.

In the twilight cool, wearing Emily's clothes wasn't as bad as it had been in the glaring midday sun of the Memorial Day parade. Margaret Kimball strutted in her robin's-egg-blue dress as though she were born to wear high-necked, pinch-waisted dresses with long skirts. The men, in fact nearly everyone besides Margaret, seemed considerably less comfortable.

"I'd forgotten what it was like to become someone else." Catherine came up beside me, fluffing her hair into a blond halo behind her. "I think I like myself better in jeans and painting shirts."

"I like you better that way, too." I blushed and shook my head. "Not that there's anything wrong with the way you look now."

"It's all right. We had to start somewhere. Let's just forget about last time, okay, without any more said." Her face was so free of guile that I could hardly believe I'd ever thought of her as an enemy or a rival, or any threat at all.

"I'd like that." I was relieved, and pleased to have another chance at her friendship. "What happens now?"

"If this were my old show, we'd wait for the director to call for our scene, so I guess that's what we'll do here."

She nodded her blond head toward Ben, who had obviously taken his own role as director to heart. He was standing outside the roped-off portion of the field, pointing at a set of lights with one hand; the other hand clutched a clipboard to his chest. Despite his easy, confident stance, Ben had no more than his high school dramatic club experience to call on. That, and our untrained enthusiasm, would have to carry the show.

Creating theater magic looked impossible to me, but then maybe this uncontrolled chaos provided some essential energy to every production. "What are the odds we'll actually pull this off?" I asked Catherine.

"Looking good. Ben was smart when he wrote this. Took everyone's virgin state into account. I do believe it's all going to be fine, if we get through tonight without someone dying from the curse of Taconic Hills past." She grimaced. "Sorry. I'm nervous, and from what I can tell, so are a lot of people."

"Nervous about the acting, or nervous about . . . ?"

"My teacher used to say that acting always has a component of fear in it. She called it organic fear—we used to joke about which organ it was in. She warned that we had to find a way to live with it, to use it." Her face became taut with concentration. " 'You are bigger than your fear,' she'd say."

She turned toward the stage, and we both watched the scene below; the chaos of it was marvelous and at the same time perplexing. Why couldn't people work together without mass confusion? My bees, with no ability to speak, performed endlessly complicated tasks. Maybe that was it—they *couldn't* talk, so they couldn't misunderstand each other.

"Places, everybody." Ruth's voice, clear and brisk, carried perfectly well without amplification from the stage.

It's not what you say, it's what you're thinking. Be physical and don't act in your head. You are bigger than your fear. I went over the pointers Catherine had given me. Prickles of anxiety traveled up my arms; my throat felt far too dry to allow air or words to pass through.

Finally, by thinking about how I was able to calm myself when I was working with my bees, my anxiety passed away and I felt as though I might actually acquit myself without bringing major embarrassment to Peter, Ruth, Ben, and anyone else who knew me. Except for my fellow actors, who I hoped would be charitable, no audience would hiss or clap at tonight's rehearsal.

"Hey, Sweets, you don't need a spotlight. You shine without any help." Ben brushed my hand with his as he passed a crockery pitcher to me, leaning close so that no one else could hear. "You're going to knock 'em dead. Can't miss."

I ignored his whispered aside, wishing that Catherine weren't so near; I wanted to remind Ben that his promise to keep talking sassy to me didn't mean our conversations had to be peppered with double entendres. He had teased me for as long as I could remember, but since the clambake the tilt had been decidedly toward the intimate. If I didn't respond, I hoped he'd get my message, or simply grow tired of the game and give it up.

"Okay, everybody, places," he boomed. "We're going to run through the fire scene first."

I cringed. Even though I knew what was coming, every time I read the words, I lived those minutes all over again when I first saw the fire roaring from the roof of Vixen Hill Lodge. The noise would be provided by a sound-effects tape, but I didn't need it. The crackling of flames devouring wood, the screaming whine of melting wires, were forever burned into my brain. I had to get through this scene, had to use my fear and the adrenaline it stimulated to move me past my paralysis.

Peter, too, looked tense, angular and pale. His hands twitched and jerked as though he'd drunk too much coffee. He set down the musket he'd been polishing and stuffed his hands into his pockets. "Why is he starting there? That's not the beginning."

As if he'd been reading Peter's mind, Ben's piercing whistle cut through the noise. He waited for everyone to stop chattering and then said, "I want to give the fire scene an extra run-through before we all get too tired. We'll do it first, then we'll go back through the whole thing, beginning to end. Please indulge me."

Ruth smiled her approval from the front row, but the disgruntled buzz of voices behind me bemoaned the prospect of being here a minute longer than they'd expected. But Ben proved to be a cheerleader as well as a director. "You all amaze me with your natural talent. I expect we'll be out of here in, say, two hours max."

The groan behind me was unmistakable; I hadn't seen my father in days. It was so predictable, Dad playing the complainer, Walter good-naturedly coaxing him to acceptance. I was glad my back was to both of them, so that I didn't have to say anything to my father.

Ben walked us through the scene, shouting orders. I looked for my mark, squinting into the bright lights, finally, finally, forgetting for a second here and there that I was performing and for a moment, here and there, actually enjoying the experience.

My arms ached as I tried to pass buckets faster, faster to save the burning house—and then I froze with the memory of my own kitchen and dropped the bucket on Deeny Lambert's foot.

"Shit!" Deeny yelped in pain.

"Take five," Ben shouted, loping over to Deeny and bending toward him. "You okay?"

Deeny blushed and nodded his head, his eyes avoiding mine and Ben's.

"I'm really sorry," I said, flushed with embarrassment. "I lost my concentration."

Deeny's smile made me feel a little better, until he hobbled away. "I'll be okay in a second," he said over his shoulder.

Ben threw his arm around my shoulder. "You want me to rewrite that scene so that you're not in it?"

"And change history? No, we'll do it the way it happened," I insisted.

"Who knows the way it was?" Ben said quietly. "I wrote what I had to to make a good play. You sure you want to go on?"

I stared at him. Ben Yarnell, playing tricks with the facts of history in order to create dramatic incidents that could be duplicated in the lives of players? I shook my head to clear away the suspicion—it was born of my own anxiety and the confusion of the situation. Ben moved away, calling for places again, and we picked up with the bucket brigade. This time I got through the scene without doing further damage to Deeny or to my own ego.

Glad for the break, I went to sit in the empty third row while Peter and the other men, Ben's colonial Trojan chorus, did the fife-and-drum going-off-to-war scene that opens the play. Ben compared it to one of the big production numbers from *Les Misérables;* I thought of it as barely controlled bedlam. In the front row, Ruth and Catherine sat shoulder to shoulder, intent on the stage. The crowd coalesced into a semblance of order; my father turned to Walter for his cue, and then looked down at his feet and took two sideways steps to his right. Music blared from a portable tape player.

"Break!" Ben called. "Take five."

"I keep waiting for him to say 'Cut and print.' He loves all that director talk. I don't think he realizes he took most of it from the movies." Catherine grinned down at me.

I did a double take; I hadn't noticed her getting up. When I looked over at Ruth, I realized it was Alicia Fitzhugh sitting next to my mother-in-law.

"He's certainly in his glory." I supposed Catherine, like most people, thought it was cute, the way Ben took to the role, but I found it affected. I half expected him to come strolling onstage in jodhpurs and a beret. "Does this make you miss your old job?"

"Nope. Not a bit. Makes me—"

"Do you have my pocket watch?"

The snappish voice behind me was Peter's. I frowned; he wasn't usually so rude, didn't usually barge into the middle of conversations and interrupt without an apology.

"No, I don't have your pocket watch. Your mother was getting the chain fixed, remember?"

He nodded distractedly and headed for the first row.

"Sorry. Does performing do that to everyone?"

Catherine was unruffled. "Does it to a lot of us. A minor occupational hazard. I've learned to put up with it. Whoops," she said, checking her script, "I'm up next."

"Break a leg," I called as she headed for the stage. I settled in to watch. I was on stage practically all the time except for the first two scenes and the last, and I looked forward to the chance to see the spectacle as an onlooker.

After a few lines, I forgot that I was watching my own husband fight off the marauding fur traders. Ben had decided to follow the opening of the play with another bang and this scene was certainly full of action, Deeny marching around in his tatters and skins, the others stumbling drunkenly through the scene, diving lustily into caricatures of frontier louts. The illusion was convincing and I found myself urging Peter to hurry up and make his appearance to save the distressed blond damsel.

"Back off, lad," Deeny declaimed, hoisting his bow onto his shoulder. "This is none of your concern." He started for Peter, but his feet got tangled in the legs of a stool. He stumbled and yelled, "Shit!"

Everyone on stage burst into laughter.

"If you're going to ad-lib, Deeny, stick to the period. Zounds! Egad! . . . Something." Ben jumped from his perch on the packing crate and righted the stool as Deeny blushed furiously.

"I was surprised, that's all. I can't remember how to move and what to say, not both at the same time." Deeny tugged at his britches and set his wig straight, then took his place. "I'm ready."

Ben called for quiet and the scene picked up again, a couple of lines before Deeny's outburst. The argument escalated, Deeny and the others attacking their roles with relish. The actual fight went off without a hitch. Peter vanquished the three bounders and suffered a knife wound for his trouble. He sat beneath a cardboard tree, staring at his arm, taking more pleasure than I'd have expected in the bladder of tinted corn syrup leaking onto his snowy shirt like a bloody badge of honor.

Catherine entered again; some intangible change happened when she stepped onto the stage, as though she couldn't help but draw your attention to her. She saw Peter. Her hand flew to her mouth. She traipsed urgently toward the fake tree, calling Stefan's name.

"I'm all right. It's only a flesh wound." He jumped to his feet. Catherine moved toward him. Peter lurched toward her . . . and tripped over the stool. His face registered shock and confusion as he slammed, chest-first, onto the stage.

He didn't move, and for a second neither did anyone else. Then Catherine ran to his side, Ben jumped down from his crate, everyone converged on the stage. Catherine got to him first.

A strange, hot tightness swept over me as I watched the slender blond figure kneel beside him and brush the hair away from his face, my own response a quick and physical desire to pull Catherine away from my husband and send her flying into oblivion where she couldn't ever touch him again. Was that what happened to Klaudia? Had she gotten too close to Stefan? Had Emily created her own destiny by making Klaudia disappear, permanently?

By the time I reached the stage, Peter was sitting up, unassisted, and my moment of blind jealousy had turned to confusion over what past I might be compelled to live out.

"Gee, I'm sorry." A grimace of regret pulled at Deeny's mouth. "I must have put the stool back in the wrong place."

"You gotta watch out for things like that." Ben shooed everyone else back to their places, then knelt beside Peter. "Everything still in working order?"

Peter nodded and rubbed his leg and looked up at the miserable Deeny. "You have to know your props as well as you know your own underwear."

Now here's a piece of advice I'm giving only to you, a secret when you're on the stage.

Catherine had been so secretive, so convincing that I was the sole person to get that precious bit of stage magic from her. But it sounded as though Peter had gotten private acting lessons after all.

I took my time walking back to my seat, not looking at the stage so that I wouldn't have to see their faces. When I did turn around, everyone was back on their marks. The scene, with only ten lines to go, would wind down quickly and then it would be my turn.

Ruth, oblivious to me as usual, beamed at Catherine as she delivered her impassioned final speech of gratitude to Peter, who clutched his shin where he'd bumped it when he tripped over the stool. When their eyes met, she must have delivered some silent message, because he stopped rubbing his leg. Had Julia Stanton and Edward Fitzhugh ever exchanged such a glance in my father's presence? Oh, God, why was I doing this to myself? Or *was* I imagining? Maybe I was seeing clearly for the first time the real drama that was unfolding.

Catherine, Ruth, and Peter: an aristocratic threesome, to be sure. I could no longer tell what was fantasy, what was superimposed on my vision by the story of the Schillers, and what was really there. And I couldn't think of a single person I would trust to tell me the truth.

Finally, I had nowhere to turn. Peter, Ben, Catherine, Ruth, Roy —no one was exempt. Somebody had created a complex, long-term game in which the goal was to convince me, and not incidentally any onlooker, that the history of Stefan and Emily Schiller would continue its inexorable path of duplication and destruction in my life.

Twenty-two

"Well, yes, my dear, I'd love to talk to you, but I promised Marge I'd finish addressing these invitations to the hospital-board fund-raising dinner. Why don't you come back, say, at three? Tomorrow." Ruth bent her head to her writing, her arm already reaching across the neat surface of her desk to the pen she'd laid atop the cream-colored envelope.

It was the kind of dismissal she was accustomed to issuing, but today I wasn't willing to be treated like another volunteer awaiting orders. Perhaps she didn't even realize she was using the same tone with me, here in her sunlit, book-lined study, as she did with her committees. With Ruth, directness might backfire; I would grant her the cover of my presumed ignorance to make the next hour easier for both of us.

"I'll help you if you like. Honestly, best penmanship and every-thing. After we talk." I sat down beside her, lacing my fingers firmly together to keep from snatching her pen away.

She kept writing, but the tiniest change in her mouth, a sucking in of her lower lip, gave me a flicker of hope that my patience would be rewarded, and when she completed the envelope she'd been working on, she looked up at me, her gaze wavering between my eyes and the desktop. "I know you spoke to Jeanie, and to your father. I don't imagine I can add anything to what they told you."

"Yes, I'm certain you can. They gave me only the very barest facts. I need you to tell me more, Ruth. But first I have another question.

What do you know about Catherine Delaney, about why she ended up here in Taconic Hills?"

The shadows beneath her cheeks darkened as she smiled; new lines webbed the corners of her eyes. I waited, not speaking. The restraint took every bit of my will, but pressure would only make her resist.

Finally, she spoke.

"Catherine Delaney is a lovely young person who needs friends right now. She came here because she wanted to escape city pressures. That's all. She's making big changes in her life, and anyone who is doing that should have the support of friends. I'm not her contemporary, but I *can* help her feel at home here. I can give her my acceptance."

Of course it was simple as that, and not some trick of destiny ensuring that we replay an old story. I might have momentary attacks of jealousy when I saw Peter and Catherine together, but that didn't mean the facts confirmed my fears, nor was I bound to take drastic measures to protect my marriage, as I now believed Emily had. Maybe I'd miscalculated other things, too. If I accepted Ruth's explanation of her connection to Catherine, I could press on to the real business of this meeting.

"You have a unique vantage in town, Ruth, and you always seem to know about *everything*. I heard some about that day in the shed." I swallowed to help the rest of the words out. "How could Julia Stanton and Edward Fitzhugh have been so reckless? Didn't they know it would end in disaster if Roy found out? Or was that what she was after?"

"I thought Jeanie told you." Ruth fiddled with the cap of her fountain pen, lined up the stack of envelopes on her desk, rerolled the stamps and secured them with a paper clip.

"No. Jeanie only told me about the day in the shed, the day my father caught them. The day I found . . ." I had to stop. I was too near to dissolving. I wouldn't do that in Ruth's presence. "My father spoke about that day, too. But all he really did was repeat his old line about evil. I'm tired of hearing slogans, Ruth. I want to know *why*. You're the one who's been writing to her, so you're the one who knows whether she got what she wanted."

Her patrician nose wrinkled. She smoothed her skirt with long strokes and finally looked up at me. "It's true. I write to her. About you. About what I see of your life. But she doesn't communicate with me at all. Except for that letter she wrote this spring, the one I told you about.''

The small satisfaction that Julia hadn't given any more of herself to Ruth than she had to me or even to my father in those old letters was short-lived. "Then tell me how she got involved with Edward Fitzhugh. I need every bit of the past to understand.''

Ruth uncrossed her legs, lay her hands on her desk, and then looked up at me by small degrees. In her eyes I saw a readiness to comply with my request, and I felt a surge of triumph.

"All over this country, and especially here in Columbia County, the fifties were a magical time. I doubt there will ever be another time like it—safe, prosperous, hopeful. Which didn't mean we grew up without our fears, without certain dangers. Ours was the first generation to come to terms with the knowledge that we could wipe out all of humanity with the touch of a button.''

A music had come to her voice; even the pauses seemed like rests perfectly timed, the melody pleasant, the rhythm soothing.

"Families, those days, were under less pressure to have *things*. There were fewer *things* to have, Lord knows, and it was the rule rather than the exception for children to be raised to work hard, respect their elders, and fulfill the expectation that they'd one day take over the family farm or business, or in some way be steady and self-supporting.

"Julia drifted into town on a hot summer day and changed everything. She was fifteen, and already more a woman than the rest of us even dreamed of being. At least in her body, and in her way of looking at the boys, as if she knew a secret and sharing it with them would bring them pleasure they'd never imagined.''

Her face had been soft in the remembering, and when she looked at me, I noticed something—embarrassment, perhaps, or a recollection of her own naïveté. But did I see, too, a flicker of longing that the magic of the young woman she was describing had rubbed off onto her?

"Do you mean she was provocative, sexually?''

Ruth hesitated. "Do you want tea, Sarah? Lemonade?''

I shook my head and waited. I knew she wouldn't forget the question, but she might censor the answer.

"Not in a movie-star way, not outright like that. More like everything she did was behind a gauze curtain and you could almost see it and you'd have to imagine the rest and your imagination allowed you to possess her." She flushed. "I don't even know what I mean by that."

But I did. It fit so well with everything else I knew about Julia—her ability to shift and become what other people wanted her to be, without having her own boundaries.

"So she was different from the other girls?" I had never before considered that Ruth had been one of the girls of town, a child and then an adolescent. I tried to picture her walking down the hall of the old high school, chatting with Jeanie and Marge Hoysradt. I couldn't.

"The biggest difference was her capacity to want something. It was like she knew how to dream. The rest of us weren't very good at it. We'd spent all our lives watching calves get born, bloody and slippery from birthing, watching our dogs get hit by cars, attending to the demands of the seasons that kept repeating, over and over and over, predictable. She . . ." Ruth shook her head, stared down at the neatly written invitations and then at the cluster of late-summer flowers on her mantel. "She yearned for things. To go to France. To paint. To own beautiful objects."

Hearing Ruth only confirmed the picture I'd already formed of Julia. What was new was that the information had come from my mother-in-law. She seemed to want to tell me about herself—and suddenly I realized that everyone, really, had spoken as much of themselves as of Julia each time they believed they were telling me about my mother.

The light shifted and fell in a slant across one of her shoulders. I almost had dismissed her words because it hadn't suited my purpose to hear them, but now I realized what it must have been like for this community, so of a piece, so involved in the earthbound tasks of farming, drawing stone each spring from newly plowed fields. The people of Taconic Hills weren't accustomed to seeing the poetry in those cycles. If the earth's darkness yielded up hard, flinty rocks, then it meant backbreaking work to cart them away, that's all. To have a dreamer come down, to remind them of the other world . . . it must have made some people feel a lack in themselves. That's what I heard in Ruth's voice. Could she still be a little sad about that? Was it awe or envy Julia had provoked?

"I'm sorry. I got lost in my thoughts for a moment," she said.

"Me too. It's so easy to imagine—easier than knowing her, isn't it?"

Ruth's wry smile surprised me. "That's a thing a young person would say. Now, looking back, I do think she wasn't as hard to know as some of us thought. She was a dreamer is all and we were doers. If anyone had told Edward Fitzhugh's mother that she really had nothing to worry about, it all might have been avoided."

Now we were back on the proper ground of my investigation, and Ruth was pulling her strings and jerking me along with them. I bristled inwardly, knowing that she wanted me to ask what she meant by the reference to Fitzhugh's mother, knowing that I would if the silence stretched on much longer.

"She was afraid of Julia," Ruth said at last. "And disapproving. She didn't come from the right sort of family. Her father was a drifter, a salesman sometimes, a dealer in large manufacturing equipment one day and odd lots of ladies shoes the next. And her mother made hats."

Again, she stopped to smile. I didn't want to hear about Julia's mother's hats, not now. *My grandmother's hats.* Someday I'd want that, but now I wanted Julia.

"Julia and Fitzhugh went together in high school?"

"Oh, yes. She was the one the boys swooned over. They'd get into fights about who would sit next to her. Dan Lambert, Clayton Boice, Roy Stanton. And Edward Fitzhugh. Like moons, they circled around her. Pretty soon Roy was driving by her house every evening. But it was Ed she had chosen. And they went together, went to dances, talked to each other on the phone for hours.

"Ed's mother would call my mother and they'd talk about The Problem. It got so I could tell just from my mother's voice what was under discussion. Finally, in the middle of the last year of high school, Ed's mother hit upon the solution. She knew how much Julia wanted to study painting, so she gave her the money to go to art school in New York. It wasn't the Sorbonne, and it wasn't even a regular college. But Julia took it and went away for two years. When she came back after her first summer, Edward Fitzhugh was married to Alicia."

Ruth's leisurely telling had tumbled through what must have been years of agony and come out the other end with the entire, painful situation neatly wrapped up. Julia had allowed herself to be bought off. Had she not cared about Fitzhugh? Or had she simply been lured by the promise of art school and figured it was a fair trade? The

biggest remaining question was how Roy Stanton fit into this unhappy scenario.

"You look pale, my dear. Are you sure I can't get you something?
A cold drink, perhaps."

This was the old Ruth, back in control, at a remove again from the
story since this part didn't touch her. But I wouldn't let go yet, not
until more of those questions were answered.

"No, thanks. I know how difficult this is for you. But if you can
give me just a little more . . ."

Something soft in her eyes surprised me. "I feel as though I owe
this to you, to make up for hiding that I'd been writing to Julia."

A funny way to keep score. Maybe that was how she'd come to
have such power in this town: a mathematical equivalency that suited
her, one she could track in her head without it ever getting too
complicated. "When did Julia and my father announce they were
getting married?"

"That fall. She returned to New York for her last year at the art
school. Roy pressed her as soon as he knew things were off between
her and Fitzhugh. He never let up. Came with flowers, with books.
He even got me to help him pick out just the right silk scarf for her.
It was a beauty, white with gold threads like wheat growing right in
the middle. Every week he made her a different little carved flower.
He *pursued* her. He was something in those days. Never gave up, not
even when she told him they were meant to be just friends. I think, I
honestly do believe, that it was those flowers that did it for her. The
thought that they shared a love of art and an appreciation of the
beauty of nature."

I could barely picture my father as the romantic suitor; the depth
of his bitterness was so profound I'd never had a real sense of how he
might have been before Julia left.

"Was their marriage good?" Now my heart hammered. We were
quickly coming to the part of the story in which I played a role, and
all my old self-blame collected in a pool in my chest and made
breathing difficult.

"Who ever knows about things like that? Marriages around here
were considered good if they didn't come to blows. We measured
things differently; no one talked about personal fulfillment or self-
realization in those days. Roy and Julia got on okay, at least to
outsiders. They joined the grange, had little parties. When you were
born, everyone sent a gift. It was no better or worse than most other

marriages. Fitzhugh and his Alicia, Jeanie and Clayton, Walter and me. We loved each other, without any of the terrible awkwardness of passion. And I supposed Roy and Julia were like that, too. Or maybe I saw things that way because I wouldn't know what else to look for."

An odd admission of fallibility—and strangely unsatisfying to me. Perhaps all this new information was too much for one session. I was getting ready to offer a polite, leave-taking nicety when Ruth spoke again.

"Of course, it would have been different if Julia had married Edward. In a way, we were all relieved. It would have been something to envy, the two of them together. They were fire together, full of heat and surprises, and the rest of us could only imagine how that felt. Even after they married other people and made it a practice to stay away from each other, even when they thought they were over it, you could walk into a room and practically smell that they were both present because the air was different.

"I think they must have tried to stay apart. But there was something too strong between them, something that even Fitzhugh's calling or the weight of community standards couldn't stop. Somehow we all knew it would end badly."

Despite the unmoving air, a chill ran through me. While I was trying to understand how they could have abandoned common sense, I realized another thing: Julia had married Roy as a way of staying close to Fitzhugh. The reverend's mother only sent her to art school for two years, and Julia kept her part of the tainted bargain she'd made, but she'd outsmarted Fitzhugh's mother by managing to return and remain in Taconic Hills. She'd used my father; if I knew nothing else now, I knew that. Her marriage to Roy Stanton wasn't love on the rebound or even comfort on the rebound. It was simply a way to stay near Edward Fitzhugh.

How better to torment everyone: the community that had excluded her; Fitzhugh's mother; my father; even Edward Fitzhugh. It was masterful. "She went to church after she returned to Taconic Hills?"

"Every Sunday." Ruth sighed and closed her eyes as though she were watching a private movie. "She'd sit in the middle of the next-to-last row, and she'd wear the white-and-gold scarf on her head, summer and winter. One time I looked back there. It was a sight, and I almost gasped out loud. That window, the one with the lilies.

The light just poured onto her and her alone, exactly where she sat. To someone giving a sermon, it must have looked like a blessing from the angels. Julia would never go unnoticed."

Perhaps this was where Fitzhugh had gotten the inspiration to become the dynamic speaker Ruth had claimed he was. How he must have suffered, seeing her in his congregation week after week, deliberately seated where the light would spotlight her presence and her beauty, deliberately wearing the scarf another man—her husband —had given her.

"And my father? Did he go with her?" I could hardly bear to think about it. Beyond hope, I longed to hear that he knew, rationally and coolly, the unholy deal he had made when he married Julia. He must have, on some level, been content with his bounty. Yet he buried that truth and believed in Julia as his wife, in all that meant to him.

"I'm going to tell you something, Sarah, and it's the last thing I have energy for today. Edward Fitzhugh was a tortured man, but he kept his marriage vows and his own counsel until that day in the shed. He said so, Julia said so, and I believe them both. Why they chose that place, that day, it's one of the mysteries. It was the only time they'd—" She shook her head.

We both knew it didn't matter how many other times they'd betrayed their pledges. That was once, and for them, it was all they had.

Twenty-three

The leaves on the three willows that guarded the far side of Talley's pond had begun to yellow and would soon drift into the water to be carried over the spillway to the rocks below. It was still summer, though, and I thought Emily Schiller would have understood my excitement as I approached the hives: an anticipation of abundance, of golden honey bursting from each hexagon of comb, glistening with amber beauty.

What she wouldn't recognize was my sense of foreboding. She didn't have an inkling that the time of the honey harvest would mark her death. I had her life, and her death, to serve as a reminder that Taconic Hills had become a bizarre stage for the reenactment of those ancient, tragic events, and that warning took the edge off my pleasure.

Reluctant to go directly to the hives, I sat on the log bridge, watching the water tumble over the rocks. The fine spray was delicious against my face. I pulled off my shoes and socks and rolled up my pants so that my feet could be cooled, too, and as the first drops of the mist touched my feet, a scene from my childhood came to me as sharply etched as if it were captured in a photograph.

Dead center of my vision was Julia's face, white, terrified, speechless, staring down at me. Her eyes, as rich and brown as mink fur, long-lashed, open so wide they looked like they hurt. Her mouth, dry and pale, taut with fear.

What had I done to make her look that way?

Since I'd gathered fragments of my missing past from the offerings Ruth and the others had given me, I understood the irony that Julia, dreamy and fey, had drawn *me* for a daughter, all leaping and noises, a tree climber, a turtle fancier. This memory of her fearful face seemed connected to that essential difference between us.

And then I *did* remember: I'd gone out a window to retrieve something from the porch roof, just below. What was it?

My father's pipe.

I laughed to myself. I could almost taste the bitter pipe stem in my mouth. How I'd strutted! In his cap, with his pipe, as though I could acquire some of his swagger from those objects. Afraid that he'd be angry, I snuck into their bedroom when he was at work, and when Julia was busy with something, gardening or painting, I assumed from the stories I'd been told. Funny that I didn't have any mental pictures of her engaged in those activities. I closed my eyes and lifted my face to the sun.

I had stumbled. I could see in my memory the faded browns and yellows of a rag rug, the pipe flying out of my hand and out the window. How startled I was that the window screens or storms weren't up. Odd. But they weren't, and out it sailed, clattering partway down until it caught on an uplifted shingle. And out I went after it, in my bare feet, with my pants rolled down, onto the rain-slicked porch roof.

A nail must have worked loose—I could assume that now from my recollection of the event, but at the time all I knew was that I was snagged on something and couldn't get free, and I bellowed in anger.

What happened next? I strained to make the picture come clear in my mind, but I couldn't see anything else.

I closed my eyes.

The startled woman in my memory didn't move.

I squeezed my eyes tighter. A sandpapery scratchiness against my cheek—my father's rough chin, perhaps. Had she left me there while she called him, waited for him to come home from the garage, watched while he crawled out onto the porch? The scene faded entirely.

Angry at Julia for not climbing out to bring me in from the roof, I jumped up and jammed my feet back into my shoes and finished my hive chores. The supers were full, and I'd have to start taking honey. I was confused all over again, about who Julia Stanton was, what I meant to her then, and what I wanted her to be to me now—and what it all had to do with Emily Schiller and the coming honey harvest.

"I can't make sense of it either." Peter handed me the last, nearly woody lettuce I'd brought in from the garden. "Stefan Schiller might have been attracted to Klaudia Weigelt, which may have inspired Emily to, well, *encourage* Klaudia to leave the area. But what my mother told you about Julia brings to mind another possibility. Stefan's mother might have arranged for Klaudia to leave town so that Stefan and Emily could get together. Like Edward Fitzhugh's mother arranged for Julia to go away so that Ed and Alicia could get chummy."

"But it falls apart," I suggested, shaking the lettuce-filled colander and watching the water drops plop onto the bright enamel of our new sink, "when I try to squeeze you and me and Catherine into the same pattern."

"Unless *you're* the Klaudia/Julia character and Ruth bribes you to take off so that I can marry Catherine." He grinned broadly.

As absurd as it seemed at first hearing, Peter's hypothesis was no more fantastic to me than some of the events of the past few months. It would be a stretch to think that Ruth had created the whole, elaborate bicentennial play simply to scare me out of my marriage—a stretch, but not an impossibility.

"But don't worry, I'm not going to let you get away." He kissed my hair. "You wouldn't expect me to pay retail prices for maple syrup after all these years? I'd never give you up, Sweets, and you'll have to live with that."

Sweets. He'd never called me that before.

"Do you think I'm right about why Julia married my father? It's so easy to blame her, isn't it, without even knowing her."

"Maybe," Peter said simply, "it's easy *because* you don't know her."

"All the parallels to the Schiller story—I wonder if Julia has something to do with making it appear that history is repeating itself."

He looked at me thoughtfully, then shook his head. "On the face of it, it sounds unlikely, but who knows? Are you saying you think Julia's making these parallels happen?"

"That's no more bizarre than any of the other possibilities. I just can't figure out *why*, what it would do for her, but maybe she knows something that would make it all fit, a missing bit of information. Roy might have his own stubborn reasons for not telling me a fact, a piece of what happened that would make it all hang together. To protect me, somehow. He's been doing that all my life."

"He might be withholding something to protect *himself*."

Peter's soft voice interrupted the idea I'd been testing on myself. If I really believed that I needed to know what happened that day, there was a way to find out Julia's version of those events.

I could call Julia.

I would ask her to see me, and I would ask her to tell me what happened that day in the shed. I would ask her why she left without me. And maybe then, when I knew her answers, I could stop this cycle that duplicated a past that ended in disaster.

I wasn't willing to sacrifice my life, or Peter's, because of Roy's taboo against Julia . . . or because I was afraid of her rejection again. I'd faced those things before. I'd come to understand more, lately, of Julia and more important, of myself. It would have been nice if my childhood had been different, but I couldn't change the past. I wanted to preserve the good in the life I'd made for myself with Peter. Maybe Julia could finally help me.

I'd expected that the decision to contact her would bring with it an inner calm, but by the next morning I was more agitated, not less. My mouth was dry and my brain chased thoughts I was unable to follow all the way to their conclusion. Peter had gone to the hardware store to pick up some finishing nails. My restlessness kept me moving, pacing, looking for a source of steadiness and comfort. The oak tree was part of an old pattern; I wouldn't go sit there, not now. I was about to do something new, something that would mark a change so important that it would affect everything, my work, my marriage, how I lived in the community. I didn't want an old habit holding me back, allowing me old comfort, and old blindness.

It was settled, then. I would do it.

I dialed long-distance information; voice steady, I asked for the number of Lawrence Travis in Pearl River. After a second the computer-pitched voice recited seven digits. I dialed the number.

It was ten-fifteen. An August morning. She could be at work; she might be at the grocery store. I prayed for her to be out of the house.

But she wasn't. The phone stopped ringing, and a voice said hello. I knew right away who it was.

For a moment, I couldn't speak. Then, as though I'd been practicing the lines, the words I needed were there.

"This is Sarah Hoving. I'm sorry for calling like this, from out of the blue. I need to talk to you. It's important to me, and I'd rather not explain over the phone."

Her breath rattled across the telephone lines, and I waited long seconds, impatient for all my years of waiting to be over at once.

"Sarah." Her whisper finally broke the silence. "Thank God."

Her relief tore at me but still I guarded against exposing myself, against matching her vulnerability.

"Does Roy know you're calling me?"

Did I hear fear in her voice?

"No. No one knows," I replied. "Can I come see you? I need to talk to you."

"That's not a good idea, you coming here, I mean. Not yet. Maybe we can meet partway, in Hudson, Poughkeepsie, I don't know. The drive will be shorter if we meet somewhere. And no one we know will see us."

Her reluctance not to have me in her territory was understandable, and I was certain she was afraid of my father still. I didn't want Roy walking in on us, either. "Rhinebeck," I said, after I'd visualized the map of roads between Taconic Hills and Pearl River. "There's a new café, near the movie. My schedule's pretty flexible. What's a good day for you?"

"Today. Two o'clock. Let's meet at two."

My heart raced. *Today.* Today was too soon. I wasn't ready. I wanted to take my words back, tell her that I couldn't possibly do it today, that I needed time to prepare. But I didn't.

"Fine," I said abruptly. "I'm sure we'll recognize each other."

She hung up without saying good-bye, and I stared at the pale, stern image reflected back at me in the kitchen window.

What would she see? Would she like it? My face, my hair, my body: I'd never thought much about them. They were fine, not stunning, not quite plain. I seldom paid attention to my appearance except when I was feeling unsure of myself—when Catherine first arrived in town or when Ben told me he loved me and I tried to figure out what he saw when he looked at me.

What would Julia think of me? How would she feel when she first saw me as an adult, face-to-face?

No, that wasn't *my* question. That was her business. I had to collect my thoughts and figure out exactly what I wanted from this meeting. She might never agree to see me again. I might not get more than this chance to hear her version of things.

I puttered around for an hour, stood in front of my closet and touched every single article of clothing, but none of it was right. Finally, I combed my hair, changed into a clean shirt, and left Peter a note telling him I'd be back around dinner time. I drove off before I had a chance to reconsider.

I got to Rhinebeck at one, found a parking space half a block from the café, and walked and walked, trying unsuccessfully to work off some of my nervous energy. I passed a bookstore and a crafts boutique and a frozen-yogurt shop. Halfway down the block, a woman stood staring into a store window. She was tall and slender, and my heart hammered. I nearly fled down the street, unprepared to meet Julia for the first time out in the open, in the middle of the street. But a stout man with lank, gray hair curling around his collar appeared and put his arm around the woman. They turned, laughing, to walk in my direction. The woman, I saw, was no more than twenty.

Weak with relief, I continued down the street until I reached the spot where the young woman had been standing. Tasteful and obviously expensive sweaters and skirts graced the store window. Draped on one mannequin's arm was a scarf, a pale champagne slide of silk with water lilies of an even paler eggshell color.

Without stopping to consider, I walked into the store and bought the scarf.

"Gift-wrap it, please," I asked the dark-eyed salesgirl. Everything in the store smelled of sandalwood, even the tissue paper on which she spread the scarf. As much as anything, buying the scarf was a reminder to myself that Julia was a person of many parts and not just my mother. I was ready, finally, to offer myself as an open listener. It wasn't the same as forgiveness, but it was as close as I could come right now.

The salesgirl closed up the box and slid a gold elastic tie over it and I left, to go to the café and wait. I planned to examine every woman who entered, in case it took me a while to recognize Julia.

Twenty-four

I knew her immediately.

I had chosen a table with a good view of the door, near the back of the small café. The smell of fresh-roasted coffee, chocolate, and cinnamon filled the cheerful room; small round tables and curve-backed chairs, like the ones in pictures of Parisian bistros, were set on the black-and-white-tiled floor. If Julia had gone to Paris to study after she left Taconic Hills, this place might stir nostalgia in her. Would that make her like me less, or more, or would it not matter at all?

Thoughts like that crept in on me.

I had told myself that all I wanted was to find out what happened, but I understood at last that much more was at stake here. Much of it I had no control over. Julia's approval mattered not a whit to my real life now, but I wanted it anyway. I longed for her to feel sorry that she'd missed being part of my life. I wanted her to love me, now. At the same time, I fought an almost physical desire to run away from this appointment with a stranger who might bring even more pain into my life.

She wasn't a stranger, not really. She walked in the door looking so much like the woman in my attic fantasy that I nearly laughed aloud from nervous surprise.

Her face was smooth, glowing, the light shining on the prominences of her cheekbones and her forehead. Her eyes were brown, long-lashed, and very round, and her gleaming, chestnut hair was caught back in a low ponytail. She wore a long-sleeved, round-necked white cotton sweater tucked into a denim skirt. A blue silk scarf splashed with magenta flowers floated over her shoulder like a casual but absolutely essential brush stroke that pulled together the elements of a painting.

She walked toward my table, moving like a dancer, her hips twisting to get by in the tight space, and I could hardly breathe. I took a sip of water. Before I put the glass down, she was standing in front of me.

Her hands were long and graceful, and older looking than the rest of her, wrinkled, with a few age spots beginning to show. Then she said my name.

"Sarah."

It wasn't a question. And, mercifully, it wasn't quite the sweet melodic sound I'd conjured in the attic, but an ordinary woman's quite pleasant voice.

"Yes. Please, sit down. Can I get you coffee, or something cold to drink? Do you want a cookie? The scones are wonderful. They make a fresh batch twice a day." I knew I was chattering.

"Coffee. Yes, that would be nice. I'll get it. Don't you go away." She frowned, then turned to the counter while the waitress poured her a cup of coffee.

My mind was a complete blank. I was caught in an odd feeling of being outside of time, of being suspended in an objectless, noiseless space. But as soon as she returned, set her fragrant coffee on the table, and pulled out the chair opposite mine, the world started up again.

"This is so strange. I've dreamed about this happening." She sipped from her cup, and I noticed the lines above her lips, lines that belonged to a middle-aged woman.

"Thank you for coming." I saw that her hair made the same funny V at her temples that mine did. "This must be strange for you, to think that you had put your other life behind and then to have me call."

Her face crumpled and she reached across the table for my hand, her lips parting without making a sound. I didn't withdraw, but the touch of her skin stung me and I shifted in my chair.

As I uncrossed my legs, my foot bumped into something: the box. I'd forgotten about it. If I thought too much about what she might think or what it might mean that I was giving her a gift, I'd worry myself into a state that would bury me and the scarf beneath an avalanche of indecision.

I reached down and grabbed the white box, set it on the table, and slid it toward her. "I almost forgot. I hope you like it."

She touched the cover, then looked at me with a confused frown. I smiled and nodded, my heart hammering. This had been a terrible idea, but it was too late to undo it. She had already slipped the gold elastic from the box, was lifting the cover.

"Oh." It was a tiny sound, of surprise and pleasure. "Oh, Sarah, thank you." Her eyes swam with tears as she lifted the scarf from the box and ran it across the back of her hand, her fingers touching, smoothing, tracing the folds of the square of silk I'd bought for her. She pulled off the blue one, and then draped my pale water lilies around her neck.

Buying the scarf hadn't been a dumb thing, after all. "I'm pleased you like it," I said awkwardly, and she reached for my hand again.

Finally, she let go of me and dabbed at her eyes with a tissue, smiling crookedly. "Do you know that I came back eight months after I first left Taconic Hills? And then again two years after that."

I said nothing.

"I did. The first time, I just parked my car at Vixen Hill Lodge—no one was living there then—and sat inside. I was afraid I'd frighten you, but I had this notion, I hadn't thought it out very well, that I was going to come up to the house while Roy was at the garage and simply take you. Take you back with me. Run away together. You were something, that day, climbing into the low branches of the tree by the pond. Your hair was all wild, and your pants had a patch on the knee that someone else put there. You didn't even have mittens on. I wanted to take you home and put your hair up in ribbons, and get you into different clothes." She smiled and rolled the hem of the new scarf between her fingers. "You never did like being dressed up."

"Still don't," I said, smiling down at my jeans and plain blue shirt.

"Something happened. I don't know how, but Roy found me in the car. I never even touched you or talked to you and then there he was, pounding on the window. Scared me speechless."

I couldn't make sense of what she was saying. This wasn't what I expected to hear, wasn't about the shed or her leaving.

"Roy carried on. He frightened me, all over again. Then he made me drive to the Taconic Parkway, it was March and it had been raining, and he drove behind me, inches from my bumper. I thought about stopping the car, slamming on the brakes so that he would plow into me, but I couldn't take the chance that someone else might be hurt. I didn't know what to do." She stared at her own hands. "I've never known what to do when it comes to you."

I avoided her eyes, hiding my own small satisfaction that I'd already discovered that weakness in her.

"The second time, I never got close enough even to see you. It was like he knew I was coming and he met me at the crossroads. Maybe someone who saw my car as I drove in toward town phoned him to tell him. I didn't let anyone know I was coming, not even Ruth. I never wrote to her or anyone, even though she kept in touch with me, sent me letters every couple of months telling about you, what you were like, what you were doing in school."

"After that you never tried to come back?" As soon as the words were out, I longed to take them back. I didn't want my time with Julia to be filled with recriminations. "Please, let's not talk about that. Not now. My life has gotten pretty complicated lately, and I get sidetracked easily."

She nodded and waited. I was the one who had called this meeting and now I was the one who had to define the agenda.

"I know some of what happened. I've heard about you and Ed Fitzhugh, and about how Roy stuck a pitchfork in his chest that afternoon. I didn't remember *any* of it, until a month ago. Now I do have some memory. Ruth and Jeanie Boice have filled me in on as much of the story as they could."

Julia Stanton Travis started to cry and I wanted to yell at her. I wanted her to stop, to be the adult, and she was crying. Perhaps my face betrayed my irritation. Still sniffling into a cotton handkerchief, she said, "It still surprises me that you went this long not knowing. I was grateful when Ruth first wrote me that you had amnesia about that day. I was glad. You were able to get on with your life. It took me longer—six terrible lonely years—before I could move forward again."

I struggled to hear her words without passing judgment on her behavior. I had told myself that I would take in everything and not label it, not for a while, but I caught myself at it, assigning blame. I leaned back in my chair, aware that my movement put distance between Julia and me, wanting that space so that she knew—and I knew—that we were separate.

It took her a while of pushing her spoon back and forth on the table before she spoke. "Every letter I got from Ruth, I felt more and more like it would upset your life if I came back into it. And I had to make a life for myself. My husband's a good man, and he knows about you and Roy, but my children don't. I don't know how I'm going to tell them."

Her children. What was *I*?

"When you accepted money from Edward Fitzhugh's mother, did you know what she was doing?"

A mask came down over Julia's face. I had gone too far; she wasn't ready for this. I forced myself not to take the question back, not to spare her.

"I thought she was helping me grow into the kind of person who would make a good partner for him. I thought she was contributing to my education so that Edward and I could be together. It took me forever to realize that she'd planned my absence in order to maneuver Ed into marriage. To someone else. I was the outsider, you see, and from the city, which made things worse. And the daughter of a distinct failure. So I wasn't suitable. Oh, it was all right with them if I married Roy Stanton. He wasn't a member of the lofty inner circle of Taconic Hills. He was part of the town, sure, but not of the nobility. So that was all right." She leaned back in her chair, one hand rising to her throat.

This meeting was starting to take a toll on her. She had suffered her own agonies all these years, and for a moment I wished I could grant her peace.

"I know now that I did have other options." Julia stroked the edges of the pale scarf. "But I swear I didn't know that then. I can't undo the past. I can't go back and live it over with hindsight to guide me. But I'd like for us to get to know each other now."

I thought I wanted that, too, but I was certain that she was still holding back, that I still hadn't been told everything. I was keenly aware of a hesitation when I asked about the day in the shed, and about what happened that I no longer remembered, and I felt a spurt of anger. I thought of Peter's words, of the way he had urged me not to shut others out, not to handle it alone.

"We can try," I said finally. "I can't promise knowing each other will be the way you envision it, but we can try. Maybe we've gone far enough for one meeting."

She smiled. "Don't go yet. Please. Come for a walk and let me find out who you are. We've only talked about me and about the past. This gift, this wonderful scarf, tells me a lot about you. Please don't send me away without me knowing more. I'd like us to start making our way into each other's lives."

"Just a walk, just for a while," I said. "I need to let some of this settle in." I didn't say that she did, too; I didn't want to begin this relationship by taking care of her, even though she seemed to need that.

Being with her in a public place was unsettling.

I found myself looking over my shoulder, despite my certainty that no one in this town would recognize either of us. It was the middle of the day in the middle of the week, and everyone was where they should be, at work, at home, not spying on me in Rhinebeck, thirty miles from Vixen Hill.

Still, I directed Julia to a narrow side street. Her pace was languid; the air was still and warm, although the oppressive heat of early August had passed. Two small boys in striped polo shirts and torn jeans hammered diligently on a collection of boards in a yard. We walked in silence.

"Do you like—"

"Are your children   "

We laughed. We'd both started to speak at the same time, and we'd tripped over each other's words.

"You ask first," Julia said, her voice edged with relief.

"I just wanted to know about your children. How old they are. What they're like."

"Nate is fifteen and Sean is thirteen. They're good kids. I hope you like each other. Nate plays trumpet and does really well in science. Sean's great ambition is to be a baseball player, second base, but he's so good with young kids I think he's going to be a teacher. Tell me about your work. How did you get interested in bees?"

My brothers. This would take some getting used to.

I wasn't sure this was such a good idea. It felt odd to talk about myself in summary, but I'd match her example and try. "They kind of let me know. It sounds a little silly when I put it into words. I used to be outside every chance I got. One day, I was nine, it was still cold enough for snow to be on the ground, but it must have been early April because the forsythia were out. I was reading, sitting in a tire swing that Dad had hung from a low limb of the beech tree."

"The one by the side of the house, near the road?" Absently, she adjusted the folds of the scarf.

Her question reminded me that she had lived in the house across from Vixen Hill Lodge, and that notion startled me for a moment. "Yes. Anyway, a bee came buzzing up. I was afraid at first but something told me not to run away. It flew around me, down to my feet, then back up to my head, then traveled the span of my shoulders. It flew away, and that was that. But the next day, as I was walking back from the school bus, the same thing happened. I figured out that the bees were measuring me, getting my shape and size and storing that information and passing it on to all the members of the hive."

"You always did believe in the intelligence of the natural world."

I frowned. How did this woman, a stranger for most of my life, presume to say what I'd always believed in? "After that, it seemed as though the bees were leading me places. To the pond to see a frog. Across the stream to find a robin's egg that had fallen out of the nest. When I got to high school, I lost some of that magical feeling, but the bees had become such an important part of my life by then I just decided to keep it that way by working with them."

She nodded. I was afraid that she would hook her arm through mine and I stepped closer to the curb, not yet ready for the kind of physical intimacy I'd craved so hungrily when I was younger. Suddenly I felt as though I'd talked too long, in too much detail, and that I'd given away too much of myself. "Do you still paint?" I asked.

She smiled. "I haven't painted in years. Larry sent me to a summer study program at the Sorbonne when the boys were seven and nine. He's a lawyer, and he's got a lot of money. He's a very generous man, and I talked about it so much, he finally sent me." She stopped walking but didn't look up at me. "When I came back, I never painted again. He never said anything to me about it. No one has until now. Doing it wasn't nearly what I thought it would be."

Was that, then, why she had been so easily persuaded to leave Taconic Hills? She'd had her dream of Edward Fitzhugh, something in which she'd been thwarted. And when she finally achieved it, the reality was far less satisfying than the dream. I wondered what she longed for now. I was sure it was something. Ruth was right; dreams were necessary to sustain a woman like Julia.

Unless I was mistaken.

Unless I was making up answers that were convenient and allowed me to maintain my distance from her. I was getting confused again, and tired. I looked at my watch.

"This was a good start," I said, trying not to sound too eager or too dismissive. "Both of us should go back to our lives now. We'll be in touch later, when we're ready." I meant for her to press me, to want to make the arrangement more specific than that. But she didn't; she simply nodded and walked on, looking ahead down the street as though something important was waiting for us there.

"I'm glad you called me, Sarah. I couldn't do it first, you see, not after all these years of Ruth telling me how well you were doing, how happy you and Peter were. I couldn't disturb that for my own needs. Do you understand?"

"I think so." And, indeed, I had an inkling of that kind of protectiveness, but when she said it, it sounded misguided and didn't quite ring true. "The rest of my questions can wait."

I wanted to leave it at that, with her knowing that this hadn't satisfied all of my needs and that continuing our new relationship wouldn't be easy. I wanted her to admit the difficulties and say that they didn't matter, that the only thing that did count was that we were reunited and that nothing would deter her from remaining a part of my life.

I didn't ask for what I wanted, and she didn't say anything resembling those words. I felt myself closing up again, and I struggled against that obsolete behavior. Before I could figure out what to say next, she hugged me.

Her breasts were small, her arms cool against mine; I stiffened a little, then leaned into the embrace. She stood away from me then and stared into my eyes, her own swimming with tears. "Sarah," she whispered. "I'm so sorry."

Her words caused the lump in my throat to grow, but I couldn't absolve her, not yet.

"I'm glad we did this." I pulled back from the closeness of her body. I had come from that body, but what did that mean? A part of me wanted to deny the bond, as she had, twenty-five years before. "I'd better get back now."

Julia Travis nodded. "Yes, I have to go, too. I'm going to call home first," she said, nodding with her head toward the café.

I nodded, too, and didn't wait to see what she did, didn't turn around to see if she stopped on the street to watch me walk away. I wanted her to come after me and say, *Not yet. Don't go yet. We don't know each other well enough for me to let you leave.* But she didn't, of course, any more than she had managed to come back for me with any success years ago.

Twenty-five

"Did seeing her change anything?" Peter sliced zucchini while I dumped chopped onions and garlic and peppers into a cast-iron skillet. Another of his questions—I wasn't sure whether I really wanted to know the answer, even for myself.

"I can't tell yet. I do believe she'd tried to come back for me twice, but that's her pattern. When things get difficult, she gives up."

If she'd been around for more of my childhood, I might have learned that from her. Maybe I'd been better off without her. It was negative reasoning, to be sure, to say that I knew how to persevere because I hadn't learned the habit of quitting from my mother.

"Are you going to call her again?" He put the knife down and watched my face, his head tilted slightly, the soft, hazy afternoon light settling like a nimbus around his dark silhouette.

"No." I threw a couple of handfuls of rice into the pot of boiling water and lowered the flame. "It's her move now."

Peter reached for the zucchini and I pushed the sizzling onions around in the skillet. The warm kitchen silence was broken by a knock on the door. I hadn't heard a car; it had to be my father. I hoped he hadn't heard any of the conversation. "Come in," I called out as I tossed the zucchini atop the sizzling onions in the pan. When I turned around, I gasped.

It was Julia.

Her eyes were red, her face puffy, and her scarf hung limp and drooping at her neck. She'd been crying. My first impulse was to steer her to a chair and pass her a fistful of tissues. I half expected to see Roy looming in the doorway behind her, or her husband, or even one of her children. But she was alone, and she looked smaller than she had earlier, frailer and older than her fifty-four years.

Peter's confused frown dissolved all at once, as soon as I looked at him. He could hardly help recognizing her; the physical resemblance was far too strong.

"This is my husband, Peter Hoving. Peter, this is Julia Travis." I still couldn't bring myself to say "my mother." Peter said hello and offered her a cup of tea.

Julia shook her head. "Sarah, I have to talk to you. I had to take the chance—I've been thinking all the way over here how Roy still lives across the road. But he won't know my car, I'm sure. Can we go somewhere for a walk, just for a while?"

I teetered on a dangerous brink, drawn by her presence to step away from safe ground. She wanted me, came back because she had left something unsaid. I stepped closer to the edge, not quite blind to the looming darkness yet unable to deny her call.

"We could go upstairs. If Peter doesn't mind, he can keep a watch in case Roy stops by. He doesn't usually, not in the middle of the week, because we're all too tired from working. But in case . . ."

Peter nodded. "Sure, go ahead. I'll finish the stir-fry. It's nothing fancy, but we'd be pleased to have you join us for dinner."

Her fingers fidgeting along the sleeves of her sweater, Julia barely shook her head. "I'm afraid I can't sit still. I need to move. I'd really rather go for a walk."

I didn't know her well enough to say if it really was a note of petulance I heard in her voice. "All right, we'll go out back, near the stream. It's going to get dark soon, though."

"I'll take care of the vegetables." Peter smiled and held out his hand to Julia. "I'm glad to meet you."

She hesitated, then gave him her hand, but she was backing toward the door at the same time. Peter let her go and touched my shoulder, his gaze measuring my feelings as I passed. "We'll be back before dark," I said softly. "I'll be all right."

I followed Julia down the grassy lawn to the cover of the trees and shrubs that bordered the stream below the pond. Even if he were standing on his front step and looking in our direction, Roy wouldn't see us, especially in the dusk; only the mosquitoes would bother us. We walked in silence, the fading light still bright enough so that we could pick our way along the edge of the stream, and again I felt like an observer watching a drama unfold on its way to a grand finale.

Julia and Roy were well suited in one thing at least: They could both play a situation for all its theatrical worth. My patience was slipping away. Surely, whatever she had to say could have waited until we'd both had a little more time to absorb the impact of our first meeting, as we'd agreed to do.

As we started down the incline toward the narrow path beside the stream, Julia began to speak.

"I came back to tell you what really happened. I drove nearly all the way home this afternoon, thinking about what I *didn't* say. I wanted to protect you, Sarah. I didn't want to take away the one parent you'd felt you had. Ruth wrote to me about how Roy told you I was evil and how he wouldn't even let anyone say my name. You must have hardened against me."

I was glad she couldn't see my face, glad she didn't stop to say that I must be hardened against her still.

"I'm not going to try to excuse myself. It couldn't have happened any other way, unless I'd never moved to Taconic Hills, or unless I'd never married Roy." She stopped walking, her feet sinking a little into the soft ground.

"We loved each other, Ed and I, but we didn't plan what happened. You have to believe that, Sarah. I went to the shed to look for a piece of driftwood I'd stored there. From a trip to the beach that I'd made when I was an art student. I wanted to use it in a painting. The color was lovely, soft and sun-bleached. Roy didn't want it cluttering up the house and I didn't want to get rid of it, so I left it in the shed.

"The day was so full of promise, the way it gets here in the early spring. The air was cool but with enough bright sun to warm the edges of your skin and remind you that summer would come again. You had gone off with Roy on one of his tractor jobs. I walked up the road, singing to myself, trying to stay out of the shadows when I passed the pine trees. I was on my way to the shed, almost there, when I heard a car behind me.

"I turned to look. As soon as I saw the car and recognized that black sedan, I knew in my heart what would follow. I almost ran off into the woods to keep it from happening, but the pull was too great.

"Just thinking about him made my heart pound and my skin catch fire, and seeing him was worse. He never wore a clerical collar, of course, just ordinary street clothes. He was on his way to see to Mrs. Shook, she was old even then. I could practically feel his eyes the second he realized it was me. He pulled up and drove slow, following right alongside me."

I shivered with a chill that started at my wet feet. We were almost at the thicket of berry canes that dipped into the stream. We'd either have to stop there or go around them, and I wished she would get on with her story. My bare arms were cold; I slapped at a mosquito. Julia was lost in some moment in the past that she had decided not to share with me. She cleared her throat and went on.

"As soon as he got out of the car, I felt . . . It was as though all those years of being apart had built up this powerful need, and now there was no way to stop us from coming together. He came to me and literally swept me up into his arms and carried me into the shed. Neither of us said a word. We couldn't talk. It was a terrible and wonderful thing, for both of us. But it surely was unstoppable.

"We undressed each other as we kissed."

"Wait," I said, my voice returning to me on a wave of aversion. "Please. I don't want to hear this." I glanced at her downturned face, at the reflection of the water on her forehead where the sun angled the light up to strike her face.

"It's hard to talk about that day without giving you some sense of the strength of the feelings that were involved. It's all connected. Like a dream that won't fade after you wake up, it's stayed with me, every bit of it, for all these years."

"Please understand. I'm trying to listen as an adult, but part of me is still that child. Please . . ."

She stooped to examine a lone, pink muskmallow bloom before she resumed her story. "Ed had pulled his car up by the pines, beyond the shed, so that's why Roy didn't see it. We didn't hear you and Roy. It was the breeze and the sudden light that we felt. There we were, naked, behind that wall. I almost couldn't stand the tension, almost screamed right then. But Ed covered my mouth with his hand and we cowered in the dark, praying that you would go away as quickly as you had come. For some time, it was like the world had stopped.

"Then you jumped down from the boards Roy had set you on. I heard your little footsteps on the hard dirt floor and then your scream. That scream woke me out of my fear and I reached for my clothes. Ed did, too, but before we could put them on, there was Roy, standing in the light from the doorway. His face was contorted, purple and knotted with anger.

"He didn't say a word. Instead, a bellow came out of him, like an animal that's been stuck. It seemed to go on forever and get louder and wilder and it blinded me. I still don't understand how that happened, but I literally couldn't see because of that howl of rage that came from Roy Stanton's throat."

I looked down and saw that my hand was again clamped onto the scar on my arm. *Why didn't you see that I was bleeding? Why didn't you take care of me?* I stopped walking and sat on a grassy knob on the bank above the stream. Ruffles of green watercress bent in the forward rush of the water.

Julia sat down beside me. "There was a scuffle, Sarah—a jar of turpentine got knocked over, I remember, and I had this absurd thought we'd all burn up in a terrible explosion. You know how Roy in his anger grabbed the pitchfork and stuck Edward Fitzhugh's naked chest until he bled. I screamed. Roy threw Ed's clothes out the door and told him to get out.

"Ed went. He was hurt and Roy was bigger, stronger, madder, and quite drunk. Ed just left us alone with Roy, something I've never been able to understand. Roy's anger wasn't used up yet. He took that same pitchfork—"

A sob snagged her words as they spilled out. She trembled, knelt, and cupped her hand and splashed water onto her face. Her face was glistening now, with tears and with stream water. I didn't anticipate what was coming next; I was too involved in the sound of helplessness in her voice and how she'd been waiting to be rescued by a man who had shattered her naive expectations that he'd always protect her. I'm grateful, now that I do know what happened that afternoon in the shed, that for all of my childhood and for all the years until she spoke her next words, I had blocked the memory so terribly, so completely from my mind.

"Roy took the pitchfork and held it to your throat, Sarah. He said if I didn't leave Taconic Hills right then, he'd kill you. And if I ever came back, he'd finish what he started, with Ed Fitzhugh and with you, to punish me for ruining his life. His anger made him powerful, and the alcohol made him crazy. I was terrified he would hurt you."

I couldn't swallow, couldn't think. Light spun through the trees, water rushed beneath my feet, nothing mattered, everything did.

My father.

Willing to sacrifice me.

What proof was there to verify what she was saying? This was the heart of my past. This was why she left—or the excuse she'd used to justify running away. This explained the secrecy surrounding her departure.

I waited, heedless of Julia, until I trusted my own voice. "He's never hurt me," I said, silently discounting the afternoon he'd discovered me in his attic.

Her face was drawn into lines of sadness and confusion. "You have to understand, Sarah, I tried to explain before. I was so young, confused, and without anyone in the way of family or real friends to turn to. I was always the outsider here. As soon as I walked up to some group, in school or later in the market or in church, conversation stopped. Years—it was like that for years."

She spoke as though she were hypnotized, in a dream, and I listened.

"He followed me back to the house, and stood over me while I packed my suitcase. You were sleeping in your room, tired from the stress of it all, your arm was bandaged and he'd given you an aspirin. He made me pack and gave me the registration to the car and told me to drive and to never come back. He swore he'd kill you if I did."

She stopped for a breath; I breathed, too.

"What I did was drive right to Ruth and Walter's, the only people I could think of with the ability to help me. Or rather, help you. She told me to go to my parents' on Staten Island and she'd talk to the others, Walter and Jeanie and Clayton Boice, and Dan Lambert, and then she'd call me the next day. She promised me that they'd make sure you were all right. I didn't see any other choice, Sarah.

Ruth—I knew she'd be one of the keys to understanding Julia's story.

"I couldn't chance Roy's rage. I had to do what they told me. I didn't sleep at all that night. Walked around that tiny apartment listening to the dark, to the sirens, police cars or ambulances or fire engines, I couldn't tell, just wishing I could scream that loud."

My hands curled into tight fists; my anger sent a ratcheting shudder through my body.

"When they called, Ruth told me their decision. She said they didn't believe me, that Roy had denied threatening you, and they believed *him*. I'm telling you now because this isn't over. I can see in your face, you're going to ask Ruth or even Roy. And they're going to say that I was making it up, and I gave up and left in a selfish panic. That Roy didn't threaten you. But he did. I swear.

"They were my only hope, and when she told me the courts would never give an adulterous woman custody of a child, I knew Roy had won. Oh, he had to stop drinking forever, and he had to have a housekeeper of their choosing to live in the house, to raise you and keep an eye on things, but he had won. Ed Fitzhugh had to tell his wife, and if she forgave him, no one would mention the incident ever again."

Unbelievable: the word kept echoing in my mind. Unbelievable that this self-appointed town tribunal had such power. Unbelievable that she gave it to them. And especially unbelievable that they decided that permanent exile, from the town and from her own child, was proper punishment for one afternoon of Julia's unconsummated adultery.

Such neat justice. They had thought of everything. Everything except how their tidy arrangement would affect me. But it was over now. My father—I doubted I could face him for a while, but she was right: I would need to hear it again, from him.

She stood up and looked down at me, and started talking before I had the chance to gather my words. "I think I know how hard this is for you. I can imagine and it tears me up inside. I never wanted you to find out. I was willing to take the blame, to let you think it was my fault, that leaving Taconic Hills was a selfish thing to do. That was fine as long as you weren't asking about the past. But I didn't want you to hear everyone else's version but mine. As soon as you called, I knew I had to come see you, and I'm glad I did. I'll call you tomorrow near dinner time and we can decide what's next then. I have to go back to Pearl River now, and let you live with this for a while."

Twenty-six

Julia's black Ford rolled down Vixen Hill Road, a little cloud of dust chasing after her as though it could call her back. The last, sad edge of the sun dropped behind the western hills as a hawk swooped down over the meadow, a raptor materializing from the twilight haze. I stood in the middle of the road until both the car and the hawk disappeared, feeling as though the things I had seen and heard were important only because of the shadow they'd cast.

When I went back inside, Peter was in the kitchen, a forkful of zucchini and peppers partway to his open mouth. He shook the vegetables back into the pan and set the fork on a plate.

"No denying *that* genetic connection," he said. "Did you have a good talk? Are you glad you got in touch with her?"

Glad: that sounded like such a simple emotion. "She's going to call me tomorrow so we can make another appointment. She gave me her version of that day. I don't know what to believe."

"Tell me," he said, closing the distance between us in three steps and wrapping his arms around me, "tell me everything. But let's do it inside, while we eat. I'm hungry."

The thought of food repelled me. "I can't eat. You go ahead, though."

He shook his head. "If you can live with my stomach rumbling, I can survive a while longer without food. Want to come inside?"

I nodded, and we walked hand in hand to the dark bedroom. He folded the spread, and we leaned against the headboard, pillows stuffed behind our backs, our legs stretched in front of us and our shoulders touching.

As I repeated Julia's story I relaxed bit by bit, as though I were coming back into my body with every word. Peter said nothing for a long time. I let myself drift without direction, lulled into a comforting blankness by the song of the whippoorwill outside.

Then Peter started to speak; his voice was low and full of wonder, as though he'd rediscovered some forgotten sorcery and was amazed by it all over again. "The council of elders. I don't know how they managed it. They appointed themselves in charge of settling disputes, and the town just accepted them. It was a little bit of noblesse oblige, left over from the days of feudalism or something. My mother once told me that those three families had been solving problems, as she put it, for years."

The council.

. . . *no matter what the Council says.*

The Council finds him to be a thief.

. . . *Stefan and the Council have not said a word about K.*

For years, indeed.

He leaned back, his eyes fixed in the distance. "She said it was our obligation to serve our generation that way. Me and Deeny. I laughed at her. I couldn't believe she was serious. I was their only child, she told me, and I was endangering the moral foundations of Taconic Hills by refusing. Deeny, too. 'The Lamberts and the Boices and the Hovings have a responsibility to this town,' she said. We used to talk about it, on the school bus our senior year of high school. I wonder if someone else stepped in, or if the system has died a natural death. Canceled due to lack of enlightened self-interest or something like that."

The deluded grandeur of the so-called council was stunning. They had made the decision that sent Julia away twenty-five years ago, as their predecessors had decided that Klaudia Weigelt, too, should be exiled. They had probably advised Edward Fitzhugh's mother to pay Julia's way to art school. It would be some comfort to know that they had no power, that no one sought their advice now.

"The bicentennial," I said aloud.

Peter looked at me quizzically. "What did you say?"

"I wonder if all these parallels to the bicentennial play have anything to do with the council. The members of the council had the idea to reenact the story of the Schillers. What do you think it all means, Peter? How do we find out?"

"We ask. They got their power because people refused to confront them, because everyone just went along, me included. My mother and father—they're the key figures. That makes me really uneasy. But if we go sneaking around to find out what we want to know, we're no better than they are." Shadows filled our bedroom. Outside, one branch of the oak tree rubbed against another, the creaking like a low moan of something alive and in pain.

I was glad for the darkness, glad for Peter's warmth beside me. *He* had chosen, and it had been me. Only a very tiny voice whispered that I mustn't give myself up completely to that trust. We made no specific plan. By mutual and unspoken consent, we gave ourselves and each other a little time to be, to think.

By the next morning, the need to act had grown to a physical pressure in me. I couldn't sit at home and wait for Julia to call, wouldn't twiddle my thumbs until a member of the council came knocking on my door so that I could expose them and name their secret. And I wasn't ready yet to knock on *their* doors. While I was deciding what to do next I would make my rounds, see whether my hives were faring well in this benign season of harvest, and still return home in time to receive Julia's call.

I loaded my hive tool and bee suit into the truck, got the smoker refilled with twine, and spent the morning pulling frames heavy with glistening honey from the Hillsdale hives, all the while filled with thoughts of Julia, of how she started her day, what she said to her children, whether she thought about me when she got them breakfast, and what she hoped and feared from our new connection. The morning held a hint of the coming of autumn; the colors were definitely moving toward gold, as though the leaves were trying to make up for the diminishing sunlight of each new day.

My bees were happy, busy, smug with satisfaction that they'd provided for their winter needs. The demands of the harvest were slowing down; Maeterlinck called their urgency "the fatal ecstasy of work," and that, too, was diminishing. Bees, like people, experience a slow decline into thoughtfulness and more tempered activity as the arc of the sun and the daylight hours grow shorter.

I had nearly finished my morning rounds when I realized that I'd run out of twine for my smoker. If I stopped at the post office, I could grab my mail, pick up a sandwich at the general store, and then head to the hardware store in Copake. I'd be on my way to the Craryville hives without falling behind. I hauled the last honey-filled frame to the truck and sat for a minute in the cab, taking in the scene before me.

The hills fell away to the west in a series of paler and paler rises. The colors of summer had faded, but the sweet, flowery perfumes were giving way to the sharper, more pungent spicy autumn smells I loved.

I wondered if Julia loved the smells of goldenrod and of damp piles of fallen leaves, as I did.

If Julia was telling the truth, then Roy had lived with the knowledge of his threats all these years, ready to make good on them at any time. In his dark heart, he would relive that day every time he saw me, unless he had the same extraordinary power of forgetting that I had—or unless the things Julia described had never happened.

Part of me feared that his bitterness and hate had been fanned to such a steady fire, like the eternal flame marking the grave of a national hero, that he would carry out his old threat without hesitation, as though no time at all had passed since his discovery of Julia and Fitzhugh. The rest of me scoffed at the idea.

I was sorting all this out as I approached the post office in Taconic Hills. The sun was just reaching its peak and the town hummed with activity—summer people at the general store, farmers picking up their mail, tourists passing through and going out of their way to stop at the antique store, where they'd spend as much for an old glass bottle as they would if they'd bought it from a midtown Manhattan decorator.

I jumped down from my truck and ran up the steps to the post office, anticipating with pleasure Jeanie's smile and her greeting, until I reminded myself of her role in the council. Through the screen door, I heard Dan Lambert's voice, his deep bass ringing out into the midday bustle.

"Didn't look a bit different. I only got a glimpse of her face, but it was enough for me to see that much."

I pulled the door open and stepped inside, and Jeanie's mouth dropped open. Dan spun around, his eyebrows lifting in surprise. After an awkward moment when neither of them looked at me, Dan got his voice back. "Hi there," he boomed. "How's the bees these days?"

"Busy. Fine," I said, wondering whether they really were talking about Julia. It wasn't impossible that Dan had been standing on the post office porch when she drove by yesterday. He might have recognized a woman he hadn't seen for twenty-five years, especially if she were a featured character in the town mythology, as Julia seemed to be.

Maybe she had stopped to talk to someone. Perhaps an observer had been watching me, waiting for a chance to make it appear as though Emily Schiller's fate was playing out again in my life, and had spotted Julia.

I couldn't second-guess the entire town of Taconic Hills. If they were talking about me and about Julia, I'd find out soon enough, as I had when the fire and Clayton's murder were the main topics of local gossip.

"Anything for me today?" I asked Jeanie.

Her eyes avoided mine as she reached into the box and handed over a stack of envelopes, a couple of magazines, and a sample of a new shampoo. I tossed the sample into the trash and waved, smiling as though I had reason to smile. "See you later," I said over my shoulder. I let the screen door slam behind me, and nearly ran into Ben Yarnell.

"Hey, Sweets. I haven't seen you in ages. How goes the honey harvest?" He smiled and shaded his eyes with his hands, the worried wrinkle in his forehead at odds with the jovial tone and the smile.

"Best year so far for honey. The play is starting to cut into my work time, though."

"Next weekend. Can you believe it? The play's next weekend. How did Labor Day sneak up on us so fast? Seems like it was just February and this whole pageant idea was a twinkle in Ruth's eye."

"Feels like it's been years to me." Had it only been six months? So much had changed—and so much was still unresolved. Would Emily Schiller fade from my life, getting dimmer and less important after the pageant? "See you Thursday. God, I'm glad that's the last rehearsal." I started down the porch steps, but he hooked his arm through mine as I walked past.

"I want to warn you. The Dembowski mess has died down but a new story's making the rounds. Everyone's saying that your mother's back and that something is brewing. Is that right?"

Then Dan Lambert *was* talking about Julia.

The trees have eyes and the stones have ears in this town, it's true. Yesterday I'd been certain that Julia's trip to Vixen Hill had gone unnoticed. If Ben was right and everyone was talking about her visit, then word surely had reached Roy by now.

"Who's everyone, Ben?" Names would make it real, and I'd have a chance to unravel the tangle of lies and find out where the talk had started, although I wasn't sure why that mattered to me.

"Reporters never tell their sources, you know that." He squeezed my arm. "I see this is upsetting you and I wish I could make it better. I've heard about it from maybe eight or ten people, including Marge Hoysradt, Ike Kronenburg, and Deeny Lambert. I don't know, it's what everyone is talking about. This isn't as vicious as the Dembowski whispering campaign about the fire, Sweets, but it's going to be a hard one for you to ignore, so I wanted you to be prepared. I gotta go." He leaned down and kissed my cheek, a warm, tender brush of his lips that startled me, and he walked briskly to the door and then inside.

The hardware store in Copake suddenly seemed like an unnecessary trial. I would have to talk to Marge Hoysradt there; maybe I'd run into someone else who would look at me and think they knew secrets. I wouldn't participate in the charade of everyone pretending that we weren't keeping things from each other. They wouldn't whisper to me, as they had to Ben. Instead, they'd look at me with that mixture of curiosity and pity and never say a word, and I wouldn't put up with that.

I was worn out from trying to understand the past. I was tired of walking on constantly shifting ground into an unknown future. And I was unwilling to let Ruth believe that I didn't know how her council's decrees had affected me. Before I could talk myself out of it, I crossed the road to the general-store pay phone, fished two dimes out of my pocket, and called my mother-in-law.

She agreed to see me at four o'clock. I didn't explain why I was requesting this audience. And she didn't ask, but I was sure she assumed that Julia would be the main topic of our conversation.

Twenty-seven

At precisely four, I parked my truck under the biggest maple tree at the edge of the Hoving drive, hoping for a bit of shade from the dappled leaves so that the cab wouldn't be like an oven when I left. I almost didn't see Walter, who called out and waved as he dragged an old school desk into the barn. He kept his tools there, and had turned the outbuilding into an orderly workshop for all manner of projects. His kind face eased some of my inner churning and I made my way up the flagstone path a little calmer, a little more prepared for my meeting with Ruth.

She ushered me into the living room, dark and shuttered against the afternoon sun, and sat down on a Queen Anne chair, her hands resting primly on the curved arms. The cuffs of her blouse, white and crisp, lay on the knobby mounds of her wrists. I sat on the edge of the other chair beside the fireplace, leaning forward as though some part of me was ready to run from the confines of the cool, dim room at the slightest provocation.

"I saw Julia yesterday," I said. "She told me that you and the others had banished her. That she went away because you told her she must. Is that true? *You* decided that my mother had to give me up and go away? Who gave you the right to do such a thing?" I made myself stop; without conscious control, I might have gone on until I'd cataloged every outrageous, manipulative, self-aggrandizing bit of autocratic behavior she'd displayed in my lifetime of knowing her. That would feel good, but it wouldn't help achieve my goal of hearing her explanation, and making sure she understood the effects the council had on my life.

"Now, Sarah, you must understand. The council was always consulted about important matters. No one talked about it because it had no, well, legal power, only a moral imperative." Her chin lifted, a small defiant gesture that gave me a shiver of satisfaction—she was on her guard, posturing, justifying her own indefensible behavior.

"Since no one spoke to *me* about it, I'm sure you can understand my surprise when I found about how you changed my life. It still amazes me to think my mother's personal life became your business. That's more shocking to me than her adultery." The absence of fear had taken away some of the venom and none of my conviction. "Don't you see how patronizing it is to believe that you'd be better at resolving the problems of ordinary people than they are? Even *enlightened* despots don't make very good teachers."

From the half smile on her face, it was clear that her worldview wouldn't change based on anything I might say, at least not in the next half hour. What made it more bearable was the knowledge that Peter and Deeny, the next generation, had declined to keep the system alive.

"You and I may not see eye to eye on everything, Sarah," Ruth said, "but I'm not sorry about what I did that day. I suppose there's still some doubt about what really happened in the shed. *Somebody* had to decide what to do and it fell to us and we'll have to live with it. That's the burden of the system."

I could only shake my head at her utter presumption. How noble to assume such a distasteful task—that must be how they all thought of their roles in this whole affair. I wanted to stamp my feet in frustration and hurl her precious antique glass to the floor. "It's really just a kind of grandiose madness to think you can tell people how to live their lives."

"If only I were sure of the truth," she said finally, after long seconds had passed. "My first thought, when Julia came to us, was that she'd made up the story about Roy threatening you."

She paused, no doubt for effect, and it worked. My heart raced, and my palms were damp with sweat.

"Roy said he couldn't remember. He told us flat out that he didn't remember using the pitchfork on Ed Fitzhugh and didn't have any recollection of threatening you. Now, the one, we do know because Ed said it happened. But the other . . ." She stared at her hands. "Julia's word was all we had. And I thought she might be making up the story to seal the case against Roy. But it worked the opposite way, you see. Because I wasn't sure, because I couldn't be certain that she wasn't lying to get back at Roy. I had to give him the benefit. I told the others her story, but I made sure they understood my reservations."

Her decision twenty-five years ago had been based more on her loyalty to a native son than it had on the truth, and she was sticking to her choice. She didn't even acknowledge that the consequences of her bias had reverberated through several lives all these years.

"I want you to know, Ruth, that I mean to make sure this never happens again. I intend to expose your little group so that people can see it for what it is."

She smiled, an unattractive twist of her mouth. "My dear, you don't want to risk appearing outrageous, self-aggrandizing, or manipulative. Take care how you behave, Sarah."

She had always known exactly what to say to make me angry, but this time her words had no effect. If I had to, I'd search out others who had suffered from the supposed good offices of the council. That would come later.

I left her in her parlor, cool, convinced of her own rightness, alone among the bric-a-brac and the afternoon shadows. The air outside was clean, bracing, free of the cloying closeness of the house. I was about to climb into the truck and return to Vixen Hill when I heard Walter whistling "Greensleeves" from the barn. The sound drew me closer, a light clear piping that I could hardly believe came from a person burdened by the weight of the past.

The barn door was partway open, and the inside was cool and smelled of old hay, a sweetish grassy smell that made me want to lie down and sleep. The wide spaces between the old boards had filled with straw and seeds, ground by time into a fine, golden powder. Slats of light striped the concrete floor and fell across the old hay wagon, propped up with a stack of boards on one side where an old wire wheel used to be. Rusted old hoes and scythes and pitchforks hung on nails from every upright beam. Leather harnesses and strings of sleigh bells worn from years of rubbing against the sides of carriages, old ice skates, and an oak chest with brass hinges that resembled eagles were all lined up, Walter's projects waiting for attention.

He was bent over the desk, rubbing at the cast-iron scrollwork on the legs with a pad of steel wool. I almost turned around and walked away; this was his sanctuary, as the greenhouse was mine, and I was intruding on that. But I didn't leave. I was unwilling to be the good girl who respected the rules in a game designed to keep everyone but the rulemakers off balance.

"That's a wonderful desk," I said softly.

Startled, he jumped and then recovered quickly, peering up at me with a pleasant smile. "Not much rust on these legs. I'm glad life's going to get back to normal next week. Haven't had time to call my own since these rehearsals started."

He laid the steel wool on the floor and straightened slowly, his face in shadow until he took a step forward. When he did, the strain was apparent, circles under his eyes, his mouth held in tight. I wondered if his expression had anything to do with my situation, with Julia, with the bicentennial. The tension looked all wrong on him, surprising and unnatural.

"You didn't stop by to watch me work on this old desk," he said, brushing his hands against his pants. Tiny particles of metal glinted in the light as fibers of steel wool drifted down toward the floor.

"I want you to tell me about the day my mother left."

He nodded, revealing no surprise at my request. "You want to come up to the house and get something cool to drink?"

"No, but thanks. I'd rather talk here."

He smiled and patted a lopsided bale of hay. "You get the good seat," he said as he lowered himself onto another bale next to it.

I sat. Sharp, broken stalks of hay poked at my palms, but I ignored them. "I need to know why you sent my mother away."

The lines on his face were drawn deeper as the silence dragged on. Outside, in the west field, a tractor engine started up. The clatter of the chopper, cutting corn and firing it through the chute into the wagon, rattled through the unmoving air into the barn. Finally Walter spoke.

"When Ruth told us what had happened, we figured we had no other choice. The plan wasn't perfect, we knew that, but it was the best we could devise, better than anything else we could think of."

I clenched my fists. Even Walter didn't see how vile the council was.

"If we'd let Julia stay, Roy's anger would never die. It'd get blown up again every time he saw her. Someone was going to get hurt. We felt that would be a danger to you. We did the only thing we could."

"So you believed Julia told the truth about what happened in the shed?" My heart banged against my chest as I waited for his answer.

"I thought it might have been. I mean, according to Ruth, that wasn't the question. Ruth was the only one who actually heard Julia's story that day. The rest of us were at work when it happened. Ruth told us, explained how Roy claimed he couldn't remember. She was worried that maybe Julia was making up the part about Roy threatening you. So she could get our sympathy, you see."

She had been my mother's judge and jury, this woman whose goal it was to preserve the old Taconic Hills, to fight for a continuation of her privilege by staging a bicentennial pageant to bring the town together against an invasion of outsiders. Which was what Julia had been when she moved here, and what she remained through all the years she lived here. Perhaps her sponsorship of Catherine Delaney was Ruth's penance for what she'd done to my mother, but it wasn't enough.

I couldn't wait to get out of the barn, and away from the suffocating neatness of their world.

"I was afraid you wouldn't talk to me." Julia's voice sounded relieved.

What a strange opening, after we'd agreed to this phone call, to make another appointment to see each other. Before I could respond, she went on.

"Can I see you tomorrow? Don't worry, I don't have any new revelations, nothing like what I told you yesterday. It's just that there's so much catching up to do. I want to close the gap."

I was confused: was this a request or a demand? I held back, protective, cautious. "I'm not sure when I can get away. My hives need attention. I have about two more weeks of a really hectic schedule."

"I'll come there. Whenever you can see me. Even if it's only for an hour. I've dreamed about this for so long. Please, Sarah."

My mind whirled with reasons to say no, but I heard myself planning aloud a way to see her the next day. "I have to do some work in the morning at the hives I keep on the other side of Talley's pond. Why don't you meet me when I'm finished. At noon, at the top of Winchell Mountain Road. If you bring sandwiches, we can have a picnic lunch in the meadow."

"Perfect. I'll be there. Thank you, Sarah. You're giving me back a part of myself I'd thought I'd lost forever." And she hung up.

I pressed the heels of my hands against my eyes. I wanted her to understand that she was also giving me something she'd taken away from me. Maybe she meant that she needed me, as I did her, to be complete. And maybe she'd grow tired of me and discard me as she had all the other dreams that had become reality in her life.

Twenty-eight

The kitchen gleamed in the sharp afternoon sun. The new cabinets, replicas of the ones that had burned in the fire, sparkled with jeweled light, and all the counters and even the painted walls glinted brightly. Despite the enduring images of the fire, I finally felt safe in the house, able to sleep through an entire night without waking in a panic.

"If nothing else," Peter said as he knelt to grab the skillet from under the stove, "you've forced the council to think about what they've been doing. They might have found replacements to carry on their self-appointed work, but I doubt it. I believe their time has passed, and they can't help but admit it now."

"Hollow victory. What's the good of closing the barn door—"

"—after the horse is gone? It keeps the other horses in, doesn't it, and keeps the rats out." He smiled and pulled last night's uneaten dinner from the refrigerator. "Don't tell my mother I said that. I don't really blame her, you know. She thought she was doing right. It was a different time; she grew up believing different things."

I bit my lip against the desire to scream. Maybe I'd come to think that way after a while. I couldn't now.

"I have a confession to make," he said.

How strange that Peter chose to speak up now, when I was so vulnerable. His eyes were warm, though, and absent of secrets, and his face was open to my inspection. I raised my eyebrows in invitation for him to continue.

"I tried it once. Deeny and I talked and talked about it, and finally concluded that maybe we couldn't decide until we'd given it a try, you know, so that we could see how it really worked. We were twenty, twenty-one. It was the year you left for college, so I guess I was twenty."

He was talking in circles and I couldn't figure out the sense of his words. They flew around my head like moths attracted to a light in the darkness; as soon as one landed, it sizzled into oblivion. Instead of trying to frame a question, I waited for him to go on.

"We hated it. It just didn't feel right, sitting in judgment on one of our own. Deeny and I agreed that we couldn't do it, but at least we proved it to ourselves by trying. We both agreed, and that was that. We let it go."

He sat unmoving in the gathering dusk. Outside, a dog yapped a cheerful greeting; my stomach twisted at the thought of Prince. My head swam with the remembered sight of him. Three holes in his chest. Like the pitchfork wound my father had made in the skin of Edward Fitzhugh. One more thing I'd denied, had pushed beyond memory so I could go on with my life. Another secret I'd have to name aloud before I could go on.

"Well. You haven't said anything." Peter poured a stream of olive oil into the skillet and turned the gas on low.

"I'm glad you decided the way you did," I said finally. "Having that kind of power—it's not right."

He nodded. "The thing is, the way it turned out, Ben's probably better off for the fact that we left him alone to work things out on his own."

I was confused all over again. "Ben?"

"I don't guess the town would have trusted him to operate its only newspaper if he hadn't figured out by himself that he had to make restoration."

"Peter, you're talking in circles. What in the world do you mean?"

"I never did tell anyone. Deeny must not have, either. Come to think of it, only a few people ever knew." He seemed to be deciding whether it was right to talk about the incident, all these years later. "Oh, hell, it's so long ago. Ben broke into Mr. Inglis's house one night and stole some things. Someone saw the stuff in Ben's room and told Ruth, and Ruth told me and Deeny that we should take care of the situation, and that if we didn't take some action within two days, she would."

The thought of Ben breaking into someone's house and stealing things was beyond me. He liked adventure but his tastes didn't run to crime, unless cynicism was against the law in those days. He must have been wrongly accused, or set up by someone who wanted to make him appear to be a troublemaker. "What happened?" I demanded.

"The stuff was all returned that night. Must have happened while Deeny and I were deciding we wanted no part of enforcing some high-minded moral code for the so-called benefit of our family and friends. Anyway, that was the end of it. Ruth might even have thought Deeny and I had done something to make Ben put the butterflies back."

"*Butterflies?*" I gasped. I remembered Ben's declaration at the clambake; it felt as though it had been made decades ago, and to someone else. "What do you mean?"

Peter's forehead creased into a frown. "Butterflies. You know. Caterpillars, cocoons, butterflies. He'd stolen Mr. Inglis's butterfly collection. All these glass display boxes, maybe six of them, with ten, twelve butterflies each. All specimens that were netted within fifty miles of Taconic Hills. Whatever Ben wanted those things for I never could figure out. But he put them back. At least, we assumed he was the one who returned them, before anyone could do anything about it. Deeny and I decided that if we had taken some kind of action, it wouldn't have been as good as Ben doing it on his own. Perfect ending, right?"

A small puddle of condensation had formed around the bowl of vegetables on the counter. I emptied the contents into the pan and wiped at the puddle with a towel, wondering what it meant that Ben had stolen a butterfly collection, marveling that actions, even the absence of actions, might set into motion events that would play out in some distant future. Ben, the playwright who had admitted he'd rewritten history for the sake of good theater. Perhaps he'd had something else in mind as well . . . something that would allow a replay of Stefan's hunting accident to look like just another parallel to the events in the Schiller story.

My jars of caterpillars. My father's storing away a first-aid kit in the shed. So many acts undertaken in innocence, the seeds of present dilemmas sown in an unsuspecting past.

Peter's hand on my arm startled me from my reverie. "Thinking about the council?" he asked.

I shook my head. "Julia."

"You made an appointment to see her?"

"Tomorrow. At noon, at the top of Winchell Mountain Road. She's going to bring lunch. I don't know what I want anymore, or who I can trust. Only, I'm sure I have to see her again."

"Have you spoken to your father?" His frown wrinkled his forehead. "Are you going to do that before you see her again?"

"I've had years with him, and two hours with her, and right now I don't feel really attached to either of them. You know that odd sensation of being able to look at yourself and seeing this person doing something, watching this other person from the outside. That's kind of how I feel now."

"Sometimes," Peter said, "a little detachment can help you see clearly."

"Maybe you're right. I wonder if I can get a straight answer from my father about what he did that day in the shed. Maybe, after all these years, I'm the only one who can find out."

The risk was that I'd end up with a truth I didn't like, and I'd want both my parents out of my life, but I had to take that chance. I pulled back the curtain, peering in the direction of my father's house. His truck sat beside the pine tree. I looked again past the leafy filter of the hedge that bordered his lawn, and a light winked on in my father's workroom.

"I'm going over there." I stepped into the old penny loafers I kept beside the back door and flew into the cool evening and across the road. As I waited for my father to answer my knock, I looked over my shoulder at Vixen Hill Lodge, once more whole. Peter's dark head filled the kitchen window; when he saw me looking at him, he dropped the curtain and disappeared.

At the same time, Dad's front door opened.

"I been wondering when you were going to come over." My father held a whittling knife in one hand and a block of pale pine in the other. "Come inside."

As soon as the front door closed behind me, I felt the choking sensation of being trapped, as though something in the house itself was determined to keep me here. I followed him into the workroom, hardly thinking a coherent thought, barely even breathing.

"You saw her. Everyone knows it. Every busybody in the county's talking about how she came back. What'd she tell you, Sarah? What'd you come here to find out?"

My anger broke loose, and I felt no desire to dam it. It had been growing inside me, pressing on my lungs and my heart as it gained mass, and now it went flying out of me with each word I spoke.

"So much of my life, I've put a lot of energy into forgetting. I thought I was putting out of my mind that my mother walked out when I was just a child. I've been told things lately that make me think I've really been working to forget other things, too. That you were capable of murderous rage. That you threatened me, to hurt Julia for hurting you.

"All I want from you is one thing, only one and then nothing more. I want the truth. I've tried to remember. You can't believe how many times lately I tried to trick myself into recalling that afternoon, and there are pieces, small parts of the thing, that I can tell you about. But there's a big piece completely gone. No matter what I do, I can't remember what happened after you sent Fitzhugh away. It's blank.

"So I want to know if you really did hold a pitchfork to my throat. I want to know if you really did tell Julia that you'd kill me unless she went away. I want to know if you thought about that every time you saw me, when I was five and six and seven years old, when I was twelve and fourteen and twenty. I have to know. Tell me, Dad. Tell me now."

By the time I finished, I felt calm, clear, emptied. My father's face had drained of color as I spoke and now he was chalk white and motionless. His eyes, flat and clouded, didn't blink; his tongue darted to the corner of his mouth and then flicked back inside. His Adam's apple worked up and down, as though he were talking to himself without making any sound.

Finally, he shook his head. "I would have done just about anything to make her feel pain. But that . . . I don't know, Sarah. That's what she said I did. I tried and tried to come up with an answer, when you spoke to me in the garage, but I don't know. If I had to take an oath, the best I could do is say it might be. I might have done that."

I nodded, rose, and walked away from him.

September

A hive that does not accept a new queen will soon show their displeasure by balling, or converging in a round, angry mass and surrounding her very closely until she suffocates and dies.
  —*Everywoman's Guide to Beekeeping,* Revised Edition

Twenty-nine

There was no moon, and the deep quiet wrapped itself around me and suspended me in a void. I glanced at the clock for what felt like the hundredth time. Twenty to four. I had lain awake for three hours; I'd surely continue to toss and make noise and disturb Peter if I stayed in bed. Leaving the comfort of Peter's warm, peaceful body was the only alternative to waking him with my restlessness. Reluctantly, I got out of bed, pulled on a light cotton robe, and tiptoed into the kitchen. In the dark, I groped my way to one of the chairs by the window and sat down, staring in the direction of the pond without seeing anything.

After a while, I heard an animal worrying the leaves of the lilac bush beside the window, and a frog harrumphing his annoyance at some intruder. But those noises, momentarily distracting, weren't compelling enough to stop the tumble of my confused thoughts as I tried to decide what to do—about the coming production of the bicentennial, about my fears concerning Peter and Catherine and my anger at the council, and most particularly about my noon appointment with Julia.

I heated some milk, poured a teaspoon of honey into the mug, and took it inside to the living room. In my mind, I went over my mother's words, my father's voice, the way her hands moved, the twitch in his cheek muscle. I sipped from the steaming mug, determined to figure out who I believed, testing first one choice and then the other. Only gradually, sometime later, did I become aware of Peter, a little wild-eyed, standing over me.

"Sarah. The bed was cold and you were gone." He sat down on the couch and took the mug from my hand.

I had fallen asleep clutching it. I struggled to come back to full consciousness from the haze of images that hovered near my head, like butterflies in dappled sunlight.

Butterflies. Ben Yarnell had stolen butterflies. Was Ben responsible for the parallels?

"Sarah." Peter's voice was more urgent now. "Are you all right?"

I nodded, unable to get my mouth working to form words. I needed to brush my teeth, take a shower, have coffee. I needed to decide.

"I'll start the coffee." He leaned over and stretched his long arms down to nearly touch his toes; his back rippled and he looked like a drawing from an anatomy book. I reached up and ran my hand along the muscle on the ridge of his shoulder.

Suddenly my body burned with the need to have him touch me, and to touch him. I longed to feel his mouth on mine. I wanted him to fill me, and I didn't want to wait until dark. I reached for his belt. Peter looked startled, and he pulled away.

"Please, Peter. We'll have coffee later."

He stared at me questioningly and then he bent to me. I was counting on his warmth to help me feel real and strong, so that I could dispel the sense that I was about to split apart into thin, frayed shreds, like a child's balloon pricked by a pin.

And it worked.

At least for a while.

As we lay, our limbs sweaty and tangled on the scratchy Indian blanket, my anxiety returned, more powerful than before. Impatient with myself, I showered quickly, swallowed toast and coffee without tasting anything, and then went outside.

My father's truck was still in his driveway and the light was on in his kitchen. If I squinted, I could see his shape, smaller than in my memory, hunched and sad, as he puttered about from stove to sink, cleaning up after his breakfast. Without waiting to say good-bye to Peter, I jumped into my truck and started on my rounds.

I fought an impulse to drive to Catherine Delaney's. I longed to know what someone who didn't have all her life invested in the people and the places of Columbia County thought about the two-hundred-year-old council and how it controlled Taconic Hills. That system had touched my life with its extended reach; I was surely less than objective about it. But she might be the very person I needed most to avoid. Since Emily had been responsible for Klaudia's departure, might I not end up being the instrument of Catherine's leaving Taconic Hills? I shuddered; no use making the words clean and pretty anymore. One interpretation of her letters was that Emily had murdered Klaudia. That possibility demanded that I stay far away from Catherine, until I knew what all the parallels meant. I couldn't let myself be lured into that kind of reenactment.

Keep to my ordinary schedule, that's what I had to do. Whether I would break it and go to Winchell Mountain later in the morning, I'd know in a couple of hours. Meanwhile, the way to keep the time from oozing like thick honey was to work.

I drove directly to Talley's pond. The day was cloudy and cool, the kind of bee weather that would cause them to be agitated and temperamental, but the hive would be busy with the goldenrod coming in and the asters and that might make them more amenable to my presence.

I parked at the turnout and started for the bridge. The water was green and turgid, swollen by the rains and dirty with an upwelling of mud, rushing over the spillway as though it were in a hurry to cleanse itself. Halfway across the bridge, I stopped. An erratic procession of bees, hind legs heavy with pollen, made the return flight to the hive oblivious to the disruptive scattering of scouts going in the other direction.

The opposing stream of bees were engaged in a struggle for the right of way. The established hives hadn't yet incorporated the two new hives I'd moved to the site a few months ago. In their complex system of communication and distribution of territory, the two groups were still rivals. Between the weather and the hive conflicts, this wouldn't be a straightforward job of taking full frames and replacing them with new ones.

The bees were guarding their established claims, as Emily had protected her claim on Stefan. She had set her sights on him, had done what was necessary to make sure that nothing—not her fiancé, John, or her rival, Klaudia—stood in her way, much as Ruth, with the help of the council, went about creating a world that conformed to her ideas.

Emily and Ruth, both so busy controlling the outcome of complicated situations in their lives. I was tired of it.

Actually, another comparison to Emily—Alicia Fitzhugh, whose marriage had been so threatened in the battle for the man she and Julia coveted—worked, too. Alicia Fitzhugh: her vacant eyes had pursued me at Dad's garage when we worked on the float. When I came up to talk to Jeanie at the clambake, Alicia had been distressed, skittish. And she had called me Julia, all those months ago, at her husband's funeral, and had started me on my search for my mother.

Whether or not Catherine knew about Julia and Alicia and Ed, she was aware of the Schiller-Weigelt triangle; perhaps she'd taken protective measures, to break the pattern. I'd never hidden my feeling that she was a potential threat to my marriage. To keep me off balance, to sap my strength, she might have set up these bizarre events as precedents so that everyone would be ready to believe that any disaster that might befall me was a consequence of the mysterious power of the past reaching out to Taconic Hills and recreating centuries-old events.

I had to give her credit for resourcefulness. Fresh from New York City, Catherine had to learn a lot of new skills—how to sabotage the milk tank and the cannon—unless she had someone helping her, someone who was familiar with farm equipment, and with the traditions of Taconic Hills. Perhaps she was working in concert with Ruth . . . or Peter.

My mind whirled with confusion.

Two bees clasped together in a death spiral in front of me. Their erratic flight pattern set the hairs on my arms in motion and warned me to be careful. Even smoke might not calm these irritable creatures. And then I realized just how preoccupied I'd been this morning. All my equipment—my hive tool, my smoker, the empty frames —were still on the screened porch at home.

In my distracted state, I'd be susceptible to errors that might further anger the already-disturbed bees. I closed my eyes and felt for my calmness, but was instead greeted with an internal buzzing, as though I were the hive and some large, ungainly animal had stuck its fist through the wooden cover and reached down to pull up a clawful of honey.

I ducked as a bee flew at my face, then pivoted and marched to my truck.

As I drove back to Vixen Hill Road, I watched the clouds gather, darker in the west and heavy, as though someone were pulling a curtain across the sky. End of act three, as Catherine might say, and the velvet curtain descends.

I parked in the empty driveway. Peter's van and Dad's truck were both gone. Glad for the time alone, I leaned back against the oak tree and stretched out my legs. Brown decay curled toward the center of some of the leaves; the change was beginning, the descent toward the long dark of winter.

Other things were dying, along with summer's richness.

The old order of my life, for one thing, the notion that Julia was the one person responsible for the pain and the deficiencies of my growing up. I entertained scenarios, considered how my childhood might have been different, wondered which parts I really did believe of the tales Julia and Roy and Ruth and the others had told.

Time wove fantasies for me, but I jerked upright with a start as a splat of rain hit my face. Two more fat drops plopped onto my skin. Then nothing. It would be like this all day, judging from the look of a sky too heavy to stay dry but not yet ready to let go and rain properly.

All at once, the hand that had tried all through my long and restless night and the distracted haze of my morning to wring tears from my heart simply let go. The sensation was like sliding into a warm bath after a hard day of physical work, soothing and right and totally enveloping.

I would go to meet Julia at the crest of Winchell Mountain.

I didn't care what really had happened in the shed. An event had occurred, twenty-five years earlier, and decisions had been made. Surely my life had been changed irrevocably that day. But I couldn't take it back. I couldn't make time stop and then rerun the reel more to my liking, and neither could any of the other participants.

My father had proven himself to be a flawed but caring parent. My mother was trying to make up for lost time. Peter was with me. The rest I didn't care about. Yes, I would go see Julia—and if I left now, I'd just make it by noon. It might not even work out that we could grow into a relationship that would satisfy either of us. But at least I'd be able to say I had found my peace.

The newly built wing of Vixen Hill Lodge stood proud and peaceful as a sliver of sun cut through the thick clouds. I loaded my equipment into the back of my truck, filled with a rush of gratitude that we'd been able to recover so quickly from the fire. A niggling voice of unease whispered that whatever had been responsible for the fire and for Clayton's death, and for Prince's, still hadn't been identified. But I wouldn't dwell on that. This meeting with my mother marked a beginning. History had lost its hold on me.

Here and there along the road, farmers on tractors made their way along the outermost rows of their cornfields. In the gray light, the colors of the trees and shrubs intensified, richer and closer to their final blaze before dying. I drove through my valley, every house and shed, every tree and boulder familiar, and marveled again at its beauty. To think that I hadn't seen it, not really, all these past months of my involvement in the bicentennial and the events of Emily and Stefan's life.

I parked at the top of Winchell Mountain, in the gravel alongside the road. The view unfurled toward the Hudson Valley to the west, skimming lush meadows bordered by evergreens and the hardwoods whose colors had barely started to turn. Deeny's house, only the roof visible behind his apple orchard, poked up from the first incline. But I didn't see any other car on the three roads that converged at the peak.

She would probably come in from the west, from Pine Plains. I focused on that ribbon of blacktop, but nothing appeared. I looked at my watch. A minute before twelve. I smiled at my own impatience; she had a two-hour ride, and it could be ten, even twenty minutes before I'd start to consider her late.

If I hadn't been afraid of missing her, I would have run into the wind, straining to push against the invisible wall of air, building up to a sweat until the tension dissipated. Instead, I walked in circles.

I kicked at a stone and watched it sail into the grass. I followed the flight of a hawk as it circled the meadow, swooped down, then soared again on an updraft. I sat in my truck but hopped back out. It was almost twelve-thirty, and I finally let myself say the words.

Julia wasn't coming.

She had decided during the night that her life, the one she'd constructed without me, was threatened by our reunion, and she had stayed home. I could hardly bear the humiliation. Now that I'd finally found my own strength and generosity, Julia had betrayed me yet again. She didn't even have the courage to call and tell me she wasn't coming.

My breath was short and the light bright and hard; my palms were damp with sweat and my throat ached from dryness. It was as though my body was at war with itself, half of me profoundly hurt, and the other half furious at the insult.

Dimly, I allowed the possibility that something had come up, some emergency, a problem with her car, an accident even. I needed to work from the premise that it wasn't an intentional slight, not a betrayal at all, but some odd and malicious twist of fate that prevented Julia Stanton Travis from keeping her appointment.

Maybe someday, the reality of my life would match my dream of it.

But no matter how I tried, I couldn't transform my anger or my hurt. Perhaps Julia had succeeded, finally, in helping me construct a wall around myself to keep me from being hurt again. The notion was oddly soothing.

How silly to neglect my bees in favor of some ephemeral promise of wholeness.

Thirty

As soon as I rounded the curve beyond Talley's white frame house, a chill gripped me. It was as though a sudden wind from a frozen region had blown in through the window to surround me. A white Chevy sedan was parked in the turnout. I tried to remember: did Tim Talley have a car like that? But I couldn't picture him driving or even getting out of a car, except for the old Volkswagen bus his wife, Rina, had driven for years. I parked beside the strange car, all my senses alert as I gathered the smoker and my hive tool.

I walked toward the bridge. I stopped once to look over my shoulder when I thought I heard the snap of a twig behind me. But I saw nothing, except perhaps a flash of brown that I dismissed as an animal making a quick escape in the presence of a human intruder. I was keyed up from waiting at Winchell Mountain, I warned myself, and seeing things that weren't really there. I was partway across the bridge when I did hear the creak of a footstep on the log behind me.

I whirled around and saw only a blur of brown dress and blond hair. A small woman lifted a heavy stick and brought it down in one swift motion. *Catherine*. I ducked to avoid the blow; my equipment clattered onto the bridge, then splashed into the water. The stick caught the side of my head and I stumbled, blinded by pain and by the rocketing lights that obscured my vision.

The stick came toward me again. I stepped back, my head still swimming. Blond hair flying, the woman ran at me and shoved me with both hands, and I lost my footing.

The endless descent toward the water of the pond stretched time out of its ordinary shape. Suddenly Emily Schiller was with me. My limbs were heavy with foreboding, my mind flooded with words, pictures, fears. The woman on the bridge above me stumbled, her arms windmilling in space.

So long Emily and bye-bye woodcutter.

I couldn't breathe. *Emily Schiller drowned. . . .* In the time it took to form those words, Emily's story rushed at me, and pressed me with the stone weight of knowledge that this was the season of honey harvest.

As I broke the surface of the water and plunged into its tepid embrace, I heard a second splash, felt the shock of another body hitting the water a few feet away.

Peter's face when he opened Catherine's birthday gift, Catherine's look of distress when he tripped at the dress rehearsal. The water felt warm, welcoming.

Ruth and Catherine whizzing past me as I drove Dad home from Doc Verity's. The sun suddenly disappeared, the world was gone, and darkness closed over my head. I felt myself pulled by my own momentum, away from air, away from light.

The current dragged me in a direction I didn't want to go, and I was startled out of my surrender to the water's dark allure. The spillway—if I didn't fight, I'd be pulled toward the spillway. I'd be tumbled down the sharp edges of the rocky race and tossed about like a crystal ornament.

My lungs burned; I kicked with both feet and pointed my hands toward the surface. *I did it before and I can do it again.* Young Michael McClosky hadn't been able to keep me under; Catherine Delaney wouldn't either. I kicked again, my vision swimming first with black specks, then with bright flashes of light, my thoughts focused only on what I had to do to get air into my lungs.

I will not let them win this way, I vowed, and with a burst of effort made powerful by my anger, I pushed to the surface.

Grateful, exhausted, I gulped sweet breaths of air. I brushed my hair out of my eyes, wiped the streaming water from my face. How did I end up so far from the bridge? I was nearly in the middle of the small pond; I treaded water, aware that the current was pulling me toward the bridge, and the spillway.

Every bit of me wanted to be back at Vixen Hill Lodge; I longed for rest and quiet, but I couldn't relax yet. I started to swim with easy strokes, trying to feel in my pockets for the keys to my truck. That would be the final irony, to have lost the keys somewhere on the bottom of the scummy pond.

My truck—I had parked next to a white Chevy. *Catherine drives a Ferrari.* I was dizzy with questions: I swiveled around in the cold water to check the bridge, the banks of the pond, for any sign of another person.

I saw nothing.

Too spent to make sense of the strange car and the attack on me, I hauled myself onto the shore. If I could just lie here, on the soft grass, and wait until I regained my strength and my breath. But I couldn't. She might be coming back.

I struggled to my feet, shivering now from the chill. My shirt and my jeans matted wetly against my cold skin like heavy armor.

And then, like an apparition materializing from the leafy border of shrubs to the right of the bridge, a wet and disheveled head appeared.

It wasn't Catherine Delaney at all.

It was Alicia Fitzhugh, dazed, consumed by the effort to hoist herself up from the rocks and onto the bank. Her brown dress clung to her thin body; water streamed down her face like tears spilling from the tendrils of her hair.

She started for the road, her head bent, muttering vague and twisted sounds. She raised her arm, fingers splayed toward the sky in mute accusation. I was embarrassed, as though I were eavesdropping on an intensely personal moment, but I couldn't turn away from her.

She came closer, her eyes on her own feet. I knew at once, in the way a puzzle comes together all in a moment after you've found the single, key piece, that she was the element that would help me understand the events of the past several months.

She began to shiver, great tremors shuddering down her arms and her legs. I started toward her, but she was too occupied with her own demons to notice. Her face contorted, the skin around her eyes and mouth crumpling like thin, white paper etched with sorrow.

I stepped on a twig; my ankle twisted and I cried out in surprise. And when I did, Alicia Fitzhugh's head snapped up.

Her face, already stretched against the bones of her skull, seemed to tighten again and she paled. Bulging and ringed with dark circles, her eyes fixed on me as though her stare could dissolve me with its poison.

With small steps, I kept moving toward her, talking softly as I advanced, the way one does with an animal or a child who has been badly frightened.

"It's all right, Alicia. I have a blanket in the back of my truck. You need to get warm again. You look so cold." I babbled, keeping up a steady stream of comforting sounds. She remained rooted to the ground, her mouth moving now, her head shaking as though she was denying what I was saying. I blinked the sweat out of my eyes and continued my slow, steady approach.

She pivoted and raced thirty feet in the other direction, stopping only when she reached the center of the log span. She stared down into the water rushing over the spillway, following it with her gaze toward the rocks. Her body swayed, but then she became still. She swiveled her head in my direction and screamed, a piercing sound that cut through me with its terror.

Why did the sight of me cause such a reaction in her? And then, as though I'd known it all along, I realized that for Alicia Fitzhugh I was no longer Sarah Hoving, hadn't been since February. I was Julia Stanton, the embodiment of everything that threatened her marriage, her security, her self-respect.

Somewhere in the back of my consciousness, I heard a car pull to a stop behind me; a door slammed shut. I took another step, now close enough to the bridge to see the moss on the north-facing edge of the logs.

From behind me, a voice called out. "Sarah, wait." It was Ruth.

I felt compelled forward, pulled toward the bridge. My legs moved without any effort. The pond, on my left, glistened and sparkled with a golden reflection as the sun broke through the overcast for a moment. A breeze carried a floating leaf toward the spillway.

Ruth's voice called out again from behind me. "Sarah, wait. She's confused and she's feeling very hurt. She called me this morning to ask which hives *Julia* tended on Thursdays. She's all mixed up about time. She thinks it's twenty-five years ago. Alicia, come off the bridge and we'll get you warmed up."

"Stay out of this, Ruth." I took another step toward the bridge, holding my anger at my mother-in-law's meddling as a beacon drawing me forward. "You've done entirely too much damage already. Back off, Ruth."

Alicia Fitzhugh stepped away from me, her hand pressed against her mouth, her eyes still staring. If she took a wrong step, if she missed her footing and tumbled into the water . . . Emily's past wasn't behind me yet.

I was nearly at the bridge now. Alicia stopped midway across, as though she was no longer in the shared present; she had, indeed, retreated into some extraordinary past.

Where was Julia?

For the first time, the chill of fear I'd felt when I drove up was no longer a question but rather the answer to that question.

Alicia Fitzhugh's gaze followed the swirling, tumbling water past the spillway to the rocks below, and I knew in an awful instant why I was afraid.

Thirty-one

I raced toward the log bridge, almost slipping on a wet patch of grass. Alicia remained planted, as though she'd set roots into the logs.

Her mouth opened, wide and silent. Then a piercing scream echoed through the valley. "Julia! No, it can't be! The bees . . . Julia!"

I skidded to a stop as Alicia Fitzhugh took a backward step. "Be careful," I warned. "Step away from the edge."

But my voice seemed to terrify her. Her face twisted. "What do I have to do? The council said you'd never come back, but you did. I had to make you stay away, out of my life. Leave us alone!"

She thought I was Julia. Ruth had said so. Alicia's own words delivered the same message.

"It's all right, Alicia. Nobody's going to hurt you." I took another step toward her.

A loud peal of high-pitched laughter ripped through the air. "Hurt me? You hurt me plenty. Before I married him, and then after. He never wanted me, he wanted you. He never stopped. I caught him last week staring at your picture. Made me so mad I told him you were waiting for him in the shed. He never came back, you know. Got lost in the snow. Served him right."

"My God, Alicia, you as good as killed him." Ruth's voice was barely louder than the stream. "You killed Edward."

Alicia ignored Ruth and went on talking. "The play was a godsend. God sent me the chance and I was smart enough to know it and to use it. You might think of me as a good little minister's wife. Enough imagination to maybe knit booties for some pregnant parishioner, that's all. But you'd be wrong. I told you a couple of minutes ago, but you don't listen very well, Julia.

"I get all the credit this time. Council be damned. The milk tank was easy. Even the cannon didn't take more than a book I found—used bookstores are wonderful, don't you think? The dog, that gave me the most satisfaction. I was afraid you'd know right away because of what Roy did to Edward, but you see, you and your husband aren't so smart. You didn't even remember about the pitchfork I stuck in the tree. If you'd been a little smarter, you'd have caught on. The fire was harder, but I managed."

Alicia Fitzhugh had been confused, hurt, angry for at least as long as I had. I moved toward her as slowly as I could, but she went on rambling, seduced by the pleasure of taunting her victim face-to-face after all these years.

"You had all this time since the town started working on the pageant to worry about your death coming, to know it was going to happen because of the evil of the past." This time the sound that came from her throat was a growl. "The water must fill your lungs. You're going to drown, like she did. You're going to play the part of Emily Schiller to perfection."

But I had already freed myself from the weight of Emily's destiny. Despite her best intentions, Alicia Fitzhugh would not be the instrument of my death.

"You didn't have to kill Clayton," I said softly, stepping closer, trying to make her meet my gaze so that she wouldn't be aware of my forward progress. "That wasn't going to bring your husband back."

Her head tilted and she leaned her cheek against her shoulder. "I only meant to just injure him. The fire was a real disappointment. They got to it too soon. But everyone got the message. You do have to drown, you know." She swatted at her face.

A bee flew away, then circled around her head and landed on her arm. At first she didn't notice. I took a few more steps, closer to her, near enough to see the bee arch and jab its stinger into her.

Her body went rigid, all the color drained from her face; she swatted at the air above her head, lost her footing, pitched forward.

Close enough to catch her, I broke her fall with my body. Instead of tumbling into the water, she slid to the logs. I let her down gently and was about to push myself back up when a movement in the water below caught my eye.

It was the champagne-colored scarf, snagged on a rock. *She had a thousand. Flowered and plain, short and long, bright and dark.* Julia lay in an eddying pool, one leg twisted behind her. Blood traced a lacy pattern over her right temple.

A madness of anguish overcame me then, and I was filled with the need to do something. I translated that terrible sight into a message that I could bear: Julia was hurt, I told myself, and I had to help her.

I ran off the bridge and pushed past a startled and immobile Ruth.

"Wait!" she shouted as I hit the matted spot where I'd slipped earlier. "Don't go down there. Don't touch her. I've already called an ambulance. They'll be here any second."

What did she mean? Had Ruth seen Alicia, did she know that Julia was lying among the rocks? I pushed my questions away. I had to get down there, had to free that scarf.

I had to save my mother.

I scrambled down a series of natural steps in the rocks; places to set my feet miraculously appeared as I needed them. The rocks were damp with spray, slick with moss. Halfway down to the rushing water, a sheer rockface slowed me.

I caught my breath and searched frantically for a toehold.

I twisted my head to look down at Julia, still a few feet below me. She hadn't moved. "I'm coming," I shouted.

Still, she didn't look up.

I kept going, needing to complete the passage to the bottom of the stream where the broken body of my mother lay. Somehow I managed to negotiate those last, treacherous feet.

Her hair, I remember, was wet and cold as I freed the tattered scarf from the rocks and then lifted her face out of the stream. I don't know how long I stayed there, Julia's head on my knees, the water lapping at my feet. I experienced a merciful blankness, needing only to touch Julia's cold cheek occasionally so that I could soothe her.

Eventually, hands reached down to lift her from me, then helped me to my feet and guided me up the slippery rocks to the grass.

It was Peter's voice that finally broke through to me.

"Sarah, it was too late. You did what you could, but she was dead already."

"Dead because I bought her a scarf," I whispered as he led me to his van. "Dead because I forgave her and wanted her back in my life."

She was buried in Pearl River, in her husband's family plot.

He was a kind man, solid and warm, even in his grief. "She was so thrilled to have you back," he told me when I came to see him on the day of her funeral. "That morning she said she was going to come early and surprise you. Something about wanting to see you in your natural element, working with your bees."

Her sons sat beside each other on the sofa, holding hands like two scared children, each trying not to let the other get lost.

Because I felt like an intruder, I didn't stay for the funeral; instead, I arranged for a memorial service at the Taconic Hills Methodist Church a week later. I hadn't anticipated wanting the comfort of a church service, but it had seemed important. She had touched the lives of so many people in this town. They should be reminded of that.

The day was beautiful, sunny, the kind of weather in which dreamers take off on flights of fancy and painters get out their brushes. The light seemed to pull every drop of richness from the last of the summer flowers.

The church was nearly as full as it had been that day in February when Edward Fitzhugh was buried. Julia finally had gotten everyone's attention here in town.

"I hope she's watching all this." Peter put his arm around my shoulder. He stayed close to me, and I welcomed that.

Catherine, Ben, Deeny and Nancy, Jeanie Boice, Ike Kronenburg, Dan Lambert, even Riley Hamm and Harris Del Santo were seated somewhere in the crowd. Walter was next to Peter; Ruth sat beside her husband.

I had by then let go of any questions about her involvement in my mother's death and had accepted her explanation: She had become alarmed by Alicia's strange phone call, had arrived at Talley's pond to find Alicia wandering dazed, and had followed her to the edge of the stream, where she discovered Julia's body. Nobody had seen Julia's car until later, when Riley Hamm had found it parked under a hickory tree, a quarter of a mile away.

The voices of the choir swelled the air with a sorrowful hymn, and I cried. My tears were for Roy, who hadn't come, as I knew he wouldn't, and for Alicia Fitzhugh, still living out the fruits of her anger and her fear in a hospital ward. But mostly, they were for Julia and for me. Everything in our lives had conspired to keep us apart.

"She would have liked this," I said as I turned to look behind me. Motes of fine dust danced in the soft, golden shaft of light that stretched from the lilies of the stained-glass window as though pointing to the empty space in the center of the next-to-last pew.

Perhaps Julia would have suspected that the people of Taconic Hills had come out for this occasion to satisfy themselves that even in death she and Edward Fitzhugh were not to be together.

I comforted myself with the thought that my mother, for all eternity, would have something to long for, an unfulfilled dream to sustain her.

X